AN UNFORGETTABLE NOVEL
OF AN AMERICAN FAMILY...

# BREAKER BOYS

*Euan Morgan:* At age eleven he left his childhood behind to become the newest "breaker boy" in John Markham's mine—and the first union man.

*Gwladys Protheroe:* She had lived for her dreams and ambition—and they plunged her into a nightmare of depravity and abuse.

*Zakrzewska:* No one could harness his madness—and from the day he came to the mine Jeddoh would never be the same.

*Mother:* She was a seventy-year-old woman pitted against the most powerful men in the country. She was determined to bring the union to Jeddoh—and she wouldn't leave until she'd won.

"Vivid...each person is real for the reader. This is not just about mining and unions, but also about love, passion, growing up, and the various emotions that constitute life at the edge of survival."
　　　　　　　　　　　　　　　　—*Library Journal*

"A vivid reconstruction of the period."
　　　　　　　　　　　　　　　　—*Kirkus Reviews*

"Terrifying...the ending is novelistically thrilling... *Breaker Boys* {is a} burly ancestor of John Updike's early 'Rabbit' novels."
　　　　　　　　　　　　　　　　—*Los Angeles Times*

# BREAKER BOYS

## A Novel by
## Jan Kubicki

**WARNER BOOKS**

A Warner Communications Company

For
Peg and Frank

# A Note about Names

At first glance, the names of some Polish and Welsh characters in *Breaker Boys* might seem to be unpronounceable. In truth, they are quite easy to pronounce and are rather melodic when accomplished correctly. Below are some that appear most frequently throughout the text along with their correct pronunciations.

| | |
|---|---|
| Zakrzewska | Zak-shef´-ska |
| Gwladys Protheroe | Glad´-us Pró-tha-ro |
| Moczygemba | Mo-chi-gem´-ba |
| Maciejewski | Match-i-jeś-ski |

### In the Morgan family

| | |
|---|---|
| Myfanwy | Miv-awń-way |
| Euan | Yú-an |
| Rhys | Rees (rhymes with Greece) |

# PART ONE

## EUAN

PART ONE

JUAN

THE boy stared down at his clean sheet of paper, afraid to begin, afraid to sully its perfect whiteness. His hand, clasping a black sheath pen with a no. 2 nib, hovered over the inkwell at the corner of his desk while all around him other pens clinked deeply, then scratched across paper, leaving trails of ink like tracks of coal through snow.

At the blackboard, Miss Protheroe mouthed every syllable she inscribed for the class to copy.

"... one na-tion in-di-vis-i-ble ..."

Penmanship! How he hated it, hated school and his *mam*'s foolish wish that he spend his life reading books, writing words, figuring numbers, whose purpose he neither understood nor cherished. There were thirty-eight in his class, mostly girls, mostly English and Welsh girls. He was the oldest boy, except for the Polander, Antoni, whose leg had gotten crushed underground and who never spoke, even if called upon, but just sat against the back wall near the older girls, mostly Markham girls, who were skilled in penmanship.

The room in which they met, this "school," had been the builder's shed when G. B. Markham erected the town of Jeddoh, Pennsylvania, and everything in it in 1868, some thirty-two years before. There were windows on three sides, a blackboard, brought all the way from Philadelphia, and a door on the other; thirty wood and cast-iron desks, which the younger children shared; and plain pine flooring. Except for the Stars and Stripes, which hung from a lopsided pole above Miss Protheroe's desk, no adornments or pictures graces the whitewashed walls. It still looked like a shed.

"Almost finished!" Miss Protheroe said crisply, nudging her spectacles, which were constantly slipping down her long and narrow nose, back into place. By the end of a trying day, the bridge of her nose looked red and sore. This was such a day, and it was not yet two o'clock. "I'll be coming around to inspect in a minute," she added sternly.

The English and Welsh girls pursed their lips, making anxious sounds as though they would never finish in time. The younger boys frowned and gripped their pens even more tightly with their stubby fingers. And still, the boy's paper lay untouched, tormenting him with its whiteness.

The Markham girl across the aisle spotted his blank page, saw the look of anguish on his face, and her eyes knew that he would fail. He had no taste for that, for her knowing. "She practices at night, I bet, but then she's got no chores either," he fumed to himself. He glanced at her paper, at her neat letters in neat rows, at her blue pinafore and starched collar, at the velvet bow that tied back her long black curls, the gold ring she wore on her little finger. He was wearing a shirt of his brother's that was too big for him and pants that were too small and shoes that fit just right but needed new soles. And he didn't have a gold ring.

"I can do as good as her, even if her father is John Markham," he told himself and dipped the pen with the no. 2 nib into his inkwell. (Not too deep! Too deep and the ink would blot when the pen first touched the paper; not deep enough and the nib would trip or sputter, sending ugly black flecks across the page.) Boldly he made his first stroke.

"There!" he said to himself, relieved, then gritted his

teeth. It was too long! "You always start too big!" his *mam* scolded him once when she tried to help him learn to print his letters. "You'll never get more than a few at a time like that on a page!" Ever since, he tried to mind her, but his letters still started out giantlike and got smaller by degrees till, by the time he finished, if he finished, they were shrunken and hunched over like old men.

He bit his lip and pondered whether to go on or begin again on the back but was suddenly distracted by something outside the window. ("Always sit at the window," his brother, Rhys, had told him. "Then you'll never be wanting for something to do.") It was Pretta-moor, the peddler, pushing his rickety old cart down Frog Street, calling "*Pretta-moor, pretta-moor!* Big potatoes!" From where he sat, the boy could see much of the busiest part of Frog Street, which ran the length of Jeddoh, roughly a mile. There were no other streets. Frog Street was Jeddoh. He could also see the long side of the company store, the side with the pay window, where the miners lined up to get their monthly wages, and across Frog Street to the colliery beyond, clear up the hill to the pit head even, but not the breaker itself. And the western spur that carried the coal to market passed not twenty yards from the school. He wondered with each car that passed whether it carried his *dada*'s coal or whether Rhys's mules had hauled it up. He kept track, too, of the number of cars that rolled out each day. He knew when the shipments were over quota or under and proudly recited this to his *dada* each evening as his *dada* washed up, and he was always right.

"I learn more looking out," the boy thought, "than I do being in."

The pit head looked quiet now, and the cars had stopped rolling down from the breaker long since. "They'll be quitting early," he decided. Frog Street looked deserted, too. Except for Pretta-moor, there were no peddlers, only Crawley & Marshall's Powder Works wagon unloading in front of the company store. This week's shipment was smaller than last week's, just as last week's had been smaller than the one before. Nobody had to tell him what that meant. With summer coming, there would be less demand for coal, less work, less need to keep powder at hand, powder that, if ignited, would blow the store half-way to the moon, a prospect he fancied at moments like this, for such a shot would surely take with it the school and maybe, with luck, Miss Protheroe as well, a fancy from which he was suddenly and sharply jolted by a resounding thwack and a yelp from across the room.

"Have I not told you, Michael Figmic?" Miss Protheroe demanded as she raised the frightened Polander in the front row by the hair at the back of his neck. A shrill chirp replaced the usual soothing resonance of her voice. "I expect neatness from you, and what do I see? A dirty, filthy paper!"

"She sounds just like a tea kettle, whistling her head off," the boy thought, bemused by the idea of steam shooting from her top. "Somebody take her off the stove! Empty her! Stuff up her spout!"

Under her harsh grip, the Polander gyrated as though he were trying to climb the very air he breathed to escape the pain. It was almost comical to see, although only the older girls in back, who today were cutting paper for the younger children to use, dared giggle.

Miss Protheroe wasn't at all like his last teacher in Sugar Notch, back before they moved to Jeddoh, back before the trouble began. Mr. Gingreich let the boys plays boys' games, like Rotten Horses and Kick the Wicket. He didn't make them sing or play girls' games. Singing was for church, and girls' games were . . . well, the boy couldn't even figure what *girls* liked about them.

Miss Protheroe finally released Mickey Figmic, who turned away to hide his tears. As she moved on down the row, the boy eyed her warily as she complimented this girl or that, stroked their hair, smiled and nodded, then held up their prim scribbles for others to see.

"What am I to do?" he wondered. He wished Rhys had told him to sit by the door. He could have escaped by now. Instead, he was trapped.

There was still one way out. Once before he'd gotten

almost through before he'd messed up, and then only when someone bumped his arm. "But if I did it once . . . ," he reasoned, turning his paper over, "I could, I bet I could again!" then, holding his breath, rescratched the first stroke near the top, carefully, in human scale. The "p" was harder, but his hand moved urgently and, maybe for that, more deftly. The "l" was easy, then the "e." (Scratch, scratch, across the page; he was doing it, and it was fine.) Dip for more ink, then the "b" and the "g"—an upside-down "b" with a tail—another "e" and on to . . . "allegiance" (not knowing what it meant, nor caring, more confidently now, dipping to the ink again, moving on, moving on) with an "a," double "l," another "e," another upside-down "b" with a tail, and the "i" - "a" - "n". . . . "Allegiance," he mused. "It looks almost like 'all giants.' I pledge 'all giants' to the United States of America!" He liked the sound of that and vowed to say "all giants" next time the class recited it (he wouldn't even care if Miss Protheroe heard him), then finished his "c," the final "e," and paused to admire his progress.

I pledge allegiance

"Not bad then. Maybe I'll get to be a regular penman yet," he crowed to himself, then dipped into the ink once more, and . . . and . . . then it happened. While dotting his "i," ugly splats shot out from the nib. He stared at the paper, disbelieving at first, then kicked his desk, angry that he had allowed himself to imagine that it would end anyway but this. "What's the use?" he thought dully and dropped the pen, which rolled across the paper and through the splats of inks.

He heard a sigh, turned, and saw the Markham girl looking at her paper in dismay. She had finished printing her words and had begun to write them in longhand to impress Miss Protheroe, when an errant stroke had scattered black splats across her page.

"See, you're no better," the boy wanted to say.

"Don't tell," she implored, whispering, seeing him. She was near to tears. "Don't tell."

"Do I hear talking?" Miss Protheroe warned. "Talkers are not workers! You can't be talking and working at the same . . . ," but her voice was suddenly drowned out by a long blast from the steam whistle at the colliery. The boy looked out to see a huge white plum belch from the steam vent near the pit head, then rise, all soft and curling, like cotton candy, till it dissolved in wisps.

"I'd like to be that smoke," the boy thought. "I'd float out of here and never come back. I'd float right out."

The younger boys ran to the window shouting, "Quittin' time! Quittin' time!" and craned their necks to be the first to see the cage reach top.

"Away with you now!" ordered Miss Protheroe, shooing them back to their seats while the rest of the class made ready to end school early.

The boy felt nothing but relief. Safe for another day, he covered his inkwell and wiped the excess from his pen on the sole of his shoe. Across the aisle, the Markham girl folder her paper and slipped it into her desk, but it was the boy Miss Protheroe's eye fell on.

"Not so fast, Euan Morgan!" she admonished, peering over her spectacles. "And why are you in such a hurry? Let me see your paper."

"I . . . I'm not done then," the boy stammered, his heart pounding.

"You never finish!" Miss Protheroe snapped, her temper worsening. "Sit down then, every one of you! They can do without you for a few minutes more!" The disgruntled children returned to their places as Miss Protheroe picked up her ruler and approached the boy's desk. "Let me see your paper, Euan Morgan! Hurry! Hurry!" she said as he dallied, then snatched it from his hand.

To the boy, Miss Protheroe looked old and sour, older than his mother even, where in truth she was younger; she was thirty-two. She had come from the old country, from Merthyr Tydfil, where her father had been a miner, but she was spared the harsh life of most girls of her class who went to work in the silk mills and stayed there, just stayed there. Instead, she became a teacher, an occupation for which she possessed no particular charm or skill. John Markham hired her to school his five daughters and the miner children of Jeddoh, whom he was obligated by law to educate until they graduated or reached an age when they were old enough to quit for work in the mills or the breaker.

Gwladys Protheroe was a plain woman, uncommonly tall and large-boned, but not ungainly. Her dresses were colorless, ill-fitting. She wore no pins or rings, no ribbons at her neck or about her flame-red hair, which she combed back from her face and pinned in a tight knot. As gossips were wont to say, she was not found attractive by most of the eligible men of Jeddoh or of the neighboring town of Freeland, where she lived. Those who did, Polanders and stable boys, she rebuffed. She put aside what money she could for her wedding day or for passage back to Cardiff and her Merthyr Tydfil, but the jar in her room contained only nine dollars and forty-five cents. She had escaped the silk mills but lived in another kind of prison entirely of her own creation.

"Look at his, Euan Morgan! You can no more write than a pig can walk on two feet!" she said, her voice trembling with rage. "I'd expect this from Michael Figmic, but from *you*? You're no better than the 'hunkies!' I see six, seven . . . nine splotches! What's nine times two, Euan Morgan? Shall I give you eighteen then?"

" 'Cause I dirtied my paper?" he wanted to say. "They don't worry about dirt in the colliery. You can get as dirty as you want over there and nobody minds, 'cause the harder you work, the dirtier you get. It's only the likes of you cares about things like that!" he wanted to say.

"Or would you rather stay after and . . . ?"

The boy extended his hands, palms up.

"You'll have it then," she said, ready to oblige. "Hurry, stand up!"

And so it began. With each swat, Miss Protheroe kept count, alternating the hand she hit each time so that neither alone bore the brunt of the stinging blows or, rather, so that both hands suffered equally. With each swat, the boy flinched. He had taken his licks before from his *dada*, from Mr. Gingreich even, but never in front of everyone and never from a lady.

"Look, he's cryin'," a voice in back sniggered. He wanted to say, "I'm not! I'm not crying!" but he was; the words choked in his throat. Across the aisle, the Markham girl, secure from discovery, sat smirking.

At eighteen blows, Miss Protheroe kept going. Punishment in advance, she called it. At twenty-three, she stopped abruptly, walked to the front of the room, and, without another word, rang the brass bell that sat on her desk, dismissing school. Perplexed by her odd behavior, the children stayed seated. Then some boys, leery that she might change her mind, rushed for the door and the dusty yard beyond. The girls followed more tentatively in groups of three or four; a few remained behind and began to clean the erasers and straighten the room for tomorrow's lessons. Euan Morgan lingered beside his desk, slowly rubbing his hands on his pant legs, waiting for the schoolyard to clear so he could leave. Miss Protheroe, her mouth twitching in an angry pout, eyed him over the rims of her spectacles.

"You're nothing but trouble, Euan Morgan," she told him. "You can barely read; you don't know your numbers; you can't write neat! You're only good for looking out that window! Tomorrow I'm moving your seat up front by the little ones, and if you don't take part I'll talk to your *mam* about how poorly you're doing. Do you hear me?" but Euan just stared silently at the top of his desk, at names and initials carved there by others before him, at Rhys's he'd carved there himself. "I asked a question! There's plenty more of what you already got. Would you like another eighteen then?"

He shook his head no.

"You're *worse* than the hunkies! They don't know better. Now tell Miss Protheroe you're sorry for being lazy and ignorant and you aim to do better in your lessons."

"I . . . I'm sorry, Miss Protheroe," Euan heard himself say. It might as well have been Antoni, the Polander, who spoke. Or Pretta-moor, the peddler.

"And do you aim to do better with your lessons?"

"Yes, Miss Protheroe."

"I don't think you ever will; I don't think you can," she added curtly. "Now be gone with you! And fix your shirt! You look a sight."

He tucked his shirttail in and smoothed his straggly brown hair as he hurried toward the door.

"What do you say?" she called out, stopping him.

"Thank you . . . Miss Protheroe," he answered, feeling light-headed. His hands were tingling. His fingers felt numb. Outside the door, he gasped the air deeply, like a diver escaping from a watery grave. Then he ran. He ran to get away from *her*, away from girls in cotton pinafores and long curls, from Mickey Figmic, from the smell of chalk on blackboard erasers, from pens with no. 2 nibs, from splats of India ink, and from his own utter sense of failure.

Each night, four or five empty coal cars were left on the siding next to the company store ready to be moved up to the breaker at morning. It was here, nursing his hurt and shame, standing on a coupling between cars, where he could see the pit head but not easily be seen himself, that Euan waited for his *dada* and Rhys. He could always pick them out, even from halfway up Frog Street, even with their faces blackened with coal, by the way they walked— shoulders slightly hunched, eyes fixed down at the ground— unaware that he carried himself the same way. He wondered if he'd missed them while he was getting the gab from Miss Protheroe, but finally the gate of the cage lifted, and they appeared, fell in line to "peg out," then joined the stream of men and boys heading down the hill.

They were a solemn lot, these men and boys, at quitting. There was no boisterousness, no laughter or singing, just the crackling of feet on crushed slate and the "... pah ... pah ... pah ... pah ..." of steam rising in puffs from the funnel above the boiler shanty. At the foot of the hill, the stream split up. Some crossed over to the company store, the "pluck me" store they called it, maybe to buy powder or fuses or a quid of tobacco, or maybe just to stand and smoke cigarettes, which they were forbidden underground. Some walked up Frog Street to Emerald House, Jeddoh's one saloon, to forget their troubles or listen to "Owney" Riley play his concertina. The rest went home to "Cheesetown," where only Welsh and English lived, or Irish Flats or up to Polish Hill.

Euan jumped down from his hiding place, then took a circuitous route to Frog Street, behind the company store and along the walkway that separated it from the stables, to see if his favorites—the two black mules—were out. He liked to see them each day and, when he could, brought them salt that they licked from his hand just as Rhys had shown him, careful not to let them bite. But as he rounded the corner back of the store, he ran hard into a man who has just descended from the payroll office and was pausing to take out a cigar. The impact knocked him off his feet.

"That'll teach you to watch where you're going," the man said testily, as though the boy were some pesky gnat he'd swatted from his sleeve. But his words had no effect. Indeed, the boy heard them not at all as he sat, dazed, blinking his eyes back to clearness. "Come on then, or shall I get Dr. Koons?"

There weren't many in town who wore starched collars, silk neckties, and brown suits unless they were on their way to church. Still, it took a moment before the boy realized that the man standing over him, the man he'd collided with full tilt, was John Markham, the man who owned Jeddoh. He had only seen Markham up close a few times, and then in church, but usually at a distance as he rode in his carriage or strode across the colliery yard, and always in ill-humor. Markham's face sported a perpetual scowl.

" 'Tis the curse of rich men," was how Rhys had explained it to him. Rhys told him, too, that Markham fired men on the spot who angered him or who even so much as looked at him the wrong way. And, once fired, they were cast from their homes by nightfall and left with all their worldly goods by the side of the road, be it clear moon, or rain, or deepest snow.

"What's your father's name, boy?" Markham asked sternly as Euan leaped to his feet. He thought to run, but Markham blocked his path down the narrow way. "You speak English?" the owner barked with increasing impatience.

"Yes, sir," Euan answered, trying not to look at the man for fear of looking at him the wrong way.

"Then what's your father's name?"

"Morgan, sir."

"Ivor Morgan?"

"No, sir, Hugh. Hugh Morgan," Euan told him with a growing fear that Markham meant to report his careless tumble to his *dada* or, worse, that the owner had been so angered that they'd be tossed from their home before nightfall. "We've only been two months," he added.

"I see. Well, that's no excuse then, is it?" the owner chided. "You should know how easy it is to get your block knocked off around a mine."

Euan, confused, shook his head no, then said, "Yes!"

"Which is it, boy? Yes? No? You can't say both now, can you?"

Euan remained silent. "Better that than make it worse," he thought.

"You've got to keep your eyes and ears open," Markham warned. "Men and boys are getting hurt every day in the mine, some killed even, and all because they walk around looking up when they should be looking down or down when they should be looking up. I remember one man once who . . ."

Euan breathed easier. Whenever the gab started, he knew the worst was over, so he listened dutifully, concentrating on the colored paper band that Markham slid laboriously down the length of his cigar, and automatically held his hand out as Markham was about to toss it aside. The owner paused in his peroration, puzzled, then remembered that boys sometimes collect cigar bands, but at a loss to reason why, and gave it over.

"Thank you, sir," Euan said and saw, just then, his *dada* and Rhys on Frog Street, passing. "May I go now, sir?" he asked anxiously.

"Go! But keep your eyes open!" Markham warned. "One thing more...," he added. Euan stiffened. He knew he'd gotten off too easily, but Markham only reached into his vest pocket, took from it two copper cent pieces, and tossed them to him one at a time. "Buy yourself some red hats," he said, his face refusing to relinquish its scowl.

"Yes, sir! Later, sir. Thank you!" Euan said, his eyes glowing with surprise. He tucked the coins into his pants pocket and dashed off, failing in his haste to notice that the black mules were out, swatting flies and eating their measure of oats.

Once on Frog Street, Euan weaved through the homeward procession till he caught up with his *dada* and Rhys in front of Emerald House. Without a word, he fell into step beside them, as though he'd been with them all along, and reached over for his *dada*'s empty lunch pail. Carrying it home made him feel important.

"I got a ring then. Look!" he boasted, showing off the red and gold and black cigar band that he'd placed on his finger. "Fancy, isn't it? Mr. Markham gave it."

"That's about all you'll ever see from that pinchfist," Hugh Morgan said and ran his hand through his young son's hair.

Rhys laughed his throaty laugh at his father's gibe. "Pinchfist," he said, repeating the word that tickled him. Even Hugh was amused by the sound of it, by its aptness. "Pinchfist."

"No, he gave me two coppers, too, and I didn't have to do a thing to earn them," Euan told them as he dug the coins from his pocket. "Here, see!"

"Where'd you find them?" his brother asked, his curiosity piqued. "We can go back after supper. Maybe there's more."

"He gave them, I told you!" Euan insisted.

"And I'm the King of France!" Rhys scoffed and flipped his lunch pail in a circle through the air.

"He did! He gave them!"

"Now, now!" Hugh cautioned indifferently. He seemed preoccupied, as though engaged in some argument with himself. Even Rhys noticed it.

"He did!" Euan fumed under his breath, annoyed more at Rhys for ruining his mood than for disbelieving him. "I was going to give you one, too," he said aloud, but Rhys just laughed and tossed his lunch pail in the air again, turned, and caught it behind his back with one hand.

"Can you do that, nipper? Bet you can't!" Rhys taunted, but Euan just ignored him. He hated to be called nipper, an errand boy, the most lowly job underground.

"I warned you!" Hugh said more firmly, giving notice for them to stop their shenanigans. Euan puzzled over his *dada*'s lack of interest in his cent pieces. "Was it any better today? In school?" his *dada* asked instead.

Euan had forgotten his run-in with Miss Protheroe. Now it came rushing back, but he remained silent. He was learning that the less he said, the less trouble he caused for himself.

They walked the rest of the way home in silence, Hugh with his brawny hand on Euan's shoulder, Rhys slightly apart, listening to some music in his head that wouldn't quit, an air he'd heard whistled by a miner in the dark as he rolled by with a trip of five.

It was the usual with them.

Beyond the weathered houses in Irish Flats, Frog Street began a gentle rise toward Holy Trinity, the wood-framed Catholic church that stood at the crest of Polish Hill. The Morgans lived in a company house several down from the church. Like the scores of others that lined both sides of the street, it was little more than a two-story brown box with windows. Some had porches; others spread out in back with added-on rooms, shanties, and lean-tos.

When Hugh Morgan came to Jeddoh one gray day in February, he felt his luck had changed. The strike at the Dundee #2 had lasted over three weeks. There'd been trouble. He knew he had to leave, so he took what little money remained in the tin box on top of the stove and set out to find another job. After eight days of looking in the outlying coal towns, he was desperate. By chance, he came to Jeddoh, where he found work, not just as a laborer or yardman, which he was prepared to take, but as a miner. He was assigned a house, which had become vacant through a sudden eviction, and he was assured that Rhys would have work as a driver, too. It was a break in the clouds.

He rushed back to Sugar Notch that night to break the news to his wife, Myfanwy, who had no desire to leave her home, to say nothing of her daughters, for a crude company town in the mountains. Gwen and Meb worked at the Hess-Goldsmith silk mill in Wilkesbarre, the nearest city. There were no jobs for them in Jeddoh, nothing nearby. Moving to Jeddoh would mean breaking up the family, but there was simply no choice. The strike was getting worse. Each day, more Coal and Iron Police arrived. The trouble would not go away. On his first night back, Hugh was set upon and beaten by the Coal and Irons, or so he said. Myfanwy knew her husband was lying. The next morning, he and the boys moved Gwen and Meb into Mrs. Archer's boardinghouse in Wilkesbarre, then they packed most of their belongings onto a wagon and set out for their new home. Jeddoh was twenty miles away, but to Myfanwy it was twenty years back. It meant starting over, giving up, doing without.

When Myfanwy saw her new house, she cried. It was old, cramped, dirty. The stove was small. Windows were cracked. Some were missing. There were no gas lamps. The water pump was on the back porch, the privy in the yard. The morning after they moved in, the boys awoke with tiny red spots across their faces, necks, and chests.

"It's the measles!" she thought, but closer inspection revealed that they were actually bug bites. The house had been built of hickory, which was abundant in 1868 and cheap; it was also favored by bedbugs. Their house was infested. So, in fact, was all of Polish Hill. That morning, Myfanwy scrubbed her floors with kerosene; she tore apart her beds and doused the springs with kerosene; she emptied her drawers, then rubbed them down with kerosene and sprinkled it over their clothes.

"I don't know what's worse," Rhys groused, reeling from the smell, "the kerosene or the bugs!"

Every morning, even now, Myfanwy took her beds apart and rubbed their springs down with kerosene. But this was not the worst. The worst she could not scrub away or fix with paint or otherwise accommodate herself to. On both sides and across the street, up the street and down, she was hemmed in by the people she despised—the hunkies. In double blocks meant for two families lived the equal of five, sometimes six, all sharing a single pump and a single outdoor privy. By day, the hunky women worked barefoot in the house and yard, shouting their gibberish and singing while their babies cried unattended. At night, when the men came home, there was arguing, endless arguing, an endless racket. She kept apart from these neighbor women, never greeting them in the yard or passing in the street. As she saw it, living in their midst was just another of life's trials. God was testing her endurance.

Once a week, Myfanwy would walk down Frog Street to Cheesetown to visit with the pastor's wife, or Mrs. Jenkins, or Mrs. Owen Williams, who played the organ in the church. Once a week, she would write a letter to Meb and Gwen in her careful hand, and each week, they wrote in return, enclosing a portion of their wages, part of which Myfanwy tucked away in two envelopes in her bureau drawer as dowries of sorts. The rest went into the tin box atop the stove to be used for food and other necessities.

Myfanwy missed her daughters, but they were always with her. She spent her days musing about them, how they were eating, what they talked about, whom they met, whether they went to church on Sunday. At times, she imagined them with her, sharing in her chores, keeping her company. Sometimes she thought she even heard their laughter upstairs or in the backyard. It helped her to shut out the rest. It was her comfort.

When she heard the whistle blow for early quitting, Myfanwy put aside the shirts she was wringing, Monday being her wash day, and set about getting hot water ready for Hugh and Rhys. This meant filling two pails out back with water, lugging them inside and lifting them onto the coal stove, there to heat till the men reached home. She gripped each handle with a pad to keep it from cutting into her fingers, which were red and swollen from lye soaps, kerosene, and endless scrubbing. Then there were their clean shirts and trousers to be put out, and dry stockings and boots. This done, Myfanwy stood at the front window and waited, absentmindedly twisting a loose strand of hair around her finger, as was her habit. She would do no more till her men were home safe. "They're always the last. The slowpokes," she thought, finally seeing them a few houses down, then said her usual short, silent prayer of thanks to God for watching over her family. A knot loosened in her stomach. Her day's work was not yet over, but her day of worry was.

When the men came home from the colliery, they stripped off their work clothes and boots in the backyard and scrubbed down with stiff brushes, soap, and hot water. Once the day's accumulation of coal dust was gone, they rinsed themselves with cold water poured from a bucket, dressed in clean clothes, and went in for supper. This ritual was performed every day the mine worked and was brought indoors only in the worst of weather. Myfanwy had made Hugh build a high fence out back for these daily ablutions, for it galled her that their Polish neighbors, for lack of morals or animal ignorance, as she saw it, conducted their bathing openly, with great carryings on, and allowed their young girls to tote and pour water for their naked fathers, uncles, older brothers, even their boarders.

In the Morgan house, Rhys had toted and poured, and

his *mam* before him, but not Gwen and Meb; Myfanwy would never allow that. Now it was Euan's turn, and he assumed the duty with fervor, taking great pains to see that every step in the ritual proceeded smoothly. As they neared the house, he left his *dada* and Rhys behind and raced ahead to the back porch, up the steps two at a time, past his *mam*, who waited there to greet him, into the kitchen.

"No kiss for your *mam* then?" she asked.

"No time!" he called and set his *dada*'s lunch pail on the table, then turned to the stove to lift down the first pail of water. Myfanwy moved to help, but the boy protested. "I can do it myself!" he huffed as some water lapped over the side onto the floor.

"I beg your pardon then," she said, feigning indignation. " 'Tis sad when a mother can't even squeeze one kiss out of her son."

"I got my *work* to do," he said and lowered the second pail to the floor with the same spillage.

"And you're getting more on my floor than's in the pail," she pointed out, refusing to be intimidated by his self-importance.

"You filled 'em, not me," he replied matter-of-factly and lugged both pails outside, grunting every few feet to let her know how hard he was working. A moment later he was back, rummaging through the cabinet next to the stove where his mother kept the yellow soap and towels.

"Where are they then?" he asked impatiently.

"Under your nose. You can't see for looking!" Myfanwy said, opening the cellar door to take out her mop.

"The soaps! The soaps!" he demanded. "They're needing them now!"

Myfanwy was not used to being ordered about in her own kitchen. "Open the new!" she said. "I used the slivers that was left in the wash."

"Why didn't you say then?" he grumbled and grabbed a fresh soap, scrub brushes, and towels, and headed for the door.

"It's slippery! Watch!" she warned too late. That same instant, Euan lost his footing on the wet oilcloth. He reached for the back of a chair to break his fall but only succeeded in pulling it down with him as he thudded to the floor.

"Owww!" he howled, rolling over to uncover what it was he'd fallen on. It was the bar of soap.

"Oh, Lord! You'll be the death of me!" Myfanwy exclaimed. "You're just like your brother. Always in a hurry. Run, run, run! Now, see?"

"It hurts," he whined, feeling that he'd not gotten the proper sympathy he deserved.

"You'll get worse than that before you're old," Myfanwy told him as she righted the chair. "Now get up!"

"No, I'm hurt."

Just then, Rhys called from outside. "Come on, nipper! Hurry up!"

"Hold your horses!" Euan exploded with all the anger inside him. He'd taken people's guff all day, and now he wasn't going to move until his *mam* had soothed his hurt, but Myfanwy had no time to mollycoddle imaginary aches. She set aside her mop, knelt beside him, and began to gather the scattered elements of his fall.

"It hurts," he repeated, in case she hadn't been listening.

"Where?"

"All over."

"Even your belly?" she asked, piling the towels back into his arms. He looked at her puzzled. "I made some biscuits. Can you smell them?"

The boy sniffed the air, but the aroma was safe inside the biscuit tin. Even so, his face brightened.

"But I guess you wouldn't be after a taste, hurting like you do," she said, dismissing the matter. He started to protest, but she cut him off. "You can have a few *after* you finish out back. Does it hurt less now?" He nodded. It did. She tousled his hair. He was her baby, the youngest of her four who lived. She hated to see him growing up so fast.

"Maybe if you didn't try so hard," she said quietly. "You always try too hard, and you see what happens? You fall down, or something breaks."

" 'Tis a queer way of putting it," he thought. "Miss Protheroe gives me whacks for not trying hard enough. Now *Mam* says the other?"

"Euan!" Hugh yelled from outside. "Are we to start without you then?"

"Coming, *N'had*!" Euan hollered and took the soap and brushes from his *mam*. He had a job to do, and he'd hurt worse if he didn't get moving.

His *dada* and Rhys sat on short benches out back loosening the laces of their boots. Even their undressing was part of the ritual and followed a set procedure. First, Euan detached the kerosene lamps from their caps and placed them on the top step for later filling. Next, he hung their caps and coats on hooks on the porch. His *dada* wore gum boots to keep his feet dry, even though the rest of him was soaked to the skin all day long. Pulling his *dada*'s boots off was the hardest of Euan's chores and was accomplished only after a certain amount of swearing and a greater measure of sweat. Sometimes he would strain with one while Rhys struggled with the other. When removed, Euan set the gum boots on the second step, then turned back to Rhys's, which were too large for him and slid off without difficulty. These he placed on the third step. Euan helped pull off their stockings next, then their inner and outer shirts, pants, and, last of all, their longjohns. These he piled into a wicker basket so his *mam* could hang them by the stove to dry overnight. Finally he filled two more buckets at the pump, set them beside the others, then sat on the top step and watched his *dada* and Rhys lather and scrub themselves clean, although neither soap nor brush had yet been found that could scrub away the years of coal dust that had accumulated in the creases of his *dada*'s skin. His hands, his arms, his back and legs were peppered with blue scars from picks or sharp pieces of coal that had ripped under his flesh and left traces of black dust beneath his pale skin.

Rhys was muscular like his *dada*, just beginning to fill out. "Puttin' meat on my bones," Rhys liked to say, flashing his grin. Euan couldn't wait till he was taller and strong like his brother, husky-voiced like his brother. Euan remembered the day that Rhys had proudly shown him his first hairs "down there," and how his "dingus" had grown. Rhys pointed to it and laughed like a silly girl, and then his voice cracked, and he never sounded the same. He was still Rhys, but he was different, the same but different. Each day now, Rhys seemed older. "It's not fair," Euan thought. Everyone else got older, yet he stayed the same. He wanted to be a man, look and sound like a man, work like a man. Men didn't have to listen to teachers or follow kid rules. They had money. They could come and go as they pleased. They could tell other people what to do. Yes, he longed to be a man.

In adjoining yards, Polanders lathered and scrubbed amid the deepening shadows of the afternoon sun. Their former solemnity now ran to laughter and gab. The whoops and cries of glistening men doused with frigid water echoed off surrounding hills. In a few minutes, Euan, too, would pour the cold water over his *dada* and Rhys and squeal with laughter at the little jig that Rhys always danced to "warm his blood again." As they dressed in dry clothes, Hugh would tell of how many yards he'd loosed that day and how many wagons he'd filled; Rhys would repeat tales he'd heard on his rounds, and Euan would get to tell how many cars he'd seen move out, whether or not the mine had reached quota, and, of course, he would always be right.

"Two Welsh boys came through at noon, looking for work," Hugh said that night at supper, breaking finally the brooding silence he had brought with him to the table. He didn't look at Myfanwy as he spoke, nor the boys. His words sounded flat. They were tired words, words he didn't believe in. "They've only been a week or so. From Aberystwyth. Good boys, too. I told them I'd hire one of them in a minute, but I've got my laborer. 'Can't use another,' I said. Not now, with summer almost here. But Harry Tempest took one on. They had to toss a coin to see which'd get the job. The other's going to stay on a spell, keep looking. Now they need a place to live." He paused to clear his throat. His voice became tighter, more tentative. "I said I'd . . . I'd talk it over with the missus."

Euan and Rhys exchanged puzzled glances. Myfanwy sat, unblinking, her lips pursed, her eyes cast down at the table.

"We could put both in with Rhys and Euan. For a spell, not for long. Just through the summer till we get ahead again," Hugh explained, gaining in confidence, having at least broached the subject without an immediate refusal. "I know it would mean more work for you, and you've got plenty, but Rhys and Euan could help you more and . . ."

"I'll not have strangers living in my house," Myfanwy said curtly.

In Sugar Notch, with a bigger house and the girls to help with laundry and cooking, Myfanwy steadfastly refused to take in boarders. "First thing you know, they'll be making eyes at the girls," was her objection. "Then they'll be wanting to marry them, but I'll not have my girls married to miners, not as long as I have my breath to put a stop to it."

"These are good boys is what I'm sayin'," Hugh argued. "And they're needing a roof over their heads."

"If it's a meal and a room for the night, that's one thing, but you'd have them move in for good," she protested. "Let them find their own places."

"I know the house is small," Hugh continued to press, "but there's just the four of us now, and Ned the Splicer told me today there's a good chance we could have a bigger house before long."

"So we could take in more boarders?" she snapped. "Then we could cater to the whole town! And after I'm worked to death and six feet under, then you can marry one of them hunky women who's used to scrubbing and doing for eight or ten or sixteen! You bring boarders in here, Hugh Morgan, and we'll be no better than them . . . them *animals* over the fence and across the street, them and their caterwauling and their indecency!" Then, shaking her head, she repeated adamantly, "I'll not have it! I'll not have it!"

Euan had never heard his *mam* so angry before. It upset him to hear her so riled, but his *dada* persisted. "How much is in the tin then?" he asked.

"Enough," was her terse reply.

"And if we're idle a good part of the summer?"

"We'll make do."

"And the debt?" he asked. "What of that?" When Hugh was hired to work in Jeddoh, the company advanced him money against his future wages to move his family and possessions. The debt was a sword over their heads.

"We'll make do," she repeated firmly.

"That's not good enough," he said. "I'm trying to hold things together the best I know how, and I've got to look ahead to the day after tomorrow and the month after next. Now Tom Pryor was down to Wilkesbarre. He said there's talk beginning of a strike across the anthracite fields by fall. This Johnny Mitchell and his UMW boys came through talking up the union, setting up locals and the like. They've already organized most of soft coal, but they're saying anthracite'll be the real test."

"By fall?" Myfanwy asked skeptically.

"By the time of the elections, maybe before. When demand is high. And they're saying it could be long, maybe months this time."

He paused to let this grim prospect take hold.

"How big is this union now?" Rhys asked.

"Six, maybe eight thousand."

"And they figure to get the rest organized by summer?" Myfanwy scoffed. "Why, that's folly! There must be eighty thousand miners in anthracite."

"I heard more'n twice that *Mam*," Rhys piped in.

Euan had no interest in this talk of debts and boarders; he had never even heard of a union, and strikes he didn't understand. He knew they were supposed to mean that men didn't work, but hadn't his *dada* worked during the strike in Sugar Notch? He stifled a yawn and continued to trace patterns on the tablecloth with his finger.

"This Mitchell says he can do it," Hugh said. "Now's the time to look ahead. If we took in boarders, come fall we could have a good bit of the debt paid off and some to see us through a strike. If things happen like they say, a man won't be able to just pick up and go twenty miles to work another mine. He'll have to go to West Virginia or Colorado, and things is worse there."

"I won't have it. No! No boarders!" Myfanwy said.

Hugh sat silently for a moment, running his hand back through his thinning red hair. In matters of the household, Myfanwy had her way, but when it came to the boys, Hugh's word was law. "When I talked to Ned the Splicer this morning," he said finally, trying a new tack, "he told me there was an opening for a breaker boy and asked if Euan would be wanting it."

Euan perked up when he heard his name. Out of the corner of his eye, he saw his *mam* stiffen and her hand slide across the table till it rested on his arm.

"Would you then?" Hugh asked the boy.

"What?" the boy replied, looking from face to face, anxious now that he had missed something important.

"Would you be wanting a job picking slate in the breaker?"

"Yes, *Dada*," Euan answered, still puzzled.

"You can start tomorrow then. We'll walk down after and tell Ned."

"I can start tomorrow?" Euan asked, the news finally sinking in.

"That's what I said. You do want to, don't you?"

A broad smile crossed the boy's face. "Yes, *Dada*."

"Then it's settled," Hugh said, but it wasn't as easy for him to smile. He had no taste for what he was doing. He tried to sound chipper for Euan's sake. A boy's first job was an important event, even if it was in the breaker. "Your pay goes to your *mam* for the tin, and you get your spending share from her, same as me and Rhys."

"Yes, *Dada*."

Hugh turned to Myfanwy, whose eyes were dazed and

sad. "Well, *Mam,* our Euan's to be a breaker boy. He'll be needing some clothes then."

Myfanwy sagged momentarily in her chair, then looked at the boy, whose face was lit with pride. "And boots, too," she said.

And so, Euan was fitted up with some of Rhys's old clothes and Rhys's old boots. His own coat and hat would do, but he would carry no lunch pail of his own till better times. Now he would be like other boys his age; he would have a job. He would be in the breaker, working, not sitting in school. He would be earning money to help at home, growing up, finally growing up.

As if in a dream, Euan walked down Frog Street after supper with his *dada* and Rhys to see Ned the Splicer, past the black breaker, whose upper windows, reflecting the setting sun, burned orange . . .

"Is this my new breaker boy?" Ned the Splicer asked.

"It is," his *dada* answered. "Say thank you to Ned then."

. . . past Irish boys, kicking a rag ball in the dusty street, boys who worked in the breaker . . .

"Ned's a good man," Hugh told Euan. "He could've chosen any boy, but he took you, because he knew you could do it."

. . . past the finer, newer houses in Cheesetown to get his working papers from the town magistrate, John Jones Owen, who also ran the boardinghouse, for the law of 1899 allowed a boy aged fourteen to sixteen to be employed in the breaker "if he could read and write the English language intelligently."

"And do you read your Bible now, lad?" John Jones Owen asked, leaning forward over the registration desk in the front hall.

"Yes, sir," Euan told him.

"And can you write your name?"

"Yes, sir."

"Then write it here, lad." and Euan wrote his name

neatly, without any splotches, on a paper that John Jones Owen put forth.

"And how old do you be?"

"Fourteen, sir."

"A fine lad of fourteen, are you?" John Jones Owen asked and winked at Hugh, then handed him the paper to sign, and Hugh signed the paper, which John Jones Owen then witnessed and sealed, and Hugh paid the magistrate his fee of fifty cents. With that, Euan, who was actually a fine lad of eleven, was now a breaker boy.

The old Glen Ellen #1 breaker that towered over Jeddoh had been built by G. B. Markham and named for his wife. It was a remarkable structure for its day and was widely copied, but newer machines and better designs now rendered it obsolete. John Markham loved the Glen Ellen, so it continued to roar and rattle, to ingest wagonloads of coal and disgorge them in consumable pieces, thus keeping tenements in New York, schools in Boston, factories in Hoboken, and stores in Philadelphia warm throughout the winter.

It was also a splendid target. The southeast side rose a dizzying ten stories from ground to top, presenting a flat, windowless wall of tempting proportions. If a boy had a good arm, stood on the far bank of the creek that skirted the colliery, and heaved a good-sized stone at the breaker, he could hit the wall some sixty yards away. Most nights after supper, boys gathered on the bank of the creek to "hit the wall," as they called it. Or if there was nothing to do on a Sunday afternoon, someone would say, "Let's go down and hit the wall," and in no time the bank of the creek would be swarming. Bets were placed; arguments broke out over the scarcity of stones; champions were declared or toppled. Or Ned the Splicer came by and chased them all away. If stones became too scarce, teams would be appointed to sneak over the fence into the colliery to throw some back. Sometimes weeks went by and not one stone would be thrown, then suddenly the wall would be rediscovered. Or boys grew old enough and strong enough to hit it every time, lost interest, and left the wall to the younger ones.

So far, Euan had hit the wall but once, and only then, as Rhys laughed, "through the courtesy of a friendly breeze." Euan vowed that if he did nothing else by the end of summer, he would hit the wall five out of five times or die trying. But it was still only April.

Rhys hardly ever missed. He liked to hit the wall on a moonless night when he couldn't see the breaker, just hear the slap of the stone against the wood or the ping as it hit the iron stairway that ran partway up the side, or better still, the slap as it first hit the wall, then caromed off and pinged against the metal steps.

Whenever Irish boys were at the creek and Polish or Welsh boys came to hit the wall, the newcomers waited until the first group left before they took their turn. There was room for all, but the custom was to keep a distance from those not their own kind. It made no sense to Rhys that Polish and Irish boys he caroused with at work, boys who laughed at his stories at lunchtime, would barely greet him at the creek or when they passed on Frog Street. He and Euan were even rebuffed by other Welsh boys because they happened to live on Polish Hill. Rhys didn't care, but he had no taste for others, treating the boy like that. So, he and Euan kept to themselves, not from choice but "custom."

After they left the magistrate's, Hugh went home to prepare cartridges and fuses for the morning's blasting, leaving Rhys and Euan to their nightly prowl. They decided to head for the creek to hit the wall but stopped first at the pluck me store to squander Markham's coppers on "coffin nails." Euan had never smoked before and thought he should before he started work.

"In case somebody asks," he reasoned.

"Nobody goes around asking you things like that. Nobody cares!" Rhys tried to tell him. "They got better things to do." But Euan had made up his mind. The two cents bought eight Turkish Trophies, four for each of them, one of which Euan managed to lose before he'd left the store.

"How'd you lose one?" Rhys chided as they headed back into Cheesetown.

"I don't know!" Euan grumbled. "It fell out of my pocket I guess. I don't know. Give me one of yours then."

"Four for you, four for me. If you lost one, that's your tough luck!"

"I bought them!" Euan shot back. "It was my two cents!"

"And what about the sweets I buy you all the time?" Rhys reminded him.

"You never buy me," Euan said just to be contrary.

"I'm always buying you!" Rhys shouted, appalled by Euan's ingratitude. "Tell me once I didn't! Licorice sticks! Jawbreakers! And what about those chocolate and jelly things you spit out after I paid a nickel for?"

Euan walked ahead, kicking up small clouds of dust in the middle of the street. "That's the last time I buy you," he announced blithely.

"Here then, Indian giver!" Rhys said, exasperated, and discreetly gave back one of his Turkish Trophies so no one on the street or prying from windows would see, but Euan, pleased that he had prevailed, pulled out his cache to add Rhys's to it.

"Now what are you doing?" Rhys asked. "You want the pastor to look out and see you? Or Mrs. Owen Williams? Cripes Almighty! They'll be tripping over themselves to tell *Mam* they saw her boys smoking in front of the church!"

"I was just counting them."

"That's probably how you lost the first one. Put 'em back!"

To get to the creek, Rhys and Euan always took a shortcut through Dr. Koons's yard down near the end of Frog Street. Dr. Koons, the company doctor, was an old crank who, it was bruited, lay in wait each night to catch boys sneaking through his yard. No one in memory had ever been caught, but the story was told and retold of how some *had* been years back and were forced to swallow a whole bottle of castor oil as punishment. Euan hated castor oil, and his heart pounded every time they took the shortcut, but Rhys was dauntless. Euan was certain he purposely made more noise then necessary just to let Dr. Koons know he was in his yard, defying the old crank to come out and nab him. To add to the danger, Dr. Koons lived next to John Markham, and a picket fence was all that separated their yards. Angering the doctor was one thing, but John Markham was something else.

"Rhys, can't we go around?" Euan begged nervously.

"Oh, no!" Rhys cried with mock grief. "My brother's a scaredy-cat!"

Euan offered to give Rhys back his coffin nail, but it was no use. His brother had already forged into the darkness along the fence, and Euan had no course but to follow.

As luck would have it, some Irish boys, Digger O'Shea and the Morrissey twins, Patsy and Dick, were coming down from the creek at the same time. Rhys had gotten into a fight with Digger, who was younger than he but big for his age and a bully to boot, during his first week in Jeddoh. Some yardmen had pulled them apart before any blows were struck, but Digger had been itching to have another crack at Rhys ever since. As they brushed past each other, Euan held his breath and stood as close to the fence as he could, trying to appear inconspicuous.

"Well, if it ain't Morgan," Digger said to Rhys in a voice too loud. "Lookee, Patsy, it's the Welsh hunky, takin' his little sister for a stroll. I been lookin' fer ye all over town."

"I'd say you found me then, didn't you?" Rhys asked in a more subdued voice. He wasn't one to run from a fight, but Markham's backyard was hardly the place for it. Besides, he knew that Digger, like all bullies, was a coward at heart. "Now what are you going to do about it?" he challenged.

Digger wore a plug hat, an old suit coat, a vest buttoned to the top, and flannel pants patched at the knees. Everything was a year too small. He wore gloves to give his opponents the impression that he was hiding something underneath besides bare knuckles. "I'll give ye three to get runnin'," Digger said, ramming one fist against the palm of his other hand, "or I'll beat the livin' piss outta ye. One!"

"I didn't know you could count that high, Digger," Rhys said, holding his ground, while Euan tugged nervously at his sleeve.

"Jest fer that, I'm gonna bust up yer little sister when I'm finished with ye!" Digger said, pumping up his courage. "Two!"

But he never got to three. Instead, Mrs. Koons poked her head out of her back door and shouted, "What's going on out there? Be off with you, or I'll be getting the doctor!"

"See what you did now?" Rhys snapped. "You'll get us all in Dutch!"

"Not me, buddy!" Digger chortled and gave Rhys a push. At that same moment, Patsy stuck his foot out behind Rhys, and Rhys toppled backwards into a hedge. Digger guffawed, then hightailed it with his cronies down the path to the street, yelling, "In the ya-ard! In the ya-ard!"

"All right, you ruffians, I'm getting the doctor!" called the irate Mrs. Koons. "You'll be sorry you came into this yard, you will!"

"Get me out of here!" Rhys cried to Euan in a hoarse whisper, "or it'll be castor oil for both of us!"

This jolted the boy into action. He rushed to Rhys's side, and anchored him while Rhys thrashed to his feet again. Together, they groped and stumbled their way up the yard to the back fence, where Rhys collared Euan, hoisted him over, and followed with a leap himself. All the while Mrs. Koons bellowed her threats at the top of her lungs. They headed straight for the creek, running till they had crossed the footbridge that spanned the swift current, stopping only when they were out of breath.

"That was a close one!" Euan said, still gasping. "I saved your neck, didn't I?"

"That you did, little brother, that you did!" Rhys

laughed. "I could almost taste the castor oil! I swear I heard the missus pull the cork from the bottle! We almost had Markham after us, too!" Rhys was exhilarated by their close call, even the scrape with Digger. He seemed born to be forever leaping over fences, streaking recklessly through the night a few steps ahead of his destiny.

"It was a good thing I was there to save you," Euan boasted.

"Watch out for that Digger, you hear? He's trouble," Rhys warned him. "You hear?"

"I hear!" Euan said, looking around for a stone to throw at the wall. "I bet they didn't leave stones for us either."

It was dark now and clear. The breaker loomed in the moonlit sky like a black giant. Euan found the first stone, ran to the edge of the bank, and threw it with all his might, but it fell far short, landing in the bushes just beyond the fence that rimmed the colliery.

"What's the matter? Thinking about tomorrow then?" Rhys asked, picking up an odd-shaped stone for his first throw. "You barely got that one across."

"It slipped," Euan said, shrugging, then knelt to search for another.

"Take your time," Rhys said. "Think of right where you want it to go, and then aim for that spot. Like this!" And he hurled his stone into a high arc, then listened for the report above the sound of the rushing water...

("Crack!")

"See? Just take it easy. Don't hurry so," Rhys continued. "The wall's not going anywheres. And you're throwing too high. All your strength's going up, not out. Throw it out!"

Euan had had about all the advice he needed for one day. Still, it was Rhys telling him. He always tried to do what Rhys told him, so he took up another, this time smaller, and threw it more out than up, hoping against hope, but it sounded on the shale, short of the wall.

"That was better!" Rhys shouted. "I bet it went twenty feet farther at least! Keep trying, you'll do it." His own sailed off into the dark, slicing its way through the night air . . .

("Crack!")

"What's it like?" Euan asked after a moment. "In the breaker? What's it like?"

Rhys was silent. It was a question he didn't want to answer and wished the boy hadn't asked. "It's not easy . . . ," he said somberly.

"I can't wait," Euan glowed. "Then I'm going to be a driver like you!"

"You'll have to hit the wall first, nipper! Like this!" Rhys shouted, full of the devil again, and threw another stone at the huge black form, then held his breath . . .

("Crack! Ping!")

Emerald House was run by "Owney" Riley but owned, like everything else in Jeddoh, by John Markham. Every day after quitting, miners and laborers came by to "take their wet." Some never left until Owney closed at midnight. The Emerald was popular with "foreigners," many of whom had no women or family or place to call home, unless a straw pallet in a room shared with six strangers could be called a home. Men from Cheesetown stopped at the Emerald, too, but sat apart from the Irish, who separated themselves from the Polanders. Fights were a common, almost tiresome, interruption in the night's drinking, but when Owney played his concertina, there was tranquility.

Boys congregated with their buddies on the steps in front or along the side near open windows, listening to the music and stories from inside and watching the fights. Many were sent by worried mothers to make sure tippling husbands got home without falling facedown into some ditch.

Rhys and Euan made the Emerald their final stop before home. They sat out back on some barrels and listened to Owney's concertina while Rhys showed the boy the proper way to inhale a coffin nail. Euan tried to do as instructed but swallowed the smoke instead.

"This is fun," he announced gamely, coughed, rubbed his stinging eyes and coughed again.

"You don't have to keep puffing like a steam engine either," Rhys said. "And blow the smoke away so it don't smell up our clothes, or *Mam*'ll know what we were up to. Sometimes I step in dog dirt going home so she don't smell the smoke so easy. You can't do that too many times though, or she'll catch on."

Just then, a fight erupted inside the Emerald. Before long, it spilled out the side door into the adjoining yard. The fighters, Chicken Eye Joe and Jack Mulhern, were both drunk and could hardly stand up. Except for the handful who leaned from the windows to shout encouragement, few inside and none of the boys outside took much notice.

"Weren't they at it last week?" Euan asked.

"And the week before," Rhys snorted. "You think they'd find somebody else to fight once in a while."

Euan yawned and rubbed his hand over his tired eyes.

"Ready to head home?" Rhys asked.

"Not yet. Tell a story first.

"It's late. We got to be home."

"Come on, there's time," Euan insisted. He liked Rhys's stories as much as Rhys liked telling them. Rhys had an uncanny ear, a knack for stories.

"All right, but a short one," Rhys groaned, sounding more indisposed than not. It was all part of a nightly turn. Next Euan would say to Rhys that if he really didn't want to tell a story, he didn't have to, but Rhys would admit that he'd agreed to do it and would keep his word. All that was left was the choice of the story itself. Tonight it would be "Hudsonryder's Ghost," one that Euan never tired of hearing.

"And don't you fall asleep," Rhys warned, "or I'll leave you here."

"Come on then, start!"

"It happened in the summer of '63," Rhys began, "down Killickinnick way in the old Big Vein colliery. Now the Big Vein was a deep shaft mine that had the richest seams in all of Pennsylvania. 'Enough coal for a thousand and one years of mining, not a day more,' its owner, Big Tom Wilcox, used to say. Now that summer there were over two hundred God-fearing miners working the old Big Vein and one dyed-in-the-wool atheist. Hudsonryder was his name, and all the church-going miners shunned him like the plague. The boys in town threw rocks at his rickety old house. 'Sinner!' they called him and 'shame of the devil!' Finally Hudsonryder could take it no more and vowed that one day he would seek revenge on the people of Killickinnick for the sorrow they had caused him, but the people just laughed and went about their way.

"One day, Hudsonryder was heading down the gangway to his workings, and didn't the fireboss, a regular church-man, stop him and say that he'd found a feeder of gas in Hudsonryder's chamber. 'Walk in there wearin' that flame, me bucko, an' 'tis sure you'll meet the God that created ya!' the fireboss warned him. Well, Hudsonryder became angry at that and pushed past that fireboss and walked straight down to his breast, and sure enough, his lamp set off the gas, and he was blown to kingdom come.

"All that was left for the miners was to go in and pick up the pieces of Hudsonryder that were scattered across the chamber—a leg here, an arm there. His head was blown clear off at the neck. When they found it, they thought it was a lump of coal, it was burnt so black.

"'Alas, Hudsonryder is no more!' one miner cried. 'He paid the price for his ungodly ways,' said another, and they piled the pieces into an empty mine wagon.

"All of a sudden, an eerie cry rattled their teeth, and Hudsonryder's voice echoed through the mine. 'Behold, you mortals who have scorned me! Now you shall feel the weight of my revenge!' The miners quaked with fear, then fell to their knees and prayed to God to deliver them of this godless ghost. The mule hitched to the mine wagon kicked and reared and refused to move. 'The mule can see the ghost!' they said and quickly brought down an old blind mule and hitched it up. Unable to see the ghost, the blind mule pulled the wagon through the gangways to the cage, and Hudsonryder, or what was left of him, was brought up, and the pieces were dumped in a wooden box and driven to his house at the edge of the patch. When they set his clothes over top the fence, they burst into flames. The men dropped the box on the porch and ran with fright.

"On the day of the funeral, an undertaker showed up with a fine old hearse and a team of matched white horses, but at the sight of the casket, they bolted and ran wild through the streets, and again, the voice of Hudsonryder's Ghost filled the valley. 'Behold! I have kept my word! And now you shall feel my scourge!' The people of Killickinnick trembled in their boots. Grown men fell to their knees and wept. Women and children ran to hide their heads. The sky turned dark as pitch, and thunder and lightning split the air.

"So they hitched up the blind mule again, and the mule carried off the casket, but instead of stopping at the graveyard—for the good folk of Killickinnick didn't want an atheist buried in their holy ground—they drove a bit farther to Papoose Lake and threw the casket in.

"'Glory be to God! We're rid of that wrongful man! Now may we live in peace!' the miners cried, but when they got back to town, they saw hundreds of rats running from the mine shaft, followed by clouds of black smoke. 'There's a fire in the mine!' they shouted. The flames from Hudsonryder's chamber had smoldered since the explosion and now were burning out of control. Once more, the vengeful laugh of Hudsonryder echoed through the valley.

"'Please, Hudsonryder,' they cried, 'forgive us for tormenting you, but don't let our mine burn! It's all we have! Please, put out the fire!'"

"Suddenly there was a mighty roar, and the earth rumbled and shook. A gigantic crack opened at the foot of the colliery and ran right up the middle of Main Street, splitting Killickinnick in half. On it went, past the graveyard, all the way to Papoose Lake, and the water of the lake flowed into the crack and down into the mine, flooding the shafts and gangways, drowning the fire! Hudsonryder's revenge was complete. He had also drowned the mine!

"The people of Killickinnick had one hope left—to bury Hudsonryder's casket where they should have in the first place—in a piece of holy ground! So, they rushed back to Papoose Lake and, lo and behold, the casket was gone! The water had carried it down, down, down into the mine. Old Big Vein would be the resting place of Hudsonryder—forever!

"With the mine gone, the town was doomed. The people left their homes and moved to other towns, other mines. But the Ghost of Hudsonryder followed them for sure, for whenever a miner crushed his hand or twisted a leg or was killed by the damp or a squeeze, 'twas Hudsonryder's Curse they blamed. To this day, his ghost is not at rest. It's down there, deep under the ground, and it won't quit till all those who put it there are dead in their graves."

Rhys's voice was barely a whisper when he finished. He told the story as though he believed it, as though it were true, as though he'd been there to see it all take place. As for Euan, no matter how many times he heard it, Hudsonryder's Ghost always enthralled him. He loved the way Rhys affected a brogue and how at times his eyes grew wide with terror, then trimmed to slits with talk of wickedness and evil. But most of all, he loved it because the story gave him the shivers. The story seemed real to him, too.

Back in Sugar Notch, when Rhys told the story, Euan tried to imagine it happening right there where they lived. There was even a house at the end of their street that looked like Hudsonryder lived in it, although it was empty and since had fallen down. There was a pond nearby, too, and a cemetery, and a big, ugly man who worked in the ice house and wore a patch over his eyes whom Euan pictured whenever he thought of Hudsonryder, but everything was different now in Jeddoh. He had to find all new people and places to go with the story. There were plenty of houses to pick from and not just one but two cemeteries. He hadn't seen any lakes nearby, but there was Crystal Pond just a short walk over the ridge, and Rhys had promised to take him there next time the colliery was idle. Mr. Markham was just how Euan pictured Big Tom Wilcox, and Ned the Splicer became the fireboss, but he still hadn't found a Hudsonryder, and he'd looked everywhere—in the stables, in the pluck me store, at church, all up and down Polish Hill. There wasn't a decent Hudsonryder to be found.

"It's not really true, is it? The story?" Euan asked on the way home.

"Not likely," Rhys told him, not really sure himself. "Things like that only happen in the Bible, not in Pennsylvania."

"Where'd you hear it?"

"Remember Red Nose Mike? In Glen Lyon? He told it first I heard. At a 'come all ye.'"

"Red Nose Mike. Ain't he dead then?"

Rhys didn't have to answer. They both remembered vividly the day that Red Nose Mike was carried up. There'd been a cave-in. Red Nose Mike had run back to warn his crew, but a falling rock sent him sprawling on his back over the narrow, bladelike track. As he struggled to lift himself, a timber fell and caught him across the waist. The impact cut him in two.

◆◆

As the night surrendered to day, the Morgans joined the procession down Frog Street to the colliery. Euan walked between his *dada* and Rhys, proud and nervous, folding, opening, then refolding the paper sack that held his lunch. One by one, overhead, the stars flicked off, as if to save their light.

"Even the stars are pinchfists," Euan thought.

At the foot of the colliery, the yard was thick with men, somber gray faces in the somber gray light. He was one of them now. One of them.

"Roll your leg up," Rhys told him as they waited in line to peg in.

"What?" Euan asked, screwing up his face.

"Your britches!" Rhys said louder and pointed to Euan's cuff, which was dragging along the ground. "They won't let you be a breaker boy if you look like a 'billy cups.' "

"What? I can't hear!"

Rhys gave up. It was useless to compete with the rumbling machinery, the venting steam. Besides, their *mam* had stuck pieces of rolled-up string into their ears to keep out noise and dust. It was easier for Rhys to stoop and roll up Euan's cuff himself.

The line to peg in was long and grew longer behind them. Euan stayed at his *dada*'s side as they inched up the hill, excited to be able to watch the cage be loaded up close and hear the gate groan as it slammed into place, to feel the shudder as gears unlocked and hoisting sheaves as big as a man spun, dropping the miners a thousand feet into the belly of the earth, to smell the tar grease the yardmen globbed onto the straining cables, to feel cinders fall onto his face from the steam loki as it shuttled empty cars to the breaker.

"We're needing a number here!" his *dada* shouted to Ned the Splicer when they neared the peg board.

Ned opened his book and perused his lists. "Number two ought seven!" he called back and wrote Euan's name in the book with a stubby pencil.

"Remember it now," his *dada* instructed. "It's to be your pay number, too, and don't forget to peg out at quitting, or . . . if anything happens." He didn't have to explain. Euan already knew that if there was a disaster underground or in the breaker, the workers had to peg out when they reached safety. Any pegs remaining belonged to those who were not as lucky.

"Hurry along there! Yer holdin' up the road!" a voice called from back in the line as Euan scanned the board for his number.

"There it is!" Rhys said, pointing. "Five down, seven over." Euan's heart pounded as he dropped the peg into the slot.

"Till quitting then . . . ," his *dada* said and patted Euan on the shoulder. His *dada* looked awkward, as though he wanted to say more but couldn't find the words. "Do your best . . . and do everything Ned the Splicer tells you now."

"It's us, *N'had*!" Rhys said, poking his father, then called, "See you at quitting, nipper!" as they hurried to board the cage before the gate fell. Euan felt a rush, a fear of separation. He wanted to go with them. Somehow he thought that Rhys at least would stay with him awhile longer, to show him what to do, to help him out. He didn't want to be left here with strangers. Before the cage dropped from sight, he saw Rhys wave.

Ned the Splicer told Euan to wait beyond the peg board till he had time to take him across to the breaker. Euan sat past last whistle, till every man and boy had pegged in and Ned had recorded the names of those who had now shown up to work, till Ned discharged a chronic latecomer, a foreigner who was bewildered by what was happening to him, till Ned checked out some trouble in the steam shanty. Three times Ned passed by, and three times he ignored Euan. Out of boredom, Euan opened his lunch and ate a piece of cheese, although he wasn't hungry, nor was he sleepy, although he'd been awake most of the night, wondering what his first day would be like, thinking about Hudsonryder's Ghost. Then came first whistle, a piercing shriek loud enough to wake the dead.

"Markham's alarm clock," Rhys always called it, but Euan was certain it was a warning from Hudsonryder's Ghost. Then it was get dressed and run down for oatmeal the way he liked it—left to cool overnight—sausage and eggs, biscuits and tea, then to the privy for him and Rhys while his *dada* gathered together the clay and cotton wadding and blasting cartridges he'd prepared the night before and kept in a shed out back. Then there were flour and sugar and potatoes to be carried from the cellar for his *mam*, string to be stuffed into his ears. By the time they left the house, second whistle had already sounded. It was hurry, hurry all morning. Hurry to get dressed, hurry to eat, hurry to do your business, because you won't get another chance all day; now it was sit and wait and wait, hurry up to wait.

His eyes closed. His head nodded. He dozed off.

"Morgan!" a voice called sharply.

Euan looked up. Ned the Splicer was towering over him.

"You're not paid to sleep, boy. There's a nickel you'll be docked."

"But I . . ."

"Follow me then. Haven't got all day," Ned said and turned toward the breaker. Euan jumped to his feet and followed the man's broad strides across the yard, taking two or three for every one of Ned's. Ned was a big man, tall and lean, too tall to work underground. "I got tired of picking splinters out of my head," he'd say. Still, he knew the mine and the breaker as well as any man who worked them, and for good reason. On the day that G. B. Markham opened the Glen Ellen, Ned started as a slate picker. Sitting astride the next chute was John Markham; the two became fast friends. By the time John took over the mine, both he and Ned had worked every job, from shoeing the mules to stoking the boilers, from shoring up timbers in the gangways to tippling wagons in the breaker. Once, a cable on the cage snapped, stranding it and twelve men three hundred feet down the shaft. Two men were lowered to fix it. One fell to his death. The other lost all the fingers of his hand. Ned volunteered for the job. Markham had no choice but to let him try. It took twelve hours, but Ned strung a support cable down and spliced it to the broken one. The cage was brought up, and the men were saved. Since that time, he had been known simply as Ned the Splicer, although few remembered or bothered to ask why.

The sun shone brightly on the breaker as they crossed the yard. Euan had watched it with interest while he was waiting. He especially liked the loaded wagons that inched up the steep, narrow track from the pit head, barely squeezing by the empties coming down from the top house, but there was little to see beyond that. The breaker, bulky and oddly shaped, gave no hint outside of its inner muscle and guts. As they neared the door, Ned took small wads of clay from his pocket and stuck them into his ears, then raised his neckerchief like a bandit, until it covered his nose and mouth. Euan had already knotted his, as Rhys had shown him, and did the same. All at once the breaker started to rumble. Wheezes and whines of the most curious sort filtered out through cracks in the walls.

"The grinders," Ned the Splicer told him. "They're startin' up again."

"It sounds alive," Euan thought, "like a giant black beast that grinds up coal." Ned unlatched the door, which flew open, blown by the beast's hot, dusty breath. Ned bade him follow, but Euan held back.

"Come on, boy!" Ned the Splicer called and entered the dark orifice.

"Don't be a baby!" Euan told himself. "It's a big shed, not a beast. It's where you work then," and he followed Ned in, feeling that he was not so much entering as being swallowed up.

Ned led him through dark halls, up twisting stairs, past old men with brooms who spent their days sweeping coal dust, thick and never-ending, that settled everywhere like black snow. As soon as a passage was cleared, a new layer had fallen, and the sweeping began anew. They passed the screens, rows of huge sievelike frames that tilted and jounced and somehow separated the newly picked coal into its marketable sizes, screens that had been known to tear apart careless boys who fell asleep up top and were swept down with the coal into their dispassionate arms. From where he stood, Euan could look down into the bins that held the coal till it was loaded for shipping and, if he leaned far over the wooden rail, up through the maze of chutes to the picking room. Even farther above, unseen, were the rollers themselves, the grinders, with their massive, interlocking teeth that crushed the raw chunks as easily as his *mam* broke apart a lump of sugar. Ned nudged him to move along.

As Euan followed Ned through the interior, the noises grew louder and more varied. Each machine, each chute drummed its own peculiar rhythm, added its own jangle to the deafening din. The noise made Euan dizzy.

When they finally reached the picking room, Euan's mouth fell open in astonishment. What he saw was a crowded, high-ceilinged vault, crisscrossed with rickety catwalks and crooked stairs, lit only by a wall of grime-choked windows. Patches of sun glinted in, sending bright shafts through the thick, dusty air. It looked to him like the inside of an old church he'd seen in a picture book. But it was the center of the room that caught his fancy, where the breaker boys sat astride six metal chutes, four to each, slowing down the steady stream of coal with their feet. Here they picked out slate and "bony," which was half coal, half rock, as well as sulfur balls and any other foreign objects Markham could not in good conscience sell, and dropped them into the "rock box" below. What impurities the boys on top of the chutes missed, the ones behind picked out.

Ned motioned Euan to set his lunch on a shelf with the others, which he did, grateful that his was in a bag with his name on it and not in a pail like the rest, which looked all the same to him. Then Ned waved him to the bottom of chute no. 3, where an empty place, his place, waited. Ned picked up a piece of slate and held it next to a piece of coal. Slate was dull and black; coal was shiny and black. He took a piece of bony next and smashed it in two with a mallet. The good half he threw back with the coal; the rock was tossed into the rock box. Keep the coal, throw out slate and bony. That was it, that was his job.

While Euan was watching Ned the Splicer, he felt a presence behind him and smelled a most disagreeable odor—the stench of foul breath and soiled underwear. Turning, he confronted the "cracker boss," a grim-looking, barrel-chested man by the name of Daniel Bryfogle.

Bryfogle had a red, bumpy nose and mean eyes. His bloated cheeks were covered with hard, thick stubble, which he sometimes rubbed across the tender faces of his boys as punishment if they misbehaved. He wore the same clothes day in, day out—a battered derby; a coat he could no longer coax across his belly to button; a collarless shirt spotted with meals long lost in memory; a faded velvet vest, secured in front but flapping loose in back; and checkered riding breeches, worn not for riding but to accommodate his peg leg. With the thick oak rod he carried to keep his boys in line, Bryfogle shoved Euan backwards to the empty spot on the bottom of chute no. 3. Euan looked to Ned the Splicer to intercede, but the man had already fled, driven perhaps by the unholy smell that Bryfogle wore like a shroud.

"Is this to be my boss?" Euan wondered. "This . . . this 'billy cups'?"

Bryfogle read Euan's mind. "I could plant this here stick up yer nose, boy," he said with a raffish sneer. Euan could in no way hear the man, but he wasted no time climbing to the splintery plank that extended over his chute. Before he could dig his feet into the rushing stream, Bryfogle jabbed him with the oak rod, nearly knocking him headfirst into the flow. There would be no further instructions. The oak rod was law. That was all he needed to know.

The pain shot through Euan like a jolt of lightning, bringing tears to his eyes. He looked around, hoping that his ignominious arrival had gone unnoticed, but everyone seemed intent in his duties. Most, like him, had their noses and mouths covered with neckerchiefs, which periodically they raised in order to spit tobacco juice onto the coal. Some looked no more than eight or nine, the rest, his age. Only a few looked older. The biggest and brawniest of the lot sat at the top of each chute. Euan wondered if that was some sort of privilege and what they'd done to earn it.

In no time, Euan had mastered his job. Coal was coal; slate was slate, and little scrutiny was needed to tell them apart. Besides, sitting as he did at the bottom of the chute, he saw less slate and bony than the other boys and soon was able, like them, to watch the coal and also keep an eye on Bryfogle, who kept vigil over his errant crew from the catwalks overhead. For a man of his girth and infirmity, Bryfogle was unusually agile. Using the oak rod as a crutch, he negotiated the treacherous pathways with alarming speed and, thus, was able to deliver vigorously aimed clouts and heart-stopping jabs to nodding laggards without warning. But whenever the overseer had his back turned, the boys bombarded him with a riot of obscene gestures. They also talked to each other, despite the noise, using a sign language of their own invention, which fascinated Euan as much as it confounded Bryfogle.

To pick slate, Euan had to hunch as far forward as he could, bending his legs at an odd angle in front of him. He felt his first cramp when the crooked board on which he sat began to cut into his thighs, when he tried to shift to a more comfortable position. It was only a cramp, but it felt like someone was twisting off his leg. "If I could just . . . stand," he thought, "I know the pain'd go." He tried to rub it when Bryfogle wasn't looking, but then his back started to hurt, and his shoulders. And then a sharp piece of slate cut his finger. He yelped with pain, but of course no one heard. The only comfort he got was an angry look from Bryfogle. "Wish I had a pair of gloves and a bottle of N'had's liniment and N'had to rub out the cramp," he said to himself. "He'd rub it out good."

(Pick slate, pick slate, pick bony, pick slate . . . )

The coal streamed by in an endless, mesmerizing blur. Sometimes the flow thinned till he could see the bottom of the chute. Then it rushed, fast and deep, threatening to push him back off the edge of his board. His fingers grew red and sore. "It's like trying to catch bits of glass floating down a mountain creek," he thought. "If I stop to nurse a cut, ten other pieces get missed, then the cracker boss'll come, and the cracker boss'll come, and . . ."

(Pick slate, pick bony, pick bony, pick slate . . . )

Euan smelled Bryfogle behind him. "What now?" he wondered, and turned to see the cracker boss, eyes glaring, holding a handful of coal he'd found in Euan's rock box.

"Don't let it happen again!" he seemed to say, then gave the boy a jab in the ribs as an inducement. Euan had never hurt in so many places at once. He tried to think of one part of him that didn't ache. His ears! They didn't hurt. Nor did his elbows and toes. He wiggled his toes— they were fine!—and tried to wiggle his ears. Rhys could wiggle his ears, but he never could. He tried to think of things that took his mind off the hurt. Miss Protheroe! He wondered what she had to say when his *mam* delivered her note. ("Oh, dear me! A breaker boy so soon? I shall miss him, Mrs. Morgan!") Miss Protheroe! He had no tears to shed for the loss of her. No more penmanship! And twenty whacks and punishment in advance! Yes, he was better off rid of her, and that made the pain seem less.

(Pick bony, pick bony, pick slate, pick bony, pick slate . . . )

He thought back to last night, to their adventures, how he'd smoked his first cigarette. "And when we came home, when we came in the door, *Mam* lifted her nose in the air and sniffed. 'Who stepped in something?' she said right off, and Rhys said, 'He did,' and I said, 'I did,' and Rhys nearly busted out laughing, and *Mam* grimaced and said, 'Get out with you then! And make sure you scrape every bit off!' and she swatted Rhys and called him a 'divil' for keeping me up so late, and I went out and scraped my boot over the edge of the porch, and *Mam* said, 'If there's a dog that done his duty within half a mile near my house, my boys'd find some way to step in it as sure as I'm living!' And she swatted Rhys again for laughing while she was trying to scold us, and we went up to bed and got in bed, and Rhys said, 'Who stepped in something?' and we started to laugh all over again until our *dada* yelled to us to be quiet or he'd bring in the strop. . . . ''

(Pick slate, pick bony, pick slate, pick bony, pick . . . )

Suddenly the cascade of noise fell away. The coal slowed to a trickle and stopped. "What is it then?" Euan wondered. In the stillness that followed, he could actually hear chatter above the screens and rollers, which continued to rumble, coal or no coal. Across all six chutes, boys groaned and stretched as they began the laborious process of standing up. Stiff joints cracked.

An older boy at the head of Euan's chute climbed atop his board, bent over, and farted loudly in the direction of his buddies, then turned, smiling, to accept their jeers.

It was Digger O'Shea.

The lag, it seemed, would last but a few minutes. The boys never would learn why the coal had been stopped-up underground, nor did it matter. It was a common enough occurrence, and they were grateful for the pause, for it broke the tedium, gave their blood a chance to course unrestricted again. Some used the time for a game of tag over the chutes and catwalks. Bryfogle thought the time was better spent separating bony but had to catch the offenders first to prove his point.

On the chute next to Euan, a lank boy whose face and hands were black with dust, raised his neckerchief, held a finger against his nostril, and blew a thick gob of black snot into the chute. "Black outside, black in," he said when he noticed Euan's stare. "What's your name, greenhorn?"

"Euan Morgan."

"Ain't I see you in church?"

Euan nodded. "What's yours?"

The older boy regarded Euan coolly. "Jenkin Davies."

"How old are you?" Euan asked.

"Fourteen. We're all fourteen here. I been fourteen for three years now," Jenkins answered.

"Well, if it ain't Morgan's little sister!" a voice shouted. Without even looking, Euan knew who it was, and his insides started to churn as Digger and the Morrisseys came toward him, gingerly straddling the chutes, scattering anyone who happened to be in their path. Euan knew Digger worked somewhere in the colliery, but he supposed it was underground, not here, where he looked like a grown cow among spring calves. As for the twins, neither had a face burned by intelligence. Patsy—or was it Dick?—had a wandering eye, and the other had lost his front teeth in a fight, which caused him to spit profusely when he spoke. No one dared address him for fear he'd answer back.

"Lookee, Patsy! They're jobbin' girls now! Maybe they'll give yer sis a go next.''

"Git to work, ye lazy galoot!" Bryfogle roared from the catwalk above and swung the oak rod in a broad, threatening arc. Everyone laughed as Digger scurried back to his perch, protesting his innocence. "All of ye! Git back to work! There's bony enough!" Bryfogle bellowed. The boys picked up their mallets just to satisfy the blustery grump, who retreated to his office after a moment, not to be seen for the rest of the morning.

Suddenly the air rattled with the sound of new coal being dumped into the hopper up top. The boys cheered and tossed their mallets back into their dump chutes. Euan wondered as he raised his neckerchief why they were glad to see the coal again. He was only beginning to get the kinks out of his body.

Just then, Digger swung around and waved his thick fist at Euan. "See ye at lunch, ye little pisspot! Teach ye to git me in Dutch!"

Euan was taken aback by Digger's fury. Now, besides the monotony and pain, he had the threats of a bully to contend with.

The sound of the coal moving down through the breaker toward them grew louder and more ominous. The top boy on each chute pulled his cap down over his ears, reached out, and locked hands with those next to him, then set his legs, knees together, squarely in the flat of the chute. All began a low yell that rose higher and higher as the coal approached, climaxing in a delirious scream as the coal crashed with startling velocity into the front rank. Coal flew into the air, hitting boys in the face on the way up, on the head coming down. It was like an explosion, the force of which nearly knocked some top boys, like duckpins, onto the rows behind. Only the grip of their mates saved them. Now Euan knew why only the biggest and brawniest sat atop each chute.

A cloud of thick dust settled once more over the picking room. Shafts of light that sliced through the gray air became Euan's measure of time. As the sun rose higher in the sky, the shafts tilted more steeply. Patches they lit crept slowly across the backs of boys in front of him, then converged in a single gash of light on the window before disappearing altogether. With the sun beyond the top of the breaker, the only evidence that morning had passed was his enormous hunger, that and his fingertips, which were bleeding.

In school, Euan lived each day for the noon whistle. When it sounded, he squirmed until Miss Protheroe dismissed the class, then he was out of his seat like a shot, up the street to home and a bowl of hot broth, sausage left from breakfast, his bread and tea. If there were chores, he helped his *mam;* if not, the rest of the hour was his. He would spend it sitting on the steps of the pluck me store, sucking on a licorice, listening to the conversations of bosses who stopped in for supplies. He imagined that when the noon whistle sounded in the breaker, everyone stopped what he was doing, pulled up a stool or bench, and sat down to eat his lunch, much like Emerald House without beer. And without fights. It was a time to rest, to gab, to tell stories.

Euan barely heard noon whistle today above the noise. He felt it more, felt it in the change of mood in the picking room, in the heightened anxiety that set the boys squirming on their boards. No one was allowed to grab for his lunch until Bryfogle had given the word, which he could not do until the wagons that had started to the top house had been dumped into the hopper and all that coal ground and picked. The last few minutes before lunch was called were always the most aggravating, especially when the flow diminished quickly, like today, and Bryfogle was nowhere to be seen. Finally Digger hurled a rock from his box at the boss's door.

"Hey, lumber foot! Git off yer fat arse!" Digger yelled. Immediately a barrage of missiles from other rock boxes crashed against Bryfogle's door until the boss, still groggy from his morning sleep, appeared on the catwalk.

"What the hell ye tryin' to do? Scare a man to death?" he roared.

"It's noon whistle," some boys shouted back. "We're hungry!"

"Then eat, ye sons of whores! And I hope youse all choke!"

Before he could finish, the boys were gone. Euan held back from the stampede, waiting to see what the others did, half expecting or hoping that someone would take him in tow, but he was painfully ignored, even by Digger and the Morrissey twins, who vanished as soon as they plucked their grub off the shelf. There were no stools or benches to sit on. Everyone grabbed the nearest open spot, blew the coal dust off his lunch pail, and devoured his food before someone else did. Euan's sack had been torn open and inspected. His bread had fallen out and been trampled by half the crew's boots.

"Be glad you got any left," one boy said. Others near him sniggered. No one moved or offered a place on the floor or steps, so Euan clasped what was left of his paper sack under his arm and moved to an empty spot near the windows. His hands were dirty and smelled of the tobacco juice the boys had been spitting onto the coal all morning. His fingers were sore and covered with cuts and dried blood. He had trouble opening the sack, trouble lifting the food to his mouth, but before he could take even one bite of his cheese, Digger and his cronies emptied a bucket of coal dust on him from the catwalk above. The picking room erupted with laughter. Everyone had anticipated the prank, had even see the culprits creeping into place, but no one said a word. The same fate had befallen each of them when they were greenhorns.

When the shock of the prank wore off, Euan was heartsick. He shook as much dust as he could from his head and clothes, but what food he had left was covered. He had thought of his lunch a good part of the morning, in the last hour, of little else. Now this!

Everyone waited anxiously to see what Euan would do. Most in his place had thrown their food away or started to cry. Someone had chased the culprits once, boxed their ears good, then ate *their* lunch, but Euan was in no mood for that. He wanted food more than he wanted revenge, even more than a good self-pitying cry. He was so hungry he hurt inside. "It's just coal, not dirt," he reasoned as he tried to scrape it off. "Coal can't make you sick. Mules chew it, Rhys said so. the blasting powder makes it salty. And what'd Jenkin say? 'Black outside, black in'? What's the difference then?" he asked himself and bit into the cheese.

"Disgustin'!" Digger groaned from above. Others were equally repulsed, but Euan wolfed it down, the coal crackling between his teeth as he chewed. He ate all his meat, too, and drank his broth, although it was cold. Even so, he was left hungry.

The boys soon lost interest in him and drifted away to their separate mischiefs, leaving Euan to contemplate his aching fingers, the tips of which had been rubbed nearly raw by the coarse dust and rough-edged coal.

"Red tops," Euan heard a voice say. He turned and saw a surly-looking boy slouched against a beam, finishing off a piece of meat.

Euan looked at him, puzzled.

"Red tops we call 'em," the sloucher said, then held up his hand, palm out, to show the thick calluses he'd grown. "Your hands get like this. If you last."

"How long then?"

The sloucher smirked and turned away. He'd said all he wanted to say.

Huddled beneath a set of stairs was a scrawny Polander who, like Euan, seemed alone and friendless. The two watched each other, neither wanting to be the first to speak, neither sure that the other was someone he wanted to speak to. Finally, the Polander left his niche and offered Euan a piece of sausagelike meat from his lunch. Euan demurred but relented once the aroma hit his nose. The meat was spicy and greasy, unlike anything he'd ever tasted, but he was famished, and it filled him. The Polander gave Euan a plug of his chewing tobacco, too, which Euan stashed in his pocket for later.

"Thank you," he said, then hiccoughed for having eaten so fast.

The Polander was Tadeus Harakal. He'd been in America four months and spoke only a few words of English. Once they exchanged names, they had little else to talk about, "*Icz szczac! Na reke. Icz szczac!*" Tadeus said when he noticed Euan's fingers. At the same time, he waved his hands in front of him and went through the motions of what looked to Euan like urinating.

"I don't . . . I don't understand," Euan said, shrugging.

Tadeus's big, dark eyes rolled in frustration. "*Icz szczac! Na reke!*" he repeated. Finally, in desperation, he took Euan by the shoulders and led him down to the dank, smelly privy, where Euan managed with difficulty to undo his buttons and relieve himself. When they returned to the picking room, Bryfogle was standing at the bottom of chute no. 3.

"This yer place, boy?" the cracker boss asked in a low growl. At once, a dozen jeering boys surrounded him.

"I . . . I guess so," Euan stammered.

The boys sniggered with anticipation.

"Look what I be findin' in it," Bryfogle snapped and pointed to Euan's rock box, which was unaccountably overflowing with coal. "How ye 'spect Boss Markham to be makin' any money if'n ye throw away all his profits?"

"But I . . . I didn't . . ."

"Then who did? Are ye sayin' these pitiful lads put coal in yer box jest to git ye in Dutch?"

Euan looked around at their smug faces. "No," he said weakly.

"Well, yer not thinkin' 'twas I who'd be doin' it?"

"No."

"Well, who then?" Bryfogle demanded, pulling the boy closer to him.

"I don't . . ."

"*Who* then?" Bryfogle repeated and set the tip of his

peg leg on the toe of Euan's boot, then pressed down hard. "*Who* then?"

Euan twisted with pain. "I did! I did!"

"We don't shine to liars 'round here, boy, ye hear? I'll have yer pay docked fer ever' piece of coal in yer box!"

"I said I did it! I said!" Euan pleaded, near to tears, but Bryfogle wouldn't let up. Instead, eyes glinting, whiskey breath panting, he pressed down even harder.

"Hold still while I'm puttin' manners on ye, boy! Ye ain't in no prim schoolhouse now, ye hear? And I ain't no schoolmarm!"

Suddenly coal crashed into the hopper up top. The boys groaned loudly, disappointed that their sport had come to an end. This time it was Euan who wanted to cheer. Bryfogle reluctantly loosened his grip on Euan, then barked his usual threats as the boys scrambled back to their chutes. Euan hobbled in circles for a moment to regain the feeling of his foot before hoisting himself up to his board, which, to his amazement, had been removed and replaced by a sawed-off broomstick. He stared at it dumbly, uncertain what to do.

"Ye there!" Bryfogle bellowed, brandishing the oak rod. "If'n yer not goin' to work here, git home with ye! Go back to yer mother's teat!"

The boys pulled down their caps and began their low yell as the coal rushed nearer. Euan had no choice. He yanked his neckerchief into place, sat across the narrow handle, and hunched forward, grasping the sides of the chute as best he could. He clenched his teeth, his eyes, his whole body against the onslaught. The roaring coal and the boys' rising scream mingled till both were the same, till both exploded at once over his head, under his feet, filling him with terror.

"What am I doing here?" he cried desperately. "This is what hell must be like! What am I doing here?"

And he thought for the first time of leaving this place.

"The sun's gone down," he thought at first. "No, too early for that. Must be a cloud. It's gone cloudy."

(Pick slate . . . pick bony, pick slate . . .)

The picking room had grown dark, darker than usual, like a tomb. The air was gray and thick, so thick he could hardly see the top boys. Hours had passed since lunch.

(Pick bony. . . pick slate . . .)

His mind had grown dull. The pain had worn him out, pain and lack of sleep. He couldn't think, didn't want to think. Thinking didn't shut pain out; it let it in, left room for it to come in, to sneak in between thoughts. It was better to blank it all out, all, all his thoughts, both good and bad. Better to be thick and dull, like the air he breathed. Gray outside, gray in. "That's how the others do it, day after day," he'd told himself. "That's how they last; they shut it all out. They don't see patches of light or think of comical stories to pass the time. They shut it all out. All."

(Pick slate . . . pick slate . . .)

"All they see is bony and slate, not coal. Coal don't matter, only bony and slate, bony and slate."

(Pick bony. . . pick slate . . .)

Sitting on the broomstick didn't hurt anymore. It did, but he didn't think about it anymore. His fingers didn't hurt either, because he didn't think about them. He shut them out. And the fire was gone from his stomach, the fire from the spicy meat Tadeus had given him, or was it the tobacco he'd chewed, the juice he'd swallowed, although he knew he wasn't supposed to but forgot? Digger no longer worried him, nor did Bryfogle. He was too tired to worry. All he wanted was . . . all he wanted was . . .

(Pick slate . . . pick slate . . .)

. . . was to sleep . . . to sleep.

(Pick slate . . . pick . . . pick . . .)

He didn't even think of running anymore, of escaping the picking room, because every path, every passage led him back sooner or later to his *dada* and to Rhys, and how would he tell them that he'd run away or look them eye to eye and say, "I couldn't . . . I'm too sore . . . too tired . . . I'm afraid?"

(Pick . . . pick . . . pick . . . pick . . .)

There'd been a stir on top of the chute earlier. A holler. A fuss. He didn't know what. He didn't care to look, but Digger suddenly rose up on his board, holding something he'd found, something in the coal, and waved it for the others to see. Euan didn't look. He shut it out.

It was a finger. A grown man's finger, blasted off or torn off, and loaded with the coal. They were always finding things—blasting cartridges, shoelaces, crucifixes— and now a man was without his finger, and Digger was waving it for everyone to see. He stuck it up his nose and in his ear. The boys all laughed, then Bryfogle came, and Digger tucked the finger under his cap, but Euan ignored them both. He didn't even realize the coal had stopped, that the room had grown quieter, that he could hear the weighmen shouting and cursing in the top house.

"Get ready, greenhorn," Jenkin leaned over and said snidely.

"Get ready?" Euan asked. "For what?"

"You'll see. You'll see."

"A boy! Send up a boy!" a voice called down from the top house. "Send up a boy!"

Bryfogle charged across the catwalks, reached down, and nudged Euan with the oak rod. "Hey! Yer wanted! Up there!" he shouted and pointed to the top house. Euan looked about suspiciously. Their faces were smug, so cruel. Was this another prank? Why would *he* be wanted?

"Send up a boy!" the voice called, growing more impatient.

"Now, boy! Or by God, I'll be draggin' ye up there meself!"

Euan struggled to his feet, stiff and cramped, and made his way up the side of the chute, half hunched, to the landing up top, stepping over boys who grinned like he'd done something wrong and got caught.

"Last to come, first to go," the sloucher gloated.

"Good-bye, greenhorn!" Digger called as Euan passed and goosed him with his newfound finger.

"Good-bye, greenhorn!" the boys chimed in chorus.

Euan was in a daze, like one awakened from a long

sleep. He looked at Tadeus, who sat in silence, his only expression an unmistakable look of fear, an expression more unsettling than the others' jeers.

The top house was bigger than Euan thought, bigger than it looked from the ground. The wagons entered through a wide passage after their precipitous climb. On the flat was a scale, where they were unhooked from the cable that hoisted them, then weighed. Each wagon was then pushed down a slight incline till it reached the tipple, a circle of track and floor that locked the wheels in place, then tipped like a cradle, dumping the cargo into the hopper below. When righted, the empty wagon was shunted to another track, reattached to the cable and sent back down to the pit head.

The hopper was a huge, fifteen-foot-deep trough with four tin-covered walls that tapered in at a steep slant. Its bottom was filled to the height of several feet with chunks of coal.

Before he knew what was happening to him, someone, the man they called McGuinness, tied the end of a long rope around Euan's waist. Another led him to the edge of the hopper. It was Mr. Powell, whom he knew from church.

"Down you go then," Mr. Powell said.

Euan looked at him blankly.

"Come on, you're holdin' the works up, boy!" Powell added testily, as though Euan should have known what to do. Finally, unceremoniously Bryfogle pushed Euan over the edge, and he slid to the bottom of the trough. At once, the men started shouting orders at him.

"Get that chunk! The big one!"

"Throw that one up there!"

"No, that one!"

"I said over there! Over there!"

Euan's head spun around, trying to sort out their conflicting commands, trying to move the chunks from the center to the sides, trying to figure out just what it was he was doing. The rope kept getting in his way, too, and it was hotter here with the sun beating down on the roof. He stopped to wipe the sweat off his brow.

"Hurry, boy!" 'Tis all day yer takin'!"

"Jump up and down! In the center! Harder! Harder!"

"That one next! The big one! Yes!"

"Jump now! Harder!"

Suddenly the coal shifted under his weight. It was a slight, almost imperceptible, shift but unmistakably in a downward direction. "What's down there then? What could be at the bottom to make it slide?" he wondered, and suddenly he realized. Surrounding him on four sides were slanted walls, all slanting toward him. It reminded him of the funnel his *mam* had a home, the funnel she used for pouring. This pit was like a funnel—a funnel for coal! The coal was ready to pour out the bottom, and he was standing right over the hole!

"Put your weight into it, boy! Jump now!"

"You got it, lad! One good jump'll do it!"

"Harder! Jump harder!"

But the hole was clogged, jammed with coal, and he was trying to open it, free it so the coal could pour again. But where? Down where? The he remembered what was below, and he could hear them, rumbling, turning, their giant teeth, hungry for coal, ready to crush the coal after it fell through, down, down, to the rollers! The grinders!

"Don't stop now, boy! You're almost there!"

"Jump hard, boy! Jump!"

The jam shifted again beneath his feet. He froze.

"Come on, boy! You're takin' too long!"

"Jesus, lad! Ye'll have us here all day!"

Euan was afraid to move, afraid that one step would break the jam, and he would pour out the bottom with the coal. The rope! Yes, the rope! That was why they'd tied it around him! To keep him from sliding through with the coal! One end was tied around him, but what of the other? He traced its path by sight across the coal, up the side of the hopper, till it disappeared over the edge of the deck. No one was holding it!

"Look at 'im, Bryfogle! He thinks he's goin' down with the . . ."

"Let 'im! He's jest a little fart, a lazy little fart! Who's to miss 'im? Not me! I got me a bunch more, and they's all trouble if'n ye ask me!"

"You goin' to stand there all day, lad?"

"Get me out!" Euan yelled. "Pull me up! Pull me! Pull me!" but the men just laughed at him. They enjoyed his fear. In his fright, his panic, he stepped forward, causing the jam to give way. The coal resumed its relentless slide. He scrambled across the sinking bed, screaming for help, yelling for his *dada* to come, or Rhys. He clawed at the side wall, trying to get a grip, but the tin was too slippery. He felt the coal falling away beneath his feet, heard the men laughing, looked down, flailing still, and through his tears saw the last chunks slide into the hole. Yet he did not.

"You didn't think we'd let you fall through, did you, lad?" McGuinness said as Bryfogle tugged Euan up the sloped wall.

"Nuthin' to be feared of! Had me foot on the rope the whole time, ye little fart, ye stinkin' little fart!"

Euan could barely stand when they lifted him to the deck. He was safe, but he couldn't stop trembling with fear.

"Nothing to be scared of, boy!" Powell comforted.

"His first day," Bryfogle sneered. "Prob'ly his last."

Euan pushed past the men, found the stairs, and went back down, running, stumbling down the stairs, till he saw the rollers, huge and hungry, rumbling round and round, but he couldn't . . . couldn't run past them. Something kept him from running past.

"Stay, stay!" they said, the rollers said. "We're hungry . . . so hungry! We want you . . . stay, stay! Come closer . . . ," their teeth enticed, and he drew closer still, closer, fascinated as another wagon was tippled into the hopper, and its coal dropped through the maw into the waiting teeth to be chewed into little pieces, which dribbled through the teeth into the chutes below.

"No, no! That could've been me," Euan thought. "Could've been me."

"Come closer, closer. We will grind you. We *want* you."

"No, no!" the boy said.

And he heard the yell from below, the long, rising whoop, the delirious scream, and he wanted to be with the boys, wanted to scream with them, because now he knew why they screamed. Each of them had been lowered into the hopper, and each, like him, had cheated the grinders. They screamed because they were alive, still alive to scream! That was why, and now he screamed, too, because *he* was alive. He screamed until he couldn't hear himself anymore, until the roar of the grinders and the coal being tippled into the trough was one roar, and he raced down to his chute, and his board was in place, and the broom handle was nowhere to be seen.

◆◆

WHEN he opened his eyes, Rhys was standing over him.

He forgot at first where he was, how he'd gotten there, gotten out. It had ended somehow. Had the whistle blown? He couldn't remember, but the boys had flown off the chutes and disappeared. He found his way outside, following their footprints in the coal dust. It had turned cool. He buttoned his coat and sat against a fence by the loading bins to wait for his *dada* and Rhys. He fell asleep, then woke in the fading light.

"You didn't peg out," Rhys said.

"I forgot. I forgot my number."

"Five down, seven over. I did for you. You all right then?" He could see tear streaks through the coal dust on the boy's face. Then Euan held his hands out, turned his bloody fingers for Rhys to see.

Rhys gasped. "Didn't they help you at all? Didn't they tell you what to do?"

Euan shook his head no.

"Those bastards!" Rhys snarled under his breath and started to rub his brother's shoulders. "Raise them every chance you get, and keep moving them, or they'll get stiff. Did you piss on them?''

"What?"

"Did you piss on your fingers? It's the best thing. Makes 'em cure up faster. Didn't they tell you?''

"No," he answered, dimly remembering something Tadeus had said or tried to say or tried to show him.

"G'head. Piss on 'em now," Rhys said. "I'll wait."

Euan tried to undo the buttons on his pants, but his fingers were too sore. Rhys tried to do it for him. "Aw, hell," he said, more quickly undid his own and urinated on the boy's outstretched hands. Euan cringed from the stinging bath. "They'll be better in a couple of days," Rhys told him. "But save all your piss. You'll need it."

Halfway home, Euan could walk no farther, so Rhys hiked him onto his shoulders and carried him piggyback. Hugh was waiting with soap and towels, and together they washed him with warm and rinsed him with cold, wrapped him in a blanket and carried him to bed. He was too tired to eat. Myfanwy sat with him in case he woke. She bathed his fingers.

He looked fragile to her, almost helpless as he slept. "Is this why we had a family?" she asked when Hugh came in to look at the boy. "We owe them better than we had."

Hugh thought for a long time. "It'll give them the strength they need to pull themselves out of this place."

"If it don't kill them first," Myfanwy added, brushing away a tear before it rolled down her cheek.

Just then, the boy stirred.

"Don't let him get me," he mumbled, still in sleep. "He's after me, don't let him . . . !" Myfanwy pulled the cover up and tucked it under his chin. "He's . . . he's after me!"

"It's all right," she said, soothing her hand across his cheek. "It's all right now."

". . . after me, after *me*!"

"Who?" she asked. "Who's after you?"

"The Ghost," he whispered, drifting deeper. "The Ghost. Hudsonryder's Ghost . . ."

# PART TWO

## ZAKRZEWSKA

MYFANWY brushed aside the curtain and stared in amazement at the human river that surged past her front window. "Where in creation could they all be coming from?" she asked her family. It hadn't occurred to her that Catholics also celebrated Good Friday or, if they did, that they would turn out in such large numbers to do so.

"It's getting late," Hugh said, looking at his watch. Myfanwy sighed heavily. She was beside herself with apprehension.

"Isn't it like this on Sundays?" Gwen asked. She and Meb had arrived that morning on the train from Wilkesbarre and were to stay the weekend.

"I don't know. Pastor Wheat starts Communion at nine. Sunday school don't let out till past eleven," Myfanwy explained. "They do whatever it is they do in between."

"Well, if we don't leave now, we'll miss the start," Hugh said, nearing the end of his patience, "and I do not want to have Pastor Wheat staring down his nose while I bring my family in to Good Friday service ten minutes late."

"All right," Myfanwy said, yielding, "*Dada,* you go in front with the boys. I and the girls will follow behind."

Like a barque venturing into hostile waters, the Morgans

63

stepped from their porch and broached the Catholic tide, which flowed relentlessly toward Holy Trinity. At the prow, Hugh deflected the waves, nodding at the few men he recognized, ignoring the annoyed looks of those forced to change course as his family parted their waters.

"What are you doing up on the Hill?" their scowls seemed to say. "Go back to Cheesetown, where you belong!"

Myfanwy had never seen so many Catholics in her life. Dressed in their garish Sunday best, which to her looked fit more for a circus than for church, all of Polish Hill and Irish Flats seemed to be marching in procession up the middle of Frog Street, four and five abreast. Myfanwy had confined herself to her kitchen all morning, making sure that everything was just right, scrubbed clean, tidied up, just right for the girls' arrival. The urge to drop everything and wait for them on the front porch was unbearable, but the thought of having to greet them in front of her hunky neighbors was worse, so she stayed inside, sending Euan out every few minutes to see if they were coming. Now, walking down Frog Street surrounded by hunkies, she felt choked, smothered by their numbers, as though they were filching the very air meant for her, and didn't regain her composure until several minutes after she reached the safety of her pew in the Presbyterian church.

To Gwen and Meb, Jeddoh was an affront. Neither thought Cheesetown was as dreary as their *mam* had described it. They recognized Mr. Markham's house as soon as they saw it, and the church, and Mrs. Owen Williams's with its porch swing and pruned hedges. "Once the trees bloom and there's flowers, it'll be quite the picture," Gwen told her *dada* as they walked up Frog Street from the train station, but here enthusiasm fled when they crossed the tracks into Irish Flats. The colliery was gloomy enough, both girls agreed, but the gray mounds of culm that ringed the town made it look oppressive, as though Jeddoh were being choked by its own refuse. By the time they reached the Hill, the girls were walking with their heads down to shut out not only the dingy squalor but the leering eyes of eligible young men that locked on them as they hurried up the street, the same eyes that were ogling them now as they made their way to church. Gwen didn't know how her *mam* could stand it from day to day.

"Well, girls? What do you think of our new home?" their *mam* had asked after their reunion in the parlor. She looked more winsome and youthful than either of them could remember.

"It's . . . it's lovely, *Mam*," Gwen said, trying to sound cheerful, but all her mother's efforts had failed to disguise its drab rudiments. "It's not so big that you have to spend your whole day cleaning."

Meb was not so tactful. "What's that smell?" she asked, sniffing the air. "Did someone knock over a can of kerosene?"

At nineteen, Gwen was the elder of the two by a year. If Meb's auburn hair, deep-set eyes, and thin, angular face made her the picture of her mother, Gwen was her father's daughter through and through. Her hair was reddish and more curly, her face freckled, her smile more winning, and while she was not exactly plump, her figure was more ample. Gwennie was the one suitors caught sight of first, the one they asked out to the music hall and then for a soda, even though she always insisted that Meb come along, a calamity suitors invariably avoided by recruiting a cohort to even up the clumsy threesome.

If Jeddoh was both less and more than the girls expected, it was still not the greatest shock awaiting them that morning when their *dada* and Rhys met them at Jeddoh Station. Gwen marveled at how much Rhys had grown since they'd seen him last. "He'll be breaking all the girls' hearts soon," she said.

"What do you mean? I've broke a string of 'em already!" Rhys boasted with a smile that betrayed his innocence.

"Wait till you see the other one," their *dada* told them. "He's in the breaker now."

Gwen wasn't sure at first if she'd heard him right. She turned to Meb, wondering if she'd missed that line in her *mam*'s letter, but Meb was equally shocked. And indeed, there Euan was on the porch when they reached the house, holding his hands stiffly in front of him to invite their immediate sympathy.

"*Mam*'s inside," he announced solemnly. With his white shirt and tie, dark coat and knickers, he looked like a little undertaker.

"And what about you, old sobersides?" Gwen asked, wincing at the sight of the scabs on his fingers. "Don't you have a hug and a kiss for us?"

"You can hug me if you want, but you have to be careful of my hands."

"Well if you'd rather not . . ."

"It's all right then," he said bravely. "They don't hurt so bad today. I've got dip . . . dipsenation."

"What's that?" Meb asked, not sure she wanted to know.

"*Dis*pensation," Rhys groused as he caught up, having had to carry their heavy valises from the station. "That means he gets out of chores 'cause of his red tops."

"Oh, my!" Gwen said. "I guess you can't eat the sweets I brought you then—taffy, your favorite. You got to pull it apart with your hands."

Euan's face brightened but quickly clouded over when he remembered he'd best appear forlorn if he wanted to keep his dispensation.

"I'll eat it for him," Rhys offered.

"No, you don't! They brought it for me!" Euan protested and had dogged her footsteps ever since, that is, until their *mam* announced that there would be no taffy until after Good Friday church was over.

Euan had survived three days in the breaker, but he wondered as he sat in church next to Rhys if he could survive three straight hours listening to Pastor Wheat's long and boring *hywl*. He looked forward to the hymns, because then he could stand and stretch, but his legs soon tired, and he welcomed the chance to sit again. He liked Pastor Wheat's Crucifixion story, too, especially when the roaming soldiers drove the spikes through Jesus's hands.

But most of the time he thought about the taffy waiting for him at home.

Rhys and Euan had to sit in the third row, apart from the rest of the family, because the church was so crowded. Rhys didn't mind. From there he had a better chance to eye Mary Markham, the eldest of the five Markham girls, who sat across the aisle and pretended not to be eyeing him back.

When the service was finally over, they were up in a flash and out the side door to the yard behind the chapel, where most of the boys congregated to mark time till they could go home to change out of their Sunday clothes. Tins of Yankee Boys were passed around, and everyone took greater care than usual to keep from spitting on the other boys' shoes or trouser legs. Otherwise, they all might as well have been standing at the pit head or sitting at the chutes. Euan hovered behind Rhys and the older boys, drivers mostly, near a maple that bore the carvings of countless pocketknives, and listened to a story Rhys was anxious to tell ever since he'd learned it the day before from some Irishmen.

"So, there's O'Shaughnessy, down in the mine," Rhys began, complete with brogue, "an' he's beatin' his poor old mule. An' the more he beats it, the less the critter wants to move. Well, who happens by on his way to bless the new air pump but Father Murphy? An' the good Father says, 'Is that any way to be treatin' the animal what carried our good Lord into Jerusalem?' An' O'Shaughnessy says, 'Forgive me, Father, but if the good Lord had been ridin' *this* son of a bitch, he'd *still* be tryin' to git there!'"

Euan didn't understand the story or why the other boys laughed so loud, but he laughed along so they wouldn't think he was stupid. It was funny, too, to hear Rhys swear. That was reason enough, so he laughed all the harder.

Myfanwy made it home with her girls before the savages were let out of Holy Trinity. After mass, Polish Hill erupted with a fever of celebration, the likes of which were seen only on paydays. They gathered in backyards up and down Frog Street at tables, which were really doors torn from hinges and laid across crates, to devour feasts their women had spent weeks preparing.

"Look at them," Myfanwy sneered as she watched from her window, "eating like there's no tomorrow! And the drink! They'll be dancing next, you wait. And Lord knows what else!"

"You don't have to look at them, *Mam*," Gwen said.

"Well, it'll be a sad day when I can't gaze out my own window," Myfanwy replied, craning her neck for a better look. "Agh, look at that one, sitting on his lap. like a woman of the town. I tell you, they'll be the death of me!"

The noisy celebrations continued on through their supper. Hugh had to raise his voice during grace. He knew that God could hear him, but he wasn't sure about his family. Afterwards, they sat in the parlor, listening to Hugh read from the New Testament. Gwen and Meb sang, "*Rhydygroes*," "*Blaen-Y-Coed*," and the family's favorite, "*Crimond*." Myfanwy cried when she heard her girls sing. "You've got the most beautiful voices on God's earth," she told them. Rhys and Euan read some Bible verses, too.

That night in bed, Hugh and Myfanwy lay sleepless, kept awake by music and laughter and shouting, even gunshots, from neighboring yards.

"It's worse than the strike in Sugar Notch," Myfanwy said to Hugh.

"There's a Polish priest coming up special from Wilkesbarre for Easter. Maybe he'll quiet them down. Tomorrow he's taking their confessions."

"Confessions, hah! He'll need more'n a day!" Myfanwy scoffed. "He'd better plan to stay the week!"

Rhys and Euan bedded down in the parlor while Gwen and Meb took their room. Gwen lay awake, listening to the music of a lone fiddler who played on long after the others had fallen mute, and thought of Richard, the young clerk she'd met in the five-and-dime. Then the music stopped, and she wondered if she'd dreamed it, but in the parlor below, Rhys had heard it, too.

"That was pretty... and sad," he said to his brother, but Euan was fast asleep. And then it started again, far-off, a ghostlike melody carried on the wind.

◆◆

"PUT some muscle into it, Gwennie," Myfanwy said the next morning while she and the girls and Euan made a batch of biscuits. "Here, let me show you."

Gwen sighed and brushed back an errant curl from her face. "They don't work us this hard in the mill!" she complained.

"Neither of you is going to make a good wife if you can't bake a decent biscuit!" Myfanwy warned as she attacked the dough.

"The five-and-dime sells biscuits already baked," Meb said. "They call them cookies and put them in bright boxes. They do all the work for you."

"You couldn't get me to eat them," Myfanwy sneered. "They probably rot your stomach out."

"Richard swears they're the best," Meb said without thinking. Gwen's eyes flared as she motioned for her sister to hush up.

"Richard?" Myfanwy asked, smelling a fox. "And who might Richard be?"

"He's... oh, he's just someone," Gwen shrugged unconvincingly.

"He works in the five-and-dime," Meb added.

"Oh?" Myfanwy said in a casual tone that belied her intense interest.

"How much nutmeg did you need, *Mam*?" Gwen asked too anxiously, trying to change the subject.

"Not too much, just a little," Myfanwy answered matter-of-factly.

"How much is a little?"

"Let me do it! If you don't know by now!" Myfanwy snapped, then took the tin from Meb's hand and scooped out a spoonful. "Now remember next time!"

"*Mam*, if you'd write it down, it wouldn't be so hard to remember!"

"Write it down?" Myfanwy asked incredulously. "And if you lost the paper where would you be? It's your fingers that knows, and your eyes and your taste that remembers. Write it down! Hah! Gwennie, get the griddle ready! Euan, bring over the bowl of currants! And don't drop it like last time!"

"Yes, *Mam*."

It was Euan's job to watch over the currants, which had to soften in warm water before they could be mixed into the dough.

"Now," Myfanwy said, turning back to the girls, the tone of her voice leaving no doubt she meant business, "which of you wants to tell me who this Richard is? He's not a miner, is he?"

Gwen frowned at Meb for betraying her. "He's a young man I met," she confessed, more annoyed than intimidated. "He's from a good family, and he's got a good job at Kirby's, and he's going to be moved up real soon. I like him, *Mam*. He's a gentleman, and there aren't many I've met I can say that about. Whenever he comes to call, he's real polite, isn't he, Meb? He knows how to respect a young woman. Ask Meb, she can tell you."

Myfanwy continued to work, spooning currants onto the dough and mixing them through and through, while Gwen just got herself in deeper and deeper.

"Where did you meet him then?" Myfanwy asked. "In church?"

"No . . . no, not exactly," Gwen said, getting flustered.

"Well, he does take you to church, doesn't he?"

"Not exactly, no," Gwen said, barely above a mumble.

"No?" her mother trumpeted.

"He goes . . . to a different one."

"Well, how many churches are there? I should think if he was half the gentleman you say, he'd be escorting you to church on Sunday," Myfanwy huffed. Then a dark thought crossed her mind. "He's not *Catholic,* is he?"

"No, *Mam*!"

"Thank God for that! I don't want you to see this Richard whatever his name is again. At least until he's taking you to church regular!"

"Oh, *Mam*, you act as though that was the only thing that mattered!"

"And what is that supposed to mean? Did you learn that sass from this Richard, too? Well, I won't have it in my house. You may not be living under this roof, but I'm still your mother!" Myfanwy said, her voice quivering with anger. "Euan, step outside!"

"But, *Mam* . . ."

"Go help Rhys with the porches!"

Euan hurried out the back door. He didn't understand what it was his *mam* and Gwennie were arguing about and wanted to stay to hear more, but his common sense told him to leave while the getting was good. He ran down the back steps to the gate and along the side of the house to join Rhys, who was sweeping the front porch, but when he got there, Rhys was nowhere to be seen. His broom and brushes were there but not him. Suddenly another explosion of voices, Rhys's among them, came from the kitchen, and a moment later Rhys, his face angry and flushed, came tearing out the front door.

"Jesus Christ!" he said and kicked the broom across the porch. "I work all morning, go in for a couple of biscuits, and get my head bit off! Well, to hell with their biscuits! And to hell with the goddamn porch!" With that, he stormed off down Frog Street.

Euan sat on the front step, listening to his *mam* and Gwen argue in the kitchen. It made him sad.

"We're getting just like the hunkies," he thought.

Maciejewski's yard was a gathering place on Polish Hill. It was really three yards with no fences or shrubs in between. When Karl Maciejewski moved into the right side of the double block at no. 67, he planted a garden in the corner of his backyard and apple trees along the back fence. He had been a farmer in the old country, and even though he now worked underground, not on top, he wanted to keep his hands in soil. In the rest of the yard, he planted grass, thick grass that grew better than his vegetables, and bought a goat to keep it neatly trimmed. In time, the garden grew smaller and smaller, and the grass took its place. He bought a second goat and planted Jozef Moczygemba's adjoining yard behind no. 69, and when the Zdepkos moved into no. 65 a year later, he planted theirs as well. Now it looked like one yard, and in summer, Maciejewski's was the place to go for shade when the heat bore down on Jeddoh. It was used for weddings and funerals, and today, the biggest Easter feast on Polish Hill. It had begun Friday after mass and would continue the weekend long, pausing only for everyone to go to church and to sleep, and end Monday night only because there was work Tuesday morning.

For weeks, the Maciejewski, Zdepko, and Moczygemba women, and the Gieryk women from across the street, had been baking breads and cakes of every kind, *kielbasa* and *pierogi*, roast goose, venison, pheasant, and hare. This morning, they had risen at dawn to carry baskets laden with a little of each up to Holy Trinity to be blessed by the Polish priest when he arrived. The men had been busy, too, making *polinkey*, a brew of whiskey, beer, and red peppers, which was fermented in metal tubs, sometimes for as long as a week.

Rhys heard music coming from Maciejewski's yard as he sulked down Frog Street and stopped by the fence to listen. It was a strange sound, strange to him, not like Owney Riley's concertina, which was pleasant to the ear. These fiddles he heard were shrill and whiney, but their rhythms were jaunty, and in no time he was caught up by their spell.

He could see three fiddlers in all at the far end of the yard, and one who looked like he was playing a big standing fiddle. In front of them, pairs of dancers were spinning around while others, seated and standing, clapped and whistled in time. It was lively, intoxicating, and in no time Rhys's anger had dissipated through his tapping foot.

"*Polinkey! Polinkey!*" a toothless old man called to Rhys from the path between houses, then raised his cup and quaffed it down.

"*Polinkey!*" Rhys called back with a smile, and the old

man danced some steps he'd learned as a boy in the old country. His legs were stiff, but his memory was not dimmed, and the *polinkey* made him young again.

Suddenly a girl who looked no older than Gwen or Meb ran shrieking past the old man into the street. Five or six rambunctious young swains followed close behind and quickly caught up and encircled her, cutting off her escape. One, whom Rhys recognized from the colliery, carried a bucket of water, which he threw at the girl, drenching her from head to foot. The girl wailed loudly and swung at her tormentors but otherwise seemed to enjoy the attention, while the young men laughed heartily and congratulated their buddy on his good aim. Then unexpectedly another young man emerged from the yard, also toting a bucket of water, which he emptied down the poor girl's back. This time, she was furious, as were the first young man and his friends. A fight ensued, which ended when the first young man smashed his bucket over the skull of the interloper, knocking him out cold, but the girl refused to show her pleasure to the winner. Instead, she made a great show of pouting and ran home to change her clothes, while the victor was hoisted onto his buddies' shoulders and carried back to the feast, leaving the poor loser to nurse his wounded pride and the goose egg he now sported on his head.

Rhys was mystified by this spectacle, by these people. He worked with them, lived among them, but they were strangers to him, and he to them.

"*Pierogi?*" the old man called as he patted his stomach and motioned for Rhys to join the feast. Remembering how hungry he was and having nothing else to do, Rhys soon found himself eating a cabbage *pierogi* and listening to Razor Kudla and his fiddlers play the "*Kozak Zawydija*" in Maciejewski's yard.

❖❖

No sooner had Gwladys Protheroe stepped from her rented carriage than a groom came running across the yard to tend her rented horse.

"Af'noon, ma'am," the groom said deferentially, then

hied the rig away, leaving Gwladys alone outside the picket fence that surrounded the spacious yard and residence of John Markham. Markham had built his house, all red with white gingerbread trim, in a cluster of shade trees, which was now encroached on two sides by barren mounds of gray slag.

"Like an oasis amidst a desert of culm," Gwladys thought, marveling at the house's obvious charms. "So grand and so befitting a man of Mr. Markham's character and station," character and station being the two attributes Gwladys regarded most highly in men. She had come to Jeddoh this afternoon as guest of Mrs. Markham, an invitation delivered in school earlier that week by Mary and her sisters.

"Miss Protheroe," the note read. "I would be most pleased to have you join me for tea this Saturday afternoon in appreciation of the fine attention and skillful cultivation you have so diligently provided my daughters in their educational endeavors. As an entertainment, they shall favor us with various selections from their musical lessons. I shall be pleased to receive you at 3 o'clock p.m. Yours most admiringly, Mrs. J. Markham."

"But what does it mean?" Gwladys's landlady, Mrs. Pardee, asked after her exultant boarder had shown her the note.

"It means, Mrs. Pardee, that Mrs. Markham intends to take me on then as private tutor to her girls! It's what I've been hoping for these past months, and now it's come to pass!" Mrs. Pardee had never seen her boarder so excited. The teacher charged around the parlor, fluttering her hands and striking such dramatic poses that Mrs. Pardee couldn't help but be astonished. "Just think, no more riding to Jeddoh each day in an open carriage! No more leaky schoolhouse or foul-smelling children! I shall be part of the household and live in a mansion . . . well, it's almost a mansion, but it will do just fine! And Mary confided to me that Mrs. Markham is planning a grand tour this summer for the entire family. A grand tour!"

"Oh, my dear, I'm so happy for you," the stout

landlady bubbled, "but I shall miss you, too. You've been like . . . like a daughter of my own."

"You shall have to help me get dressed," Gwladys said, hardly hearing the woman. "I *must* do something with my hair! Something different!"

"Yes, child. Of course!"

"What do you think of curls? And what shall I wear? Everything I own is so old, so drab! I have no color in my life, Mrs. Pardee! I've not got a decent hat either! Ah, this is come so sudden! If only I had more time!" She stopped suddenly in her frenzy and stared off, distracted. Tears welled in her eyes. "I'm to have tea with Mrs. Markham," she murmured with a quiet realization, then giggled girlishly, grabbed her startled landlady, and danced her in circles around the room, chanting and laughing, "The tutor's invited to tea! The tutor's invited to tea! The tutor's invited to tea!"

Thus, as Gwladys passed through John Markham's gate that afternoon with her hair fashioned as usual but with loose crisps circling her face, wearing a dowdy dun-colored dress that she tried vainly to brighten with a yellow shawl and white gloves borrowed from Mrs. Pardee, she felt she was entering into a new life, a life of belonging and acceptance, of new dresses, polished silver, and grand tours. A moment later, she heard squeals of delight as Helen, June, and Rose, the youngest three, charged down the front steps and threw their arms around Gwladys with such gusto that her spectacles almost flew from her face.

"Hello, Miss Protheroe!" Mary called from the open door. "Don't mind them. Come in, do!" Mary was a radiant girl with her mother's hair, long and black, her mother's fair complexion and smile, but her most startling feature, her piercing eyes, were her father's. She was just blossoming. In a few days she would be sixteen.

Gwladys somehow managed to ascend the steps with one moppet clinging to her side and another clutching her hand. "My word, I never knew I occasioned such affection," she said, smiling, to Mary as she entered the vestibule. At once, she was transfixed. Behind the ordinary facade and draw curtains, the decor and furnishings of John Markham's house were more grand than anything she had ever seen, could ever imagine. The panels in the hall were of white oak trimmed with hand-carved rosettes. Oil paintings in ornate gilded frames brought from England glorified the walls. Suspended above them was a mermaid chandelier of pan-hammered brass and cut crystal. Its frosted globes were tinged with ruffles of glass tinted pink and blue. Red carpeting stretched from wall to wall and up the grand staircase. The upper landing was presided over by three majestic stained-glass windows, which the sun ignited into a rainbow of Mediterranean amber, Venetian scarlet, and Munich blue.

John Markham's house was more than a mansion. It was a palace.

"Good afternoon, Miss Protheroe," Mrs. Markham said cheerfully as she emerged from the music room and extended her hand to Gwladys. "I am so overjoyed that you could visit."

"Thank you ever so kindly," Gwladys responded, taking in the sweep of the music room and grand parlor, both of which would soon be hers to enjoy. At that same moment, the elegant mahogany grandfather clock chimed three, as if to signify the start of her new life.

"I assure you," Gwladys gushed, "the pleasure is all mine!"

Rhys sought out Razor Kudla during a break in the playing and found him at a table surrounded by food and beer. Razor worked in the mine as a laborer for an Irishman he despised. Many times, he tried to bribe Rhys to bring him extra wagons. Rhys always protested vigorously at the same time he laughed at Razor's shameless antics. In the end, Rhys would bring the wagons, and Razor would conveniently forget to pay his promised bribe, but it didn't matter to Rhys. He enjoyed Razor's vitality and looked forward to seeing him each day, but their camaraderie ended at quitting. Until now, Rhys had never even know that Razor was a fiddler.

"How long you been playing that thing?" Rhys said as he tapped Razor on the shoulder.

"Rhysie!" Razor exclaimed, his mouth full of food. "I t'ought vas you! Come, sit! Sit! You vant *polinkey*?"

"No, no . . . not for me," Rhys demurred. He knew its reputation.

"Beer!" Razor insisted, and Rhys nodded to be polite. "Jozia, bring my butty some *piwo*!"

"How long have you been playing that fiddle?"

"I t'ink I vas born playin'," Razor laughed and threw back his head, which was a mass of thick, dark curls. He came from a large family and had lived in Jeddoh since he was fifteen. He was nineteen now but looked years older. "No, I vas nipper in Mahanoy City. Ev'ry so an' so, gypsies come in town, play at saloon. Give 'em cup of mushrooms and boilt chicken, an' 'dey play all night! 'Dat is how I learn. Jus' listenin'."

"Is it hard to play?"

"You vant to learn? I learn you."

"Is it hard?" Rhys repeated.

"Naw, is easy! You vant, I make you reg'lar Polish fittler!" he said and handed Rhys his instrument to inspect. Just then, not twenty feet away, another young girl was accosted by a different young man, who poured a bucket of water down her back. The same shrieks and laughter erupted.

"Why do they do that?" Rhys asked.

"Is olt custom," Razor explained. "boy pick out girl he like, vant to marry, t'row bucket of colt vater on her. She call him names."

"It doesn't seem like there are an awful lot of Polish girls in Jeddoh to chose from."

"Is big problem. All vant same girl. If girl pretty, she spen' whole damn day changin' dresses. But on day after Easter, she pick fella she vant from whole church, sneak in, t'row bucket of colt vater on him vhile he sleep."

"In bed? I wouldn't like that, I don't think," Rhys said, shivering at the thought of it.

" 'Den you never get voman, my frient," Razor added, laughing.

"Thank you," Rhys said as Jozia set down his cup of beer.

"*Dziekuje*," Razor corrected.

"*Dzie . . . kuje*," Rhys said uncertainly. "*Dziekuje*. And you, my friend? Why aren't you running around with a bucket in your hand?"

"Here is my voman," Razor said, holding the fiddle. "She sing for me. She never talk back. She eat very little. She vill take me outta 'dis place forever. She is all 'da voman I vant. In couple years, I get 'da real t'ing—big, beautiful voman. Vhen I got money an' big house."

"You get paid then? For playing?"

"Sure! Vettings, feasts, fun'rals . . ."

"Let me see your hands," Rhys asked him. "They're just as callused as mine. They're like leather. How can you play with hands like that?"

Razor shrugged. "Brain tell fingers vhat to do. Fingers listen."

"Aren't you afraid? At work? Of having your hands hurt?"

"Sure. Who is not afrait down 'dere? I am afrait for my neck, too!"

"I don't think about it. I don't feel afraid down there."

"Sure, you fella wit' easy job," Razor kidded. "Try crawlin' t'rough sqveeze sometime, vhere ceilin' creep so fast you can feel it. 'Den you know vhat bein' afrait is."

"Yes, it's awful sometimes, but it's . . . I can't explain it. Being where men aren't meant to be—there's something . . . *exciting* about that."

"An' crazy. I t'ink you crazy, you know 'dat?"

Rhys laughed at Razor's gibe. "Listen, Razor, if I could learn to play fiddle, could I . . . ? I mean, would you let me play with you and your boys?"

Razor looked more pleased than shocked. Still, he kept

Rhys dangling for an answer while he weighed first one side then the other.

"I'm like you," Rhys prodded. "I don't want to spend my life in the colliery. I want to get out of Jeddoh, too."

"I t'ought you say you like bein' in mine?"

"I may be crazy, Razor, but I'm not stupid. It kills you down there—the falls, explosions, gas. And if you live through them, you get the asthma. You die by inches, and that's worse. I want to get out, too. At least you've got a plan and some money. I haven't got either."

"Sure, you can play vit' us," Razor told him. He was intrigued by Rhys and saw great prospects for their future together.

"And I'll get paid, too, like you?"

Razor nodded. "Better you are, more you get."

"I will be the best," Rhys said with his characteristic swagger.

"No, no!" Razor corrected. "I am best. You . . . ? Secont best! Let us drink on it! Jozia! *Polinkey* this time!"

Rhys grimaced but nodded his approval. "*Polinkey* this time. Now, my friend, when do we begin?"

"Mr. Markham insisted on giving the house a name, but I thought that too pursy," Mrs. Markham said, raising a hand-painted teacup to her lips. Gwladys couldn't help notice her hostess's hands, which were as delicate as her Limoges china. Fortunately her own were well hidden. " 'Well, the Vanderbilts do it,' Mr. Markham argued, 'and the Biddles and everyone in Newport! Why can't we?' 'We're in *Jeddoh*!' I protested. 'This is hardly Newport!' Well, Mr. Markham, as always, got his way. The trouble was he could never decide what to call it, the house. It doesn't look like anything but an overgrown school, don't you think?"

Once Mrs. Markham said it, Gwladys had to agree. "But a schoolhouse I would be proud to instruct in," she thought as she raised her cup.

Mrs. Markham had greeted her guest in a morning robe of lace and white satin. "How odd!" Gwladys thought, clearly spying the woman's negligee underneath. "Here it is, afternoon, and she's not yet dressed? Perhaps it's some new fashion. Perhaps society ladies in New York receive their guests thus." Gwladys wondered how she would look in such a robe, lounging the morning away, receiving guests for tea, her coiffure swept up like Mrs. Markham's and held in place on top with tortoiseshell combs. She envied the woman's milk-white skin and raven hair, her petite frame, her taste and reserve, all of which seemed to underscore Gwladys's own unpracticed manner.

More than anything, Gwladys wanted to *be* Mrs. Markham.

The parlor in which they sat, the blue and silver music room, was dominated by a polished-ebony grand piano, the strings of which, Mrs. Markham was quick to point out, were gold-plated and never had to be tuned.

"How convenient," Gwladys marveled as she devoured every detail of the room's decor, from the modish sand-stenciled wallpaper to the velvet drapes woven with gold thread. The names alone made her head spin—Bohemian Lester glass, Royal Dalton lace, gem-embedded Sevres porcelain! "How on earth does she keep all the names straight?"

Just then, Kathleen, the plump-cheeked servant girl, interrupted to ask if Mrs. Markham would be needing further refreshments.

"Yes, another pot of tea," Mrs. Markham replied in a chilly tone. "And tell Mrs. Toole I'd prefer if it were hot this time."

"Yes, mum," Kathleen said as she picked up the tray.

"Kathleen, what is that on your front?" Mrs. Markham asked, noticing a stain on the girl's uniform.

The girl twisted sideways, trying to conceal the offending spot. "A jar of preserves broke in the kitchen, mum. It got on me shift."

"Kathleen, I don't tolerate slovenly girls," the mistress of the house scolded. "This is the third time in a week I've had to talk to you about your appearance. I don't expect to do so again."

"Yes, mum."

"You're not in the bogs now. Or the hog slops."

Gwladys discreetly ignored the exchange. In truth, it made her uncomfortable. She had known too many girls like Kathleen, had nearly become one herself, and longed for the day when she, too, would have Kathleens to order about.

"Yes, mum. Am I excused, mum?" Kathleen asked with her head bowed, her voice barely above a whisper.

"You are excused. And see what is keeping my daughters! They're trying my patience!" Mrs. Markham ordered as the girl fled and added, not caring if she was overheard, "She's a dollop, that one. Two little ones and not yet married! I would have discharged her long since were it not for them, but I can't see punishing the innocent for the sins of the mother."

"No, of course. I agree with you heartily," Gwladys observed, hoping that her shared contempt did not go unnoticed. "I, too, am confronted daily with the rude nature of this foreign element."

"I fear for my girls, of their being exposed to such wantonness."

"Yes, yes," Gwladys agreed and clucked her tongue. She wanted to say, "You are wise in removing your girls from school now before it is too late," but caught herself in time.

"Quality in domestic help is so precarious these days," Mrs. Markham observed. "And no better in the cities, I hear. Consider yourself fortunate that you needn't burden yourself with such concerns, my dear."

Gwladys smiled smugly and sipped her tea.

"Where *are* my girls?" Mrs. Markham wondered and called up for them to join her at once.

"Coming, Mama!" Mary answered from above. A moment later, a conspiracy of laughter rippled down the stairs.

"I shouldn't tell," Mrs. Markham divulged, "but the girls are planning to surprise you in their Easter dresses."

"How nice! thank you, I shall act surprised," Gwladys

said, pleased to be taken into confidence. She was feeling more and more at home.

"I bought the material at Wanamakers's on our excursion to Philadelphia in March," Mrs. Markham explained.

"I remember your going," Gwladys said. "The girls were so excited."

"As was Mr. Markham when I handed him the bills," Mrs. Markham sighed and raised her eyes to the ceiling. "Ever since Mrs. Bemis made the dresses, the girls have been pestering me to let them display them for you. I *had* to give in! I so hope you don't mind."

"Of course not!" Gwladys protested. "You know they're my favorites!"

Suddenly footsteps and nonsense sounded on the stairs. Mrs. Markham and Gwladys exchanged glances of barely suppressed delight as the girls burst into the room and circled around their teacher, each vying for her eye. All five were attired in high-waisted skirts of pink silk chenille with ruffles at the bottom and small bows in back, whose ties trailed nearly to the floor. Their blouses of white silk chenille had miniature bouquets of daisies pinned at the neck. The outfits were completed with pink parasols and straw boaters capped with more miniature daisies.

"My word!" Gwladys piped. "Who might these little princesses be? Not my Anna! And Helen? And June, my little June! You all look like strawberry parfaits, tasty enough to eat! Shall I eat you then? Look at you, Rose! And Mary, you look beautiful!"

"We're dressed for Easter," Helen chirped as the others grinned, basking in her attention.

"Let me see all of you!" Gwladys exclaimed, then motioned for them to turn around, which they did, nudging and giggling as they swirled.

"Now who shall be the first to sing?" asked their proud mother.

Immediately a chorus of "Me! Me!" rose up, and Gwladys was forced to choose among them. Mary started with "In the Good Old Summertime," which she rendered in a pleasant voice, accompanied haltingly on the piano by

Anna. The rest followed with recitations or simple piano pieces, at the conclusion of which the girls retired to their rooms with Mrs. Bemis to work on their petit point, leaving Gwladys alone with Mrs. Markham.

"More tea, my dear?" Mrs. Markham asked after the room had quieted.

Gwladys accepted with a tinge of nervousness in her voice. "Was it evident?" she wondered. "Did I sound too anxious? I must let her lead the way. I must appear gracious and . . . and, yes, act surprised!"

"They are lovely girls, aren't they?" Mrs. Markham asked as she poured.

"My word, yes! I would be proud to call them my own."

"I do hope that some day, Miss Protheroe, you yourself will experience the connubial joys, of which I consider children to be foremost."

"What a peculiar wish," Gwladys thought. While she had long hoped for marriage, she had never contemplated children as part of that design.

"I am afraid those days are far off," Gwladys answered.

"Surely there is some gentleman in your life," Mrs. Markham pressed. "A woman of your qualities must be greatly sought after."

"What is she coming to?" Gwladys wondered. "Is she afraid if I accept the post I'll run off in no time with some gentleman? That's it! She wants some assurance that I will remain for a reasonable duration."

"If such a gentleman does in fact exist, Mrs. Markham, he thus far has failed to make himself known to me," Gwladys lamented.

"Ah, but there are so many eligible bachelors these days," Mrs. Markham offered as comfort. "One never knows what course one's heart will take."

"I assure you, madame, I harbor no . . . ," Gwladys felt herself choking back the words, ". . . no ambitions for matrimony at this time."

"What are you saying?" a voice shrieked inside her

head. "You'll mouth any lie to please her, won't you? Any damnable lie!"

"My dear, I do hope you have not forsworn marriage!" Mrs. Markham said with just a hint of condescension in her voice. Gwladys shifted uncomfortably in her seat, looking for a way to change the course of their conversation.

"Why no! If anything, marriage has forsworn me!" Gwladys answered, then smiled to evidence her good humor.

"Come now! Life has many twists and turns, Miss Protheroe. We never know where it will lead us. Why, just last year my maiden aunt, Miss Claire Cummings, of Rye, was taken in marriage, and she had just passed her sixtieth year. Regrettably, four months after the nuptials, her husband, a Mr. Atwood, perished in a steaming accident. Aunt Claire nearly went mad with grief."

"Pity," Gwladys chimed.

"Ah, yes! To have found happiness so late in life only to have it torn asunder! It *is* a pity!"

Both women sighed in unison.

"There was, however, one consolation. Mr. Atwood was a man of capital. Aunt Claire's living quite handsomely now and finds herself pursued by codgers up and down the Hudson Valley," Mrs. Markham added with a mischievous smile. "So, Miss Protheroe, don't discount yourself. You still have your youth, your health, your . . . beauty, and God is on your side! What more could you ask?"

"A position of respect," Gwladys wanted to say. "Money, love, a home." The list went on.

"Which brings me to a topic of importance that I must discuss with you this afternoon," Mrs. Markham continued. "We've enjoyed your company to the utmost, but there is a professional matter that begs our attention. I hope it won't intrude on your visit."

"No, not at all!" Gwladys said eagerly.

"It harks back to what you earlier called this 'foreign element.' The Jeddoh school is simply no longer a place where my daughters can receive their education."

"I could not agree with you more," Gwladys replied. "The situation is indeed adverse."

"I'm particularly concerned about Mary. She's of an age, you know, when certain consideration must be given to her... her future. She must be prepared to meet the social obligations of a young lady of her station, and, of course, marriage."

"Of course!"

"That is why Mr. Markham and I have decided to enroll her in finishing school this autumn."

Gwladys looked up from her tea with considerable surprise.

"Mind you, Mary doesn't know yet," Mrs. Markham confided, "but we'll be sending her to Miss Cadwallader's School in Philadelphia, where I attended, of course. At the same time, Mr. Markham and I have decided to enter the younger girls in the Episcopal school in Hazelton. It's not the best, and it will mean a lengthy carriage ride for them each day, but conditions simply compel it."

Gwladys was stunned into speechlessness.

"I realize it will be a great loss to you, and my girls will certainly miss you as well. Mr. Markham, however, so wanted me to convey his utmost pleasure at your accomplishments in the Jeddoh school, and he is adamant that you continue there as long as... well, forever, if you wish. He has the utmost faith in you."

Gwladys had ceased to hear the woman's babble. She struggled to comprehend the enormity of her loss, of her debacle. No mansion, no position, no grand tour, no, none of that. No household or fine dresses or sparkling girls to brighten her days.

"She tricked me, the cunning vixen! She led me on, twisted my words, used me, humiliated me! I heard myself say it—'I could not agree with you *more*, Mrs. Markham.' 'The situation is indeed *adverse*, Mrs. Markham!' Why, I'm just another Kathleen to her, and worst of all—'I harbor no ambitions,' I assured her, 'no ambitions for matrimony!' I groveled for her favor, denied my will to please her! And what is to be my appreciation? I am consigned to the sludge, the slops, the flock with brains of culm! Forever!''

"Is something the matter, Miss Protheroe? You look unwell.''

"No, no . . . I'm fine. It's nothing,'' Gwladys lied, feeling queasy, her face turning decidedly pale, unaware that in this, at least, she had actually achieved partial, if fleeting, resemblance to her admired hostess.

❖❖

MYFANWY put off supper as long as possible, but when Hugh sat at the table, she knew it was time to serve the meal whether Rhys was present or not. She had not spoken to Gwen since their angry exchange, nor was Gwen about to apologize for challenging her mother's authority, at least to the degree that it extended over the choice of her gentlemen friends. As for Rhys, there was no speculation, no alarm, not even the mention of his name, but an uneasy silence hung over the table as they ate.

And then Euan giggled aloud.

Hugh glowered. He was already irritated that no one would come forth to tell him what had happened that afternoon while he was off doing carpentry work at the church, but he knew there'd been a tiff just the same, and Euan's levity in light of Rhys's unaccountable absence riled him all the more.

"It was a story I was thinking of,'' Euan said, explaining his outburst. "Rhys told it yesterday. After church. About a miner with a stubborn mule.''

Hugh tempered his mood, realizing he'd been unfair with the boy. "I've never heard that one,'' he said. "Why don't you tell it?''

"No,'' Euan demurred, wishing he'd never brought it up in the first place. "I don't think it would be proper.''

"Why not?''

"Well . . . it's Rhys's story.''

"We could all do with a laugh then,'' Hugh said, pressing. "Tell it.''

Euan looked at his *mam* and at Gwen and Meb, hoping

that at least one of them would come to his rescue, but he was beyond the pale. "Well . . . there was this man working down in the mine," Euan began reluctantly. "And he was working all the time, and his name was Mr. Shaunessy. And he had a stubborn mule. And he was beating the mule, but the mule still wouldn't go. So Father Murphy was passing by and . . ."

"Wait now. What was Father Murphy doing down in the mine?" Hugh asked.

"Well . . . he was there to bless the mules. I don't know. It's Rhys that told it!"

Hugh was losing his patience. "Just finish your story, Euan."

Euan's telling got more and more painful. "Well . . . Father Murphy said, 'Don't beat the mule! That's the mule that Jesus rode into Jerusalem.' And Mr. Shaunessy said, 'Oh, no! It couldn't be this mule, 'cause this mule's . . . this mule's a son of a bitch!' "

The only sound that could be heard was the scraping of the girls' forks against their plates. Myfanwy watched Hugh, fearful of his reaction, but Hugh maintained his calm, on the surface at least, and finished drinking his tea.

"And so, that's the story," Euan said, waiting for the tumult that never came. It never came, because at that moment they heard Rhys walking along the side of the house, humming a tune. The tumult was just delayed.

"Finish your stew then," Myfanwy told Euan, as though the act of eating would somehow shield them from the unpleasantness of what was surely to come.

Rhys could not have chosen a worse time to come home, but enter he did, grinning and reeking of alcohol. "*Polinkey!*" he called to his startled family and stumbled giddily to his seat, next to Euan. Gwen and Meb exchanged knowing glances and tried to keep from giggling, but both Hugh and Myfanwy refused to even look at him. It was as though he were dead, as though he had never even walked through the door. Euan just gaped, open-mouthed.

Rhys looked down at his empty plate. "What, no *polinkey*?" he said and succumbed to another fit of laughter.

"I'll do it, *Mam*," Meb volunteered warily and took Rhys's plate over to the stove. She returned with a heaping portion, which Rhys, having gorged all afternoon, simply rearranged, first one way, then another, on his plate.

Hugh finished his meal without saying another word, rose from the table, and slowly walked upstairs. A moment later, he called down for Rhys in a tone so devastating it sobered up Rhys by half. He looked at Gwen, at Meb, even at Euan, all of whom were staring at their plates, none wanting to incur further wrath from their father *or* their mother.

"Rhys! I'll not call you again!"

Rhys took a deep breath and walked upstairs.

"Euan," Myfanwy said curtly, "you are never to tell a story like that again. Ever. Do you hear? You're forgiven this time, because your brother took advantage of you with gutter talk."

Euan heard a mumble of voices from above, then the swift rush of his *dada*'s razor strop, the awful slap of leather against Rhys's bare bottom, and his cry, muffled by the biting of his sleeve. Euan flinched inwardly with each swat. Only once before, in Sugar Notch, had he seen his *dada* take the leather strop to Rhys, when Rhys had stolen a nickel from the tin on top of the stove. Rhys denied to the end that he'd done it, but Mrs. Heard had seen him in John Good English's store buying fireworks and told his *mam* in passing. He was buying them, he said, for Malcolm Jones, who'd given him the nickel because he had to stay at home with a lame foot. But a nickel *was* missing from the tin. His *dada* told Rhys never to steal and never to lie and gave him five swats with his strop, and Rhys cried like he'd never cried before and said he didn't steal and didn't lie, and the next day, the nickel was found behind the stove where it had rolled, and his *dada* said to Rhys that he was sorry, oh, he was sorry, and that he'd never use his strop on Rhys again.

Until today.

When it was over, when the last of the ten had been

dealt, Euan heard his *dada* hang up the strop, and he heard Rhys crying, and he was crying, too.

◆◆

GWLADYS returned to her boardinghouse, entering through the back gate, in hope of stealing to her room unnoticed, but the ever-vigilant Mrs. Pardee spied her coming through the trellis and ran to be the first to tell her.

"*More* good news, Miss Protheroe!" the landlady beamed as she dried her hand on her apron. "*He's* back!"

"Who?" Gwladys asked, benumbed by her visit and the long ride back.

"Who do you think? Why, Mr. Janeway, of course!"

Gwladys was abashed. "Mr. Janeway?" she managed to utter.

"Yes, Mr. Janeway!" Mrs. Pardee said, perplexed. "Surely, you remember him? The salesman? Such a lively gentleman, he is!"

(Oh, yes! Gwladys remembered. She remembered well.)

"He hasn't forgot you," the landlady babbled on. "He asked right off, 'Where's Miss Protheroe? I want to see Miss Protheroe! She *is* still here, I trust? Still here, I hope?'"

(How, how could she forget him? And that night, that inebrious night? "Let me hold you," he said. "I *want* you. I want *you*.")

"'She's still here,' I said, 'but you'd better hurry,' I said, 'better hurry. She's not long for this house. She's off to a new position and trips to Europe,' I said, and you should have seen the look on his face!"

(His face, his face, his gnomelike face! A gap-toothed smile, tufts of hair growing from his nose, his ears, but none, none on his head, his head as bald as a baby's bottom. "Touch me," he said. "Go on! Touch me!")

"I said, 'You'd better hurry, Mr. Janeway, or that nice young lady is going to get away from you, and you'll never find the likes of her again!'"

("Touch me! Touch me!" he said. "Touch *it*! Touch *it*!" he said and lifted his nightshirt, raised it higher, higher until she could see his hairy legs and chest, and there, nestled under the folds of his paunch, stirring in the dim light . . . "Touch me, touch me," he panted. "Touch *it*! Touch *it*!")

"Oh, he has eyes for you, Miss Protheroe! I told him to be sure to sit across from you at the table tonight, and I think, but don't hold me at fault if I'm wrong, I *think* he's going to ask you to go to Easter services with him tomorrow! Won't *that* be grand?"

Gwladys stayed in her room past reason, despite her hunger, hoping that the other guests—that *he*—would finish eating and retire and let her come down to eat her evening meal in privacy, in peace.

"Miss Pro-the-roe!" Gwladys heard her landlady trill from below. "What *can* be keeping you? I've called three times now!"

"Go away!" she wanted to scream. "I'm not coming out! Ever again!"

It was futile. A few moment later, Mrs. Pardee came knocking at her door, prying, fretting, urging her to appear. It was futile. Gwladys found herself descending the stairs to the dining room below, amid laughter and the smells of pork and cabbage.

The dining room was cozy—a long table, nine chairs, a noisy gaslight hanging from the ceiling, others flickering along the wall, the food placed in large dishes and bowls scattered across the table, steaming vegetables, great slices of bread, chunks of pork carved from a roast by Mr. Mellancamp, the man who fixed telephones. Mr. Janeway's seat was empty.

"Why are they laughing?" Gwladys wondered as their hysteria rose and fell in waves. Mrs. Pollitt, the ribbon clerk, who wore ribbons in her hair, clucked until her face turned scarlet. Hubert, her pimpled nephew, held out a glass of water to her, for fear that she would choke. Mrs. Wolsifer, Miss Cruickshank, Mr. Paretti, all, all laughed.

"He's under the table," Hubert confided to Gwladys. "Under there."

Indeed, he was. She felt a hand touch her booted ankle,

a fondle, a brush of hot breath across her shin. The table shook.

"Is it her at last? Can I come out now?" a high-pitched voice called from under the table, and a gnome-face popped from beneath the cloth, between her knees. Gwladys shuddered.

It was *him*! It was Mr. Janeway!

"Hello, Miss Protheroe," he said, leering, and spread her thighs apart and set his bewhiskered chin on her belly. The boardinghouse claque guffawed and applauded his antics.

"He's a pip, that one! A pip!" Mrs. Wolsifer chortled.

"Make him stop, Mrs. Pardee!" the beribboned Mrs. Pollitt yelped, her portly frame undulating with mirth, and covered young Hubert's eyes with her hand. Even so, he peered through her fingers. "Oh, Lord! Make him stop!"

"Miss Protheroe! Aren't you going to welcome me back?" the gnome-face beseeched and rubbed his hand across her thigh.

Gwladys ran, gasping, to her room and locked the door.

In her room, her semidarkened, overheated room, Gwladys lay in her nightgown, reliving her meeting with Mrs. Markham, trying to forget but not able, wondering what hope was left for her in a life that was so cruel. Her heartbeat felt erratic. Her breath came only in spurts. Sweat drenched her nightgown. She wondered if she were dying. She hoped she would.

The clock in the downstairs hall began to strike. She counted eleven, then heard footsteps creaking down the hall toward her door. Or was it Mrs. Pollitt's snoring? No, footsteps.

Creak, creak. A pause, then creak again.

She heard a knocking. "Who's there?" she asked faintly.

"It's me. Mr. Janeway," a voice whispered at the crack.

"Go away!" she huffed. "I don't want to see you. Go away!"

"I've got something for you. Open up. Something for you."

"I'll call Mrs. Pardee if you don't leave."

"No, don't! I've got something for you. Listen!" She heard a liquid splashing in a bottle. "Brandy. It's brandy, Miss Protheroe! Open up. I've got something else, too. A surprise! For you!"

She wanted brandy. She needed brandy. It would help her, help her to clear her mind, to forget. What to do? Let him in? No, no. "Leave it," she said. "Outside the door. Thank you. Good night."

"Open, Miss Protheroe. Open up, or I'll . . . I'll tell. I'll tell Mrs. Pardee. How you let me in your room that night. I'll tell."

"Go away! Go!"

"I've got something for you! Open up!" She heard a rustling against the door. "You'll like it, come see! Come see, or I'll tell! I'll tell the old hag you're a slut, a goddamn bitch of a whore."

She unbolted the door and opened it a crack. Just a crack. "What do you want? Why do you cling to me like this?" she demanded in whispers.

"Here! For you, my love!" he exulted and thrust a corset through the crack. "It's the very latest style!"

"I don't want it!" she said, shoving it back into his hand, then closed the door. "Leave me be!"

He shook the bottle again. She wanted to scream, but something more powerful inside her wanted a taste of brandy, or the smell of a man, even this man, imprinted on her. Her head was floating, floating like a leaf on a raging pond. She heard the flutter of birds lifting up, up into the sky.

She opened the door.

"Can I fill your glass?" he asked.

"I've had enough, thank you," she told him, but in truth she had not. In truth, the brandy was having no effect at all.

"There's but a bit left. A few drops," he said and spilled the rest into her glass. She drank it down, feeling its warmth tingle in her throat. "In Utica," he continued, after he'd licked the mouth of the bottle, "the women have the best figures. I sell many corsets in Utica. As well as in Buffalo. I sold corsets to twin sisters in Schenectady once. Afterwards, they modeled them for me. I wish you could have seen them, so plump, so pink, so soft. They were like . . . like two tulips."

"Tulips?" she giggled. "And what am I, Mr. Janeway? What am I?"

"You, my lovely are . . . a rose! Miss . . . Prothe*rose*!"

"Oh, Mr. Janeway!" she said, rising from her chair by the bed. "Your blandishments are so . . ."

"So . . . *what*?"

The room suddenly seemed smaller, the heat more intense. The brandy was having its way with her. She undid the buttons at the top of her gown.

"So . . . so welcome," she said.

"I want to see you in your corset, your new corset. Will you put it on for me? Will you wear it? For me?"

Her head felt light. She moaned her assent.

"Now . . . ," he said softly, "now . . ." and reached up and undid her gown and let it slip to the floor, and sighed and looked at her and sighed again, then reached around her and secured the corset around her. She sucked in her breath, and he laced it loosely up the front and touched her breast, and she exhaled deeply. His fingers gave her gooseflesh.

"Does it bind, my dear?"

"No . . . ," she said softly, loathing, fearing his touch but wanting it, too. "No . . . no . . ."

"You're not an easy size to fit, my love," he said, smoothing his hands across her midriff, down to her hips, and up again to her breasts.

Her breath came faster. Everything was happening too fast, too fast. She had had too much brandy. Or not enough.

"I've had no complaints. It's the very best corset, worn only by the very best women . . . and the very best whores," he said. "Which are you? Tell me? Which are you?" he asked and reached around and squeezed her buttocks. "I know. I think I know."

"Not yet," she said. "I want more brandy first. More."

"There is no more. You've drunk it all."

"I want more. More!" she soughed. "I must have more."

"There *is* no more!"

"Then take your corset and leave," Gwladys said indifferently, "or I'll scream. And Mrs. Pardee will find you in my room, debauching me in my room!"

"If I get more, will you . . . let me? In your corset, wearing your new corset, will you . . . let me?"

"Yes . . . yes," she said.

"I've got some cheap rum. In my suitcase," he said.

"Get it," she said.

"Miss Protheroe?" the voice called softly at the door so as not to wake the other boarders. "Miss Protheroe, are you all right?"

Gwladys covered the corset with her robe, then opened the door to find Mrs. Pardee and Mr. Mellancamp, in nightshirt, holding a candle.

"Oh, thank God, child, you're safe!" the woman cried. "I had the most dreadful fear. I heard a noise on the stair and rose to investigate. It was Mr. Janeway, prowling about in his nightshirt, and he was headed straight for your door. I fear he had lustful designs on you, my dear." And this she spoke most quietly, most discreetly, "His . . . his 'thing' was sticking out like a tent pole, and he was carrying a bottle of whiskey! Thank God I caught up with him in time! Who knows what he might have done to you, child!"

"Mr. Janeway?" Gwladys said, remembering to hold her hand over her mouth to hide the smell of her breath, her brandy breath.

"Yes! Our Mr. Janeway! The very same! I told him to pack at once and leave first thing in the morning. It's a disgrace! And tomorrow, Easter! But don't you worry, child, I've asked Mr. Mellancamp to sit outside your door the rest of the night. You're safe, my dear. Nothing will happen to you now. I pray to God I caught the fox in time. Good night. And pleasant dreams.''

Gwladys closed the door, feeling a hunger deeper than she had ever felt before. She *wanted,* wanted what, she knew not, but there was a fierce yearning inside her, waiting to be fulfilled.

(''Touch me, touch me! Touch *it!* Touch *it!* Touch the heart of it. Go to the center, quench the fire, my fire of wanting. Let me breathe free again, let me feel! Feel what? I'll know when I feel it! I'll *know!*'')

She *wanted,* wanted what, she knew not, and when she awoke that Easter morning, she was still wearing her new corset.

◆◆

''He lives! He lives! Christ Jesus lives today!''

Rhys sang loudly and with great feeling in church that Easter Sunday. In fact, all four Morgan children sang like a choir of angels, the better to make their *mam* and *dada* forget their trespasses of the day before.

''He walks with me and talks with me along life's narrow way.''

The singing soared that morning. The passion the congregation shut out of their daily lives poured forth in their singing.

''He lives! He lives! Salvation to impart!''

Iolo Morganwyg, the paymaster, sat with the elders in the front pew and sang so fervently the veins in his bald head stood out. Bronwyn Howell, tall and birdlike, sang with tears streaming down her cheeks.

''You ask me how I know He lives . . .''

And then for the final measures, the crescendo, the voices blended in exuberant four-part harmony, but more like eight- or twelve-part, notes never even written in the hymnals but improvised years ago and passed down through families so that each family had its own distinctive way of ending a song.

''He *lives* within my heart! Amen.''

The effect was exultant.

Up at Holy Trinity, all pews and side aisles were jammed, and a crowd three-deep spread along the rear wall. Most of the overflow were Polish Hill irregulars, men who wanted no part of an Irish parish with an Irish priest and only came today because Priest Jozef Ziemba was sharing the mass with Father Brislin. The two groups sat and stood apart, like rivals at a football match. Each side gave loyal attention as the priest of their choice led the service, then coughed and squirmed in their seats while the other took his turn. Two lines formed for Communion, the Irish refusing to receive from Priest Ziemba, and the Poles from Father Brislin. A shuffle broke out when an Irishman returning from the rail accused a Polander of taking his seat. Several burly men had to intervene before the antagonists could be subdued.

Frog Street was deserted at this hour, except for Fritz, the dog, who had left his yard in Irish Flats to savor the smells of *kielbasa* and pork and ham that wafted from every house on Polish Hill. He stopped at Maciejewski's yard, where five or six young men were sleeping in the grass, having spent the night where they had fallen in their drunken revelry, like so many bodies on a battlefield. One sat up, looked around vacantly, then tumbled back to sleep. Not very interesting, Fritz thought and continued on his way.

There was one living soul on Frog Street. Outside Holy Trinity stood a tall, swarthy man, his clothes dirty and rumpled, his face unshaven, as though he had spent recent nights sleeping in fields, under culverts. A worn satchel rested against his leg as he stood, listening to the singing of the children's choir, and twirled a blade of grass between his teeth. The music, the singing, reminded him of his childhood far away.

"Easter," he said under his breath. "This is Easter."

Fritz spied the traveler, sauntered up, tail wagging, and sniffed the man's boot. "Go on, get!" the man snapped and drove the dog away with a kick. Fritz, misunderstanding the stranger's rage, returned with his ears and tail down to make amends. The stranger looked at the cur dispassionately. He had little use for dogs and none at all for this one, now groveling before him.

"Here, boy," he said, kneeling, and extended his hand. Hearing this, Fritz moved in closer, his tail wagging tentatively. "Good boy. You come to me, boy."

These were the last words Fritz heard. The man raised his massive hand and smashed it down on the dog's head, cleanly, swiftly. Fritz staggered and plopped to earth, his eyes staring vacantly, dumbly dead. Blood trickled from his nose and ears. His legs twitched in the dust and then were still.

The stranger left the dog lying in a heap and headed down Frog Street, past the empty houses, past Maciejewski's yard, past the same wafting smells, stopping only at a house at the bottom of Polish Hill to dip his hands into a pie that sat invitingly on the kitchen table.

"I could go in any house on street right now and take what I want, and nobody ever know I was here," he said to himself, but these people had nothing he wanted, no property, that is, and they kept their money in banks. With his belly full; he moved on to the Presbyterian church, where the congregation was singing the final hymn of the morning.

When the service was over, Pastor Wheat greeted each family at the door as they left. This being Easter, no one was in a hurry to get home. The boys congregated as usual behind the church. The men gathered under the black oak out front, where they discussed the finer points of Pastor Wheat's scriptural message. The women and their daughters shared the street, circulating freely, admiring each other's spring dresses and hats.

Myfanwy introduced Gwen and Meb to the women, who knew of them from her stories. She had not spoken to Gwen since their dispute, nor Gwen to her, nor did Myfanwy speak her name but simply called them both, "my girls."

As Hugh stood talking to the men, he noticed a dark, familiar figure leaning against a tree alongside the church. A chill ran through his blood. Finding some excuse to break away from the group, he moved closer to the man to confirm his suspicion.

"Zakrzewska! What are you doing here?" Hugh asked, trying to quell the anger in his voice.

"They tell me you come here after Sugar Notch," Zakrzewska said coolly.

"Who? Who told you?" Hugh shot back.

"Never mind."

Hugh drew Zakrzewska farther back alongside the church to avoid curious eyes. "What do you want here?"

"Job. I need work," the intruder answered. There was no desperation in his voice, only contempt.

"See the pit boss," Hugh told him.

"No, you give me job."

Hugh hesitated. "I don't . . . I already have my laborer."

"Now you have two," Zakrzewska replied matter-of-factly.

"Zakrzewska, I told you I never wanted to see you again. I meant it! Now clear out of here and . . . !"

"Talk! Talk, talk, talk, talk, talk!" Zakrzewska clucked, his voice imitating a chicken. "I think you change your mind."

"I don't . . . *like* you, Zakrzewska. You know that." The very words were almost painful for Hugh to say.

"And I don't like you, Morgan. But I need job. And you man who give me. You say one word, and I go to work."

"It's not like that here. This is not Sugar Notch! I don't have the authority. Do you understand? It's a different company. These are different people. They don't work the same way. I can't just hire anyone I want here."

The more Hugh made excuses, the more Zakrzewska knew he was lying. "Do men here know you scab in Sugar Notch?" he blurted out. Hugh wanted to strike the man across the face but remembered where he was. "I bet they pretty angry, they find out," Zakrzewska continued brazenly. "Man who go 'gainst brothers, he no good. What you think they say I tell them?"

"What I did, I did for my family," Hugh shot back.

"And what I do, I do for my family! In Chicago. They

live on bread, beg pennies in street. I work to bring them to me so they have good home, not some . . . some rat place where death is! My family! They all I care 'bout, just like you!''

"Zakrzewska, the work is slow now. There might be layoffs soon. This is not the time . . . ,''

"Oh, man! Is never time for hunky! Is that what you say?''

Hugh squirmed uncomfortably, cursing himself for allowing this man to invade his life again, but he realized that Zakrzewska had come this far to find him and would have pursued him even farther if that had been his aim.

"It doesn't matter who or what you are, Zakrzewska. I can't hire you if there's no work.''

"I see . . . ,'' Zakrzewska answered, nodding. "I see.''

"I'm sorry,'' Hugh said, disposing of the matter. Zakrzewska shrugged as though he had expected that answer all along. "I must be going,'' Hugh said and started back.

"They your daughters? With your wife?'' Zakrzewska asked. Hugh froze. His skin prickled to hear Zakrzewska mention his family. "Too bad girls must live in Mrs. Archer's boardinghouse in Wilkesbarre. Is such big city. Many things can happen to girls alone in big city. Ah, but they very pretty; soon they find young fellas, get married, not have to work in silk mills no more. Very pretty . . . very pretty . . .''

"If you so much as go *near* them!'' Hugh warned, struggling to control himself. "No, if you even *look* at them—do you hear me?—I'll kill you! I'll find you, and I'll kill you! Do you hear?''

"Give me job in Jeddoh. Then you not worry,'' Zakrzewska said, smiling. He enjoyed seeing Hugh tormented like this.

"You . . . you, miserable, filthy dog! You are the scum of your people!''

Zakrzewska didn't answer; he didn't have to. He knew that Hugh Morgan, out of his goodness, which was really stupidity, could be counted on to follow the most cowardly course, the one that men of courage like himself would sneer at. "If man say to me what I say to him," he thought, "I would crush the life from his body. These Welshmen, they are like scared babies. They are not worth the air they breathe!"

"Be at the pit head Tuesday by second whistle," Hugh told him. "And if you're late, no work!"

"I be there," his nemesis answered, and Hugh knew that he would keep his word. That he knew.

"I be there."

Rhys hurried back into the church to find his cap. It was empty except for someone at the organ who was running through a particular passage, never quite getting it right. Finally she hit a series of dissonant chords and sat looking at the keyboard in frustration. It was Mary Markham.

"Hello there!" Rhys called, startling her. She turned, surprised that anyone was listening, doubly surprised that it was Rhys Morgan, standing not ten feet away from her.

"Oh, hello," she replied, trying to mask her pleasure.

"I saw you looking at me this morning," Rhys said, perhaps too rashly.

"I wasn't looking at you."

"Yes, you were. You always do," he blundered on, then, to salvage his introduction, confessed to looking at her, too. "What were you practicing?"

Mary struggled to maintain her composure. She wasn't prepared for such a meeting, for having him expose her so boldly. "Mrs. Williams is feeling unwell. I'm to play for service tonight."

"You play good."

That was it! She laughed giddily at his blatant lie. "I'm terrible! I only know one song!"

"It's my favorite," he lied again.

"We'll be singing it all night!"

"I'm Rhys Morgan," he said after a pause and went to shake her hand but wasn't sure if girls shook hands with boys so withdrew it again.

"I know," she said, not saying how, but she knew just the same.

"I thought your playing sounded good. I did."

"Thank you," she said, smiling for the first time. Her smile was very pretty, and her eyes were deep and dark, so deep and dark a boy could easily get lost in them. "I've only been playing for a little while now. It's not as easy as the piano, you know."

"I'm a music player, too. I and some friends, we play the fiddle."

"How long have you played?"

"Well . . . not long, but I'm getting real good at it. We're going to play at funerals and picnics to make money," he said brightly, then looked into her eyes a bit too deeply arid got lost in her eyes. For a moment, neither of them spoke. Or breathed.

"I forgot my cap," he said, breaking the spell. "I better go then."

She didn't want him to leave, but she couldn't let him see that. She couldn't tell him how she felt.

"It was fine to meet you . . . Rhys," she said, caressing his name.

"*Ta* then," he replied, beaming.

"*Ta*," she said and followed him all the way up the aisle with her eyes.

That night, the congregation winced as Mary hit one wrong chord after another, but Rhys didn't notice. To him it sounded good.

❖

COME TUESDAY, Rhys left for the colliery early with his pockets full of salt and brown sugar, which he used to coax his mules from their stalls. Mine mules, normally irritable and unpredictable, were at their worst after a spell of idle days, and Rhys had no intention of being kicked by a peevish mule.

His bribery worked. In no time, he had all five, which he'd named for Markham's daughters—Anna, Helen, Rose, June, and Mary—hitched and ready to roll.

"I've got the charm!" he called out as the other drivers

thrashed about with their uncooperative lot. A few minutes later, sitting on the front wagon drawn by Helen, with Anna, Rose, June, and a hastily renamed "Mamie," plodding dutifully behind, Rhys led his first empty trip down the still-quiet gangway. Content with himself, he bit off a chew of tobacco and sang to hear his voice echoing through the chambers:

> *My sweetheart's the mule in the mines;*
> *I drive her without reins or lines.*
> *On the bumper I stand, my whip in my hand,*
> *My sweetheart's the mule in the mines.*

Bryfogle emerged from the hovel he called his office that morning in a drunken stupor. Euan was not surprised. He'd been suspicious from the start and had often heard the boys plotting to relieve Bryfogle of his secret cache of booze. What *did* puzzle him was that he had not seen Bryfogle *enter* his office that morning.

The first wave of coal had just come down from the top house. It was leftover coal from Thursday, so it came in fits and starts. In the meantime, no one had seen or heard of Bryfogle, and then suddenly there he was, weaving across the catwalk, shielding his eyes from the sun, which was just beginning to stream in. He had also taken off, or never bothered to put on, his shirt and vest and coat, so that his potbelly hung out over his britches.

"He looks like a top," Euan thought. Indeed, he did—big and round in the middle, smaller above and below, and tapering to a point, his peg leg, at bottom. Euan expected to see him start spinning at any moment. Instead, he pissed at great length against the wall. When through—and even the boys were astonished at his capacity—Bryfogle staggered back to his office and disappeared inside to finish his morning snooze. At the same time, the flow of old coal ran out. New coal would not reach the top house for another half hour at least.

It was a confluence of circumstances too tempting to ignore.

Digger made the first move. He'd been belligerent from the moment he pegged in. As he climbed to his perch, he booted Little Jake in the behind for not moving out of his way fast enough. Jake *was* little, but he was also feisty and even Digger wasn't too big to take on as far as he was concerned. But that morning was different. He saw something in Digger's eye that told him to back off, so he gritted his teeth and swallowed his pride rather than end up with a busted lip. Euan and the others Digger terrorized at one time or another sat with their heads bowed, their eyes fixed to their chutes. No one wanted to catch Digger's eye, even by chance, for fear of being his next target. The worst of it came during the lulls, when the flow of coal slowed or stopped, and Digger got bored and started looking around for something to satisfy his mischievous frame of mind. And then Bryfogle lurched into view.

Digger looked at Patsy and Dick like he couldn't believe his eyes. It was as though a prayer long since forgotten had been answered, or as though a hundred-dollar bill had fallen from a rich man's pocket and landed squarely in his lap. No words were needed to savor his good fortune. He knew immediately how to take advantage of the windfall.

Digger ran at once to the stairs that led to the top house to be sure the weighmen were occupied, and Dick ran below to check for Ned the Splicer or roaming engineers, while Patsy dug a saw out of the tool chest in the corner. This done, all three converged on Bryfogle's office.

Euan watched in fascination as their stealth unfolded. He had no idea what they were up to but joined the others who guardedly approached Bryfogle's office to see what was happening. Euan had come to expect the unexpected in the breaker, but nothing prepared him for the odd sight he encountered when he looked inside.

The smell hit him first. It was fetid and foul, like Bryfogle himself but worse, because there were no windows in the room to circulate the stench. Thus, it remained entrapped, like a living presence, crouching in the corner, festering, waiting to assault those foolish enough to trespass, eager to leap from its confines to offend noses beyond its imprisoning walls. The room was dark and gloomy, lit only by a single kerosene lamp, which hung over the table in the middle of the floor. Empty tin cans with jagged lids lay everywhere. Bryfogle himself sat snoring in the chair next to his oversized desk. Beyond him, Euan could see a potbellied stove, a brass bed and mattress, which bore the deep impression of its owner's body. Bryfogle, it seemed, lived in this squalid hole.

The most peculiar sight was the wallpaper, or, more precisely, what he had used to cover his walls. From what Euan could see, they were pasted with pictures cut from newspapers and magazines and arranged neatly, side by side. They were yellowed now, fading and brittle. The few he could make out were of boxers—muscled men, their thick fists poised to strike or raised in triumph over vanquished opponents. "Kid" Dugan and Jack "Corky" St. John were their names, and "Big Dan" Bry . . .

"Bryfogle?" Euan mouthed to himself. "A boxer? That tub of lard?"

Indeed, there he stood—on two good legs—younger, thinner, a broad smile across his face, the face of a bare-knuckled champion. It *was* Bryfogle!

Suddenly Euan heard the sound of a saw cutting through wood. He looked down to see Digger sawing an inch or so off the bottom of Bryfogle's peg leg.

What's more, Dick had lifted the silver flask from Bryfogle's vest pocket and was taking turns with Patsy, guzzling it down. Digger stopped his sawing long enough to demand a swig and gulp down what little was left, then he ordered Dick to refill the flask with sulfur water, which smelled like rotten eggs and tasted worse. In the meantime, Patsy foraged for Bryfogle's cache of whiskey.

"Don't jest stand there gawkin'!" Digger growled at the boys who stood in the doorway. "Keep a lookout!"

Euan and the others quickly spread out across the picking room to watch for passing workmen. Euan went along, because he feared what Digger would do to him if he didn't, but for the first time, he felt as though he were part of the crew and that made him feel good.

In no time, Digger had cut off the tip and was beginning to trim the sawed edges with his knife. Dick ran back with the flask just as his twin pulled a locked metal chest from under Bryfogle's bed. It sounded as though there were bottles inside, but there was no time to pry it open. The flask was replaced, the shavings were whisked away, and everyone returned to his chute to await the coming of new coal.

Hugh spent the morning drilling into the seam of coal he'd been working for the past month. His auger weighed over eighty pounds and had to be turned manually. When his hands and arms couldn't take the pain anymore, he switched off with Zakrzewska. Together, one man drilling, the other holding the rig in place, they penetrated four feet into the face.

The breast Hugh worked was known as a "chute" and followed a fifty-five-degree diagonal seam. The steep angle made it not only more difficult to work than the more common, level breasts, but also more treacherous. Hugh did not remove the coal he blasted loose each day. Instead, he used it as a platform from which his subsequent drilling took place. While this chute itself may have been eight to ten feet wide, most of it was packed with coal, except for the manway, or escape passage, which narrowed to less than two and a half feet in places. Each day, Hugh and his laborers climbed up the length of the manway, which now stretched to sixty feet, hauling the drill, picks, a barrel of blasting powder, safety lamps, and any timbers needed to shore up the sides of the manway as its length increased.

"I can't . . . can't . . . turn it . . . any . . . more," Hugh said, tensing at the end of the six-foot-long drill.

"Let me try again," Zakrzewska offered.

"No," Hugh said, releasing his grip, exhausted. "She's in pretty far. Must be hitting rock."

"I try," the Pole said, spitting on his hands and positioning his feet more firmly on the loose surface of coal.

"No, Zakrzewska! It could break. It's in far enough,"

but Zakrzewska had already gripped the auger with his massive hands. Hugh knew there was no use protesting once the Pole set his mind to something. Either he would break the bit off deep inside the hole, thus negating their morning's effort (to say nothing of costing Hugh the price of a new bit), or he would prove his point and drive another few inches into the face. Zakrzewska alternately coaxed, then berated the bit under his breath till slowly, slowly it turned against his weight and muscle.

"I tell you I make it work! You see? Zakrzewska know what he do!"

Hugh was awed by the man's strength. "If only he weren't a lunatic," Hugh thought, "I could work with him quite well."

"Morgan," Zakrzewska asked, straining at the drill, "I ever tell you my first job when I come to America? (Easy, easy! There she go!) In Chicago. I come on train with two cents in pocket. (See? Not so bad now.) I think some day I be rich man maybe, like J. P. Morgan, but only job I get is in stockyard killin' cattle. They give me sledgehammer. I say, 'What this for?' They say, 'Hit cow over head.' I say, 'Noooooo!' (Ah, you son of a bitch, don't lock on me now!) They say, 'How else you kill cow?' 'With gun,' I say. 'Bullet cost money,' they say. 'Sledge cheaper, do same job.' So, they bring me cow. First time I miss, hit cow on nose (This bastard! You see how easy she turn now?), make big mess. Next try, I hit cow on noggin. One blow, she go down. (This face is devil, I tell you. This face no good!) Big cow, too. I become number one cattle killer."

"Zakrzewska, your jabbering uses up good air," Hugh complained. "We'll suffocate if you don't shut up.

"I talk to keep my mind off stinking job," Zakrzewska growled back.

"Let's get the drill out. She's in far enough."

"You like story? Is good story?" Zakrzewska asked as they disengaged the drill. A few feet away, Aloysius, Hugh's other laborer, worked silently and efficiently, unpacking blasting cartridges by the dim light of the safety lamp.

"I might have liked it more if I hadn't heard it already," Hugh said sarcastically. "And each time it keeps changing. Once, J. P. Morgan himself got you the job, and another time, you killed the cow on the very first try. You're paid to haul the drill down, and the powder, not tell stories."

"Haul drill down? Aloysius do that!" Zakrzewska shouted petulantly.

"Aloysius helps me set the powder," Hugh said firmly. "You take down the drill, then come back for the keg. By then we should be ready to light."

"But I always help you tamp powder. That my job!"

"Aloysius does it now."

"Aw, Jesus Christ, you stink! Hunky only good for dirty work. Right?"

"Right!" Hugh shot back.

"I show you I do good work! I work harder than you!"

"I didn't ask you to work for me! I don't need you. You need me, and don't forget who's boss here!"

Zakrzewska grumbled and started hauling the drill toward the manway.

"And be careful!" Hugh called after him. "That bit's worth more than you are!"

Zakrzewska bristled. He wanted to snap the bit in two. "I could do it, too," he muttered under his breath. "I could."

"What's that?" Hugh asked.

"Nothin'," Zakrzewska shrugged and disappeared into the narrow channel.

Bryfogle awoke with a start and looked around, confused and disoriented, feeling more strange than he'd felt in a long while, then remembered that this peculiar condition was called sobriety, that he'd missed not only most of the morning, but most of the last few days as well. Grabbing his shirt and vest, which he buttoned haphazardly, he stormed onto the catwalk.

"What are ye lookin' at, ye boneheads? Git back to

work, or ye'll be lookin' at the back o' me hand!" he yelled at his charges, many of whom were staring back at him with nefarious glee, and stalked the length of the catwalk with menacing strides to make his presence known. Feeling suddenly and oddly disjointed, Bryfogle stopped, shifted the straps that held his appendage in place, then took a few more steps, but his newly acquired limp would not go away. After one more attempt, he faltered, bracing himself against the wall, as if overcome by a fit of dizziness.

"What's the matter, Bryfogle?" Tom Monahan, an engineer, shouted on his way up to oil the rollers. "You look queer!"

"Jesus!" Bryfogle said, perplexed. "I think me bum leg is shrinkin'."

"Are ye sure it's not yer good leg startin' to grow?" Monahan chided.

Confounded, Bryfogle decided he needed a good, stiff drink, pulled out his flask, and took a swig before the foul odor and taste caught up with him, but just as he turned to spit the swill out, he came face-to-face with Ned the Splicer, who was following Monahan up to the rollers. There was a regulation against drinking alcohol on the job. The punishment was automatic dismissal. There was no regulation against drinking sulfur water, but in his confusion, Bryfogle neither spit out nor swallowed the vile stuff. Instead, he held it in his mouth nodding and smiling until after Ned had passed, hoping that the usually garrulous superintendent wouldn't stop to talk. While thus occupied, Bryfogle happened to squint down at the tip of his peg leg, which looked as if someone had taken an axe to it.

"Jesus in heaven! I been decrapitated!" he blurted out, forgetting himself, then tasted the sulfur water he'd just swallowed and began to cough and sputter and fall down and roll about on the floor as though he were dying.

The boys laughed so hard they had to hold on to their boards to keep from falling into the chutes. They made unholy faces like his and gagged and clutched their throats as if they were dying, too. But when Bryfogle realized that he would live, that it was the boys who had mangled his wooden appendage and poured sulfur water into his flask, he slowly rose, shoved his finger down his throat until he started to retch, then leaned as far as he could over the catwalk railing and sprayed the laughing boys with a huge gusher of sulfurous vomit.

"Hey, buddy!" Razor shouted when he saw Rhys approaching his headway. "Time for next lesson!"

"Soon, Razor, soon. When I can see straight again," Rhys answered. He might have added "sit again" as well.

"Next time, forget *polinkey,*" Razor told him, laughing.

"Do you think I . . . I could get my own fiddle to play?" Rhys asked.

"Easy."

"Where? Do they cost a lot?"

"Six dollars. In 'V'ilkesbarre. Easy."

"I don't know, Razor," Rhys said hesitantly. That was two weeks of his pay before Markham subtracted what Rhys owed back to the company. The rest he had to turn over to his *mam*. It would take him months to save six dollars.

"You pay for easy, you see," Razor told him, then clapped him on the back. "First, you gotta learn playin'. I come by you house. Tonight."

"No, no," Rhys said, knowing the complications that would cause. "Tell you what, I'll meet you outside the Emerald. After supper."

"After supper," Razor agreed, and they shook hands. Wherever Rhys went the rest of the day, he heard only fiddles playing in his head. Only fiddles.

"All right, which of ye little buggers filled me medicine bottle with sulfur?" Bryfogle shouted at the still-giggling boys. "Was it ye, Zdepko?"

"No, sir," Andrew Zdepko said meekly.

"Ye little liar!" Bryfogle screamed and smacked Zdepko over the back, hard, with the oak rod. "Was it ye, Davies?"

"Not me," Jenkin said, tensing his body to receive the onrushing blow. The mood had suddenly become somber, as it always did during these inevitable accountings.

"How about ye, O'Shea? And don't ye be tellin' me that ye didn't have a part in tryin' to kill me."

"No, sir, I didn't," Digger said contritely, wiping the last flecks of Bryfogle's supper off his coat. "It was Morgan."

A moment passed before Euan realized that he was the one being blamed. Nothing he could say would have mattered in the swirl of events that followed. From that moment he was accused, tried, and convicted.

"Morgan? I *knew* it!" Bryfogle bellowed. "I knew that little bastard'd be the death of me!"

"And he sawed your leg short," Digger added. "I seen him stash the saw under his bony."

"I'll squash the little turd!" Bryfogle roared and heaved his ludicrous, limping figure across the catwalk and down the stairs to the foot of chute no. 3, where he found the saw in question hidden in Euan's box. "Aha!" he gloated triumphantly. "Here it is, indeed!" Then, seeing the severed tip amidst the pile, his eyes nearly popped from his head. "Sweet Jesus!" He groaned, waving the tip for all to see. "An' here's me leg!"

"How much powder you use?" Zakrzewska asked, looking over Hugh's back as he tamped the last of the wadding into place around the fuse.

"Just enough . . . ," Hugh answered, trying not to break his concentration, for each step in setting and blasting explosives was critical. There was no room for careless work, for carelessness unleashed forces that even seasoned miners had no control over, so he trusted no one's work but his own. That was his only protection. His obsession began with his blasting cartridges and his fuses, which he made himself, even though both were sold in the company store, and extended to the tamping of the explosives into the hole itself.

He packed the hole first with two fuseless cartridges,

each about a foot long, then wet clay, to prevent air pockets, which would weaken the force of the explosion. He inserted the third cartridge next so that its fuse extended a few inches beyond the opening of the hole, then wrapped the fuse tightly with cotton wadding and clay. Because the fuse burned inside a waterproof casing, this tamped material did not interfere with rapid ignition. The entire process took patience and care. A badly tamped shot might yield a few pounds of coal and so much smoke that an hour would pass before it cleared, an hour in which no other work could move forward. With a properly fired shot, a miner could almost lay out a cloth and have the coal fall onto it in a neat pile.

"What powder you use?" Zakrzewska asked.

"Black niter. Type B fine. For shattering. Does that meet with your approval?" Hugh was becoming exasperated by the man's incessant questions.

"How much you use?" Zakrzewska repeated.

"A little more than two pounds."

"That all? Is that enough?"

"I don't want to bring the whole damn mountain down on us, man!" Hugh snapped angrily.

"I would use more," Zakrzewska insisted.

"Then you are a fool."

"I must know these things. I will be miner one day," Zakrzewska said.

"You? A miner? God help us all!" With that, Hugh finished smoothing clay over the hole and around the fuse which extended several inches beyond the opening.

Aloysius disappeared with the leather pouch into the manway. "Go with Aloysius," Hugh told him. "Now!"

"I wait for . . ."

"Now! I'm going to set this fuse, and I don't want to be stepping over you on the way down."

Zakrzewska climbed into the manway. "I would have used more," he said and lowered himself from view.

"You would, too," Hugh said to himself.

He waited a few seconds to give Zakrzewska a good head start down, then raised the glass of the safety lamp and held the flame to the tip of the fuse. The fuse hissed, sizzled, then burned white. He lowered the glass, hurried to the manway, and surveyed the face one last time. In the dim light, barely distinguishable from the wall, was the powder barrel. Zakrzewska had forgotten to carry it down.

"The powder, you fool!" he yelled.

In that moment, the fuse burned beyond the surface of the hole, burned unstoppable, deep, deeper toward its reason for being, freeing him from the burden of choice, perhaps even from his very life. A shot was about to fire, about to ignite a nearly loaded barrel of black niter, type B fine. He could leave the barrel behind and scramble down the manway as fast as legs and hands could move. Even if he made it to the bottom, which was unlikely, the blast would send sixty feet of loose coal down on top of him. And Zakrzewska. And Aloysius. If he made it only partway down, the rush of coal would catch him, bury him, suffocate him. And if the blast didn't kill him, the damp would.

No, he had one choice and, therefore, no choice—to carry the barrel down in the precious seconds remaining, even though it would slow his descent and leave him vulnerable to the shock of the blast and the deadly fumes it unleashed. Without thinking—thinking was not called for— he dropped the lamp, scrambled across the rough surface of the coal, gripped the barrel and dragged it to the narrow opening. Full, it weighed twenty-five pounds, now, just under twenty. He jumped into the manway feet first, the barrel over his head, and slid roughly down the sharp-edged rock and wood channel. He could hear Zakrzewska below him.

"Hurry! HURRY!" he shouted.

"You need help?" Zakrzewska called.

"MOVE! MOVE!"

Down below, Aloysius hollered, "Fire! Fire!" to warn anyone entering the headway or working a nearby breast of the imminent blast. "Fire! Fire!"

Hugh nearly reached bottom before the charge exploded.

\* \* \*

Euan stepped from the breaker into the blazing light of the yard. He couldn't see at first, but he heard their laughter and ran straight into its midst. Without hesitating, he picked out Digger, who was sitting, eating his lunch, and kicked him squarely in the teeth. Digger somersaulted backwards onto the shale-covered yard, spitting out blood and cheese as he rolled. Euan leaped atop him before he could recover, pummeled him with his fists, jabbed him with his knees. ("Catch them by surprise," Rhys always told him. "Never let the sucker get the best of you.") But Digger was five inches taller and thirty pounds heavier. Gathering his wits, he flipped his attacker onto his back and inflicted a stronger set of kicks and blows.

The yardmen separated them before too much damage was done. As it was, it was the second beating Euan took that morning.

"You should've thought twice before you took on Digger. He was pretty sore today," Jenkin said as Tadeus and Andrew Zdepko and Little Jake tried to stanch the flow of blood from Euan's nose.

"When ain't he?" Jake said.

"No, he's been double sore since Sunday," Jenkin told them. "You ain't heard? On Easter. Somebody killed his dog."

Hugh sprawled across the rough floor, his head in Aloysius's arms. The force of the shot, or the powder barrel, had knocked him unconscious. First Zakrzewska, then Aloysius, had pulled him down the rest of the manway through the thick smoke.

"Drink some, drink!" Aloysius urged, holding the canteen out to Hugh. Hugh took a mouthful, swirled it around in his mouth, then spit it out. The rest he emptied over his head.

Zakrzewska stood in the darkness a few feet away, skulking like a child anticipating and dreading his parent's rebuke.

"Is my fault, Morgan," he said, near tears.

"I don't want to hear it," Hugh said, softly, distantly. He loathed the man's weakness.

"I make up to you. I work extra. I never forget nothin' no more."

"I'll pay you for the whole day," Hugh said with difficulty. "Just . . . just get your things . . . and clear out of here." His eyes were closed in pain, his body racked by the violent descent from the face.

Zakrzewska suddenly moved forward and collapsed, blubbering, at Hugh's feet. "Oh, no! No! Oh, no! Morgan, I am so sorry! Please don't do this. I have nothing. No one want me. I try, I try so hard. You only good man I know. Only good man who give me chance."

"No, Zakrzewska. No more."

"Oh, God! What am I to do? Please, Morgan. Please! Give me one more chance. I would never do nothin' to hurt you. I pray to Virgin to save your life. I say, 'Please, Holy Mother, save this good man, watch over his family, don't let nothin' happen to him 'cause I am stupid, stupid man.' I say, 'Take my life, not his! Don't make his wife and babies suffer 'cause of me. 'Cause of *me*!' Oh, please, Morgan, let me stay. I be changed man, you see. I work hard. I pray to Holy Mother to make me better."

Hugh held up his hand for the man to stop, repulsed by the sentimental lies, the sloppy weeping. He didn't believe Zakrzewska for a minute, and yet he acceded, perhaps to stop the man's simpering display, or perhaps because he feared the dark side that would lash out if he refused to relent.

"We've lost enough time already," Hugh said finally. "Help Aloysius with the planks."

"You mean I can stay?" Zakrzewska asked incredulously.

For a long moment, Hugh remained silent, as if reconsidering.

"Yes, Zakrzewska. You can stay."

Zakrzewska closed his eyes and smiled inwardly. He contemplated kneeling to kiss Morgan's feet—the perfect final gesture, he thought. "No," he said to himself. "I have won. Let him kneel and kiss my feet."

\*  \*  \*

Rhys caught up to Euan on the way home. Euan's eye was nearly swollen shut, and blood was caked under his nose and swollen lower lip.

"I heard Digger busted you up pretty good," he said. Euan just walked on, kicking his feet through the dust of Frog Street. "I hope you got in the first punch at least."

Later, in their backyard, Rhys washed the dirt from Euan's cuts. The boy cringed but otherwise remained silent. "Cripes Almighty! I can see I'm going to spend my whole life patching you up," Rhys told him. "Next time, at least try taking on somebody your own size, will you? Or somebody smaller?"

"You should've seen it," Euan finally mumbled, still in pain but with a faint trace of a smile on his lips, "I kicked him! I kicked him right in the son of a bitchin' teeth!"

# PART THREE

---

# MARKHAM

WHEN John Markham was twelve years old, his father sent him to boarding school and gave him a monthly allowance of five dollars, which John found more than enough for his simple needs. The majority of the boys received far less from their fathers and, being spendthrifts, soon flocked to John for loans to supplement their meager incomes. Young John was more than happy to oblige.

To accommodate the overwhelming demand, John had each boy sign an IOU and held the boy's pocket watch as security, an arrangement he had never heard of before and one that he was quite certain he had originated. If debtors repaid their sums by the agreed-upon time, the budding financier charged no interest. Many did not. The most profligate defaulted altogether. John's cabinet began to take on the appearance of a watchmaker's safe.

Unpaid notes continued to mount, prompting John to initiate a system of double compound interest, an innovation he likewise assumed he had originated, unaware that usury, or so it was called, had been in practice long before the moneylenders were driven from the temple by Jesus of Nazareth. John's nickel-and-dime empire continued apace.

At the end of the term, when mothers descended on the school to collect their offspring, many were distraught to find that their sons timepieces were now in the possession of a certain enterprising young capitalist. Faced with the unenviable task of explaining to their husbands the disappearance of gold and silver watches, many of which were heirlooms, as well as their sons' lack of financial acumen, the anxious mothers each paid sums ranging from eighteen to twenty dollars to the boy financier, who returned to Jeddoh with a profit of over four hundred dollars.

John Markham frequently told this story to his associates and employees to illustrate his ingenious business sense, and those who knew him well in no way doubted its veracity. The part he most delighted in telling, however, was the denouement, for when young John returned to boarding school the next term, the same boys lined up to borrow money, and once again he was ready to oblige, only this time he charged triple compound interest.

"No one has ever bettered me since then, because I am more clever and ruthless than the people I choose to deal with," Markham always bragged at the conclusion of his story, which was also the point of his story, and no one had ever disputed or challenged this assertion either. Until now.

On the first Friday of each month, Markham rode to Hazelton to pick up the payroll at the Miners National Bank. He drove the wagon himself as an act of defiance. No thief would dare rob John Markham, he thought, another assumption that had never been put to the test, but not for lack of sentiment, and certainly not with two armed Coal and Iron Policemen riding behind him.

His companion on these monthly rides was Ned the Splicer, his eyes and ears inside the colliery. Most of the time they rode in silence. They knew each other too well and too long for idle gab. When Markham spoke, it was to address a problem or to offer his solution. Today was no exception, but when Markham finally spoke, Ned the Splicer detected a bitterness in his voice, a level of frustration he'd never heard before.

"They're trying to suffocate me, Ned. Slowly. They want me out. They want all the independents out—oh, not by next year, or the next couple, but down the road. They want all of anthracite to themselves—the railroads *and* the coal.''

The elusive 'they' he referred to were the railroads. Since the early days of anthracite mining, railroads were the only practical means of getting coal over the mountains to market. As much as mine owners like G. B. Markham needed the railroads, the railroads needed operators like G. B. Markham even more, for without a commodity to transport, railroads had no hope of survival, whereas coal at least had a thriving local market. Thus, the mine owners had the upper hand, and used it to exact highly favorable contracts from the railroads like the Reading, the Lehigh Valley, the Pennsylvania, and the Jersey Central. And then, almost overnight, that changed. The railroads combined into larger companies, like the Delaware, Lackawanna and Western, then bought huge tracts of undeveloped forest land, which also happened to be sitting on huge reserves of coal. The railroads went into the coal business, slowly at first, and then with a vengeance. They dropped the price of coal, charging in some instances less than the cost of mining it. The independents had no choice but to follow suit. And then the railroads raised the price of shipment to tidewater. And then they raised it again. They carried their own coal, of course, for free, but the independents had to pay dearly to keep the markets that had made them rich. Many buckled under and sold out to the railroads rather than lose their accumulated wealth. A few, like John Markham, remained, or were allowed to remain, because they were politically prominent or offered no threats to the railroads' supremacy.

''I should have seen what was happening long before this,'' Markham told Ned, then added ruefully, ''I should have gone into railroading and beat them at their own game.''

''What can you do now?'' Ned the Splicer asked, knowing the answer before the question had left his lips, asking because it was expected of him to ask.

''I can hold out for a while. The bastards just raised

their prices to tidewater again. Not by much, mind you, but I've got to raise my ton just to keep even. What are we at now? Twenty-six forty?''

"Twenty-six sixty.''

A ton of steel weighed two thousand pounds, as did a ton of wheat or a ton of feathers, but in anthracite a ton of unprocessed coal, or the long ton, as it was called, weighed as much as the operator needed to cover his cost of production, plus a small margin for profit. Every time the combines raised the price of shipment, an independent had to increase his output or lower his cost of production or both. Or lower his margin of profit.

"I want you to raise the ton to twenty-eight. By Monday.''

Ned tried to put it tactfully. He knew the mood of the men. "Twenty-seven would be easier.''

"It won't do,'' Markham said firmly. "It has to be twenty-eight. Down in Mahanoy City they're up to thirty-two.''

The wagon turned onto Frog Street. In the distance, they could see the line of men that had already formed at the pay window alongside the store. A cheer went up as soon as they were spotted.

"The men won't like it,'' Ned cautioned.

Markham grunted. "They have no choice now, do they?''

There was a stir, an excited murmur in the crowd.

"Can you see it then?'' Euan asked Rhys, then stood on the tips of his toes, straining for a glimpse of the pay wagon above the heads of the crowd that blocked the street in front of the colliery. He might have had better luck if he'd knelt and looked between their knees.

"No use getting excited all over again.'' Rhys told him. "It's probably just another beer wagon.''

A cheer had gone up when the beer wagon came through. To some, it was a more welcome sight. They knew that the pay wagon would roll in before noon, but sometimes the beer wagon didn't show up until two or three o'clock.

Euan had been up and dressed since first whistle, only there'd been no whistle, nor was there any work this day. Not on payday. If Euan had had his way, he and his *dada* and Rhys would have been first in line at the pay window, but his *dada* was in no such hurry.

"The sooner you get it, the sooner you have it spent," he told the boy, but Euan would not be put off. It was his first payday. In three weeks he'd earned more than all the money he'd ever had in his pocket in his whole life, over seven dollars, and he couldn't wait till he held it, till he smelled it, till he got to eat all the sweets his share would buy.

"Let me get up on your shoulders then," Euan begged. "I can't see."

"You're an itch, you know that?" Rhys grumbled. "*N'had*, make him stop. He's been pestering all morning."

"Now, boys . . ."

"I'm going to the steps for a look!" Euan blurted.

"Stay here," his *dada* said. "Lose your place in line, and you'll have to wait all day."

Euan let out a long exhalation of breath to show his impatience. Then a cheer rose up, and the mulling crowd—those who weren't officially in line—rushed for places behind those who'd had the good sense to line up earlier. Suddenly the road was clear, and Euan could see the pay wagon charging toward them, its horses' manes, splayed, windblown—Markham, shouting at the reins for all to clear the way—the guards' shotguns, glinting in the morning sun. A tingle rolled up his spine. It was the prettiest sight he'd ever seen.

By the time the pay window opened at noon, the line stretched all the way up to the pit head. It would take more than three hours for those at the end to reach the window, but by that afternoon, every man and boy in Jeddoh would have money in his pocket.

Women from Polish Hill, wearing their brightly colored festive dresses and aprons, waited in line with their men. Each wore the colors of her home province in the old country—fiery red; soft sky blue; sunny amber; or deep, rich green. For one day at least, Jeddoh was rampant with color.

Euan's curiosity won out, and his *dada* finally let him leave his place in line to see what was happening up front at the pay window. As he walked along the track, balancing atop the rail, past the queue of expectant faces, he could hear the children in the schoolhouse across the way, singing a song that he remembered singing and remembered hating. He walked slowly, hoping they'd see him, see how important he was. He was getting paid today, not for singing or scratching letters with a pen, but for working in the breaker.

When he got to the pay window, Euan stood on the dirt path and rested his arms on the chest-high deck. Above him towered a Coal and Iron Policeman, whose rifle leaned, stock down, against the railing.

"T'ree nine nine," Euan heard a burly Polander say as he stepped up to the barred window. Behind it, Euan could see Iolo Morganwyg, the paymaster, as he scanned his list for the man's name.

"Zoltan Ras, laborer. Miner: Con Roberts," Morganwyg read, then in his droning voice recited the man's work schedule for the month. "Worked fourteen days, out two because of a...," and here he squinted to read Ned the Splicer's writing, "...a bad back. Total, one hundred twenty-four hours; total, twenty-seven dollars eighty-six cents. If you concur, signal by saying 'Aye.'"

"*Tak*," Ras said, refusing to answer the paymaster in his own language, but Morganwyg just as adamantly refused to continue until his instruction was followed.

"If you concur, signal by saying, 'Aye,'" Morganwyg repeated coldly.

"You'd think it was his money he was giving out," Euan said to himself.

"Aye," Ras conceded begrudgingly, and Morganwyg read on, relishing each amount, however small, the company could justifiably take back.

"Less: on credit, clothing and sundries, six dollars four cents; food and tobacco, two dollars thirty-seven cents;

medical, fifty cents; spiritual, fifty cents; breakage of company property during fisticuffs on second April, one dollar seventy-four cents. Total deductions, eleven dollars eleven cents. Total pay, sixteen dollars seventy-five cents.''

Morganwyg pushed the man's pay envelope under the bars. Ras, grinning, ripped it open with one swift move and began to count his earnings.

"Next. Move along," Morganwyg said impatiently.

"Move along," echoed the Coal and Iron Policeman, and Ras shambled off, still grinning.

"One six two," the man next in line said. Euan recognized him as the man who passed the collection plate each Sunday in church.

"Elfreth Owens, miner. Worked sixteen days; mined total of seventy-two tons; less: dockage, fifty-three tons

"Wait a minute, Iolo, wait a minute! You're docking me—fifty-three from seventy-two—nineteen tons? Nineteen?''

"That's Mr. Laughran's figure, Elfreth, not mine," Morganwyg said, his eyes fixed down at his papers.

"But nineteen tons? I know coal from rock, Iolo, and I would never be bringing up nineteen tons of rock! Do you hear what I'm saying then?''

"If you wish to discuss it with Mr. Laughran . . .''

"It's thievery!" Owens shouted. Heads down the line suddenly turned in his direction. "I'm entitled to seventy-two tons, and I expect to be paid for seventy-two tons!''

Euan saw the Coal and Iron Policeman's hand reach unobtrusively for his rifle.

"Are you impugning the integrity of Mr. Laughran, Elfreth?" Morganwyg asked, staring icily.

"I'm saying, I *know* what I sent up, Iolo, and it weren't nineteen tons of rock is what I'm saying!''

"If you'll step aside, we'll look into the matter after the rest of the men get . . .''

"Where's Markham?" Owens demanded. "I want to talk to Markham.''

"Mr. Markham is a very busy . . .''

"I want Markham, dammit! I won't speak to anybody

but Markham!'' Owens shouted. The mob hushed. The only sound was the singing from across the way.

"Calm down, Mr. Owens,'' Euan heard Markham say from inside the payroll office. His voice was firm, yet so quiet Euan could hardly hear it above the children's song.

"I assure you Mr. Laughran's figures are correct,'' Markham continued. "In fact, he made special mention to me that you were sending up a high percentage of rock and how peculiar that was, for you are usually so scrupulous. If I were you, I'd take greater care loading your wagons, or dockage will be the least of your worries. I'm in the business of selling coal, Mr. Owens, not crushed rock.''

As Markham spoke, Owens shifted nervously from foot to foot, reminding Euan of himself whenever he got the gab from Miss Protheroe.

"Do you have anything more to say, Mr. Owens?'' Markham asked.

"I...I...I think,'' Owens stammered, "I think we ought to have our own man doing the weighing. That's what I think.''

No sound came from the window.

"That's all...that's all I have to say,'' Owens said, his voice barely above a whisper.

Laughing and clapping, the children finished their song.

"Shall I continue?'' Morganwyg asked. Markham made no sound so the paymaster cleared his throat and droned on. "Less: dockage, fifty-three tons at ninety cents per ton, forty-seven dollars seventy cents; setting of timber, three dollars ninety cents; total, fifty-one dollars sixty cents. If you concur, signal by saying 'Aye.' ''

Owens was too flushed with anger to reply. Behind him, the men bristled with impatience.

"Aye,'' Owens grunted finally.

"Less: rent, ten dollars; on credit, clothing and sundries, eleven dollars thirty-five cents; food and tobacco, twenty-five dollars thirteen cents; powder and fuses, three dollars sixty-six cents; medical, fifty cents; spiritual, fifty cents; water, forty cents. Total deductions, fifty-one dollars and fifty-four cents. Total pay...six cents.''

Owens stood, frozen, staring at the envelope containing his pay.

"Next. Move along, Elfreth," piped Morganwyg.

"Move along there," said the Coal and Iron Policeman.

"Keep your bloody money, Markham!" Owens exploded, tearing the envelope in half. The nickel and penny fell out, rolled across the wood deck and over the edge, landing in the path at Euan's feet. In line behind Owens, the men's impatience boiled over.

("Ye got a job, ain't ye, Owens? Shut yer trap!")

Still, Owens continued to rage at Markham as though some slow-burning fuse inside him had suddenly fired, releasing years of anger and frustration.

"How can a man keep a family going on six cents a month?"

("Some don't make that much. Where's he been?")

"I work hard, harder than most men here, and by Jesus! the hunkies are making more than me! And they just send it back to Po-land. I got a family *here*, Markham!"

("Don't fret, man, at least when you roll over at night to cuddle yer wife, ye ain't got six others in the same room cuddling, too.")

"I got little ones like you! How can I feed them on six cents?"

("They ain't starved yet. He oughta see mine.")

"There ain't a man here that gets paid what he earns. You're bleeding us, Markham, bleeding us dry! You've got that fine house! How much money do you *need*? How many of us gotta drop dead from work before you ... before you've got all ... all you ... how much ... before ... ?"

Owens drooped. His rage dissolved into sobs and back into rage again, at himself, for losing control. Ned the Splicer watched the last part of the tirade from the doorway of the payroll office, then picked up the torn pieces of the pay envelope and handed them back to Owens.

"It's all right, Elfreth. Let me walk you home," he said quietly and put a reassuring hand on Owens's shoulder.

The shaken man looked inside the halves of the envelope. "Where's my six cents then?" he said. "I'll not leave till I've got my six cents!"

Euan retrieved the coins from the ground and handed them up. He had never seen a man cry before.

"Thank you, lad."

"Come, Elfreth, I'll walk you," Ned the Splicer said and led him past the silent faces to his home.

"Next," said the paymaster.

Word spread quickly that dockage was running higher than usual for the month. Hugh had set a large number of timbers in his breast for which he was paid by the foot. That total was safe, but his tonnage would be low, because he had only begun to "clean the length," or empty the breast, by month's end. High dockage would hurt his tonnage; high dockage could wipe his total out. As he stepped to the pay window, his voice sounded more anxious than usual.

"Two three eight."

"Hugh Morgan, miner," Morganwyg read out. "Sixteen days; thirty tons mined; less: dockage . . ."

Hugh held his breath.

". . . twenty-six tons . . ."

"Only four tons," Hugh whispered to Rhys. "Could've been worse."

". . . at ninety cents per ton, twenty-three dollars forty cents; setting of timber, eighteen dollars forty-two cents; total, forty-one dollars eighty-two cents. If you concur, signal by saying 'Aye.' "

"Aye," Hugh said, relieved.

"Less: rent, eight dollars; on credit, clothing and sundries, nine dollars forty-five cents; food and tobacco, twenty-one dollars eighty-nine cents; powder, three dollars twenty-six cents; medical, fifty cents; spiritual, fifty cents; water, forty cents. Total deductions, forty-four dollars; indebtedness to company increased by two dollars eighteen cents." Morganwyg looked up from his list. "Is this your son here, Mr. Morgan?"

"Yes," Hugh answered. "One ought five."

"Rhys Morgan, driver. Worked eighteen days: sixteen, plus two Sundays tending mules; total, one hundred seventy-eight hours; total eighteen dollars forty-six cents. If you concur, signal by saying 'Aye.'"

"Aye."

"Less: medical, fifty cents; spiritual, fifty cents; damage to coal car on seventeenth April, one dollar fifty cents . . . ;"

Rhys winced. It had been a stupid accident that wasn't even his doing. Still, he'd been blamed.

". . . reduction of debt owed to company by H. Morgan, father, number two three eight, ten dollars; total deductions, twelve dollars fifty cents; total pay, five dollars ninety-six cents."

Morganwyg handed Hugh a "snake statement," a slip of paper that showed the slow decline of his indebtedness to the company by means of a red diagonal line. Hugh had borrowed heavily against his future wages to pay for the move to Jeddoh, to replace goods left behind. He still owed over eighty dollars.

Euan knew of their debt, but he never dreamed it was so high. "Eighty dollars!" he said to himself as he looked at the snake statement. "I'll be an old man before it's paid off."

"Next!" Morganwyg called impatiently. "Next!"

"Two ought seven."

"Euan Morgan, slate picker. Worked thirteen days; total, one hundred twenty-one hours; total, six dollars five cents. If you concur, signal by saying 'Aye.'"

"Aye."

"Speak up, lad."

"Aye!"

"Less: medical, fifty cents; spiritual, fifty cents; dockage for over-abundance of coal discarded, twenty cents . . . ;" Morganwyg paused, squinted, and raised his eyebrows at the next entry in his ledger. "less: replacement metal tip for damage done to wood leg of D. Bryfogle, two dollars . . ."

Hugh and Rhys looked at each other incredulously and then at Euan, who kept his eyes affixed to the paymaster's ledger. Rhys burst into laughter at the thought of puny Euan doing "damage" to a barrel of lard like Bryfogle, but Hugh silenced him with a sharp glance. Two dollars was at stake.

"Could there be some error, sir?" Hugh asked.

Even Morganwyg looked perplexed. "There's a complaint here, written by Mr. Laughran, that has Mr. Bryfogle's mark on it. If you wish to discuss the matter, you can step aside and..."

"No, no," Hugh said, knowing how useless it would be to protest such a complaint. "Was this your doing then?" he asked Euan.

Euan's heart was pounding. Two dollars lost because of Digger's prank. Two dollars! Was that worth the kick he'd given Digger in the teeth? Yet, if he denied being the culprit, the story might come out—how Bryfogle had beat him, how Digger had busted him up. Euan didn't want his *dada* and Rhys to know how weak he'd been, how he'd cried. Better to let them think what they wanted to think. "The less you say, the less your trouble," he thought.

He nodded yes.

Morganwyg read on, "Total deductions, three dollars twenty cents; total pay, two dollars eighty-five cents."

The envelope scraped across the ledge. Euan mouthed the sum to himself as he took his pay in his hand, his hand, which was shaking.

"I wouldn't do that," Euan said. "It's all supposed to go to *Mam*."

"Suit yourself then. Everybody else does," Rhys told him and shrugged like he didn't care if Euan believed him or not.

Some trappers clattered down the steps behind them, ripping open the plugs of tobacco they'd just bought in the store. Everyone who passed had a fresh quid or a handful of sweets. Some women carried cups of beer to their men who were still waiting in line.

"How much do you...?"

"Knock down? Fifty cents," Rhys said, holding his pay

envelope up to his eye, then tipping it so two quarters rolled out. "Everybody does it," he repeated as he stuffed the quarters into his pocket. "Everybody. Even *N'had*."

"Was that what you gave him then?"

Rhys looked at Euan, surprised that he had seen him hand their *dada* a dollar from his pay envelope. Euan had been so busy, counting and recounting the contents of his own, that they didn't think he'd notice. But he'd seen, seen the uncomfortable look on his *dada*'s face, embarrassed to be asking his son for money, seen him tuck the dollar into his pocket, then turn away and square his shoulders like nothing had happened.

"You don't miss nothing, do you?" Rhys said and shook his head.

"Then how much should I . . . ?" Euan asked, still uncertain.

"Twenty-five. You earned it."

Euan held his pay envelope up to his eye, spotted a quarter, and shook it out into his hand. Reluctantly. Half of him knew it was wrong, but the other half was anxious to taste the sweets the extra money would buy.

"I'm going in to get some sour balls," he told Rhys. He was halfway up the steps before Rhys told him to stay put.

"*N'had* said wait here for him."

"He might take all day."

"Sit down. He'll only be a couple of minutes."

"Where'd he go then?"

Rhys didn't answer at first. "To the Emerald."

"The Emerald? *N'had*?"

"He only goes paydays. *Mam* don't know."

"*N'had*?" Euan asked again, unable to comprehend his *dada* sitting at a table with a bunch of drunken miners.

"A man can work up a thirst in a month," Rhys said quietly.

Euan was confounded. First, he'd seen Mr. Owens cry. Then he learned of the size of their debt. Next, Rhys told him about the knock down, and now, he found out that his *dada* drank beer at the Emerald just like other men! It had been an eye-opening day.

Suddenly there was a burst of laughter and loud catcalls from the line, and a woman's voice shouted, "Move out of the road! I'd like to pass!" It had been three weeks since Euan had heard that shrill screak. He looked up to see Miss Protheroe, whip in hand, trying to drive her carriage through the line of taunting, pay-hungry men. He stepped into the street for a closer look.

"Top o' the mornin' to ye, Miss Protheroe!" one of the drivers called.

"Ye never passed *me*, Miss Protheroe!" shouted a door boy.

"Can I tote yer books for ye?" another driver asked then leered to his mate, "I'd like to tote somethin' else fer her, and it ain't her books."

Euan could see Miss Protheroe's face flush with anger, her teeth grit with anger. He enjoyed her discomfort. He laughed at the men's jeers.

"Move, you brazen lugs!" the teacher shouted back at them as her horse danced nervously. "Or I'll give you a taste of my whip!"

"Her lips, did she say? Her cherry red lips?"

"Yer not in yer schoolroom now, Ma'am. Ye gotta say, 'Please.'"

The growing ruckus drew the attention of a Coal and Iron Policeman. "Let the lady pass!" he shouted.

"'Dat no lady, 'dat Miss Prot'roe!"

But the way opened up, and her carriage passed through their ranks.

"Cheerio, Miss Protheroe!"

"Leavin' so soon? Let me buy ye a shot 'n' a beer!"

It was then that she spotted Euan in the middle of the road.

"So, there you are, Euan Morgan!" she said, reining in her horse, her eyes brimming with wrath. "You're right where you belong, aren't you? With the rest of the animals!" As she drove off, she called over her shoulder, "I hope you're happy!"

Euan felt humiliated, being singled out in front of everyone. His face reddened. "She's just an old son of a bitch of a bastard!'' he said to Rhys as they watched her carriage sweep through Irish Flats.

"Better not let *N'had* hear you talk like that."

"Son of a bitch of a bastard!'' Euan mumbled under his breath.

Another pair of eyes followed the teacher up Frog Street.

"She is not pretty, but she would make good wife," Zakrzewska said to himself, still wearing his work clothes, his only clothes, as he stood alone on the edge of the crowd, twirling a sprig of hedge between his teeth. "Woman like her stuff money in mattress, I bet. Maybe couple hundred dollars."

"Miss Proth-roe," he said aloud, testing the sound of her in his mouth. "Miss Proth-roe."

Myfanwy greeted her men at the back door with a smile. "Let's see what we got then," she said and took down the tin from the stove and held it out to each in turn. "*N'had?*"

Hugh shook his head no. She moved on to Rhys, who spilled the contents of his envelope into the tin.

"Four dollars forty-six cents," he announced.

Myfanwy looked at him skeptically.

"Breakage," he explained. "They always pick on me."

And finally Euan.

"Two dollars sixty," he said proudly as he emptied his money into the tin. "They got me for breakage, too."

"Well, next month will be better. There'll be enough to make our tin brim over," she said brightly, then reached in and took out a dime for Euan. "Here's for you. Careful how you spend it then."

"Thank you, *Mam*."

And a dime and a nickel for Rhys. "And here's for Rhys. . . ."

"Thank you, *Mam*."

And two quarters for Hugh. "And here's for *Dada*!"

"Thank you, *Mam*," Hugh said, imitating the boys. It was enough to make them all laugh.

The pluck me store did a brisk business on payday. At times it became so crowded that Mr. Beech, the manager, had to lock the front door to keep the store from being overrun.

After a struggle, Euan emerged with a sackful of red hats, licorice, sour balls, and jelly beans left from Easter. Rhys bought coffin nails. After a supper he couldn't finish, having gorged himself with sweets, Euan returned to buy peanuts and molasses. Rhys bought some Yankee Boy, and they sat alongside the Emerald to watch the mobs streaming up and down Frog Street.

"Rhys, I don't feel so good," Euan said queasily after he'd emptied his sack.

"I don't wonder," Rhys said, shaking his head. "You'd think they were giving a prize to the one who could stuff himself the most."

A moment later, Euan upchucked twenty-seven cents worth of red hats, licorice, sour balls, peanuts, molasses, and jelly beans left from Easter.

Most houses on Polish Hill had kegs of beer out back, and the din lasted late into the night. Fights began over insignificant remarks. Rivalries over women boiled into brawls. No one behaved quite like himself on payday.

Around three o'clock, gunshots crackled through the crisp night air and echoed off the surrounding hills. To Rhys, it sounded like a hundred stones, all hitting the wall at the same time.

"Damn fools," Hugh muttered to Myfanwy and rolled over.

Euan never even woke up.

It was a senseless death—two friends quarreling, one pulling a gun, friends rushing to separate them, shots firing, one of which tore through the throat of a curious bystander, killing him instantly.

Most hardly even knew the victim. He was quiet, worked diligently as a laborer, and lived as a boarder in Maciejewski's. He died after paying eight dollars for his monthly room and board and drinking three beers. No one knew that he was saving to buy a farm with his brothers when they arrived from the old country in two months. In his pocket was two dollars sixty-one cents and a bank book that listed a deposit of five dollars just that day, bringing the balance to three hundred twelve dollars.

Zoltan Ras died a nearly rich man.

❖❖

NEITHER Razor nor his fiddlers could read music. They were naturals. One of them would hear a song, learn it by ear, and the others would work in their harmonies accordingly. They approached their playing with the serious, almost grim, aggressiveness that some men directed toward digging ditches or sawing wood. They were businessmen, which is why Razor had cast his eye on Rhys long before Rhys happened into Maciejewski's yard.

Razor and his fiddlers, Blackie, Stanko, and Pauli, made a bit of money playing for weddings and funerals, but they knew they could earn even more by playing for socials and teas in Hazelton and Wilkesbarre, even Philadelphia or New York. They also knew that in their present configuration they would never get hired. *Polkas* and *kozaks* were not in demand at socials and teas, nor were foreign bands, especially Polanders. Rhys was their first step to acceptance. Next, they would learn American songs, and then they would prosper.

They practiced their playing every other night and Saturday and Sunday afternoons, usually in the cellar of Razor's house or a shed behind Stanko's. Rhys felt overwhelmed at first. His hands, clumsy and calloused, seemed ill-suited for such a delicate instrument. ''Is voman for caressin', not club for hittin','' Razor reminded him time and time again. Fortunately there were only four strings to play—the big, the middle, the little, and the baby—or so they called them. They were not musicians. They were naturals.

Rhys struggled with the strange-sounding tunes and practiced the simple fingering that Razor taught him every chance he got, while leading trips down the gangways, in church listening to Paster Wheat, in bed at night waiting to fall asleep, at the supper table waiting for his *mam* to serve his food.

(Big, middle, little, baby, baby, little, middle, big . . . )

"Is there something wrong with your hand then?" his *dada* asked.

"No, no, nothing!" Rhys shrugged.

"Keep it still then. It's enough to make me nervous."

"It's just stiff is all. Maybe a touch of the arthritis," Rhys said and chuckled, then resumed beneath the table out of view.

(Big, middle, middle, big, little, baby, baby, little . . . )

And the songs! Melodies all sounding alike to him— rhythmic, pulsing, circular, with never enough time to catch up when he got behind, and he always got behind.

"Hurry, Rhysie! Hurry!"

(Big, baby, big, baby, middle, little, middle, little . . . )

In some, Razor gave Rhys just one note to saw in time. If he found his note, all was fine. If he didn't, Razor lifted his eyebrows or winked till he found his way. Thus began a set of signals that passed between them so Razor could let Rhys know when he was flat, or sharp, or behind, or ahead. Most of the time, Razor's face looked contorted by some horrible affliction, but there were smiles of favor, too. In time, those smiles became more frequent.

(Big, little, middle, baby, big, little, middle, baby . . . )

"When will I be ready to play?" Rhys asked one afternoon as they packed away their instruments. He was using Blackie's old fiddle.

"Soon," Razor said proudly. "Next mont'. Big vettin' comin'."

Rhys smiled. "I can't wait," he said, but secretly wished that they would not have to wait that long.

❖❖

THE men glutted the yard. They stood in patches and spat tobacco juice onto the crushed slate. Their mutterings seethed like water thrown onto a hot stove.

Before his *dada* could stop him, Euan ran ahead to see if the cage had broken down or if the boilers had lost their steam, the usual causes of such delays. He weaved up the hill through a maze of sullen men to the pit head, where a crudely painted sign had been nailed for all to read. Until further notice, a long ton would weigh twenty-eight-hundred pounds.

"Is this what the huff is about?" Euan wondered. Suddenly there were angry shouts, and the crowd turned as one to see Tom Pryor grab the front of Ned the Splicer's shirt in his huge hand. Almost at once, some other miners pulled Tom Pryor back, but his face burned red with anger.

"Dammit to hell, man!" he shouted. "I've got to send up five or six hundred pounds more each day just so's I can keep up with what I earned last month! You call that fair?"

"Now, Tom," Ned the Splicer kept repeating and raised his arms to quiet Tom Pryor, but Tom was so riled he wouldn't listen. Others raised their fists at Ned the Splicer and started to shout, too. Euan climbed atop a barrel near the peg board for a better look and to see if his *dada* and Rhys were coming so they wouldn't miss the fight.

Then four Coal and Iron Policemen appeared from behind the steam shanty and began shoving their way through the crowd to where Ned stood surrounded by hostile miners. Their rifles were raised across their chests, and they didn't care who got batted across the back of the head as they passed. Anger flared in their path, flared and spread, like the sparks of a brush fire, first here, then there, then all around till the yard was lit with hate. Euan cringed at the sudden conflagration and wished he'd not left his *dada*.

And then, John Markham himself appeared, flanked by more Coal and Iron Police, and made his way to the heart of the mob where he climbed, undaunted, to the bed of an empty wagon so that all could see him and hear his words.

"Is this a strike?" he boomed. "I said, 'Is this a strike?' I'd like to know, for I'll close the mine down for good if it is!"

The mob begrudgingly fell silent.

"If you think you can make more in any mine in anthracite, go! Leave here now, and don't come back! I pay an honest wage for an honest day's work. Let no man say different! I have always been fair!"

"And what you pay us," a voice shouted from the crowd, "you steal back in your bloody store!" Others spurred on the attack, voicing discontent that reached beyond the long ton.

"Is it fair what you make us pay for powder?"

"Today it's twenty-eight-hundred! What'll it be tomorrow?"

"Why not charge us for the air we breathe, Markham!"

"If you have a grievance," Markham answered over their shouts, "I have always taken time to listen."

"And that's all ye do!" The restiveness mounted.

"When will we see an end to the dockage?"

"We want our man to weigh the coal! We're tired of being cheated!"

"And who will pay this man?" Markham demanded. "I will not. Will you? And who will keep your man honest? Shall I have to pay another to keep watch over him? You think there are easy solutions. There are none! You want more pay for less labor? That is not how it goes. From here on, you will have to work harder and take less . . . or you will take nothing!"

For a moment, there was silence. Euan searched the still-simmering faces for his *dada* and Rhys. Spying them, he jumped down and pressed through the crowd to their side.

"Ye'd sing a diff'rent tune if we brung the union in here!" an Irishman yelled as he passed, sending out sparks, reigniting the flames.

"Yes! What about a union?"

"We want a union!"

"The union! Yes! Yes!"

"We'll bring Johnny Mitch' in here, then ye'll see!"

"You think there'll be work today?" Euan blurted as he came upon Rhys.

"Shhh! This is important!" Rhys scolded.

"It's Sugar Notch all over," his *dada* grumbled and shook his head. "The fools! The bloody fools!"

"I will hear no talk of union!" Markham roared. "Today or any day!"

"Johnny Mitch' says he can get us twenty percent higher pay!"

"Then go work for Johnny Mitch'! The union cares about only one thing—jobs for its fat, bloated leaders—men who have lined their pockets with your wages! But I give you jobs, not the union! I give you money for clothes and food, a roof between you and the elements! I watch over the men who work for me, men who are loyal to me! But I will tell you this, the first day you bring the union in here, I will discharge ten of you. You will be out of your houses by nightfall! You and your families and every miserable thing you own will be huddled at the side of the road by moonlight! The next day, ten more will go, and the next, and the next! And then you can look to the heavens and give thanks to God on high for bringing you Johnny Mitch'. Johnny Mitch' *and* his twenty percent!"

"Ye can't fire us all, Markham!"

"And why not?" Markham demanded.

The men were stunned, bludgeoned into silence.

"Why not?" he repeated barely above a whisper. "I am all the union you will ever need. I am all the union you will ever have."

The men looked at one another in their shame, each hoping that the next would find words to make them feel like men again instead of scolded children.

"The ton is twenty-eight-hundred," Markham affirmed. "While you stand here, pennies are falling from your pay envelopes. Time to get back to work!"

"Let's go now! We'll have a full day today!" Ned the Splicer shouted. Slowly, slowly the men began to disperse.

"The bastard!" a man behind Euan snarled under his breath.

"I hope he rots in hell," spat another.

"Come on then, lads," his *dada* said to him and Rhys, his hands on their shoulders. "Let's move on. That's all over now."

But it was not over.

"*Pani* Markham! A vort, please!" a voice called above the grumbing and the shuffling feet.

"Who said that? Who?" Markham asked.

"Here! Me, Jozef Moczygemba!" a tall, bearded laborer said as he moved forward into the clearing in front of Markham. "I have grievance." Everyone stopped to stare at this Pole, who had the temerity to confront Markham in his foulest of moods. It was as though he were inviting his immediate discharge.

"Say *ta* to your friend," a Welshman sniggered to some Poles. "He's not long for this place."

"I vork for you," Moczygemba continued, "my brot'ers vork for you seven years. Ve know 'da vork; ve vork hart. T'ree times ve ask for miner job, an' t'ree times you say is not time. You tell us vait, an' each time ve vait, an' vait, an' still none of us is miner."

"We don't want no hunky miners!" a Welshman behind him hollered.

"My mules got more brains than a hunky!" yelled another.

But Moczygemba pressed on. "Vhen *vill* be time, *pani* Markham?"

"Never!" came shouts from the crowd. "Never! Never!"

"All ve vant is chance, *pani* Markham, chance to show ve work as goot as 'Merican miner. You see, ve make goot miner."

"Never! Never!"

"Don't do it, Markham!"

"Send 'em back where they came from! Goddamn hunkies!"

Tom Pryor elbowed his way into the open area. "If it wasn't for these bloody roundheads—they're the cause of the trouble here! Things was good till they came in. Now they want us out! Well, to hell with them, Markham! No hunky's going to push me out of my job! I was here first, and by God! I'm staying!" His words loosed a torrent of hate.

"Stop this at once!" Markham shouted when their epithets threatened to get out of hand. "You're here to work not squabble like a bunch of women! As for you, Moczygemba—yes, you and your brothers are good workers, but I have more miners than I need. Still you did come forward with your grievance with due respect, and since I am a fair man, I will consider it. As for the rest, any man not pegged in before five minutes will be discharged!''

Third whistle blew. The men, still grumbling, hastened for places in line at the peg board.

Euan looked up at his *dada*. "What's like Sugar Notch, *N'had*?''

"All of it," his *dada* said sorrowfully. "All of it.''

Markham's office was not fancy. There were no curtains or rugs, just a wooden desk two oak cabinets, and two padded chairs. A telephone hung on the wall near the door, and a green-shaded oil lamp rested atop the desk next to a brass inkstand. The room's single affectation was a Victrola, which Markham had recently bought for himself in Philadelphia.

Through one window, Markham had a view of part of the yard and the pit head. The other windows looked onto the blank wall of the Glen Ellen and the wood fence that surrounded the colliery.

"Sit down, Ned!" Markham said as his superintendent entered. "Did you see what happened out there?" Markham's eyes glowed with a fiery intensity.

"I thought there'd be trouble. It could have been much worse.''

"I don't think we're talking about the same thing. Did you see how it ended? The rancor? The hell with the long ton, it was their hatred for each other that won out. I'd forgotten how rigid those old Welshmen could be, and how dogged these roundheads are. I don't believe Jesus Christ himself could start a union here.''

"So . . . you'll play one side against the other? It's a risk.''

"Everything's a risk, Ned. Do you have an alternative?''

"Supposing they *did* unite," Ned allowed. "What would happen?''

Markham thought for a moment. "They'd probably get what they wanted, whatever that is. I don't think they know themselves." He paused and looked for a moment at the portrait of his father that hung on the wall by the door. "Can you imagine what Old G.B. would say about all this?"

"He *would* have closed the mine down."

"And burned the breaker, just for spite," Markham added with a chuckle, then turned to his Victrola, released the brake, and placed the needle onto the spinning disk. Immediately, a lively tune burst forth from the horn. Markham seemed entranced, but to Ned it was just another noise, indistinguishable from the colliery's other rattles and rumbles.

"Is . . . is that all then?" Ned the Splicer asked.

"No," Markham said. "No, I want you to find a roundhead, one who might make a good miner. Not this Moczygemba. They'll think I'm rewarding him for having a big mouth."

"There are a few I can think of who might be . . . acceptable."

"Take your time. Let me know your choice in a few days," Markham said as he sat and let the music wash over him. "I can't let it happen, Ned. This union. It would ruin me. I can't let it happen."

••

"Bore da," Myfanwy said to Mrs. Jenkins as they met near the dry goods counter one rainy Wednesday. She did her shopping early in the morning while there was still a good selection of produce and freshly killed meats.

"*Bore da,* Myfanwy. We missed you at Ladies' Aid last night."

"My Hugh was ailing. His back again."

"Nothing serious, I hope?"

"The usual. It's a wonder they can stand straight at all, hunched over the way they do, day in, day out."

"How true!" Mrs. Jenkins said, then added quite casually, "We included you in our plans for the deacons' supper this Saturday. Could you bake us two of your apple pies?"

Myfanwy was taken aback. While she had always helped

to serve supper at the monthly elders' meetings, she had never been asked to help prepare it. That was an honor reserved for the older members of the Ladies' Aid. Myfanwy had never expected to be given an opportunity to take part, to prove herself, so soon. Fortunately her pies were her strength.

"Why . . . why, yes," Myfanwy gushed. "Of course, I shall be happy to."

"And Mr. Beech just opened a new apple barrel!" Mrs. Jenkins said. "Very tart, I hear."

Just then, at the counter behind them, Mr. Beech raised his voice to a Polish woman. "No, I cannot give you!" he said. "*Nie! Nie!*"

"Then I better hurry," Myfanwy replied to Mrs. Jenkins, raising her own voice to be heard above the shouts. "Baking apples are so hard to come by this time of year."

"I cannot! *Nie!* Mr. Markham has refused," Mr. Beech repeated loudly, but his words were useless. The woman's pleading only became more desperate.

"What's going on?" Mrs. Jenkins finally asked the dry goods clerk when the confrontation became too unpleasant to ignore.

"It's her third time here this week," the clerk confided. "The husband drinks, lost his job a month ago, so Markham cut off their tick. They live in the patch beyond Polish Hill."

"Are there any children?" Mrs. Jenkins asked.

The clerk nodded. "Little ones."

"*Nie! Nie!*" Mr. Beech said, angry now. "You bring *dolary,* you buy, not till then."

"She tried to barter yesterday," the clerk added. "Some pictures and trinkets—a lot of junk."

"*Dolary?*" the woman asked and laughed a bitter, high-pitched laugh, then turned to confront the disapproving eyes directed at her. She muttered something in Polish, took a few steps and, weakened from hunger, collapsed at Myfanwy's feet.

"Get some water!" Mrs. Jenkins ordered the clerk then knelt beside the woman and raised her head. The woman's eyes were red from crying, her lips, dried and cracked. When the water was brought, Mrs. Jenkins helped the woman drink it down.

"*Dziekuje*," the woman said weakly.

Myfanwy couldn't bear to look at her. She felt nothing but revulsion. "These people—they're not like us," she thought as she walked back to inspect the new apples. "I can't feel sorry for them. They bring on their own misery."

Later, as they were leaving, Myfanwy saw Mrs. Jenkins take fifty cents from her purse and hand it to Mr. Beech.

"Here's for the water she drank," she heard Mrs. Jenkins say, her voice curling with contempt. "The rest is for food. If she needs more, put it on my tick."

"Why did you do that, Margaretta?" Myfanwy asked when they reached the bottom of the steps. "You know it will get right back to Mr. Markham."

"I'll not have the death of children on my conscience," the older woman replied. "*Ta*, Myfanwy."

"*Ta*, Margaretta.

On the way home, Myfanwy thought of nothing but her pies. When she had set aside her goods, she sat down to compose her weekly letter. For a change, there was pleasant news to convey.

"Dear Meb," she wrote. "Something wonderful has happened . . ."

◆◆

"You're to take these pies down to Mrs. Jenkins," Myfanwy instructed Rhys. "She's in the church basement waiting for them. And don't drop them! They're for the deacons' supper tonight."

"Can't Euan do it?" he moaned.

"And how's the little one going to carry these big tins?"

"He's not so little," Rhys said as she set one pie in each of his arms. "Aren't you going to wrap them in something?" he asked. He didn't relish the idea of being seen carrying two of his *mam*'s apple pies down Frog Street on a Saturday afternoon. He could hear the ribbings already.

"It's only down the street, boy."

"Something then. A towel maybe?"

"More work!" she huffed and took two clean dish towels and wrapped them around the pies. "And don't forget to bring my towels back!" she called after him as he clomped down the back steps.

It didn't take long for the worst of it to come his way. Everyone he knew seemed to be out, enjoying the warm sun.

"Hey, Rhysie! Vhat you got smell so goot?"

"Ye gonna give us a taste, buddy? Jest a taste!"

"Did you help your *mam* bake 'em, too?"

"Atta boy! His *mam*'s helper!"

"Patty cake! Patty cake! Baker man . . . !"

He knew if he set the pies down to take a poke at one of his tormentors that the pies would be gone before his fist hit flesh, so he just grinned and quickened his pace, thought of his fingering exercises and grinned some more, making note of the most irksome so he could rub their noses in dog dirt first chance he got.

("Big, middle, little, baby, big, middle, little, baby . . .")

He reached the church with his pies unscathed as choir was letting out.

"You need a hand, lad?" the sexton, old Mr. Prodgers, said and held the vestry door open for him.

"Thank you, sir," Rhys said as he entered, then froze when he spotted Mary Markham coming down the steps from the choir loft with two other girls. "Cripes Almighty!" he blurted out, forgetting himself, and backed out the door and down the stoop. The last thing he wanted was for Mary Markham to see him looking like Simple Simon. He was thinking of heaving his double burden over the fence when he backed into the old maple tree near which he and his buddies congregated each week after Sunday school. He dashed behind it just as Mary and her girlfriends burst through the door.

"Did they see me?" he wondered, catching his breath, then peeked around the thick trunk to spy. There were three in all—Alice Tuttle, another he knew only as Thelma, and Mary, in a pretty, white cotton dress. He found Mary pleasing to look at, but everything about her was different from everything he knew, different from everything he was. Still, he was taken with her. He had never been taken with a girl before.

"What did she write to you?" Alice asked Mary.

"I've not read it yet," Mary said, taking the slender red volume from the sash tied at her waist, then thumbed casually through its parchment pages.

"I'm *dying* to know," Alice fussed. "Hurry!"

"Why, that petticoat!" Mary exclaimed as her eyes fell on the entry in question.

"What does it say?" Thelma piped.

"Not here! She might come," Mary replied, glancing cautiously over her shoulder, then, to draw out the suspense, rushed down the steps to the foot of the maple tree. Rhys drew his head back, certain now of discovery.

("Big, middle, little, baby, big, middle, little, baby . . .")

"Mary Markham, *you're* the petticoat!" Rhys heard Alice chide, then Mary giggled, and the three of them plopped down on the grass.

"Cripes Almighty!" Rhys groaned to himself. "Now I'll never get away!"

("Big, middle, little, baby, baby, little, middle, big . . .")

"All right, nosy!" Mary teased, then read in a light, wistful voice, " 'When the golden sun is sinking, and your mind from trouble's free . . . ' "

"That's the same verse she wrote in mine!" Thelma gasped.

"Shhh! Let her finish!"

" ' . . . while of others you are thinking, will you sometimes think of me? Yours till Niagara Falls, Charlotte Bempkins. P.S. May the skin of a gooseberry cover all your enemies.' "

"What a snip! It's the same she wrote to me!" Thelma said indignantly.

"You'll need a basket of gooseberries with her around," Alice observed. "Look what she wrote to me: 'Man's love is like Scotch snuff, get a whiff and that's enough; woman's love is like French candy, always good but never handy. Yours till the sidewalks, Charlotte.' She's just an impudent snip!''

"Who does she think she is?" Thelma huffed.

"What did Stubb McAndrew sign?" Mary asked provocatively.

Alice grimaced and handed her book to Mary. "You read it. I can't."

" 'Love many, trust few.....' " Mary began in the same wistful voice as before, " '... but always paddle your own canoe.' " Then, trying to suppress her laughter, " 'Yours till the kitchen sinks, Stubb.' "

"I'm sorry I even asked him," Alice bleated. "Charlotte asked him to sign hers, and he practically filled the whole book! I hate her!"

"She's such a snip!" Thelma chimed.

"They're all a bunch of gossips," Rhys said to himself. His arms were getting tired, and he was bored with their silly chatter. "Us fellas work all day, and all they do is gossip and write poems to each other!" He would never understand girls.

("Big, baby, baby, big, middle, little, little, middle . . .")

"Have you got everyone then?" Alice asked Mary.

"All but one," Mary replied coyly.

"Let me guess his name!"

"Shhh! Don't you dare say it!"

"Who?" Thelma asked, always a step behind. "Who's she talking about?"

"Mary's got someone special."

("Big, little, middle, baby, big, little, middle, baby . . .")

"Don't you dare tell her, Alice, or I'll never speak to you again!"

"Who?" Thelma pumped.

"You'll find out when he signs my book."

"I know who it is," Alice bragged. "He's a driver."

("Big, little, middle, ba . . .")

Suddenly Rhys was all ears.

"A driver?" Thelma queried. "Not Theo Bakunas!"

Mary groaned.

"Thelma, I swear, you're as dumb as cheese!" Alice

said. "Anybody with a brain half the size of a pea knows it's Rhys Mor..."

"Alice Tuttle, I hate you!" Mary shrieked.

"It's no secret, Mary. Everybody knows you're sweet on Rhys Morgan!"

"I didn't," Thelma chirped.

"And everybody knows he never looks your way!"

"That's not true!" Rhys wanted to say.

"That's not true!" Mary said. "He always looks my way!"

"Then why hasn't he signed your book?"

"She didn't ask me, silly!" Rhys thought. "And I'm not sure if I would anyways!"

"I haven't asked him yet! But I will, first chance!"

"Oh, cripes!" Rhys moaned to himself. "Now I'm in for it!"

"Bet he won't," Alice teased. "Bet he don't even know who you are! I bet if you ask, he'll laugh in your face."

"I'd never do that," Rhys thought. "I'd sign my name at least."

"You're just saying that, because Stubb McAndrew is sweet on Charlotte Bempkins!" Mary accused.

("Maybe I'd write a poem, too—a short one—if I knew one, but I don't know any.")

"We'll see, Miss Mary Markham, we'll see. Right, Thelma?"

"I don't know what neither of you is talking about," Thelma admitted.

("I'll have to write something! Something pretty. But what?")

"Rhys Morgan's got better things to do than sign your book!"

"Alice Tuttle, you're awful! How could you say that?"

"If it wasn't true, Mary, you wouldn't be so upset!"

("'Roses are red; violets are blue...?' Oh, cripes!")

"You're just the worst person, Alice! I don't know why I'm friends with you," Mary said in a huff, then stood abruptly, tucking her book back into her sash. "Maybe I'll just be friends with Charlotte Bempkins from now on!"

"Go 'head! See if I care!"

"I will, too. And you'll be sorry!" Mary said crisply, then turned to leave and would have if she hadn't come face-to-face with Rhys Morgan. "Oh!" she gasped. "It's you!"

"Hello, Mary," he said, his face blushing a full and bright red.

"I suppose you heard everything then? How long have you been . . . ?"

"No, no, no!" he lied transparently. "I saw you from the road, sitting here with your . . . with them, and I thought maybe . . . " His voice trailed off as her glance fell to the pies, which seemed like lead weights in his arms.

"They smell good," she said, smiling, snaring him with her pretty, dark eyes, and he stared back, forgetting himself, forgetting everyone else around them. Maybe he could write a poem about how pretty she was, about her pretty eyes, her pretty smile, a poem to thank her for giving him something to think about besides mules and coal and playing fiddle with his buddies.

"I *said,* 'They smell good.' "

"Oh . . . oh, thank you! They're for the deacons' supper tonight."

"Apple pie's my favorite."

"It is?"

She nodded.

"Well . . . well, only *one* is," he blurted. "One pie, I mean. My *mam* made an extra, and . . . and . . . and I thought, *she* thought, my *mam* thought, it'd be nice to give one to you. To your family, that is." ("What am I saying? What am I saying? *Mam*'ll kill me!")

"But we've got Mrs. Nabby to make pies. She makes the best pies in all of Pennsylvania."

"Hello, Rhys," Alice said, smiling at him. Thelma just smiled.

Rhys nodded back. "Well, if you don't want it, it's no bother . . . "

"I'll take it," Alice offered.

"Hush up, Alice," Mary warned, then smiled at Rhys.

"I'll be happy to take it. It's very thoughtful of your *mam*. Be sure to thank her for us, and I shall thank her myself when I see her tomorrow in church."

"I...I wouldn't bother if I was you," Rhys said nervously. "She's...she's peculiar in things like that."

"Oh?"

"She'd be happier knowing that...that...that you didn't, that's all."

"Are you sure there'll be enough for the deacons now?" Mary asked. "It wouldn't do to have them calling for more of your *mam*'s pies with none to give them, would it?"

"Well..."

"And I'm sure they'll be calling for more."

"Maybe you're right. It *wouldn't* do, would it?"

"Your *mam* can bake us another pie next time," Mary said.

"Right! She bakes all the time. I'll bring it down to you myself!" he said with a smile of relief. "Next time for sure! Well, Mrs. Jenkins will be wondering where I am with the pies. It was good to see you again. *Ta* then."

"*Ta*," Mary said.

"*Ta*," Alice and Thelma said.

"*Ta*," he said to all three and turned toward the vestry steps, knowing they'd be watching him every inch of the way, terrified that he'd stumble and fall like the clumsy oaf he was. Once inside, he bumped the door closed with his behind, then leaned against it, his legs weak, his hands trembling.

"I think I'm in love," he sighed to old Mr. Prodgers.

("Big, middle, little, Mary, big, middle, little, Mary...")

"It *is* a nice day, isn't it?" Mr. Prodgers said in return. It was just as well the old man was deaf, for he was spared the epithets that flowed from Rhys's mouth a moment later when Rhys remembered that Mary had never asked him to sign her book.

❖❖

THE back road from Jeddoh to Freeland was rough and rarely traveled. It was used mostly by peddlers, because it was the shortest route. Everyone else, rather than have an axle break or a horse fall lame from the deep ruts, took the Easton highway, which was longer but less rutted. Gwladys Protheroe traveled the back road.

She had driven this road day in, day out now for two years. She hated it, hated the ride, hated the loneliness. She hated the horse that pulled her carriage. She hated her carriage. She could have taken a room in Cheesetown with a miner's family, which is what she had left Wales to get away from, or in the boardinghouse, which was cramped and bug-infested, or so she wanted to believe, because the thing she hated more than the journey to and from Jeddoh each day was Jeddoh itself. She even hated to look at the Markham girls now that they were abandoning her. And after them, what was left? Nothing. No, she had to leave Jeddoh and Freeland forever. That was clear, but her money jar now held only ten dollars sixty cents, enough for a ticket to Wilkesbarre and a month in a boarding-house, maybe two, if she starved herself. She could find work there, scrubbing, clerking, scooping ice cream, serving platters to travelers in hotels, and certainly, most certainly, in the silk mills, but not teaching, not in summer, nor in the fall, not while there were qualified men. Besides, she had lost her taste for teaching. As for the rest—servitude—life in a bawdy house appealed to her more. The life she wanted, she was not equipped to secure; the life she knew, she was not fit to avoid.

She could be Mrs. Janeway. He had left a note for her, passed through Mr. Paretti, urging her to meet him Easter afternoon outside the free library. She didn't go. And he had sent a letter, postmarked Cleveland, asking her to be his bride, to become Mrs. Janeway. He said he loved her.

("Gwladys Protheroe, do you take this gnome to be your lawfully wedded husband, to have and to hold?")

She threw the letter in the trash. How many other women had he written the same words to? How many other women had he given corsets to, had his way with after he'd plied them with cheap brandy? And what would she do while he was on the road, peddling his corsets in Utica and Schenectady, in Cleveland and Kalamazoo? Bear a race of Janeways? The thought sent shivers down her spine. And then a more ghastly thought took its place, more ghastly because of its inevitability. How many more nights would pass, she wondered, before she regretted the rashness of her refusal, before nights became too lonely to endure, before she was sorry that she was *not* Mrs. Janeway?

"Oh, God," she moaned and closed her eyes and wished she were on the road to Merthyr Tydfil. "My life is in *such* disarray!"

Later, Gwladys would remember distinctly that she was thinking about Mary Markham when she first saw him. Mary had broken the news that day that she would be going to finishing school in the fall.

"Are you excited, my dear?" Gwladys had asked her.

"Why, yes," the girl had answered. "Shouldn't I be?"

"Of course. Finishing school is a big step in a girl's life, but then some girls need to be finished . . . and some never will be ready," she answered, leaving Mary to decide which category her teacher had consigned her to. She was specifically remembering the hurt look on Mary's face and the pleasure it brought to her when she saw the man ahead, half running, half walking, in the middle of the road.

"Cleave to!" she called, for the road was narrow. He stepped aside and waved his arms for her to stop.

"Ride, please?" he shouted. "Ride?"

It was unthinkable. His face and hands were black with coal dust, his clothes still wet. She passed him by. Undaunted, the man resumed his pace. In no time, he had caught up and was running beside her.

"You give ride to Freeland?" he shouted. "Important! Very important!"

She cracked her whip, spurring the horse to a faster gait, but the man kept up, matching the horse stride for stride.

"I must send telegram! 'Mergency!"

She ignored him. In his fury, the man ran ahead, grabbed the horse's bridle and reins, then, using all his strength, pulled the animal to a halt, despite Gwladys's protestations and repeated applications of the whip.

"*Now* you give me ride," he said and yanked the reins from her hand.

"Give me back my horse! I shall speak to Mr. Markham about you!"

It was his turn to ignore her. Still holding the reins, he started to climb into the carriage when she struck him fiercely with the whip. He fell back, hand to face, a long, bloody lash mark across his cheek, eye, forehead. He grabbed the whip with one hand, her arm with the other, and pulled her from the carriage in one quick move, then smacked the horse across the rump and sent it galloping off with the empty carriage bouncing behind.

"Now you walk, too," he said, wiping blood from his cheek, and resumed his journey.

"What is your name?" she demanded, hurrying after him. "I am going to report you to Mr. Markham!"

"Zakrzewska. Teofil Zakrzewska."

"You will not get away with this so easily, Mr. Zak . . . Zak . . ."

"Zakrzewska."

". . . and you will be responsible for any damage done to that horse and carriage, which are not mine!"

"Don't worry. Horse find way home."

"Oh, my God!" she gasped. "What will Mr. Price say when his horse returns to the stable without me?"

"He will say, 'Thank God! My horse is safe!' "

"And what about me?" she shouted.

"Shut up, lady! Nobody care about you."

"How dare you speak to me like that?"

"Shut up. Is long walk to Freeland. "

She halted at once. "You don't think I'd walk it with you, do you? I shall wait here until some *civilized* person happens by, and tomorrow morning first thing . . ."

"They find your carcass by side of road, eaten by bears and wild dogs. Good night, Miss Proth-roe!" he said, then picked up his former pace, a half-run, half-walk, and left her standing resolutely in the middle of nowhere.

* * *

"Damn him anyway!" Gwladys said under her breath as she tried to adjust her spectacles, which had been forced out of shape by her sudden descent from the carriage and so sat crookedly across the bridge of her nose. She cursed herself for dallying at school, never considering that darkness might be upon her before a Samaritan came by. She paced back and forth, thinking of bears and wild dogs, then, more out of impatience than fear, started walking toward Freeland.

The road was rough, her shoes not suited for such terrain. Twice, she tripped over ruts, the second time landing on her hands and knees in a puddle. Her spectacles slid off and splashed into the water. Her third fall came when she stumbled on a pebble and twisted her ankle. She walked on, hobbling now, but the road ahead of her and behind remained deserted. As she rounded a bend near a high outcrop of rock, muddied and disheveled, she wondered if she would see Freeland before nightfall.

"Gwladys Protheroe!" she shouted aloud, chastising herself, "*you* are in disarray!"

"Is long road, no?" a voice behind her said. "Always longer on foot."

Startled and embarrassed, she wheeled about and saw Zakrzewska sitting in a niche among the rocks, smiling smugly. She picked up a stone and hurled it at him, missing by a wide margin, then turned, totally frustrated, to resume her journey.

"I make sure nothing bad happen to you," Zakrzewska said, grinning, as he caught up to her.

"You also make sure nothing good happens. Leave me alone, will you?" she said and walked on, her ankle causing pain, which even she in her resolve could not hide.

"I cannot leave lady 'lone by side of road. With me you are safe."

"I thought you were in a great hurry to get to Freeland."

"You do better if you take off shoe. For fifty cents, I carry you."

She halted suddenly and looked at him, looked beyond the grime. He was easily as tall as she, as muscular and imposing as any man she had ever seen. His face was broad, his forehead high, his nose large and flat from repeated breakings. The mark from her whip was still a red, raw gash across his face. She couldn't look at his eyes. She was afraid of his eyes.

"Do not think, Mr. whatever your name is, that I have changed my mind. You have stolen my horse—Mr. *Price's* horse *and* carriage—and you have put me in jeopardy, and I am going to the constable as soon as I reach Freeland. *You* are in deep trouble."

"You are always teacher?" he asked. "You are never woman?"

"You, you . . . animal! How dare you speak to me like that?"

He grabbed her wrists, subdued her, and studied her features carefully, like a schoolboy investigating a butterfly he'd pinned to a board.

"What do you want of me?" she asked, uneasiness telling in her voice.

"Whatever you want. What do you want?" he said.

"I want . . . I want you to unhand me . . . to leave me alone, to get out of my way, do you hear? You are in deep trouble."

"It is you who are deep, deep in trouble, lady," he said, then laughed at her and held his hands aloft, free of her. "You see, I am not bad man. I do nothing to hurt you."

"I am not afraid of you, nor am I afraid of bears and wild dogs!" she said as she backed away.

"No, it is *you* you are 'fraid of, lady. I see it in your eyes. I hear it in your voice. I watch you, riding through Jeddoh. You are 'fraid to look at people, 'fraid people will see *you*!"

She shut out his harangue. Her head felt light. In the moment before she toppled, earthward, she heard a sound from far off. A cry of deliverance.

"Shhhh!! Quiet!" she said, gathering her wits.

"'Fraid people will see you are no better than them!"

"Quiet, don't you hear it? The horse! It must have stopped," she said and hurried up the road to meet it.

The horse whinneyed again. This time, Zakrzewska heard it, too.

The road twisted, then dropped to a wood bridge that spanned a creek. The horse had careened too close to the side. A wheel had caught. The horse slammed into the rail, then toppled over, pulling the carriage with it. Both now lay tangled and broken in the swift water below. It was a horrible sight that Gwladys and Zakrzewska came upon.

"Oh, my God!" she cried, breathless. "My God, look what you've done!"

The horse thrashed in terror, trying to free itself from the carriage, trying to keep its head above the rush of water.

"Oh, my God! Do something!"

Zakrzewska shrugged. "What can I do?"

"*Do* something! Do *something*!"

At the creek's edge, Zakrzewska found what he was looking for, a thick, three-foot section of timber from the railing, too short, Gwladys thought, to be of use in freeing the horse from the wreckage. He waded in just short of the flailing animal, raised the timber high, waited for the right moment, and brought it crashing down, skullward. Gwladys screamed.

The animal slipped beneath the water.

They walked down the road—she, a few feet ahead, still weeping; he, perplexed and brooding. In the distance, the steepletops of Freeland rose above the trees.

"Why cry over dead horse?" he asked. "I save it from misery."

"You *caused* its misery!"

"Wasn't even your horse!"

"Oh, God!" she said with dread. "What am I going to tell Mr. Price?"

"Tell him . . ."

"Oh, shut up, will you? Shut up! Just shut up!"

"Miss Protheroe! What happened?" Mr. Price exclaimed as she entered his stable looking haggard, distressed.

"Your horse almost kill Miss Proth-roe!" Zakrzewska blurted before she could even open her mouth.

"Where's Ranger? Where's my carriage?" Mr. Price asked anxiously.

"Your horse go crazy! Why you give such crazy horse to lady?"

"Miss Protheroe, are you all right? Where's Ranger?"

"Ranger at bottom of creek!" Zakrzewska ranted on. "He dead! He crash through bridge, almost kill lady. I see whole thing. Lucky I came 'long."

"Miss Protheroe, is this true?"

Gwladys hesitated, looked at Zakrzewska, looked into his eyes. Looking deep, she found herself. She found release there, and respite, and looked no further. She nodded yes. Now she was this man's accomplice.

"Why . . . why, that can't be!" Mr. Price said, distraught.

"Are you saying I am liar?" Zakrzewska asked ominously.

"No, no . . . ," Mr. Price said uncertainly.

"And Miss Proth-roe, she is respectable lady. Would she lie?"

"I don't . . . I don't think so. No."

"Oh, it was awful!" Gwladys exclaimed dramatically. "I couldn't stop him. Poor Ranger, he just . . . he just went over and . . . and down! It was awful!"

"This is your fault, Price! You give lady bad horse!" Zakrzewska accused. "Tomorrow, you have best horse and carriage for her, you hear?"

"Why, yes . . . yes, of course!"

"Best horse and best carriage! Or you have devil to pay!"

The two conspirators walked side by side down Main Street in the cool night air. A crescent moon crept overhead, like a prying eye.

"There was no emergency, was there?" Gwladys concluded. "No telegram." The tension, the calamity, the absurdity of that afternoon still roiled inside her. Her life never seemed more haphazard, or more dangerous.

"Man get very lonely without woman."

"You plotted this whole encounter then."

"All except horse," he admitted. "I see you many times in Jeddoh, but you never see me. You look right beyond me. I say to myself, 'How can I get Miss Proth-roe to see me?' "

They walked on in silence, past storefronts and banks, past churches. She felt unexpectedly at ease in the company of this man, safe even. He had more strength than she had ever seen in a man, more candor. His soul seemed bared to her, like an open wound.

"There is story of farmer . . . ," he began, then choked back his emotion, unable to speak.

"Go on," she said. "I'm listening."

"I hear story once of farmer in old country, in Poznan, who have young wife but no farm, no job. Land was bad, soil thin, like paper, so farmer say to friend, 'Why not leave this place? Go to 'Merica, find good job.' Friend say yes but wonder how to pay for such, since farmer have wife. Friend have no wife. So, farmer say, 'I will go 'lone, make money, send for you, send for wife, then we all be 'Mericans; we all live good.' So, farmer go to 'Merica and make money and send for friend, and friend come. They celebrate. Farmer ask friend, who by now is drunk, how is his wife, and friend smile and say, 'She is goot. I keep her warm while you gone.' Farmer ask what is meant by that, and friend boast of having intercourses with farmer's wife while he was away. This broke up farmer for some time. He could not work, could not eat, and finally he say to friend that some day he do same to him let him taste same medicine. Farmer bring wife to 'Merica. For while, things is good, but wife then seem far away, sad. Farmer not understand; wife not understand. He get angry; he hurt her; he say he is sorry, but nothing ever same again. She tell him 'bout friend who have his way with her, and they both cry. Wife say she is not worthy of husband no more. One day, wife become so sad she jump in river and drown. Then, farmer have no one. He is far from Poznan with no wife, no friend, no family, only stinkin' job.

"I am like that farmer," he said, weeping softly. "I know his sorrow. I have no woman. In place where my heart should be, there is just . . . ache."

"You *are* he, aren't you?" she said, touched. "You *are* that farmer."

Zakrzewska said nothing. He said nothing.

"Where will you go? For the night?" she asked.

"I walk back." He shrugged.

"The wound on your face, it could fester. It should be cleaned. Come, I have salts in my room."

Gwladys preferred to escape Mrs. Pardee's prying eyes but ventured no farther than the vestibule before the landlady charged from her parlor.

"My goodness, Miss Protheroe! I was so worried when you didn't arrive as usual," Mrs. Pardee chirped, then froze when she saw the dark stranger and stared, speechless, as Gwladys led him upstairs.

He closed his eyes.

He heard a cloth being swirled in a basin of water, being squeezed of its excess. He felt her breath on his face, the coolness of the cloth as she touched it gently across his grimy wound. He smelled her, a faint sweatiness masked by dusting powder, which she had discreetly applied to her cheeks and neck when they had first entered the room.

"It will not scar," she said.

He reached up and touched her breasts and pulled her close to him. He heard her soft moans.

The cloth dropped to the floor.

On the bed, he fumbled hungrily with her clothes, groped underneath her skirt, moving alternately to her various parts with increasing frenzy, wanting to taste them all at once. She surrendered herself. Each new sensation, each step toward ecstasy, intensified her guttural abandonment.

He entered her.

Below, Mrs. Pardee, Mr. Mellancamp, and Mrs. Wolsifer listened to their rutting in bewilderment and disgust—her moaning, a shriek, exclamations in a foreign tongue, a boot striking the floor, a devious laugh, the bed driving rhythmically against the wall. Then silence.

There was a knock at the door.

Gwladys answered after carelessly draping herself in her robe, unaware, or perhaps aware, that her breast was exposed. Her hair floated wantonly about her face.

"Miss Protheroe," said the mortified landlady in a hushed tone, "I . . . I cannot have this behavior in my house."

Gwladys closed the door. They coupled three more times that night.

At daybreak, Mr. Price hitched his best horse to his best carriage, but Gwladys never arrived to claim it. Hugh Morgan waited near the pit head, but Zakrzewska never pegged in. In the schoolhouse, Mary Markham read a story to the children. Some drew on the blackboard. At ten o'clock they went home.

In a bedroom in Freeland, Gwladys lay naked under the snoring hulk that was Zakrzewska. She felt stretched, sore. Her breasts bore teeth marks, her buttocks, bruises. Her hair was blowsy, matted with sweat and blood from the wound on his face.

Once again, Gwladys Protheroe was in disarray.

◆◆

On Saturday, two mornings later, Zakrzewska finally showed up for work.

"Where were you?" Hugh asked as they rode down in the cage.

"I had a sickness. In my bowels."

"Tom Pryor saw you two nights ago in Freeland. Coming from a tavern." The Pole just stared in surly silence. "I could discharge you right now. I am at the end of my patience," Hugh told him.

Later that morning, Hugh sent Zakrzewska to the saw-mill for a timber he needed for propping.

"Why can't Aloysius? I can do more than fetch like dog!" Zakrzewska griped, but Hugh refused to be baited. Finally he left, muttering under his breath, "I hope the whole damn mine fall down on your head." A short while later, he returned, carrying with him a timber of the approximate size Hugh wanted.

"Where did you get that?" Hugh asked.

"Miner in gangway say, 'Here!' He did not need it."

"Who? What was his name?"

"Mr. O'Something. He glad to be rid of it, glad I come along."

"You're a damned liar! Where did you get it?" Hugh demanded and looked the timber over for a miner's mark-ing, some sign of the chamber from which it had come. "I'll not be party to bobbing pillars. Tell me where you got it!"

"Irishman give it to me," Zakrzewska said coldly.

"How dumb do you think I am? You stole this from some other chamber you lazy, lying . . . !"

Before Hugh could finish, Zakrzewska lunged at him, driving him against the wall of the headway, knocking the wind out of him. But Aloysius was just as quick, just as strong. He tackled Zakrzewska and held him at bay till Hugh recovered.

"Get out of here! You're finished! Get out!" Hugh shouted, summoning the courage that had eluded him till now.

Zakrzewska shook off Aloysius's grip. "You are traitor to your people," he snarled at him, then retreating to the gangway, lashed out at Hugh, "You will be sorry for treating me like dog! Wait! I will make you suffer! Just wait, Morgan!"

That same morning, Gwladys Protheroe, having been evicted by Mrs. Pardee for lewd deportment, moved her belongings into the boardinghouse in Jeddoh. Her quarters, small and cramped, were not intended for extended residence. With her trunk in place, she barely had room through which to squeeze in passing from the door to the bed, from the bed to the chiffonier . . .

"It is well that I am just passing through," she told herself.

The move had been costly—a dollar for the carriage, a dollar for the driver, and a like sum lost, because she had paid her rent through month's end.

"When one's life is so . . . disarranged, one must take pains to preserve one's resources," she reminded herself and rattled her money jar to hear its reassuring clink of metal and glass. Nothing, however, could compensate the loss of pride she had suffered at being turned out into the street while Mrs. Pollitt, the ribbon clerk, and Hubert, her pimply nephew, gaped on gloatingly. And what had she to show in the end for her quirk of passion? A sore back and an airless room in the place she hated above all else.

. . . from the chiffonier to the basin, from the basin to the closet, from the closet to the bed.

"Please stay; I want you to stay," she had said to him as he dressed to leave, realizing at the same time that she wished him gone, not from her life but from her bed. Her time of month was at hand. There was only so much that she could give.

"Will I see you again?" she asked.

"Yes," he said.

"When?" she asked.

"Soon," he said. "You will be my woman." And then he left her left her to ponder what it would mean to be his "woman."

His wife? Was marriage to him thinkable?

("Gwladys Protheroe, do you take this 'hunky' to be your lawfully wedded husband, to have and to hold till death do you part?")

His concubine? His servant?

"What do you want of me?" she had asked him on the road.

"Whatever you want," he had said. "What do you want?"

And then, perhaps, she had seen the last of him.

"These are, indeed, suspenseful times," she lamented and clutched her jar of cash ever tighter to her bosom.

Zakrzewska went to the colliery office and there found Ned the Splicer. "I am discharged," he said.

"Under what circumstances?" Ned the Splicer asked.

"I am told I am no longer needed. That Morgan, he give man job, then take away for no reason. That man stinks!"

Ned the Splicer tried to calm the highly excited man. "I have no power over what miners . . ."

"Just give me money that is mine!"

"That will take some time," Ned said. "Come back in an hour."

Zakrzewska started to go, then hesitated. "I would watch this Morgan," he said very deliberately. "He rob timbers. From east slope. And last week I saw him take tag from other fella's loaded wagon and put on his tag. He is shady character."

Zakrzewska squatted in the shadow of the breaker and wondered what he would do next. He felt safe in Jeddoh. No one from Chicago had come through looking for him, not like in Denver. If he left now, he might easily be discovered, for surely he was still being sought. And then there was his golden opportunity, Gwladys Protheroe, to consider. He feared she was too headstrong to make a good wife, unlike his wife in Chicago, his Ewa, but Gwladys was too valuable to let slip away, not with the money he was certain she had secreted in the hem of her coat or at the bottom of a box of dusting powder. No, his fortunes lay in Jeddoh. All he needed was another job. Another job.

He was distracted from his musings by John Markham, who emerged in his neat gray suit from the company store, looked at his pocket watch, and turned down Frog Street toward his home.

"I think is time I meet Mr. John Markham," Zakrzewska said and hurried down the hill to intercept him.

It was exactly ten twenty-five by his watch, Old G.B.'s watch, the one Old G.B. had carried till the day he died, but looking at it reminded Markham less of his father than of his days of usury, the memory of which never failed to provoke in him a smile. He still hoarded a box of unclaimed watches somewhere in his attic, a selection of which he'd kept to pass on to his sons, the sons he was sure he would have. He remembered that box and vowed to look for it one day soon. Some were of gold and chimed the hours. His girls might enjoy playing with them if nothing else.

Ten twenty-five. There was still time to stop at home before he had to leave for Wilkesbarre and his meeting with McCandless and Glasscock, the only other major independent operators besides himself, now that Stillwell had caved in to the railroads. They were to talk of strategy, a possible merger to give themselves strength, ways to keep the packs of railroad wolves from the door, a futile effort at best, for McCandless was weak and Glasscock stupid. He knew he could depend on neither for the long haul but had to prop them up or face his own annihilation that much sooner.

Ten twenty-five. He replaced his pocket watch and began a brisk walk down Frog Street toward his home.

"Ho, John!" Dr. Koons called as he left Mrs. Owen Williams's.

"Hello, Henry!" Markham said and waited till his friend caught up. "I see you less and less these days. Come, walk with me," he invited and put his hand on the doctor's shoulder. "And how is your patient?"

"Failing, I'm afraid. There is little more I can do." His face looked drawn from having spent the better part of the night on his call.

"She's a good woman. I shall keep her in my prayers."

"Tell me, John . . . Ned informs me that you're reopening the west entry."

"I'm thinking of it. I haven't decided for sure."

"It's hexed, John. I'm not a superstitious old woman as you know, but I've seen too many good men brought up from down there, dead or pretty near. I think it would be a mistake."

"There's a lot of coal in those veins, and I can't afford to let it sit anymore. Not these days."

"There's only a lot of worthless rock, from what Ned says."

"If I listened to Ned all the time," Markham scoffed, "I wouldn't have any fun, you know that."

"It's hexed," the doctor repeated, unamused, but Markham just laughed.

"I *have* my reasons, Henry," Markham said more persuasively. "Besides, I've not made up my mind for certain. There are many other things to consider, superstition aside." Then, as they reached the doctor's gate, "You must come visit soon. Emily is forever asking about you."

"I will, John, if you will agree to consider what I've said."

"Agreed. By the way, I've just got my new supply of Havanas."

"All the more reason to stop by," the doctor said, brightening. Then, nonchalantly under his breath, "I don't mean to alarm, but I do believe you're being followed."

"I believe you are correct," Markham said calmly. "I've seen him from the first. I thought, however, he was following you."

"Now, why would anyone . . . ?"

"A jealous husband, perhaps?"

"John, be serious! Who is he?"

"Probably a disgruntled hand. These roundheads are a disagreeable lot." Then, wryly, "Do you think I might be able to outrun him to my door?"

"John, I think you can do anything you set your mind to."

"Then wish me luck!" Markham replied and hastened away.

"Good day, John! And think of what I've said!"

"I will, Henry, I will!" Markham called without looking back. A moment later, he turned up his path, bounded up the steps, and disappeared behind the safety of his door.

Thwarted, Zakrzewska cursed his luck. "If not for damn doctor, I would get satisfaction by now! Goddamn gadfly, if I stick knife in his throat, that would knock smile off his goddamn face!" His bitterness fueled his anger; his anger fueled his desperation. He strode defiantly to Markham's gate, and yet his knees shook. Sweat dripped off his face.

Markham's house stood before him, like a fortress. Around it stretched the yard, like a moat. Its curtains, like bars, shut out the offending world, his world. He had seen great wealth before, but he never despised it as much as he did right now. And yet, his very life lay in the hands of this man.

"I must see Markham, I must!" he told himself and started up the path, feeling light-headed, not knowing what he would do or say.

A sudden wind rustled through the trees; the porch swing rocked gently. Beneath his feet, the wood steps squeaked. His hand reached out.

"If I knock, I will not get in."

He murmured a prayer as he turned the brass knob. The door opened with a faint click.

From the vestibule, he could see into the music room, the front parlor, the dining room, up the grand staircase. He had never seen such splendor nor smelled such richness. And yet, he felt at home here, as though this were *his* home, that if he sat at the table, *his* table, a legion of servants would bring him cognac and pheasant, that the photographs on the wall were not Markham and his family but Zakrzewska and *his*—*his* Ewa, *his* Mary and Tillie and Bruno.

He laughed giddily and smelled the smell of baking bread.

Suddenly a child started down the steps. Zakrzewska stepped back into the parlor where she could not see him.

"Papa! Papa!" she called and ran past into the music room and the room beyond.

"There's my angel! My precious little angel!" he heard Markham say, words he had heard himself say, and heard the child laugh and hug and kiss her father just as his Mary and Tillie had hugged and kissed him not so long ago, and yet, so long ago. He stole across the hall to spy as Markham raised young Rose above his head and whirled her in dizzy circles, unaware that, as Markham set the laughing child down, he glimpsed a portion of Zakrzewska's dark figure in the hall mirror.

"Have you been good today for Mrs. Bemis?" Markham asked the child and stroked her long black curls.

"Yes, Papa!"

"Then go into the kitchen and tell Mrs. Nabby that your Papa said you are to have a special treat for being such a good girl."

"Yes, Papa!" young Rose said, hugged her father one last time and ran to the kitchen for her treat.

Markham rose and when she had left, turned toward the front hall. "I see you," he said. "Who are you? What do you want?" Zakrzewska retreated a few steps. He contemplated bolting for the door, but it was too late. "How dare you?" Markham demanded, approaching, when he saw Zakrzewska more clearly.

"Please, sir. I mean no harm here! Please, listen!"

"I could have you shot for coming in here!"

"No, please! I have stuff to tell! Important! There is big trouble coming. Danger to mine!"

Markham looked hard at the intruder. "What do you mean?"

"I hear men talking. There will be . . . be trouble. In mine!" Zakrzewska repeated, fishing for words.

"What *kind* of trouble?"

"I am . . . I am not sure."

"Get out of here!"

"*Union!* Union trouble! Men . . . men go to Wilkesbarre, talk to union."

"Who? How many?" Markham demanded.

"I don't know," Zakrzewska demurred. "I could find out."

"Why are you here? Did they send you?"

"No, I come on my own. I have . . . deal."

"What kind of deal?"

Zakrzewska hesitated, then plunged ahead. "You give me what I want . . . I tell you 'bout trouble."

"Union trouble?"

"Yes!"

"Who are you?"

"My name is Zakrzewska."

Markham bade the intruder to follow him through the music room into his study beyond. "You had better be all you say, Mr. Zakrzewska," he warned, leaving no doubt that he meant business and closed the door behind them.

An hour later, Zakrzewska returned to the colliery office.

"I thought you had forgot," Ned the Splicer said, pushing an envelope across the desk. "Count it if you wish. It's all there."

Zakrzewska said nothing, instead handed Ned the Splicer a note written on Markham's personal stationery.

*This man is now a miner. See that he has the tools to commence work Monday next.*
*J. M.*

Ned the Splicer thought it was the most peculiar thing he'd ever seen. Had Markham lost his senses?

"So, what do you think of me now, hey?" Zakrzewska asked grinning. "Now, now *I* am big-shot miner!"

# PART FOUR

RHYS

NED the Splicer accompanied Zakrzewska to the store that same afternoon and had him outfitted with the tools he would need, and powder. Mr. Beech was astonished and later told Tom Pryor, who told Caradoc Williams while they were having a beer at the Emerald. "Tug" Brennan overheard their conversation and told the Milligan brothers, who told Harris Meighan, who told Karl Maciejewski that Markham had hired a Polish miner.

"Moczygemba?" asked Maciejewski.

"He worked for Hugh Morgan," Meighan answered. "Don't know his name." Neither did Maciejewski, nor anyone else in town, except Hugh Morgan.

That night, there was elation on Polish Hill, and uncertainty. "Who *is* this man?" they were left to wonder. They'd seen him often in the past month. He was clearly one of them, but he kept apart, never attending mass or joining them after work for a sausage and beer.

"*Dzien dobry!*" they would say, tipping their hats each morning, and he would say, "*Dzien dobry!*" and nothing more. "*Dobranoc,*" they would say at the end of the day, and he would smile and nod and go in his own direction. "What a strange man," they said to themselves. "He must be very sad, very lonely." But many of their brothers

171

missed their homeland, the lives, the families they had left behind, and yet they took comfort in fellowship with their own kind. Each man walks his own path, they reminded themselves. It was not their place to pry or pass judgment on their brothers.

The mystery continued unabated the next day. In church everyone talked of little else, and by second whistle Monday morning, a delegation from Polish Hill had gathered at the pit head to give this new hero their blessing.

By the time Hugh joined the line to peg in that morning, Zakrzewska was telling the story of his promotion to an ever-increasing field of admirers for the third time. He had accosted Markham on the street, he bragged, to protest the plight of the Slavic labor force in Jeddoh. Markham was so impressed with Zakrzewska's forthright appeal, or so the story went, that he decided then and there to make him a miner. That there were no witnesses to this extraordinary event seemed to bother no one, nor did they appear to notice that Zakrzewska's passion for his fellow workers and Markham's admiration for him increased with each retelling.

"Ho, Morgan!" Zakrzewska called with a broad grin on his face. "I tell you one day I be miner just like you, did I not? And look! I am miner!"

Hugh looked at the hero coldly. "Then I shall have to count every trip I make to the pits as my last," he said, "for no man can be safe down there as long as you are packing powder."

Zakrzewska's admirers laughed, thinking Hugh's gibe was meant in jest, but Zakrzewska did not laugh. Hugh had soured his mood.

His eyes would blink open at first whistle, not a moment before, even if he was already awake. "Why open them if I don't have to, while I can still get my rest?" he reasoned. It was a game he played with himself, like when he listened to Rhys's breathing. Euan could tell from the sound Rhys made, either full and steady, like a bellows, that Rhys was asleep, or soft, almost silent, like now, when he was awake. Euan thought Rhys made sleeping sound like work, but for all he knew, everyone slept the same way. He'd only ever slept next to Rhys. This morning, they both lay awake, savoring the smell of bacon their *mam* was frying below. The smell was tantalizing, but neither wanted to be the first to rouse himself. It was another sort of game they played between them, seeing how long they could stretch their time in bed before their *dada* threatened to use his strop if they didn't get moving.

"I'd like to get my hands on the man that blows the whistle," Rhys said out of the blue. "I bet that's all he does, too—sounds the whistle."

"Rhys? Euan?" their *dada* called from below.

"I wish one day he'd forget and blow second whistle instead of first, or third instead of second. That'd cause a stir on Frog Street."

"Rhys! Euan!"

"I wonder who wakes him up, the man who blows the whistle? Suppose he forgot some morning or fell sick? Who'd blow it then, I wonder?"

His reverie was interrupted by footsteps on the stairs.

"Coming, *N'had*!" Rhys said, and both of them jumped out of bed, pulled on their britches, then stepped into their boots. Their *dada* was a player in the game, albeit unwittingly, but he always seemed to win.

For Euan, the morning routine never changed—jump out of bed, dress, hurry down to eat, run out to the privy, help *Mam*, grab lunch, hurry off. It never changed. The smell of bacon frying on the stove never changed, nor did the taste of his *mam*'s preserves or the brown sugar she sprinkled on his oatmeal. There was always more to eat if he wanted it, and he always wanted more. Rhys always had a story to tell, and his *dada* always had chores to add to his list. His *mam* always had to remind him to sit up straight and keep his mouth closed when he chewed, and he always forgot.

The walk to work never changed. The grim faces and

houses were always the same, always silent. At the stables, he always looked to see if the black mules were out; they were still his favorites. He could peg in without even looking for his number—five down, seven over—and he knew his way through the breaker by heart. His body still grew stiff, bending over the chutes, but he no longer felt like a worn boot by the end of the day. He had friends— Little Jake, Tadi, Andrew Zdepko, and Jenkin Davies, when he wasn't sulking—although his *mam* would never let him carouse with them at quitting. More and more, Bryfogle ignored him. Even Digger ignored him now that he was no longer the greenhorn.

He found comfort in the sameness of his life, its certainty, even its monotony. He looked forward to climbing to his perch each day, to the first coal hurtling down the chutes, to Mickey Figmic, the new greenhorn, trudging to the top house whenever there was a jam, to emptying his rock box at quitting. Euan still hadn't hit the wall or found a Hudsonryder, and he wondered where Rhys sneaked off to each night after supper, why his *mam* spoke only of Meb or "the girls" but never of *Gwen*, but whatever loose ends plagued his peace of mind, they vanished at the touch of his *mam*'s hand as she cleaned his ears with warm sweet oil before Sunday church, at the sight of his *dada* winding his pocket watch each night after supper, at the sound of Rhys next to him, in bed, breathing, just breathing.

"Me *da* says Morgan's old man's a scab!" Digger announced as he strode into the picking room followed by Patsy and Dick.

Euan's first reaction was to laugh. How could his *dada* be like the crust he got over a cut?

"Ye don't even know what it is!" Digger jeered, seeing Euan's puzzled expression, then broke into a forced laugh. "Jesus, yer a dumb one! Patsy, yer li'l sis got more brains than this here dumb son of a scab!"

Patsy and Dick started to cackle, too, and the other

boys, but Euan was convinced none of them knew what "scab" meant either.

"What is it then?" Euan asked, and just as he thought, Digger lost his smirk.

"Me *da* says he heard yer folks was run outta the last place ye lived!" Digger sneered. "He says scabs is worse'n hunkies! Scabs ought'na be 'lowed to live near respectin' folks!" Then he spit in Euan's face. "That's what me da thinks of yer old man." He spit again. "An' that's what I think of *ye!*"

Digger stood with his legs wide, ramming his fist into the palm of his hand, daring his target to strike back. His eyes were slits of hate.

Euan was angry but confused. How could he feel bad about something he didn't understand? Digger might just as well have called his *dada* a bucket or a sneeze. "You ain't said yet what a scab is, or don't you know yourself?" he chided, wiping Digger's spit from his face.

"*I* know, ye pisshead! It's *ye* that don't!"

"Then say it if you know so much!"

"Yer the son of a scab! If ye don't know what ye are, I ain't tellin' ye!" Digger bluffed. "Son of a sca-ab! Son of a sca-ab!"

Patsy and Dick picked up the chant, and soon it spread around the room. Euan's heart sank. He thought he was through with the tricks, the names, the fights. And then an anger welled in him. He wanted to push Digger down, to kick him with his boots, to wipe the arrogant smirk off his face once and for all. He wanted to hurt Digger as much as Digger had hurt him.

"Son of a sca-ab! Son of a sca-ab!"

All morning long the chant echoed in his head. He saw boys staring at him across the chutes. Greenhorns were common, but none of them had seen the son of a scab before.

"Whatever it is," he thought, "it must be terrible."

What had Digger said? That they'd been "run out" of Sugar Notch? What did that mean? They *had* left suddenly, but nobody had chased them. There had been trouble, fights at the colliery, in the streets. Coal and Iron Policemen were everywhere. His *dada* came home one night, beaten and bloody. "The Coal and Irons did it," his *mam* told him. Is that why they left Sugar Notch then? The Coal and Irons ran them out? Was his *dada* afraid of the strike, afraid of the Coal and Irons? But his *dada* had kept on working during the strike while other fathers stayed home. They were the ones afraid, not his *dada*. The Coal and Irons had scared them off, not his *dada*. Then why *did* they leave? Maybe they *had* been run out. Maybe his *dada* was a scab, whatever that was, whatever that meant.

"What is it then? A scab?" he asked his friends at lunch.

Only Jenkin spoke. "My *dada* says scabs steal food from families of men that's on strike."

"My *dada* would never do that! My *dada* would never steal anything! And there's no strike here!"

"My pa says strike comin'," said Little Jake.

Jenkin had the last word. "*Dada* says, too, if you scab once, it makes it easier the next time."

That night at supper, no one mentioned the "word," but Euan could feel its presence at the table, like an unseen visitor.

"Did . . . did *N'had* do what they're saying?" Euan asked Rhys later as they made ready for bed.

"Don't pay it no mind. It's a lot of gas," Rhys said, but Euan wasn't convinced. "Who's saying it? Digger?"

Euan nodded.

"I hear it some, too, but if they want extra wagons from me, they keep their mouths shut. It'll pass."

"What does it mean then? A scab?"

"He's a man who goes against a strike. A man who . . . never mind!"

"Like the boss? Or the Coal and Iron Police?"

"No. It's different. A miner who . . . who doesn't stand by the rest . . . by the rest of the men who's on strike."

"What do you mean 'stand by'?"

"Join. He doesn't join. He keeps . . ."

"... keeps on working?"

Rhys blew out the lamp. The truth was too hard to face in the light. "Yes," he said.

So that was it, a man who kept on working in a strike, like his *dada* had kept on working? Was that so bad then? As bad as Jenkin said? As bad as a man who stole food from families of men on strike? Or was it the same somehow? His *dada* was a scab. Did that mean he was a scab, too? His *dada* had done something bad. Did that make him bad, too? What would make a man want to be a scab? Why wouldn't he stand by the rest? If his *dada* hadn't been a scab, everything would be all right now. Why did he do it? Why?

Euan buried his face in his pillow so Rhys wouldn't hear him crying.

The next day it got worse.

"Mister Bryfogle?" Digger whined abrasively as he approached his chute. "Do I hafta sit near the son of a scab? I fear I'm apt to be tainted!"

"Ye already got lice, ye big galoot!" Bryfogle retorted. "Now shut yer bazoo an' git to work!"

"Oh, dear Jesus! Save me!" Digger pleaded. "I'd rather be dead than sit near the son of a scab!"

"Shut up, Digger!" Euan exploded.

"An' who's gonna make me?" Digger snarled back, then scooped up a handful of coal dust from the floor and threw it in Euan's face. "That's what we do to scabs 'round here! Scabs is dirt 'round here!"

At lunch, Digger and the Morrisseys lay in wait for Euan beneath the stairs to the privy. The twins held Euan down, and Digger sat on his belly.

"You leave him alone!" Little Jake shouted as Euan gasped for breath.

"Shut up, ye little sis, or ye'll be next!" Digger warned, then called for Dick to haul out their surprise. Dick ran to the privy and returned with a smelly bucket tied to a rope. "Hurry up, do it! Do it!" cried the bully, and Dick emptied the wretched contents over Euan's head.

"C'mon, boys! Let's see what a scab looks like with his britches off!" Digger shouted next and began to yank at Euan's buttons. "Ain't never seen a scab's dingus before!"

"I bet he ain't got one," said Patsy. In no time, Euan felt the rough boards beneath his bare bottom.

Suddenly Bryfogle appeared on the stairs. "What's this? Havin' a li'l fun, are youse? All right, games is over! Git back to yer chutes!" Then he saw Euan squirming on the floor, heard his breathless whimpers.

"Who's that then?"

"It's Morgan, sir!"

"Jesus in heaven, Morgan!" Bryfogle gasped. "Ain't that bitch of a mother ye got ever showed ye how...? Ye stuck the wrong end in the hole!"

At quitting, Euan ran behind the breaker and climbed over the fence to the stream to wash off the mess, the smell. When he returned home, his *dada* scolded him for dawdling after work, for not being there to help with the toting and the pouring. His *dada* looked gruff and sour, the way Miss Protheroe had looked. He barked at Rhys, too, and at their *mam*, when she tried to calm him. They ate their supper in silence. It was as if Hudsonryder's Curse had fallen on their heads.

After supper, his *dada* prepared his blasting cartridges at the table in the kitchen. His *mam* sat in the corner, twisting her familiar strand of loose hair around her finger. Rhys was off on his nightly prowl, leaving Euan alone on the back steps to watch the neighbor children catch lightning bugs in cans.

"Zakrzewska talked," he heard his *dada* say.

"I knew it," his *mam* said bitterly. "I knew it."

Zakrzewska. Euan knew the man's name but not the man. He'd never seen him, only heard his *dada* speak of him. His *dada* came the closest he ever came to swearing when he spoke of Zakrzewska. Was he the cause of this?

"You've been hearing things about me," his *dada* said later when he came and sat next to Euan on the steps.

Euan was glad it was dark. He didn't have to look at his *dada*, didn't have to see the shame that spilled from his eyes.

"They're saying I'm a . . . a scab, or worse, aren't they? You know what a scab is then?"

Euan dropped his head. His eyes filled with tears.

"It's never easy, this life. Only a few have it easy. We have to work for what we get, work to hold on to it, and even then . . . even then. . . . My *dada* worked every day of his life, even when he was so sick he could barely hold up his head. Down in the pits, like me. He told me and your uncle Davey one day if anything ever happened to him down there, it'd be up to us to take care of our *mam*, and our sisters. A week later he was killt in a fall. He knew somehow, I think, his time was near. They never even got his body out. Davey was ten then; I was twelve. Our uncles helped some, and the church, but they were as poor as we. The mine owner, Mr. Lovecroft, let us stay on in our house; he said our debt to the company store was too . . . too great to forgive, that Davey and me would have to work it off. We had no choice. We worked for nine years without a penny of pay. Nine years. And everything we earned went toward the debt, but our *mam* and our sisters never went without. We'd made a promise to our *n'had*, you see, and when your *mam* and I was wed, I made the same promise, and I've kept it and will keep it as long as I have breath left in me. Do you see that, lad? Do you hear what I'm saying?"

"I think so."

"There's people don't understand that, or don't want to. And some just want to be mean. In Sugar Notch, it was their strike, not mine, and I put my family above their strike. They'll never forgive me for that."

"Even here? In Jeddoh?"

"Many here've got family there, too."

"What if they cause a strike here then?"

"They won't. Markham's too strong. In a couple of days, they'll forget all this scab business. Meantime, anybody says it to you, don't listen. They're just riled up, that's all."

"Yes, N'had."

That night in bed, Euan told Rhys the story their dada had told him.

"*Dada* didn't do a bad thing then," Euan explained. "He didn't steal food from families, like they're saying. He was just working to feed his own."

"Who said he was stealing food?"

"Jenkin said."

"Jenkin's a plughead. *N'had* didn't join the strike, that's why they're burned up."

"So what? I wouldn't either if it meant *Mam*'d go hungry. Would you?"

"*Mam*'s not going hungry. There's more to it than that. There's more," Rhys said, but he couldn't tell Euan what he didn't want to hear.

The next day, neither Tadi nor Andrew greeted Euan in the picking room. Whenever their eyes met, Little Jake lowered his glance. Euan ate alone, but he didn't feel bad. "In a couple of days," he told himself, "they'll forget. They're just riled up, that's all."

After pegging out that afternoon, Euan went with his *dada* to the pluck me store for a keg of powder. The usual crowd of men gathered there, smoking, passing time; most were men Euan knew from church.

"Scabs use the back door, Morgan!" Tom Pryor said, stepping forward to block their path to the steps.

"I have done no wrong to you, Tom," Hugh said quietly.

"You're a scab, ain't you?"

Euan looked from face to face. The expressions they wore were not the same they showed in Sunday church. "If they only knew what I know, they'd say different," he thought. "But they'll see; they'll see."

"You are quick to accuse," his *dada* said. "The Lord would have you be just as quick to forgive."

"The Lord never worked in a coal mine," Pryor replied.

Just then, Euan spied a man leaning against the railing, staring down at them, a man he didn't know, a dark man with hard features and the biggest hands he had ever seen. The man was smiling. The others looked pained, as though they had no taste for taunting his *dada*, but this man was enjoying it.

"Come on then," his *dada* said to him, took his arm, then pushed their way past Tom Pryor.

"Who was that man then?" he asked his *dada* inside the store.

"Tom Pryor, you know . . ."

"No, the one sitting on the rail. The big man. With the grin."

"Zakrzewska."

Euan shuddered. He had finally found his Hudsonryder's Ghost.

❖❖

THEY called themselves the "Sons of Thunder"—a crew of five laborers with Zakrzewska as their leader, all working together to extend a headway that had long lain dormant. After this was done, two of the five would be chosen to become miners and would, along with Zakrzewska, dig their individual breasts. They worked fast and hard, determined to prove themselves. Their shots, for which Zakrzewska used twice the powder necessary, resounded through the entire mine, giving rise to their name, but while seasoned miners shook their heads, the Sons of Thunder loosed enormous amounts of coal and rock, sending up some thirty-two wagons on their best day.

And then it all went horribly wrong.

It was to be Digger O'Shea's first day in the pits.

"I'm a trapper now," he told Bryfogle that morning as he hovered in the doorway to the man's office. "Ye can't boss me 'round no more."

"Good riddance!" Bryfogle huffed. "Never did like ye! I hope the rats down there eat ye alive!"

"There's rats down there? Jesus, I hate rats!"

"Big, ugly buggers!" Bryfogle hooted. "As big as coal wagons!"

Digger looked at him skeptically.

"It's true, I tell ye! How do ye think I lost me leg?"

"Go on!" Digger gasped.

"It's true!" Bryfogle exclaimed. "And may the good Lord take me good if'n I be tellin' ye a lie! I was workin' up Nanticoke way wit' me brother, Billy. Had me two good legs then. Had us a bootleg shaft, too, steep-pitched— 'twas murder to work—but we made good till it begun to spoon out. One day, we was gobbin' the bone, and the mine rats begun to run out of the drift. Next thing ye know, the whole damn ceiling fell, knocked us out cold. When I come to, there was these big, ugly rats chewin' on me leg. 'Twas nothing' left below me knee but a naked bone!"

"Jesus!"

"Watch out fer the rats, boy, they'll eat ye alive! First they go fer yer eyes, then yer lips, yer tongue, yer privates—the juicy parts—then they nibble on yer brain!"

Digger's eyes flared wide with terror. His jaw fell slack; his breath came short and fast.

"Fact is, there's one crawlin' up yer leg right now!" Bryfogle screamed and pinched Digger's thigh.

"Yiiieeeeee!"

Digger bolted halfway across the picking room, brushing off imaginary rats with his plug hat, before realizing he was the brunt of Bryfogle's joke. By then, the rest of the boys were rolling over the chutes with laughter.

"Good ribbons to ye, too, Bryfogle!" Digger yelled. "Now I won't hafta smell yer stink no more, or look at yer ugly puss! An' 'twas me who sawed yer leg, short, ye dumb ox! An' puked all over yer cot! An' ripped yer . . . !"

"Out! Get out!" Bryfogle growled, like a huge bear, and hurled the oak rod across the picking room at Digger, who ducked in time and turned to see it smash against a far beam and crack in two. The boys cheered.

"So long, scab!" Digger said to Euan, who was standing nearby. Then he tore down the steps and disappeared into the belly of the breaker.

It was a prayer come true. The boys couldn't believe their ears. Only the Morrisseys were sad to see him go.

"This is it. This is your door," Ned the Splicer told Digger, pushing open the canvas-covered wooden frame that stretched the width of the gangway. Immediately a stiff draft whistled through the opening.

Digger looked around the dank, deserted gangway and wished he'd never left the picking room. The passage was only twelve feet across at its widest point, barely enough room for two wagons to squeeze by. Pools of fetid water lay between the tracks, along the walls. The ceiling, low in spots, higher in others, was crusted with brightly colored lichens.

"All you do is make sure the door is closed after a trip passes," Ned continued. "If you don't, the air currents'll shift, and the roundheads down at the bottom of the slope won't get ventilation in their chamber. The smoke and gas'll build up something terrible. You understand?"

Digger didn't but he nodded anyway.

"You can sit here by the side," Ned said, motioning to a tiny niche in the side of the wall. "Watch your toes as the wagons roll by. Watch out for kicking mules. The water's bad; don't drink it. And don't *ever* fall asleep!"

There was a scraping noise on the wall behind them.

"What was that?" Digger asked nervously.

"Nothing. Just rats."

"Rats?"

"Any questions?"

"I just stay here? All day?"

"Keep your lantern low," Ned said, walking on. "If it gets wet, you're out of luck. You leave when the round-heads leave, not before. And always do your business downwind of the draft."

Suddenly Digger was alone thousands of feet below the

earth with only dripping water and gnawing rats to listen to. He turned his lantern up full.

Drip . . . drip . . . drip . . .

The Sons of Thunder were preparing another shot. The Gieryk brothers, Stanislaw and Wincenty, worked the drill. Peter Moczygemba helped Zakrzewska fill six blasting cartridges with coarse niter, while Leo Mucka and Jac Drozda cleared the headway of loose rock.

Drozda started singing a song from the old country, from his days as a farmer, and Mucka joined in. Sometimes, one knew verses the other didn't and sang his version. It was rare to hear singing in the pits. Old-timers thought it brought bad luck, but Drozda and Mucka didn't care; they liked to sing.

> *I'll not go to the field for plowing.*
> *Let my father go alone.*
> *I would rather go a-walking.*
> *Where the pretty girls are staying.*
> *Where the pretty girls are staying.*

Moczygemba heard their singing and moaned lugubriously. " 'Dey are like dogs in heat," he laughed. "Have only vun t'ing on brain."

"Listen who talks!" Stanislaw chided. "Vun who have t'ree girls hidden in Freelant!"

"Vhat you mean, you liar? I got four!" he bragged and tied off the top of the last cartridge. Then to Zakrzewska, "Is 'dat enough?"

"No, we make one more," Zakrzewska replied and raised the powder barrel for pouring. "One more! Make big blast!"

"Hey, door boy!" Rhys shouted as he pushed open the trap. The draft whistled through behind him. "Hey! Trapper!"

Digger awoke with a start. "What? Who is it?"

"So, it's you!" Rhys said as the bully scrambled to his feet.

"Morgan, ol' buddy! Ye gave me a fright!"

"Don't let Ned catch you snoozing. He'll give you the boot as soon as look at you," Rhys said, sorry now he'd awakened the big lug.

"Thought I was never gonna see nobody again!"

"You'll get used to it," Rhys said and cracked his whip twice over his head. A moment later, Rose, Helen, and Anna plodded through the open trap behind him, pulling eight empty wagons.

"And the rats! They're everywhere! I killed one over there. With a rock. Jesus, I hate rats!"

"Don't ever kill a mine rat! Ever!" Rhys warned. "The rats know when something bad is near. A fall, or gas. If they take off up the gangway, you better run, too. Run like hell!" he said and followed in the direction of his mules.

"When'll ye be back?" Digger asked. There was an edge of desperation in his voice.

" 'Bout an hour. Haven't you forgot something?"

"What's that?"

"The door, trapper!"

Digger had forgotten the one thing he was put there to do. He scooted across the tracks and pushed it closed. The rushing wind stopped.

"Why don't you do what Ivor, the trapper before you, did?" Rhys called back. "Feed them scraps from your lunch. Take care of the rats, and they'll take care of you!"

Digger followed the dim light on Rhys's hat until it disappeared around the bend. He was lonelier now than before, and the talk of food had made him hungry. He crawled back into the niche and opened his lunch pail.

"I'll take care of the rats all right. If one comes *near* me," he said as he bit into a hunk of corned beef, "I'll bash his head in!"

The track had not yet been extended into the headway where the Sons of Thunder worked. Rhys hitched up

Helen to the loaded wagons he found waiting at the mouth and unhitched four empties. He listened to the camaraderie, the singing that spilled out of the chamber.

"They're having too good a time," he thought.

A minor incident marred his morning. Helen refused to move beyond the headway. All his pulling and cajoling failed to budge her.

"Hee-yah!" he shouted, whipping hard across the mule's rump! "Heey-ah! Hee-yah!" Only when his whip was wet with blood did the animal bolt forward. Rhys had seen other drivers whip their mules viciously as a matter of course, for sport even, but he used his own whip sparingly.

"Sometimes," he thought, "there is just no other way."

"*Pozar! Pozar!*" Mucka bellowed as warning at the mouth of the headway. "Fire! Fire!"

Deep inside, Zakrzewska lit the squib with the lamp from his helmet and ran toward the monkey heading, or cleft in the wall of the headway some twenty yards back, where the others stood or crouched shielding their eyes and ears from the imminent blast.

They braced themselves and waited. But nothing happened.

"You sure it light?" Moczygemba asked.

Zakrzewska nodded. "Wait. It will fire." But it did not fire.

There was no way of telling whether it was a "blown-out" shot or if the fuse had just sputtered, in which case it could reignite at any moment. There was no way of telling.

Digger cast shadow figures against the walls with his hands. He tried to remember Patsy and Dick, and sunlight. Between chews, he pronounced words and names just to hear the sound of his voice, any voice. He would have sung, but he didn't know any songs.

When he reached into his pail for the wedge of cheese

he had saved for last, he grabbed instead a scruffy, wet rat. Annoyed, the critter squawked, then went about its forage unimpeded.

Digger leaped across the tracks, wailing with horror and disgust.

Zakrzewska walked slowly down the headway toward the face, like a cow in a slaughterhouse waiting for the fatal hammer to fall, only this time, cow and cattle killer were one in the same. He had faced death before but never dreamed his demise would come from something as insignificant as a burnt-out shot. For the first time, he wished he had used less powder.

But Zakrzewska would not die that day.

In the moment before the explosion came, he heard an odd wailing in the distance. Distracted, he turned. The blast caught him, thus, from behind and flung him against the wall of the headway like so much detritus.

Digger was jolted from his hysteria by the roar of the blast. Before he could cover his ears, the aftershock threw him backwards onto the tracks.

"Holy Mother!" he thought. "There's men down there!"

Then, as the echoes of the blast died, from every crevice, every ditch, from every dark hole up and down the gangway, came a high-pitched screeching, an alarm, a pandemonium of fear, and hundreds of squealing rats teemed forth and ran blindly up the tracks toward the trap door. The gangway was suddenly alive with rats, and Digger, merely an obstacle in their flight. They surged across his legs, his chest. He felt their feet and hairy bodies, clambering across his face, falling into his screaming mouth, before slithering in their frenzy under the wooden frame.

Then, when the last of the rats had skittered across his brow, a miasma of smoke and dust swelled from below, enveloping him in noxious fumes, ripping at his throat with arms of hot gas. His body heaved and coughed, refusing to succumb, till somehow he crawled across to the stagnant water that lay beyond the track, and there immersed his face and drank to soothe his scalded throat. He lapped greedily from the pool, ignoring its smell of sulfur, its taste of blood, the small, hairy body that brushed against his cheek. Then, sated, he pulled away and saw a dead rat floating in the swill. He screamed.

It was the rat he had boasted earlier of killing.

"Teofil! Vhere are you?" Peter Moczygemba called over and over as the men stumbled, choking, through the thick smoke. Stanislaw heard a groan along the wall, and there, under a pile of rock, half buried, was Zakrzewska.

"Goddamn shot!" Zakrzewska muttered as they pulled him out. One side of his face was scraped raw. His shoulder was battered.

"Qviet, Teofil! Lie still!" Stanislaw said and poured water over his handkerchief, then placed it over Zakrzewska's face.

"No, no!" Zakrzewska answered, pushing to his feet. Only then was the full extent of his aching evident.

"Ve take you up to doctor," Moczygemba said.

"No, I stay here!"

"You are not fit. Look at you," Drozda argued, trying to steady him. "Peter is right. Peter, Leo—help carry him. Ve put him in empty vagon."

"I can walk! Save yourselves!" Zakrzewska boomed, shaking them off. "Leave me be! You are the ones need help!" and he lurched past them toward the mouth of the headway.

Digger huddled in his niche, still shivering with fright. If he lived to be a hundred, he never wanted to see another rat. He could still feel them running across his face. He touched his lips, his nose, his cheeks. There were scratches everywhere, and blood.

"They coulda killt me! An' who'd of knowed down

here in this goddamn cave? Goddamn rats! Ate all me food, too. Didn't leave me nothin'!''

He peered from his niche. The dust and smoke were drifting slowly back down the gangway, sucked by powerful fans in the west entry. It was strangely quiet now. Even the dripping seemed stilled.

"Don't care what Morgan says," he swore, looking at the trap. "I ain't goin' through there. Those damn rats're prob'bly waitin' beyond so's they kin finish me off. Hah! I'm too smart fer 'em! Jes' let 'em try an' come back! I'll be ready this time!''

He picked up his empty lunch pail to heave at the first rat to return. He waited, but no rats came. His stomach growled.

"I could do with a piece of bread right now, or cheese. Those hunkies got grub, I bet. Hunky grub," he said to himself and looked down the gangway for signs of life. "Maybe I should mosey on down there. Maybe they're hurt. Or dead. Maybe they're needin' me."

He picked up his lantern, then started down the tracks, even though Ned the Splicer had warned him against leaving his door. Suddenly a figure loomed at him out of the darkness ahead, a dazed, burly figure, hunched with pain.

"Are ye all right, mister?" Digger asked, but the man brushed past him and walked on. "He looks like a dead man," Digger thought. The man gave him the shivers.

It was then that he heard voices coming from the mouth of the headway. He raised his lantern and picked up his pace.

Zakrzewska stumbled on. He reached Digger's door and pulled it open, pausing for a moment to feel the rush of cool, clean air on his burning face. As he passed through, the current pushed the door open wide, freeing the full force of the powerful draft.

He stumbled on, oblivious.

\* \* \*

"He is more stubborn 'dan mule," Digger heard one say as he approached.

"Mule has bigger brain," said another.

"Vhat ve do now?"

"Ve stay here, finish up."

"Hello there!" Digger called, seeing their dim light through the haze.

"Who is 'dat?" a voice called back.

"It's me!" Digger said as he arrived at the mouth of the headway, where two of the men stood. "I'm the trapper from up the way. It's me first day."

"Vhat you vant?" Moczygemba asked grumpily. " 'Dis no place for boy."

"I ain't no boy! I jes' never been down before. I'd like to see what it's like. Inside."

"You want to see dark hole?" Drozda laughed.

"I 'spect to be a miner meself one day," Digger said proudly.

"Come, 'den, trapper boy!" Drozda said, leading the way. " 'Den maybe you t'ink you vant to be farmer."

"There's no rats in there, is there?" Digger asked, trying to mask his fear.

" 'Da rats know better," Moczygemba said.

" 'Dey come here, ve put 'em to vork first t'ing!" Drozda said.

"Youse do?" Digger asked, following them in. "Little bastards ate me lunch this mornin'. Jesus, I hate rats!"

Outside the headway, the air coursed briskly. Inside it was stagnant and foul. Digger felt as though he were entering a tomb.

At the monkey heading, Drozda lit a long, slender lamp, lowered its glass chimney into place, then attached it to the end of a stave. The others readied their tools for work.

"What's that for?" Digger asked.

"Big 'splosion leave gas. Fire damp. It rise to roof. Vun spark an' boom!" Drozda raised the pole and moved the lamp slowly beneath the roof as he walked deeper into the headway. "Flame burn bright means 'dere is damp."

"Won't yer lamp set it off?" Digger asked warily.

"Is special lamp," Drozda explained, moving deeper. "Only let in bad gas.

"Better leave this behind then," Digger said and set his lantern down on the floor of the chamber.

"You learn fast, trapper."

"What if ye find this . . . this damp?" Digger asked, catching up.

"Ve sit an' vait till fan blows all avay."

As they wandered off into the darkness, neither noticed the flame in Digger's lantern diminish sharply, flicker, then die.

❖❖

RHYS's route covered two miles and was roughly circular in shape—up the length of the central slope to the northern veins, where the richest coal deposits lay, through a connecting air passage, past Digger's door, to the tip of the west entry, a desolate section worked by the Sons of Thunder, then back along the western seams to the cage, where the coal was hoisted up to the pit head and the breaker.

As soon as Rhys entered the air passage on his second trip, he felt the draft and knew that something was wrong.

"It's that fool trapper," he thought, jumped off his lead wagon, and ran ahead of his mules with his lantern. The air passage descended gently for two hundred feet, then curved before coming upon Digger's door. As he rounded the curve, Rhys could see what his ears had already told him—the door had been left open.

"Trapper! Trapper, wake up!" he shouted, but there was no answer, just his voice echoing into silence. He reached the door out of breath and pulled it closed, cutting off the fierce flow of air. "Trapper!" he shouted one last time, but the trapper was gone. Rhys found his plug hat lying in the ditch. He ran on.

Down below, he found the empty wagons outside the

headway, just as he'd left them, but there were no voices now or sounds of work from within. Ground smoke and dust drifted slowly from the mouth toward the fans.

"Maybe they've all gone up," he thought. "Maybe there was trouble up top, and I didn't hear. Or maybe they're still in there hurt."

"Halloo! Is anybody there?" he called again.

"Should I run for help?" he wondered. "I'd look like a fool if I did, and they were all sitting up top having a laugh on me."

"Halloo! Is anybody in there?"

Something was wrong, he knew that. Men didn't just leave their jobs in the middle of the day. Not even these greenhorns. He raised his lantern, paused, then entered the chamber.

Rhys found them twenty yards in, sitting along the walls, eating, their lunch pails open, their hands holding cheese or bread or tins of soup. Digger was there, his mouth stuffed with a chunk of Leo Mucka's *kielbasa*, which Leo had just sliced off with the knife he held in his hand. Stanislaw Gieryk, Jac Drozda, and Peter Moczygemba sat across from them. Stanislaw had just opened a tin of coffee. They were all dead.

Rhys froze at the eerie sight. There was no struggle, no horror, only four men and a boy who settled down to eat in a cloud of smoke and dust, fell asleep, and died. He dipped his lantern into the drifting cloud; the flame diminished. When he raised it again, the flame glowed bright.

"It's the damp!" he said aloud. "Black damp."

His first instinct was to run from the smothering gas that brushed past his legs, but he remembered that there were six who worked in this gang. Two were missing.

"Halloooo! Is anybody there?" he shouted once more.

The answer came as a faint tapping of rock on rock.

He found the man—it was Wincenty Gieryk—clinging to an outcrop of rock, trying desperately to keep from falling back down into the damp. He had left the others to do his business and had dropped his drawers and squatted in the deadly cloud. His britches were still down around his knees. Rhys ran to him and helped him to his feet. Then, with Wincenty clinging to his shoulder, he carefully retraced his steps past the sprawling corpses to the mouth of the headway, to safety.

The colliery whistle blew three short blasts over and over.

Up and down Frog Street, women put aside their laundry, their baking or sewing to say a silent prayer. Then they gathered in their parlors and waited for the dreaded Black Maria—the death wagon—to roll to their doors.

Myfanwy was boiling wash on the stove. She moved to the rainspattered window through which she could see the top of the breaker. "God help us," she said. "Please, please don't let it be one of ours."

A thousand feet below, Hugh was preparing to set a timber when Aloysius came running from the sawmill.

"Trouble in vest entry!" Aloysius said breathlessly. "Some die. 'Dey say Rhysie vas 'dere."

"My Rhys?"

"I hear his name, 'dat's all."

Hugh dropped his tools and ran toward the main shaft.

In the breaker, the boys heard the "three shorts" above the roar of the coal and stopped working. They all had fathers or older bothers underground.

"Keep yer eyes on yer chutes, or they'll be blowin' it for youse 'next," Bryfogle shouted. One by one, they resumed their picking, the only way to relieve their minds of the agony of not knowing whether their fathers and older brothers were dead. Not knowing was worse than knowing.

"How many?" Markham growled as he arrived at the pit head. Before anyone could answer he saw the bloated brown faces for himself.

The bodies had been carried up and set across the gravel

yard. A light rain was falling, but no one thought to cover the faces of the dead. Digger's mouth was still gorged with food. Leo's hand still held a piece of sausage.

"Jesus God Almighty!" Markham gasped.

"Black damp," Dr. Koons said pointedly as Ned brought over the tags of the dead from the peg board.

"We've never had black damp in this mine!" Markham fumed.

"I know, John! I also know black damp when I see it."

"They sat right down in it," Ned added. "They never knew."

"Are there any more?"

"Just these five," Ned answered. "One got out. A driver came by and pulled him out in time." Ned paused, then said, "They're Zakrzewska's crew."

Markham's face turned livid. His eyes flared. "Where is he?"

The whistle ceased its doleful shriek.

"Maybe it sound for me," Zakrzewska mused. His face half bandaged, he sat waiting in the infirmary for Dr. Koons to return. "Maybe I am dead after all." But his face throbbed; his shoulder felt as if someone had wrenched it from its socket. He was very much alive.

Heavy footsteps approached. The door behind him opened; a man stepped in. Somehow he knew it was Markham. His body tensed, feeling the man's eyes burning at his back.

"I cannot see you," Zakrzewska said, unable to turn. "Who is there?"

"Tell me," Markham replied, trying to suppress his rage, "what do you know of the damp?"

"Markham, is that you?"

"The damp!" Markham exploded. "You've heard of fire damp?"

"Yes," Zakrzewska answered, bewildered.

"Then what of black damp? And white damp? And after damp? What of them?"

Zakrzewska remained silent.

"I thought so. Come, then!" Markham beckoned. "Come, see what your ignorance has wrought."

"Have they taken up the ones from the west entry yet?" Hugh asked the headman at the cage.

"They've been goin' up all morning," the headman answered.

"I'm looking for a boy. He may have been . . ." Hugh couldn't finish.

"There was a boy. There were five dead. Others hurt."

"His name is Rhys. He's a driver."

"I don't know, mister. Best you go up an' see."

Hugh stepped into the cage just as the gates were closing. Next to him were the Moczygemba brothers and Stefan Drozda. The ride up was interminable.

For the seventh time that year, Gwyndaf Pugh and his helper, Ben John Evans, wheeled Black Maria from the stables next to the pluck me store. The compartment was ten feet long, maybe five feet high, and four wide. The sides were closed in; two doors opened at the back. Once it had been a dairy wagon. Now it was painted black, inside and out.

"How many?" Ben John asked.

"Five. Maybe six."

"Might need two trips then."

"One'll do."

Pugh and Ben John brought out the mules and hitched them up. The same ones were always used—Euan's favorites— the blacks.

Zakrzewska followed Markham to the yard. He saw the corpses lying on the ground, saw the doctor and Ned huddled in the rain.

"What has this to do with me?" he wondered. "My hands are clean." And then, moving closer, he saw the faces of his crew. "Oh, no!" he groaned. "Oh, no! How could this be? How?"

"You tell me," Markham said bluntly.

When the cage gate opened, Hugh, his heart pounding, rushed forward to where the dead lay. He searched frantically from face to face, expecting the worst, but these men were strangers. Confused, he turned and saw Rhys sitting outside the steam shanty, huddled under a blanket with Wincenty Gieryk.

It had been the longest day of Rhys's life, and the worst. Afraid to leave Wincenty behind, afraid the man would crawl back in to save his brother and the others, who were beyond saving, Rhys tied Wincenty's leg to the wheel of one of the wagons, then ran to the western slope, the nearest working breast, for help.

At first the miners there wouldn't believe him, the sight described was so grotesque, but then, reluctantly they followed him back and heard, long before their destination was reached, the wails of the lone survivor echoing off the chamber walls. The unearthly sound filled them all with fear, for was not this chamber cursed? And then, with their own eyes, they saw and believed the tale of this boy, this hero. The bodies were lifted, carried out, and set into the empty wagons. Twice, men faltered, overcome by the still-deadly gas that still swirled around their feet, and had to be lifted lest they, too, succumb.

During the long ride up, Rhys blamed himself. If he had not dallied on his first run, he might have arrived at their headway sooner, or if he had run faster in running for help, help might have arrived in time to lift these men from their cradle of death. When finally he saw his *dada* up top, Rhys turned away, afraid his *dada* would rebuke him for not saving more lives. Instead, his *dada* rushed to him and embraced him with tears in his eyes.

Drozda and the Moczygembas confronted the corpses of their brothers in stunned silence. "What is this black damp?" they wondered. "And why has it come now? Why now?" They were accustomed to sudden, disfiguring death in the mines, but this quiet, painless death confused them. It felt wrong.

Hugh had seen black damp before at Sugar Notch, in Wanamie and Huddersfield, but as Rhys recounted his discovery in the west entry, something seemed wrong to him as well. He left Rhys's side for a moment and returned to the men gathered near the bodies. As he drew closer, he heard the unmistakable voice of Zakrzewska. Zakrzewska! He should have known!

"When I leave, they were alive!" Zakrzewska shouted at Markham. "How is it I am blamed when I was not there?"

Hugh couldn't remain silent. "You killed them just the same!"

"Keep out of this!" Zakrzewska warned.

"You and your explosions!" Hugh said with contempt. "Every shot gives off *some* black damp, man! It's nothing! But yours were three or four times too big! The damp must have been enormous to do this!"

"The fans in the west entry would have carried it away all the same," Ned the Splicer interjected.

"You see?" Zakrzewska shot back. "You think you know everything!"

"Then there's something else to it! Something! For as sure as I am standing here, you caused these five boys to die!" Hugh saw the futility of saying more and turned to leave, but his heart held him back. "Can something be done?" he asked. "Something to cover these boys? Can they at least have some dignity in death?"

"The wagon's coming now," Ned the Splicer said.

Hugh walked back to Rhys, and together they returned to the cage. The last thing they saw before it descended was the bodies of Zakrzewska's crew being laid atop one another in the back of Black Maria.

"I've not done with this!" Markham said as Zakrzewska started back to the infirmary with Dr. Koons. Zakrzewska glowered at him and defiantly trod on. "Damn his pernicious soul!" Markham muttered to Ned the Splicer. "This will bring trouble. Keep your ears open, Ned. Let me know everything."

It was a shivery sight—Black Maria leaving the colliery, behind it the brothers of the dead, straggling in the rain. Parlor curtains were drawn aside. Unseen watchers followed its progress up Frog Street and prayed for deliverance. After each house was spared in turn, the curtains were dropped neatly into place, and the watchers breathed again.

The first house not spared was Digger O'Shea's. When the wagon stopped in front, a cry went up inside, and a small, gray-haired woman reeled onto the porch, her eyes filled with sadness and disbelief. In her hands were Digger's rosaries. From the parlor behind her came a man's thick, persistent coughing, the sound of a man dying of miner's asthma.

"Gerald O'Shea?" Pugh asked.

"Yes, that's our boy," Mrs. O'Shea said.

Pugh and Ben John opened the back doors, lifted Digger's body out, and set it on the porch.

"Can ye bring 'im inside, lads? Me husband's sickly."

"We got a lot of stops to make," Pugh said and returned to the wagon.

"Is it Digger, *Mathair*?" a raspy voice called from inside.

"Yes, *Da*."

As Black Maria rolled on to Polish Hill, the Moczygembas carried Digger inside and laid him across two chairs in the parlor.

"You don't leave him here! Not my house!" Big Mary Bakunas shouted as Pugh and Ben John carried Leo Mucka to her door. "He got no family here! He just a boarder!"

"But he lives here!" Pugh argued.

"Not no more. He dead!" she said and slammed the door.

The issue was the cost of a coffin and the inconvenience of arranging a burial, both family matters. Leo Mucka was practically a stranger. Pugh and Ben John returned his body to Black Maria and moved on.

Anton Gieryk and two of his sons ran up Frog Street from the colliery. They arrived at their door just as Stanislaw was being lifted from the wagon. Anton looked at Wincenty in amazement.

"Ve hear 'dat you . . . ," Gieryk said, his eyes filling with tears.

Wincenty shook his head. "*Nie*. Stanislaw."

The brothers carried their own into the house. Their women wailed with grief. It went the same at the Moczygemba house.

Myfanwy sat in her parlor, darning socks to keep her fingers busy, her mind occupied. She heard Black Maria approaching, heard the wailing down the street, finally saw the black rooftop through the window. Her body tensed.

"Please don't stop here," she said quietly. "Please, not here."

Only after it passed by did she notice that she had pricked her finger with the needle. A drop of blood stained Rhys's good stocking.

It took all three, Pugh, Ben John, and Stefan, to carry Jac Drozda into the house at the end of Frog Street, for he was a big man. Pugh and Ben John then turned the mules around and drove back to the colliery to inform Ned that Leo Mucka's body had gone unclaimed.

◆◆

HE opened his eyes from a sleep and saw her. "Gwladys," he murmured.

"I've come to tend you then," she said, removing her wrap. "Mrs. Koons said it wouldn't be proper, but I insisted."

Zakrzewska lay in a small room at the rear of Dr. Koons's house that was used for patients who were too sick or injured to return home.

"I inquired at the company store after school," she continued. "They told me you'd been killed."

"Doctor say I have con . . . con . . ."

"Concussion."

"He say I need rest. Plenty rest . . ." He drifted off.

"Don't worry, Teofil," she said, holding his hand tightly. "I'm here. I'm going to take care of you from now on."

Hugh and the boys sat on the front steps, watching the activity on Frog Street, which was busy in those early evening hours, busy with the commerce of death. The carpenter, the ice man, the beer man, each had four stops to make. Neighbors carried food to the houses of mourning. Others collected money. A carriage brought paid criers from Mahanoy City to the O'Shea house, where they would keen throughout the night.

"How'd he look then?" Euan asked Rhys matter-of-factly.

"All . . . all puffy," Rhys said. "His skin turned brown."

So, Digger was dead. Euan found it hard to believe. He could still taste the bully's spit in his mouth.

Black Maria rolled up Frog Street for a second time that day, carrying Leo Mucka in a pine box. He would be buried in an unmarked grave behind Holy Trinity, wearing his work clothes. No mourners would be present, just Father Brislin, Mr. Ryga, the gravedigger, and Gwyndaf Pugh. The cost of the casket would be borne by G. B. Markham and Company and garnished from Mucka's wages.

"There aren't many who would have gone into that chamber," Hugh said to Rhys. "You saved a man's life today. I'm proud of you."

When Black Maria passed, they stood.

It was late that night when Zakrzewska woke again. Gwladys had left. The room was dark, but he was not alone.

"I'm very disappointed," Markham said from a chair in the corner. "I trusted you. I kept my part of the deal. All you've done is kill five of my workers. You promised information, names. I have heard none."

Markham stood and lit his cigar. "If you do not give me what I want," he said, "I will make you wish you'd died down in that mine."

With that, he left.

(A warm, golden glow spilled from their chamber. He heard laughter and smelled food—rich, pungent smells that made him hungry. He entered slowly, as if walking through water, and found them, sitting in the midst of a golden cloud, eating, drinking, laughing.

"Come, Rhysie!" they said. "You hungry? Come eat! Come sit vit' us!"

And so he sat and ate their food. It made him feel good, and he began to laugh, but when he looked again at their laughing faces they were all dead, and they were laughing, because he was . . . )

Rhys gasped and sat up. He was in his room, in his bed. He was safe.

"What is it then?" Euan asked, startled.

"A dream. I was dreaming."

"I was, too. About Digger."

Rhys lay back down.

"Were you scared?" Euan asked. "Today?"

"Yes. It's all right to be scared."

"What's it like, do you think, being dead?"

"I don't know. Cold prob'ly. Quiet. I don't think you feel nothing. You just sit around somewheres and wait till they tell you where you're going—to heaven or to hell."

"Then what?"

"I'm not the pastor," Rhys said and rolled over on his side, but it was a long time before either of them got to sleep.

Drip . . . drip . . . drip . . .

In the O'Shea house, a candle flickered in the parlor. The paid criers keened softly next to the open casket where Digger lay in his Sunday suit, the suit he had long outgrown. His rosaries were twined between his fingers. The pine casket rested atop two slabs of ice that sat, in turn, across a frame of wood. Underneath, basins were set to catch the slowly melting ice.

Drip . . . drip . . . drip . . .

❖❖

THE colliery was closed for the second day in a row. It was time for Jeddoh to bury its dead.

Four caskets were borne to Holy Trinity on the shoulders of family and friends. Mourners poured from every house in the Flats and on the Hill. The church was too small to hold the crowd. Many had to stand at the back of the sanctuary or on the front steps or below the side windows in order to hear the words of Father Brislin. The mass lasted for two hours, but the funeral would continue for two more days.

They left Razor's yard, their caps pulled low, their fiddles disguised in canvas sacks like baseball bats and gloves, then ran across Frog Street to Bakunas's, where they hopped the fence into Stankiewicz's and squeezed through the hedges to where the mourners had gathered in Maciejewski's yard.

"Are you sure this is the right thing?" Rhys asked Razor nervously.

"I am sure. Just follow an' keep your head low," Razor prompted before plunging through the crowd to the platform where Blackie and the others waited.

"Kudla!" Karl Maciejewski shouted and grabbed Razor by the collar as he passed. "You late!"

"Sorry, *pan* Maciejewski," Razor said, forging ahead. "String break on fittle, but ve make goot music."

"An' who is 'dis?" Karl asked. "New fittler?"

"*Tak,*" Razor replied, trying to nudge Rhys forward.

"*Czekaj!* Is 'dis not . . . ?" Karl pulled off Rhys's cap. "I t'ought so! You Morgan's boy, son of 'dat blackleg. You not velcome here boy! Get out!"

"But *pan* Maciejewski!" Razor begged.

"Leave 'dis house!" Maciejewski insisted. "You have no place here!"

"Vhat is wrong, Karl?" Anton Gieryk asked, drawn by the disturbance.

"Razor bring 'dis son of Morgan. I say he don't belong here."

"Vait a minute, Karl," Gieryk said, looking intently into Rhys's eyes. "You are . . . Rhys? Rhys Morgan?"

Rhys nodded.

Gieryk put both hands on Rhys's shoulders. "You save my Wincenty. My boy live 'cause of you. You velcome anytime in my house," he said with great emotion and embraced Rhys and kissed him on each cheek. Wincenty joined them and embraced Rhys also, as did Jozef Moczygemba.

Razor led his astonished friend toward the platform, and a way opened up for them through the mourners.

"Hey, Rhysie!" Razor said under his breath. " 'Dey t'ink you are hero."

"Criminy dick! Wait till they hear me play!"

Rhys hadn't talked to Blackie, Pauli, or Stanko since the trouble began with his father. None of them wanted anything to do with the son of a scab. Only Razor had stood by him. Rhys approached them now with apprehension, but they treated him with the same deference as did the others.

"See? I say t'ings be all right," Razor said as he slipped his left suspender off and let it hang down the side of his trousers. Razor liked to be comfortable when he played.

The mood of the crowd shifted again when Rhys raised his fiddle to his shoulder. They thought he had come as Razor's friend, to watch, to listen, not to play. Never before had they seen a Welshman in a Slavic string band. The mere thought of it seemed blasphemous.

Rhys saw the confusion in the crowd, heard their gasps, their mutterings of discontent, and wished he'd never entered into this scheme. He forgot the tunes they'd carefully rehearsed, forgot which strings were which. His hands became sticks.

"I can't do it!" he said to Razor under his breath. At the same time, accidentally, his bow slid across the strings, making a comic, drooping sound.

Razor motioned to Blackie and the others to get ready before Rhys lost his nerve, when suddenly he heard laughter from the crowd. "Vhat means 'dat?" he wondered and looked at Rhys. Then it came to him. "Do again," he urged.

"What?" Rhys replied, perplexed.

"Vit' your strings! Vhat you just do."

"This?" Rhys asked and made the same drooping sound with his bow. The crowd laughed again, harder this time. Razor and the boys laughed, too.

Rhys was dismayed at first, but he had to admit the sound was comical, so he drew his bow across the strings again in an upward stroke, producing the reverse effect. The crowd laughed harder still.

Razor gave the downbeat, and they began to play the "Oberek Pulawiak." The laughter continued. The people were grateful for any diversion from their grief, and a whimsical Welsh boy, who grimaced with each wrong note he hit—not all of which were unintentional—accomplished this with laughter. Razor soon added to the clowning by casting threatening glances at Rhys's sour notes. The laughter grew.

Once they discovered their "comic act," for thus it was perceived, the boys wisely avoided overworking it. Still, they were besieged that afternoon to repeat their antics, which they did later on with the same success. And then they sat down to eat *ziemniaki* and *szynke* and drink *piwo*.

"You see, Rhysie? I tolt you I make you reg'lar Polish fittler!" Razor boasted, beaming with pride at his pupil.

Rhys had trouble catching his breath. "I haven't worked this hard since my first days in the breaker," he said and brushed the sweatsoaked hair from his eyes.

"Is just startin'," Razor said, toasting his fiddlers. "*Na zdrowie!*"

"*Na zdrowie!*" they responded and emptied their cups.

Just then, they heard a commotion from the path between the houses, and a voice shouted, "He's here! He's here!" Rhys turned and saw Zakrzewska, his head still bandaged, coming up the path, leaning on Maciejewski's shoulder for support. The crowd rose as one and applauded his arrival.

"Ah, Zakrzewska!" Razor crooned. "He goot man, 'dat Zakrzewska!"

"He's a murderer," Rhys said.

Razor was stung by Rhys's remark but let it pass.

"Is fault of Markham!" Zakrzewska later exhorted as he held court from a stuffed chair in the corner of the yard. A plate of food rested on his lap, untouched. In his hand was a glass of whiskey, from which he sipped sparingly as he spoke.

Rhys hovered on the periphery of the crowd that listened in reverence. It was time for him to be home, but he lingered instead to hear Zakrzewska's lies.

"Markham, he say, 'I give hunkies old, worked-out pit filled with gas. What do they know? Dumb hunkies! Pretty soon, they all dead!' That man, he know what he do, 'cause next time hunky say, 'I want job as miner,' he gonna say, 'Look what happen to last bunch!' You think he care about our brothers? He devil, that man Markham! He is greedy son of a bitch, and now, *pan* Gieryk, your son and your brother, pan Moczygemba, will not walk on this earth again."

He paused to let his words have their effect. Men and women among the crowd wiped tears from their eyes.

"I tell you," he continued, struggling to hold back his raw emotions, "I am sick at heart. Why could not I be dead, not these good boys? I would have gave my life to save one . . . just one!"

"Vhat now, *pan* Zakrzewska?" asked Wincenty Cieryk. "Vhat do ve do?"

"Tonight we sit with our sorrow. Tomorrow we talk how to keep these things from happen again."

"You mean union?" asked another.

"We must do something," he answered vaguely. He looked tired and drained. "But union take time. We must make Markham feel our anger now."

"*Pan* Zakrzewska?"

"Please . . . no more," he begged, near the point of

exhaustion. Against his protests, four men came forward and lifted his chair, then carried it to the street, where it was placed on the back of a wagon and borne back to the house of Dr. Koons.

Rhys watched and listened and was enraged. Before leaving, he heard talk of a clandestine meeting to be held in the woods the next night, where the men could talk freely, where they could plot to avenge the deaths of the Sons of Thunder.

He hurried home to tell his father what he knew.

❖❖

"WAIT UP!" Euan called as he tried to free the foot he'd caught between two rocks. "I'm stuck!"

"Come on then!" Rhys snapped as he doubled back. "You weren't supposed to come in the first place." Freeing Euan's leg was a simple maneuver. In a moment, they were both racing ahead to catch up with their *dada*.

"Are you sure this is the way?" Hugh asked.

"It's just ahead. There!" Rhys said, and they saw lanterns through the trees and some forty men gathered in a clearing near the crest of the ridge.

"Ve are zero to Markham!" Jozef Moczygemba said in the clearing. "His mules get better 'dan us. Mules get fed reg'lar. Hurt mule, you get docked! Kill vun, you lose job! But hunky get killt, Markham not even pay for box to plant him in! I say time has come ve go 'gainst him! Ve show him how strong Polonia! Tell him no more kill our brot'ers! No more!"

The other voices but one rose in assent. That man was Anton Gieryk. "I t'ink vhat you say is wrong! I teach my Stanislaw to be man of peace an' respect. Now you vant to bring violence in his name? No, no! You can blow up whole damn mine, burn breaker, do vhat you vant, but 'dat vill not bring my boy back to me!"

"Vhat vould you have us do, Anton?" asked Stefan Drozda. "Moczygemba is right. Mules is vort' more to Markham."

"Only vay to hurt Markham is vit' union. 'Dat only vay.

Union is our strengt'! An' more an' more in my mind, I am not so sure 'dat Markham is for blame. Is easy to point finger. Is not easy to dig out trut'."

"Gieryk is right," Hugh said and stepped forward from the shadows into the circle of light. Rhys and Euan stayed close at his side.

"Who is 'dis?" the men questioned.

"Morgan," others spat, as though his name were a malediction.

"Zakrzewska is quick to blame Markham for his own mistakes!" Hugh said, forcing his point.

"Who 'da hell you t'ink you are, comin' here?" Moczygemba growled.

"Get outta here!" others shouted. Rhys and Euan moved closer to their father. Euan gripped his father's sleeve.

"Wait! Listen to Gieryk!" Hugh shouted above their voices.

"Ve t'ink you better get goin', mister," Jozef Moczygemba warned him. "An' forget vhat you see an' hear tonight."

"Listen!" Hugh said. "You are starting something here that you do not understand. You're being lied to and misled, for God knows what reason!"

"These are strong words comin' from scab," a voice at the edge of the clearing said. All eyes turned as Zakrzewska rose from the rock where he had sat, unseen by Hugh, and walked forward. "If you did not bring your babies to hide behind, you would be dead now."

"I have come to tell these men who is to blame for the deaths of your brothers!" Hugh retorted. "I wouldn't give one rusty nail for Markham, but his only sin was sending those boys down into the pits with you in the first place! They were killed by gas from a shot fired by you, Zakrzewska! You!"

"Ned Splicer say fans take gas away!"

"Right," Hugh agreed. "Then why didn't they? Have any of you asked yourself that question? The fans were working, yet the gas remained. Why?"

"I left after shot was fired," Zakrzewska said. "I was hurt. I went up to doctor. I was not there!"

"I know," Hugh said coldly. "Rats always leave the mine at the first sign of danger."

"Say vhat you come to say," Anton Gieryk told Hugh. "Vhile I am here you have free to speak. 'Dis is my sorrow more 'dan 'deirs."

"My boy Rhys was in the west entry that day. Tell them, Rhys. Tell them what you saw."

Gieryk motioned Rhys forward.

Rhys looked around at the same faces he had confronted the day before in Maciejewski's yard. They had come to accept him, had even laughed at his clowning with Razor. Now they looked confused and angry again.

"I made two trips through the west entry that morning," he started in a quiet but confident voice. "When I passed through the trap the first time, I told the door boy to shut it behind me, and he did. But, when I came through again an hour later, it was open . . . wide open."

"And where was the trapper?" Hugh asked.

"Gone."

"And what happens when that trap is opened wide?"

"Well, the draft is . . . is too strong to pull the bad air from the side chambers. The draft just . . . just blows through."

"And then what did you do?"

"I closed the trap. And the draft got cut off, and the fans started to pull out the bad air."

"Could it have blown open by itself?" Hugh pressed.

"No. When the door's closed, there's no draft. The air's still."

"So, after your first trip, somebody opened the trap again and didn't bother to close it?"

Rhys nodded.

"For God's sake!" Hugh shouted indignantly. "Close the traps! That's the first thing you learn when you go down to the pits! And all that bad air stayed in the headway because the trap was left open! Who in the name of God could have done such a thing? It wasn't you, was it, Zakrzewska? You went up that same gangway, through that same trap on your way to the doctor. Could it have been you? Could you have been so stupid, so careless?" And then, as to leave no doubt in anyone's mind, "Dear God, those boys went on working in that chamber, thinking it was safe, and then they sat down to eat! Five are dead, because *you*, Zakrzewska, left a door open!"

The men stood silently, waiting for Zakrzewska to refute Hugh's charge.

"I think your boy is liar," Zakrzewska said finally. "I would lie, too, to save my father's dirty name."

"You go to hell, Zakrzewska! You all know my Rhys! Gieryk? Harakal? Moczygemba? Would my Rhys lie about a thing like this? Would he?"

The men averted their eyes and shook their heads no.

Just then, a boy ran from the woods. "Cossacks! Comin' up 'da hill!" he said breathlessly. The men quickly extinguished their lanterns and listened in silence. Indeed, they could hear the voices of Coal and Iron Police approaching in the distance. Without another word, the assembly scattered in all directions.

"This way!" Rhys said, grabbing his *dada* and Euan, then led them over the ridge to a thicket and a creek beyond. As they crossed to the other side, they heard gunshots.

"Are they shooting at us?" Euan asked, frightened.

"Not yet. They're shooting at air," Hugh assured him. They could see the lanterns of the Coal and Iron Police moving up the hill. "Come on, let's get home."

As they walked in the back door, Myfanwy rushed in from the parlor. "I was worried sick," she said. "I heard gunshots."

"It was Owney Riley," Rhys said, "scaring off some wild dogs."

As much as she wanted to, she didn't believe him.

The mine reopened the next morning after being idle three days. At the pit head, Markham, Ned the Splicer, and two Coal and Irons studied the faces of every man who pegged in.

"What is it they're looking for?" the men wondered. No one mentioned what had happened the night before in the clearing on the ridge, and by quitting, everyone thought the trouble had blown over.

❖❖

RHYS awoke first.

"Was it a dream?" he wondered. He thought he'd heard men shouting, the sound of feet pounding across porches. He sat up and threw his legs over the side of the bed. No breeze rustled the branches. No owls shrieked. He slid to the floor and knelt at the open window. The sky was starry. Hidden beyond his view, the moon shone full.

He heard weeping, or thought he did, heard a door slam and a crash of glass. From his window, Rhys could see only a slice of Frog Street. His view was more of backyards and trees that lined yards farther down the Hill, trees that looked golden in the blue-soft light, trees that churned with shadow and flame but not with fire. Then he understood. The leaves were reflecting the light of torches and silhouettes of men passing between those torches and the trees. There was trouble on Frog Street.

"What is it?" Euan asked, waking behind him.

"I don't know," Rhys answered.

"Is it first whistle?"

"Not yet. Something else."

Euan joined Rhys at the window in time to see three horsemen ride down Frog Street carrying shotguns.

They found their father in the kitchen already dressed, putting on his boots by the light of a kerosene lamp.

"What's happening then?" Rhys asked.

Their father's face looked troubled. "I'm going out to see. You two stay here."

They ran upstairs for their trousers and boots.

It might have been the middle of the afternoon—a family loading its worldly possessions onto a flatbed wagon, leaving town for a new home perhaps and better jobs, their friends gathered to bid them off amid weepy farewells. Instead, it was the middle of the night, and the gathered were not friends but Coal and Irons, there to assist meanly in the going.

Hugh and the boys joined others in their nightclothes who, drawn by the spectacle, moved hesitantly down Frog Street for a closer look.

"Move along now! There's two more!" a large man with a booming voice commanded as he strode from the house. A blaze of torchlight swept across his face, revealing the deep-set eyes that hid beneath his broad-brimmed hat, the thick mustachios that curled toward his cheeks, the glinting badge of William Frostbutter. *Sheriff* William Frostbutter.

"Oh, my God!" Hugh moaned when the truth became clear.

"What is it, *N'had*?" Rhys whispered.

"The Zdepkos. They're being evicted."

"Evicted?" Euan asked too loudly. "Why?"

Hugh hushed him. "Rhys, do you remember seeing Zdepko or anyone in his family in the woods last night?"

Rhys thought for a moment. "I think so. It was dark."

"They're the scapegoats. This is Markham's warning."

The Zdepko family huddled outside their house, the house that was no longer theirs, and watched passively as beds, chests, baskets, tables, chairs—the accumulated substance of their life in America—were carted out and pitched indifferently onto the bed of the wagon. Glass, furniture even, was broken by thoughtless bearers, curtains ripped, keepsakes ground into the dust under heavy boots, all in a senseless haste to get the job done. The last to be carried out, the *babcia* Zdepko—old, feeble, her eyes agape with fright—was lifted onto the wagon on a mattress, like a fragile doll. Finally, the family itself was heaped on board, and the wagon trundled up Frog Street under the cold, uncaring moon.

"Where will you go?" Hugh shouted to Aloysius Zdepko, his laborer, as the wagon passed.

"I dunno," Aloysius said dully. "I dunno."

"Let me know where you are."

"Hey there! Get back!" a deputy on horseback warned Hugh.

"God be with you!" Hugh bid them as the wagon rolled off.

Euan got one last look at Andrew, his friend from the breaker. Their eyes met; the boys were too dumbstruck to speak.

"*N'had*, look!" Rhys said, pointing urgently as a second wagon rolled up Frog Street. Suddenly he remembered what the sheriff had said—"There's two more!" It wasn't just the Zdepkos. Two more families were being evicted!

"Come along, boys," his *dada* said, trying not to sound alarmed. "Let's get home."

Frostbutter had regrouped his men a few houses up. "Anton Gieryk, are you in there? Come out, if you are. This is Sheriff Frostbutter." The door opened slowly, and Gieryk stepped onto the porch. "Are you Anton Gieryk?"

"Yes," Gieryk said. Wincenty and his other sons huddled behind him.

"I have here a Declaration of Eviction from this premises," Frostbutter continued. "Your employ with G. B. Markham and Co. terminated as of midnight last night, and you are no longer entitled to inhabit this domicile. You are hereby ordered to vacate immediately. These men will help you remove your..."

"Ter-min-ate? Vhat means this, this 'terminate'? You make mistake."

"Now you aren't going to make me read this whole goddamn document, are you? It says here you incited union activity, and Markham wants you the hell off his property."

"Incite union?"

"Are you going to go quietly, Mr. Gieryk?" Frostbutter asked testily. "You'll go one way or the other."

"Go? Vhere? Vhere you take us?"

"Off Markham's property," the sheriff said bluntly and motioned to the Coal and Irons to move into the house. The old man resisted and was brutally knocked aside.

"*Ojciec!*" Wincenty cried, rushing to his father's aid but was struck in the head by a billy club and went sprawling across the porch. Women's screams went up inside as the rest of the Gieryk sons were dragged forth and subdued.

Across the street, Rhys moved to join the fray, but Hugh held him back, at the same time, fighting his own urge to help this man, whom he had come to respect. "There's nothing we can do," Hugh told his son. "Nothing!"

The Gieryks did not go easily. Their women as well as their men fought fiercely, but they were clubbed into submission in the end. They emerged, one by one, dazed and bloodied, the battle lost.

All that remained was the emptying of the house. Instead of loading their goods onto the wagon, Frostbutter ordered them dumped into the street. "All this over a pile of junk," he said, surveying the mound that resulted. He picked up a kerosene lamp, dashed it against a table and lit the spilled contents with a torch. The flame flashed bright; within seconds, everything the Gieryks owned was ablaze.

Hugh saw the third empty wagon heading up Frog Street and feared that his house was next on Frostbutter's list. He felt an overwhelming desire to get his boys home. Others who had ventured out hurried to their doors.

"What are you waiting for?" Frostbutter barked at the Coal and Irons. "Get 'em out of here!"

The Gieryks were lifted or thrown onto the bed of the empty wagon while the sheriff led his deputies up Frog Street to their last stop. Hugh and the boys, their shadows cast long by the flickering fire, walked some twenty feet ahead of the group on the opposite side of the street.

"Any of you ever work in a mine?" Frostbutter asked his men. None had. "I did once, for four days. Worst four days of my life! Don't know how these dumb bastards do it."

"Shut up, you worthless ox!" Rhys wanted to shout at him. "Any man or boy here is worth ten of you!"

"Course, these roundheads don't know better," Frostbutter continued. "Don't have feelin's same as us. They're just a step up from animals. Some of 'em ain't even that."

The wagon rolled past with the Gieryks huddled silently on the back. Rhys looked up at their bloodied expressionless faces, lit by the crackling orange flame. They had lost their son, their brother, their jobs, their home, everything. It was incomprehensible to him. Where would they go? What would they do? He had held Wincenty's life in his hands, had risked his own life without a second thought to save him. That he could do at least; that was easy—a simple choice, a direct action. The pain he felt for them turned to rage because he was so powerless to do anything to help them now.

A deep sob tore through the silence. "Dear God," Rhys wondered "how much suffering can they endure? How much suffering is there?"

An object fell off the wagon and landed in the dust a few feet ahead of Euan. He picked it up—a small religious picture probably brought from the old country. "Hey, this dropped," he said, approaching the wagon. At once, a deputy cut him off.

"Give it here!" the deputy demanded. Euan handed it up to him.

"He's only a boy," Hugh said anxiously. "He doesn't know."

The deputy pitched the icon off into the darkness. "You'd better get home," he warned, "before you get into real trouble."

They hurried ahead. The last ten paces seemed the longest. The boys reached the porch first, vaulting across the banister and through the door, which Myfanwy held open for them.

"N'had, what in . . . ?" Myfanwy said before Hugh cut her off.

"Shhh!" he said, closing the door behind him as the sheriff and his men approached. The light of their lanterns played across the parlor wall; a foot fell across their step. Inside, no one breathed.

"Is this it, Martin?"

"I can't tell. Bring over the torch."

"This is eighty-nine. Which do we want?"

"Up two. Ninety-three."

The men and horses stopped before another door.

"Pavel Gaca! Are you in there? This is Sheriff Frostbutter!"

"Thank God!" Hugh said under his breath. "Thank God it wasn't us."

"Why should it be anybody?" Rhys asked.

At sunrise, the men on the Hill walked to the colliery past the still-smoldering heap in front of the Gieryk house, past the Zdepko house, where curtains, forgotten in haste, flapped in an open window. No effort had been made to remove the rubble. It was left instead for all to see.

"A warning," Rhys thought. "*N' had* was right. This was only a warning."

Shock and gloom prevailed in the colliery that day and—God, yes!—even glee. The hunkies had been put squarely in their place. For many, that was an occasion for glee. But after the shock and gloom had worn off, there was one question every man wanted answered. How did Markham know? And then, a fierce anger set in.

They had been betrayed. There was an informer in their midst.

In Wilkesbarre, Fernando Decker got a day's work pasting fly bills onto telegraph poles, fences and walls. JOBS FOR MINE LABORERS AND YARDMEN one proclaimed. IMMEDIATE HIRING— G. B. MARKHAM & CO.— JEDDOH, PENN. Decker tucked one into his vest pocket, brushed a glob of thick paste across the back of another, then slapped it over the face of a weathered poster that read:

## WANTED FOR MURDER
## TEOFIL ZWIARDOWSKI

❖❖

"WHAT do you want here?" Hugh asked the four men who confronted him as he descended the monkey ladder from his breast. Without a laborer, his work was slowed, and he had stayed beyond quitting to catch up.

"It vas you, vasn't it?" Karl Maciejewski asked.

"What are you talking about?"

"You tell Markham 'bout meetin'. Up on hill."

"Get out of my way!" Hugh threatened, but two of Maciejewski's cohorts grabbed him from behind and pinned him against the wall.

"Ve know!" Maciejewski said. "Ve know you tell. Everybody know it!"

"That's a damned lie!" Hugh shouted.

"Is it?" Maciejewski asked and punched Hugh hard in the stomach. " 'Dat come from Anton Gieryk!" He punched Hugh again, even harder. "An' 'dat come from Zdepko!" Hugh twisted to his knees, gasping for breath, but his attacker kicked him in the chest and stomach, driving him to the ground. " 'Dat is from Gaca!" he snarled and picked up a length of board. "An' dis is from me!"

"Sit still, will you?" Rhys snapped. "He said he'd work late."

"This late?" Euan asked, walking across the banister railing as though it were a railroad track. "He never works this late."

Rhys squinted down Frog Street into the setting sun for any sign of his *dada*. "He's alone now. Everything takes more time. I was thinking I'd talk to him tonight about taking me on as his laborer. If they'd let me. I'd make more, too."

"And I could drive your mules!"

"Hah!" Rhys scoffed. "They'd make nipper pie of you!" Suddenly he saw a figure turning onto Frog Street from the colliery.

"I wish he'd get home," Euan moaned. "I'm hungry."

In the distance, the figure faltered and fell to its knees.

"It's him!" Rhys blurted and tore off down the street.

"Wait up!" Euan called and raced after.

Hugh was struggling to stand when Rhys reached him. Blood ran from his nose, his mouth. His eyes were nearly swollen shut.

"*Dada!*" he shouted. "What happened?"

"A fall!" Hugh rasped. "Ceiling . . . fell . . . fell on me!"

Euan ran up. At first he didn't recognize the bloody mangle that was his father, then his face turned white.

"*Dada?*" he whimpered, then began to scream, "*Dada? Dada!*"

"Stop! Stop it!" Rhys shouted as he shoved the boy hard, stunning him into silence. "Now help me," he told Euan. "Help lift him—take his arm!" Together, they raised their *dada* to his feet. "Come on, *N'had*. Come, we'll get you home."

❖❖

GWLADYS threw her head back and laughed mischievously.

"Teofil! Here's one even you will appreciate," she said, her red hair glinting in the late afternoon sun that streaked across Dr. Koons's porch. It was her custom to read to Zakrzewska from the *Philadelphia Journal* during her daily visits, a custom he increasingly dreaded, for no matter how enthusiastically she rendered articles that suited his taste, she invariably concluded by reading the latest wedding announcements.

"My head!" he moaned, holding his still-bandaged face in his huge paw. "No more! You fill my head with too many thoughts."

"Nonsense!" she exclaimed. "If you're going to learn to read, you've got to know the words."

"I know all the words I need."

"One can never know too many words, just as one can never be too rich or too happy or too respectable."

"I know enough words."

"Why, you're worse than my pupils," she scolded him, then adjusted her spectacles and began to read in a wistful voice. "'On the evening before the wedding, the groom-to-be gave a supper at Delmonico's for his intended ushers. While skylarking, Colonel William C. Reiff, who was to have acted as chief usher, slipped and displaced some bones of the foot and regrettably could not attend the wedding at Saint Bartholomew's the next morning, having been confined to his couch ever since.' Poor Colonel!" she giggled. "Missed all the festivities!"

"What?" he asked distracted.

"You're not even listening, are you?"

"Read story again about robbery in . . ."

"We get enough coarseness in Jeddoh. What we need is more beauty and refinement."

"And this is beauty? Man fall down, hurt leg?"

"Patience!" she pouted, then smiled coyly. "I'm getting to that. 'The Reverend Dr. Tiffany and Reverend Mr. DeCamp officiated at the wedding ceremony. The cathedral was filled to overflowing with relatives and intimate friends of the families who were admitted only by engraved tickets, which were necessary to insure accommodations for one and all.' Hmmmm, fancy! 'The altar was banked with rare tropical plants of all descriptions and flowers of all hues and fragrance. A most unique contrivance was that of a gate of flowers placed about midway up the aisle, which, by an ingenious arrangement of silken cords drawn over the edge of the pews to the rear of the nave, was made to open and close when the bridal party passed to and from the altar. The bride . . .' "

"Enough! Enough!"

"But I haven't read the best part yet! 'The bride was attired in white satin and wore magnificent diamonds—a present from the groom—and her entire person was covered with her bridal veil.' "

"Stop!" Zakrzewska pleaded, but Gwladys was merciless.

" 'After the ceremony, the wedding party repaired in decorated carriages to "The Folly," the beautiful home of Mr. J. Hood Wright at . . .' "

"Enough! Please, no more! I am not so dumb as you think!" he accused. "I see what you are about!"

"But I've not finished yet!"

"I can't take no more!" he said. Then, his eyes affixed to the floor, his voice barely above a whisper, Zakrzewska told her what she wanted to hear, "When I am well . . . when I can work again, we will be married."

Gwladys beamed devilishly, then read on, " ' . . . to "The Folly," the beautiful home of Mr. J. Hood Wright at Fort Washington, where, extending in all directions were over five hundred illuminated Chinese lanterns of all shapes and sizes, which made one feel they were, indeed, in a land of enchantment.' "

* * *

"He'll be all right, won't he?" Rhys asked his mother anxiously as she left her bedroom. Two hours had passed since they'd brought his *dada* home.

"Here, fill this with hot," Myfanwy said curtly, handing Rhys an empty basin, then turned back inside.

"*Mam . . . ?*"

"What is it?"

*"He'll be all right then, won't he?"* His voice showed his nervousness and his fear.

She nodded, then closed the door behind her so Hugh couldn't hear. "I don't want the little one to know, you hear?"

"Yes, Mam."

"It wasn't a fall," she said bitterly. "He's too careful to let things like that catch him unawares. I knew as soon as I saw him it was them filthy hunkies did it."

"Just because of Sugar Notch?"

"There's more, he won't say what. It's a wonder they didn't kill him."

Hugh called out for her.

"Coming, *N'had*!" she called through the door.

"When can I see him?" Rhys asked.

"Hurry with the water then! And don't let on I told you," she said, but paused before going in to wipe the tears that rolled down Rhys's cheeks. "You're looking more like your father every day."

❖❖

"Wake up then," Rhys had to tell him. "Get up. It's time."

Euan moaned and stretched but didn't open his eyes.

"Come on, nipper. I'll go without you."

"Is it first whistle?"

"There's no whistle today," Rhys explained, rocking the boy back and forth, like a log. "It's payday. We've got to get *N'had*'s for him."

"So early?" Euan asked, rubbing his eyes.

"So early?" Myfanwy echoed downstairs a few minutes

later. "They'll not be opening till noon. You're going to stand there all morning?"

"The later we get there, the longer we got to wait," Rhys argued, even though he knew that wasn't true. He wanted to be near the head of the line to avoid the stares, the gibes he knew would come their way if they stood farther back.

"I've wrote a note then to Mr. Morganwyg, saying you're to collect your *dada*'s snake statement. Don't forget to take it."

As much as Rhys wanted to be near the front of the line, even he had to admit it was foolish to show up before seven o'clock. As it was, they arrived just past seven thirty and still had the pay window all to themselves.

It was a fog-shrouded morning, a Hudsonryder morning. The Glen Ellen was hidden from sight, hugged by pillows of thick, wet mist. All they could see was the deck on which they knelt, the wall of the pluck me store, the pay window, and forty feet of track. It was as if the rest of Jeddoh didn't exist.

"It's how I feel sometimes, living here," Rhys said. "We're cut off. There's a world around us we're not part of, a world we don't fit into. They don't want us in Cheesetown, and we don't belong on Polish Hill. People are afraid of outsiders, afraid of each other."

"Are you sure it isn't Sunday?" Euan asked. His taste for this kind of talk ran short.

"Sure, I'm sure."

"Where's everybody then?"

"They'll come. They want to get paid as much as us."

"We could hit the wall for a while. We never did in fog."

"And lose our place? I'm staying here. You can go if you want."

They stayed, and the line grew long behind them, but it was a different payday from the rest. Gone were the celebration, the feverish anticipation of money to be had, money to be spent. With summer coming, the colliery would be idle more often than not; the long ton was sure to get longer. A man couldn't even count on having a job come payday a month. His might be the next family to be evicted. The only relief many had to look forward to was inebriation come nightfall.

Rhys read their grim faces, saw their fear. These men looked cut off, too—from each other, from the world, from Markham's world which used them and discarded them like worn out parts of a machine, from hope.

"We're all the same," he thought. "We're all just outsiders stumbling through the fog."

The pay window finally opened a few minutes past noon.

"Two three eight . . . ," Rhys said, handing Morganwyg the note his *mam* had written. His mouth was leathery, his legs stiff from sitting cross-legged so long on the deck. ". . . and one ought five."

Morganwyg scowled, then scanned his list for the name. "Hugh Morgan, miner," he read. "Twenty-one days; ninety-three tons; less: dockage, sixty-one tons, at eighty-five cents a ton, fifty-one dollars eighty-five cents . . ."

"Wait a minute," Rhys interrupted, but Morganwyg read on, like a clock that wouldn't stop until its spring had wound down.

". . . setting of timber, two dollars eighty cents; total fifty-four dollars sixty-five cents. If you concur, signal by saying 'Aye.'

"A ton is ninety cents!" Rhys said sharply.

"Read the sign!"

"I don't see no sign!"

"Out front on the board, if you'd look." Morganwyg said. "Markham's only paying eighty-five cents now."

"On top of the long ton?" Rhys snapped. "Sounds like robbery to me!"

"Mind your tongue," the paymaster warned.

"Does that mean I can choose to pay one seventy-five for a pair of two dollar slippers if I like?"

"For your sass, you can step aside and wait till the rest go through. Step aside!"

"I waited for my turn. I waited all morning!"

"That's not my worry. Step aside!" Morganwyg insisted as two Coal and Irons came forward to enforce his words.

Rhys backed off, fuming. "It's not fair!" he huffed. "Every day it's something else! It's not fair!" Rhys could see Markham glaring at him behind Morganwyg's shoulder, but Rhys didn't care. He was glad Markham was there to hear him, glad to give Markham a piece of his mind. "It's not fair!"

"Next!" Morganwyg piped.

Euan froze at the window and stared at Rhys as though he were about to be swept off and beaten by the Coal and Irons, or worse.

"Next!"

"He's . . . he's with me!" Rhys sputtered.

"Then he can stand with you, too!" Morganwyg snapped. "You!" he said, glowering at Euan. "Clear the road. Next!"

Rhys yanked Euan back to the railing. He was so angry, his hands were trembling.

"Shall I go tell *Mam* then?" Euan asked.

"No!" Rhys growled through his clenched teeth, never once taking his eyes off Morganwyg. "We'll stay here, and we'll wait!"

The sun had long since burned through the fog. Like a cruel torch now, it arced through the sky. Men took off their jackets, rolled up their sleeves, and wiped their heads with sweat-drenched rags. A few pressed themselves into the ever-shrinking furrow of shade that sheltered the wall along the company store till it, too, disappeared, leaving them to scorch with the rest.

Rhys and Euan stayed at the railing. Euan brought them water, but Rhys refused to drink it. "I'll not let Morganwyg think I'm weak," he said to himself. "I can stand here all day if that's what it takes. That crapper won't get the best of me!" Only when Morganwyg retired for a moment did Rhys take the cup that Euan had left sitting on the railing. Only then did he take off his cap to wipe the sweat that soaked his brow.

Worse than the heat were the stares, the secret smiles

that hid behind righteous, squinty faces, smiles that enjoyed his ordeal. "Good! Morganwyg's put you in your place," they leered. "Serves ye right, ye mis'rable son of a scab!" "You t'ink you know it all, big boy! Now you see!" Their eyes seared worse than the sun; their hate was hotter.

"I'm hungry," Euan said softly. "Can't I go home and get some . . . ?"

"And what'll you tell *Mam* when she asks where the pay is?"

"I'll tell her . . ."

"No you won't! She's got enough worry as it is. Stay here."

It took more than three hours for all the men to pass in line, till all the men were paid. When the last went off, clutching his dollars, grateful he had only been docked for twenty tons, not thirty, like the rest, Rhys stepped forward and slid the note a second time beneath the metal bars.

"Two three eight," he said firmly, distinctly, "and one ought five."

"Two three eight!" the paymaster called over his shoulder. Rhys saw Markham lean forward and hand Morganwyg a separate ledger.

"Hugh Morgan, miner," Morganwyg read in his familiar drone, "twenty-one days; ninety-three tons; less: dockage, sixty-one tons, at eighty-five cents a ton, fifty-one dollars eighty-five cents; setting of timber, two dollars eighty cents; total, fifty-four dollars sixty-five cents. Less: rent, eight dollars; on credit, clothing and supplies, thirteen dollars forty cents; food, twenty-four dollars twenty-eight cents; powder and fuses, three dollars twenty-seven cents; medical, fifty cents; spiritual, fifty cents; and water, forty cents; total deduction, fifty dollars thirty-five cents. Indebtedness to company decreased by four dollars thirty cents."

"And one ought five?" Rhys asked.

"Rhys Morgan, driver. Twenty-two days, two hundred ten hours. Total, twenty-four dollars fourteen cents. If you concur, signal by saying 'Aye.' "

"Aye."

"Less: medical, fifty cents; spiritual, fifty cents; breakage to wagon, twelfth May, two dollars; sixteenth May, two dollars twenty-five cents, eighteenth May, one dollar; injuries inflicted on mule, twenty-sixth May, one dollar; reduction of debt to company by Hugh Morgan, sixteen dollars eighty-nine cents. Total deductions, twenty-four dollars fourteen cents. Total pay, nil. Next!"

"Wait then!" Rhys protested. "How could you be taking it all?"

"Are you next, lad?" Morganwyg asked Euan.

"Yes, sir," Euan answered. "Two ought seven."

"Mr. Morganwyg," Rhys continued, "I ask you how you could ... ?"

"Euan Morgan, slate picker," Morganwyg read on, ignoring Rhys's objections. "Eighteen days, one hundred eighty-one hours; total, nine dollars twenty-one cents. If you concur, signal by saying 'Aye.'"

"Aye."

"Less: spiritual, fifty cents; medical, fifty cents; dockage for discarded coal, eighty cents; reduction of debt owed to company by Hugh Morgan, seven dollars forty-one cents. Total deductions, nine dollars twenty-one cents. Total pay, nil."

"You can't do this!" Rhys shouted.

"Mr. Markham is tired of carrying scattergoods like you on his back!" Morganwyg said as he slid the snake statements across the ledge. "This is a coal company, not a charity." With that, he slammed the pay window shut.

Rhys scoured Frog Street looking for Razor. He felt light-headed from the heat and the sun, from his disgrace. It was simple enough—collect his *dada*'s snake statement and his pay—he could've done it in his sleep. He'd done it all right! He'd fixed things good this time! There'd be *no* pay this month. No pay.

Razor was his only hope now, the only one who could help him.

Rhys looked in the pluck me store, behind the Emerald, but there was no sign of Razor, nor was he with Blackie or

Pauli. Rhys even ventured into Maciejewski's yard, only to learn that Razor had just left. He finally found him walking up Frog Street. Razor had been everywhere looking for him.

"Did he give it to you?" Rhys asked.

Razor nodded. "But not so much. He say Gieryk owe us."

"Give me what's mine then."

Myfanwy was waiting at the door when they returned. Her twisting lock stood out from her scalp, like a gnarled finger. Rhys wanted to kick himself for not sending Euan back at noon to tell her what had happened.

"What took you?" she said, barely concealing her fury.

"The wagon was late," Rhys lied. "They didn't start till past two."

"And why didn't you send the little one to tell me?"

"I didn't want you to worry."

"All I did all afternoon was worry!"

"I'm sorry."

"And I saw some with their money long before. How was that then?"

"They took it all against the debt! Except for this!" he blurted and dropped the two dollars that Razor had given him, his share for playing at the funeral, into the tin. Euan looked at Rhys in astonishment. "A dollar from each of us," he told her.

"Well . . . that's not so good now," she said, staring at the tin.

"I didn't want to tell you. I didn't want *N'had* to know."

His *mam* never looked smaller to him, or more frail. "So, we'll pay off our debt to the store that much sooner," she said and reached into the almost-empty tin. She handed a dime to Rhys and a nickel to Euan.

Later, Euan ran his fingers across the glass candy case in the company store. All around him, boys and girls clamored to buy their favorite sweets.

"What are you getting?" Rhys asked.

"I don't know. It's all so dear," Euan answered, wishing he had some of the pennies he'd squandered last month. He finally settled on licorice.

"What did you get?" he asked Rhys as they headed home.

Rhys remained silent. He had no taste for sweets. Not today.

"What did you get then?"

"I bought something for *Mam*. Raspberry drops. They're her favorite."

❖❖

THE choir sang in Welsh that Sunday. Rhys never once took his eyes off Mary Markham. He hadn't talked to her since they'd met in the churchyard two weeks before, but he still thought about her and about signing her book, about what he'd write when he did. He worried that she'd given up on him, that she didn't care anymore whether he signed. But *he* still cared. ("Roses are red; violets are blue. When I see the sun shine, I think of you.") Still.

"That won't do at all," he thought. "She'd likely laugh at that. (I'd like to take a walk with you and hold your hand, too.) No, then she'd think I was being fresh. But why not? What's wrong with holding hands? (I'd like to hold you hand in mine and look into your eyes. Too.) I should have brought a pencil to write these down. These are getting fairly good then."

When the choir returned to their pews, Mary smiled at him, then glanced over her shoulder at regular intervals to see if he was staring back. He was.

("Roses are yellow, daisies are white. Your smile's so pretty...")

Rhys didn't hear Pastor Wheat's sermon.

("... bright ... sight ... bite ... might ... fight ...")

He was occupied with his own cascade of words, his need to give vent to the giddy feelings she loosed in him.

("... it makes my day go right ... it fills me with delight ... I'm floating like a kite!")

She was a mystery to him. Why above the others, and there were others in Jeddoh more handsome and less coarse than he, did she take a shine to him? Was it his looks she fancied, his smile? What about him singled him from the rest? If he could only figure out what she saw in him, maybe he could understand his feelings for her. He sighed. His mules seemed far less mysterious. He knew all about a mine and how it worked, but he knew very little about Mary Markham or himself. He knew how to use his mules to brake a trip while going down a slope so the wagons wouldn't overrun the lead team, but he didn't know any words to write in a girl's book. His verses were blather, he decided. He hated them and hated himself for thinking them up. He was only grateful he'd not written them to her, that she'd not read them, and he prayed by now she'd forgotten about asking him to sign.

After countless choruses of the last hymn, *"Cwm Rhondda,"* Pastor Wheat delivered the benediction, and the service came to an end.

"Wait for me outside," Rhys told Euan. "I want to talk to Pastor Wheat about coming to see *N'had*." What he really wanted was to talk to Mary without having Euan around, and Euan, who disliked church only slightly less than he did Pastor Wheat, was happy to oblige.

The pews emptied one by one. Rhys lingered in the aisle at the back of the line waiting to greet the pastor. Mary had left her family to hang up her choir robe in the hall closet outside the vestry. Rhys could see her, gabbing and laughing with her friends. "How is it I never see you outside of church?" he said to himself, repeating the words he'd carefully chosen as his opening. His hands were sweaty; his throat felt tight. It would be their first meeting by design, not chance.

The line inched forward.

"How is it I never see you outside of church?" he mumbled to himself.

The line dwindled. Every few seconds, Rhys looked anxiously over his shoulder, but Mary still dawdled with her friends. Pastor Wheat seemed less talkative than usual. "Talk it up, Pastor!" he wanted to say. "You usually talk up a storm! There's nobody on this earth talks more and says less than you! Once you get started, there's no stopping . . .''

"How come I only see you Sundays in church?" a voice behind him said. Rhys whirled around, startled. It was Mary.

"Uh . . . ,'' he said, groping. "Uh . . . I never . . . I never see you either.''

"My mother keeps me busy with chores and lessons and taking care of my little sisters.''

"Uh . . . and no time for yourself?''

"And no time for you is what you're meaning,'' she said coyly. "Why not join the choir? We're needing another tenor.''

"I have other musical pursuits,'' he boasted, regaining his confidence.

"Or Christian Endeavor.''

"I'm not a joiner.''

"*Bore da,*'' Pastor Wheat interrupted, extending his hand to Rhys. The rest of the line had passed through.

"*Bore da,* Pastor.''

"I hope your *dada* is mending.''

"He is, thank you,'' Rhys said, backing as politely as he could toward the doors.

"Tell him I shall come calling tomorrow morning.''

"I will, Pastor. Thank you, Pastor.''

"I was reminded of your *dada* as I was preparing my sermon last evening. One passage in particular . . .''

"Not now, Pastor. Please!'' Rhys moaned to himself.

"Did you enjoy our singing today, Pastor Wheat?'' Mary interrupted.

"Why yes, Mary! As always, child.''

"Thank you. Good morning then, Pastor,'' she said sweetly, at the same time nudging Rhys ahead to the safety of the vestibule.

"Good morning, Pastor!'' Rhys chimed cheerfully.

"That was close!'' Mary whispered, then smiled guiltily.

"I'll say! What a bag of wind he is!''

"We could have been here all day!'' she added, then

realized that that might not have been so bad after all. At least they would have been together.

"Have you even been to Crystal Pond?" Rhys blurted.

"Why, no. I've never been."

"It's nice there. You've never been?"

Mary shook her head no, delightfully anticipating the question that was next to come.

"Would you like to take a walk there with me? Next Saturday? It's so pretty. We could meet here, out front. At two o'clock."

Just then, Mrs. Markham appeared in the doorway, squinting as her eyes adjusted to the dimmer light. "Mary, come along! We're leaving now!"

"Just a moment!" Mary answered, trying to shield Rhys from her mother's sight. "I'd love to," she whispered to Rhys. "And I'll bring along my memory book for you to sign. Two o'clock then!"

"Two o'clock," Rhys murmured to himself as Mary ran off. ("At two o'clock I'll walk with you, to Crystal Pond . . . to see the view!")

Rhys was delirious.


"It was so pleasing to hear them sung as they were meant to be sung," Mrs. Markham said as she and Mary walked home in the company of Mrs. Jenkins and Mrs. Ethel Howell. "Don't you agree, Margaretta?"

"You're so right, Mrs. Markham. Soon we'll hear no Welsh at all."

"I think we're in need of a new piano, though. I shall have to speak to Mr. Markham about that first chance I get."

"In Caernarvon, we sang without a piano," Mrs. Ethel Howell said. "It sounded lovely."

"In Caernarvon, you didn't have Sal Lloyd to sing off-key," Mrs. Jenkins remarked.

Mrs. Markham agreed. "Can't someone speak to her? She is simply . . . she simply can't sing! Did you ever hear of a Welsh woman who couldn't sing?"

"She's from Ffestiniog," said Mrs. Ethel Howell. "What did you expect?"

"The Lord calls, and the willing listen," Mrs. Jenkins said, stopping in front of her house. "Good day, ladies."

"*Ta,* Margaretta."

"*Ta.*"

A few doors down, Mrs. Ethel Howell took her leave. "We'll see you at Ladies' Aid then, Mrs. Markham?"

"Yes, of course. Tuesday evening. Good day, Mrs. Howell."

"*Ta. Ta,* Mary."

"*Ta,*" Mary called absently. She had other matters on her mind.

Mrs. Markham and Mary continued on their way. "I saw your glances to that boy in church," Mrs. Markham said without fuss. "You are not to see or talk to him again. Do you hear? Ever! He's not the right sort."

And that was that.

◆◆

FROM the window of his office, Markham watched the men peg in and file past the sign. He had not wanted to raise the ton again, not this soon. If he had raised it higher last time, he would not have had to raise it to three thousand now. There were looks of anger on the men's faces—some even spat at the sign—but in the end they filed past it and pegged in without a word of protest. Not that he anticipated a rebellion, not after the evictions, not with the extra Coal and Iron Police he'd brought in to guard the pit head. No man was foolish enough to risk his house and job with such rash behavior. By now, they'd learned their lesson.

When the last had pegged in without incident, he turned to his Victrola and placed on it a new phonograph record, one Mrs. Markham had bought for him during her latest shopping tour to New York City. The song, "Woodsman, Spare That Tree," was a favorite of his.

*Woodsman, spare that tree; touch not a single bough.*
*In Youth it sheltered me, and I'll protect it now.*

*Woodsman, forbear thy stroke; cut not its earthbound ties.
Oh, spare that aged oak, now tow'ring to the skies.*

Markham saved, indeed savored, this moment every
morning as a means of clearing his mind for the day's
work. His underlings knew better than to interrupt this
ritual. One did not and knocked on his door.

"What do you want?" Markham called out angrily.

"You say 'come in'?" Zakrzewska asked, entering.

"No."

"I am sorry. I come back."

"Dammit, man! You're in! What do you want?"

Zakrzewska closed the door. "You did not notice?" he
asked, grinning. "I am walking! Bandages gone! I am
ready for work in mine again!"

"No," Markham said curtly.

"But I am fit as fiddle."

"I cannot send you down into the pits again. God only
knows what you'd do next."

"That was accident. Anybody have accident!"

"You don't understand, man! You are worth nothing to
me. I could get fifty qualified miners here at the snap of a
finger. Your 'offer' interested me, and our deal was suc-
cessfully carried out. I have no more need of you."

"So . . . I am out? Like that?"

"Ah, you *do* understand. I could send you down again
as a laborer . . ."

"No! No more laborer! I am miner!"

"Then go elsewhere. I'm sure you can find some
other . . ."

"No!" Zakrzewska repeated adamantly. "Now *you* listen to me, mister! You are not done so easy with me. What
is done can easy be undone."

"Meaning?"

"I could tell these men, who follow me around like
puppies, you send me down to spy on them."

"Go ahead, tell them," Markham scoffed. "They'd
shoot you on the spot."

"I could lead them 'gainst you," Zakrzewska threatened in desperation. "We form union with me as boss."

"Then I'd shoot you."

"I could tell them meeting on hill was your idea!"

"You could tell them anything you want!"

"And they would *believe* me!"

"You think so?" Markham said with a sly laugh. "If your brothers up on Polish Hill want to work for me, they will believe *me,* I assure you. This is a fierce world we live in. There are men out there, some of them good, decent men, who would do anything to survive. 'I could hire one half of the working class to kill the other half!' Jay Gould said that, and it's true! You think your idle threats scare me?"

"What does scare you, Markham? Do you have a gun here? Now? Then you better use it on me, 'cause in ten minutes I could ruin your stinkin' life. I know where kerosene is kept in breaker. One spark, one gunshot, and breaker go up like firecracker, take forty, fifty people with it!"

Markham shifted uncomfortably in his chair.

Zakrzewska continued slowly and deliberately. "Or maybe I walk out of here like you say, come back in month, or year, come back in middle of night when Markham and his family sleep quietly and set fire to beautiful red house. Ah, what a pity! What a pity that your babies—I watch from doctor's porch while they play in yard—that Mary and Helen and June and Anna and Rose—ah, little Rose, the prettiest of all, who look most like her mother but who still wet her bed—what a pity these lovely flowers never grow up to marry, have babies."

"You are a despicable animal," Markham shouted, rising from his chair.

"And you are scared, no?" Zakrzewska laughed. "You see? Our business is not yet over," he added and lifted the needle from the phonograph, which had been tracing endless, silent circles at the center of the disk. "That is very pretty song. I like that song. Very pretty."

Zakrzewska set the needle on the rim of the disk, then sat in the chair opposite Markham. "Maybe I tell you what I want. Then you think of what I am best to do for you, then we both be happy. That is all we hope for, is it not—to be happy?'' he asked, then leaned back in his chair and waved his hand in time with Markham's favorite song.

Zakrzewska burst into the schoolhouse just as the children were leaving at the end of the day.

"Teofil, what in heaven's name?" Gwladys gasped.

"Come with me! Come!" he shouted exuberantly. Gwladys had never seen him so excited.

"But why?"

"I say so! Hurry!" he said and started pulling her toward the door.

"It's all right, children! It's just a game!" she told her startled pupils, who had begun to fear for her life. She laughed and smiled all the way across the schoolyard as he led her brusquely by the arm. "What's the meaning of this?" she snarled when they reached the street. "Where are you taking me?"

"You will see!" was all he would say as he led her down to the boardinghouse, up the steps to the front hall, where John Jones Owen sat snoozing in his rocker, and slammed the flat of his hand atop the registration desk.

Owen awoke with a start.

"Mr. Owen, you are magistrate, are you not?" Zakrzewska asked.

"Why . . . why, yes!"

"Can you marry us? My Gwladys and me? Now?"

"What?" Gwladys gasped before muffling her surprise.

"Have you changed your mind?" Zakrzewska asked.

"No, but . . . but I didn't think it would be like this. I mean . . ."

"There is no better time. Marry us, Mr. Magistrate!"

"It'll cost you," Owen said drowsily. "Two dollars."

"Two dollars?" Zakrzewska asked, taken aback. "Do you have it?" he asked Gwladys. "My money is at doctor's house."

"Teofil, why don't we wait?" Gwladys suggested. "We

could invite our friends. I could . . . *we* could be dressed properly. It could be very nice."

"Like society wedding? Or maybe you change your mind."

"No . . . no," she stammered. "It's . . . it's just that . . ."

"If we don't wed now, then maybe I change my mind."

"Wait here," she said, exasperated, and hurried to her room for the two dollars.

The ceremony was memorable. Mrs. Owen, the inn-keeper's wife, served as a witness along with Mr. Rooney, a traveling salesman, who insisted on singing "Oh, Promise Me" as he escorted the bride-to-be from the parlor to the front desk, where the groom-to-be waited in his work clothes for her hand. All the while, gawking guests excused themselves, passing to and from their rooms.

Gwladys hardly heard a word that Owen read, hardly recognized the voice in her that said, "I do." When it came time to sign her name to the marriage certificate, her hand slipped, splattering ink across the clean white paper.

"This time, it will be better," Zakrzewska thought, remembering his first marriage a lifetime ago in Chicago. He became nostalgic for his children, his Ewa, the fleeting moments of happiness they once had known. "Ewa was prettier than Gwladys," he decided. "And more devoted, more respectful. She knew how to make me happy." He was suddenly sorry he had killed her.

Gwladys saw Zakrzewska's tears of remorse, assumed they were shed for her, and was touched. "He is crude, impulsive, childish, and cruel sometimes, but he can be sentimental, too," she thought. "I am going to have my hands full reforming him."

The rotund magistrate pronounced them man and wife, and the bride and groom kissed. The strangers that had gathered in the hallway applauded; the traveling salesman hummed Handel's "Wedding March."

After all the men had kissed Gwladys, some twice, and the two were left alone, she asked her new husband, "Teofil, where are we going to live? Here?"

He smiled and led her through the door to the porch, down the steps...

"Where are we going now?" she asked.

"You will see. You will see."

...past the school, the colliery, the store, past the Emerald House he led her, up to Polish Hill he led her, to the Gieryk house he led her.

"Here!" he said. "Here you will live!"

"You mean...this house? It's ours?"

"Yes! Ours!" he said and led her onto the porch and through the door.

"My God! A house! A house of our own!" she shouted. "Teofil how on earth? *How?*"

He didn't answer. Instead, he took her in his arms and kissed her, and afterwards they made love on the bare floor of their new parlor.

In the morning they were awakened by sunlight that streamed through the uncurtained windows.

"Don't go," he said as she scurried for her clothes.

"It's the last week of school. There's so much to do."

"I will bring your bags from boardinghouse."

"How can we live here? We've no furniture, no dishes! Nothing!"

"These we will get," he said confidently. Then, more delicately, "Now that you are my wife, Gwladys, is time to put together our money for new home. I have...little since I am new here, you see.

"Well, you don't expect I have any with what Markham pays me, do you?"

"But...don't you have—how you say it—nest egg?"

She laughed.

Later that night, she emptied her glass jar for him. It held a little over ten dollars, having recently been diminished by two. "There! Take it!" she said, laughing. "Buy us a bed and a chamber pot to stick under it!"

The sound of her laughter began to grate on his ears. "Have I married a silly woman?" he wondered. "I know! I *know* she have more! But where?"

As it was, his friends on Polish Hill provided most of

their household needs—dishes and knives, chairs, curtains, a rug, even a chamber pot. The carpenter came by one day and made them a table. Gwladys rode into Freeland and bought a bed. Hardly the canopied type in which she had fancied finishing out her days, it was functional nonetheless and only cost five dollars.

Hugh Morgan, venturing outside for the first time since his "accident," walked down Frog Street with Rhys and was startled to see Zakrzewska helping the driver of a delivery wagon carry a large mattress into the Gieryk house. Gwladys Protheroe held open the front door.

"They were married last week," Rhys told him.

"Married?" Hugh said, remembering Zakrzewska's tiresome references to his wife and children in Chicago. *"Married?"*

❖❖

EUAN was stumped. Lately Rhys had had a way of disappearing for hours on end, then showing up suddenly, acting as if he had never been gone at all. Euan was determined to find him, to get to the bottom of Rhys's mysterious behavior, but he'd searched Jeddoh without success. Frustrated, he sat in front of the company store.

"Sooner or later, he's got to pass by," Euan thought, prepared to wait until he did. He waited and waited, but hardly a soul passed. The only sign of life was a wedding celebration on Polish Hill, the music of which carried throughout the town. Finally he walked back home in disgust, stopping for a moment outside Maciejewski's yard to listen to the fiddle music.

"Bread of heaven, bread of heaven...," he found himself singing as he listened to one particular polka. "That's strange," he thought. It sounds just like *"Cwm Rhondda,"* the Welsh hymn that always ended Sunday church. He listened more closely. ("Bread of heaven, bread of heaven; feed me now and evermore!") The tune was the same; the words fit. It *was "Cwm Rhondda"*! "How would the hunkies be knowing our song?" he wondered and squinted at the fiddlers at the far end of the yard. To his utter amazement, Rhys was among them.

Seeing Rhys play fiddle in a polka band was a bigger shock to Euan than learning that his *dada* drank at the Emerald, bigger even than the news of Miss Protheroe's wedding. Was this where Rhys was sneaking off to all the time, to play music with the hunkies? But why? And why keep it from him? He resented Rhys's secrecy, being shut out of Rhys's life. Euan didn't like sharing his brother with others. Rhys belonged to *him*.

Without saying a word, Euan made his way through the crowd to the platform where the fiddlers stood and sat on the edge near Rhys. He wanted everyone to know he was Rhys's brother, that he was *with* him. Rhys didn't let on that he saw him, but Euan knew he did and understood; that was just their way.

After the song finished, the crowd called out to the head fiddler, the one named Razor, to "make vit' 'da funny business." Razor promised them that "Rhysie, the storyteller" had a new tale to tell, so the crowd hushed, and his brother came forward, but before he could say a word, everyone began to laugh, and then to applaud.

" 'Der vas carpenter vunce down Shamokin vay," Rhys began, amusing the crowd at once with his Slavic accent. "His name vas Stanley Gzyb, but ever'body call him 'Stashu.' Now Stashu, he vas good man, but he never *ever* go to church. Not vunce! An' not vunce in his whole life is Stashu sick. 'Den vun day, Stashu get pain in chest, an' Stashu's missus, she say, 'You lay down in bet, I call doctor.' So, doctor come, an' he listen to Stashu's heart, an' he say, 'Goot heart go "pitta-pat, pitta-pat," but yours, it go "ker-plunka, ker-plunka." ' An' Stashu's missus say, 'Can you save my man, doctor?' An' doctor say, '*Tak*, but 'da cure cost you t'ousant dollar.' 'T'ousant dollar?' Stashu shout," and Rhys rolled his eyes and clutched his head in horror, all to the delight of the crowd. Even Euan, in his amazement, couldn't help but laugh.

" '*Tak*,' say 'da doctor. 'I never make vun penny from you, 'cause you never get sick vun day in your whole life,

so now you make up for it. Pay me t'ousant dollar.' 'To
hell wit' you!' Stashu holler. 'I *die* 'fore I pay you t'ousant
dollar.' Sophie, go get 'da priest! He come gimme last
rites.' So, Stashu's missus bring 'da priest, an' priest
come, an' Stashu say, 'Fat'er, I gonna die! Sprinkle me
wit' holy water!' but 'da priest say, 'Sorry, Stashu. You
gotta pay 'da money first.' An' Stashu say, 'How much?'
An' priest tell him 'T'ousant dollar.' "

Once more, Rhys rolled his eyes, then clutched his
head, and the crowd, anticipating Stashu's anguished reply, chanted, "T'ousant dollar!" along with him. " 'Vhy I
gotta pay so much?' Stashu ask, an' priest say, 'I never
vunce see you in church in your whole life. You never
vunce put vun nickel in poor box. You vant last rites? Cost
you t'ousant dollar.' ' 'Da hell wit' you, too!' Stashu say.
'I rat'er die! But 'fore I go,' he tell 'da doctor, who is
stantin' next to priest, 'I vant you come 'round to 'da ot'er
site of my bet.' 'Vhy?' 'da doctor ask him. An' Stashu, he
look up at doctor and say, 'Our savior, Jesus Christ, he die
'tween two t'ieves. I t'ink I like to go same vay!' "

Everyone laughed, as they always did at the end of
Rhys's stories, only this time Euan saw tears in the eyes of
some. They applauded too and chanted, "Rhysie! Rhysie!"
over and over. Euan was puzzled by their odd behavior, by
the strange effect his story had.

"It was just a story," Euan told himself. "Nothing to
get weepy about. It was just a silly story."

After the fiddling ended, and Razor and his players took
a rest, Rhys settled beside Euan on the platform, carefully
choosing the words to explan what he wanted to say.

"These . . . these people up on the Hill," he began
somewhat uncertainly, "they . . . look different from us and
act different, but inside . . . inside they're the same. *Mam*
may not think so, and most of them don't either but . . .
but . . ." His thoughts trailed off inarticulately. "There's
*got* to be something better than this . . . this *hating* all the
time," he began again. "Let it be Markham we fight, not
each other. We got to start somewheres. We got to break

down the walls between us, is what I'm saying. Can you understand that?''

Euan nodded.

"I guess . . . I guess that's what I'm saying by being here,'' Rhys added.

Euan ate his first *kielbasa* that afternoon, and *kopytka* and *kapusta,* and *placki* and *knedle.*

"Hey, Rhysie! 'Dat your brot'er?'' Mrs. Angieski asked.

Rhys nodded.

"He look just like you.''

"Little Rhysie!'' laughed Mrs. Kudla as she spooned more *kapusta* onto Euan's plate. From that day on, he would be known on Polish Hill as "Little Rhysie.''

❖❖

JUNE brought green to the mountain town of Jeddoh. Trees, hedges, and patches of grass grew lush from May rains. Wildflowers defied the rocky soil.

June brought healing. Hugh grew stronger every day; his wounds mended. He spent much of his time out back in Myfanwy's vegetable garden, weeding and planting, but he longed to return to the colliery. One afternoon, he walked down to tell Ned the Splicer that he would soon be strong enough to come back to work.

"Good, I'm glad to hear it,'' Ned told him. "When you're ready, Hugh. Not before.''

June brought pain. Mary never kept her rendezvous with Rhys. All week long, he fretted about what to write in her book. He tried to compose verses of his own, with each one worse than the last. He asked Stubb McAndrew where he'd gotten the verses he'd written to Charlotte and the others.

"You got sisters, ain't you?'' Stubb reminded him. "Copy the good ones out of their old books. That's what I did.''

Rhys thanked Stubb, but his sisters were twenty miles and a train ride away. And then one day, while carrying the family Bible, which was heavy and filled with old clippings and mementos, upstairs to his *dada,* an old postcard dropped out and landed on the floor at Rhys's feet. He started to slip it back when something caught his eye. It wasn't the message scrawled on the back—"Arrived late. We're all tired. Scenery lovely."—which his Aunt Olwen had mailed after arriving safely in Ontario, or its tinted picture of the sun setting behind a summer lake, but the verse printed across the upper evening sky.

> *When twilight drops its curtain*
> *And pins it with a star,*
> *Remember me, my faithful friend,*
> *Ere you be near or far!*

"How pretty," he thought. "I bet Mary'd fancy this verse. If I change a word or two, it might do just fine."

It hardly mattered though; Mary wasn't there to meet him at two o'clock or quarter after or half past or quarter of. In Sunday church, she never once looked his way and scooted off with her friends before he could even get close enough to say hello. He walked home alone; he swore he would never talk to or look at another girl as long as he lived. That was it! He was done with them all! "Just forget her," he told himself. "Forget her! Forget her!" But the verse he'd tried so hard to find was locked in his memory now, and it wouldn't go away.

June was a time of singing and buying on tick.

The choir from the Presbyterian church traveled to Edwardsville for the *eisteddfod* at the Welsh Baptist, but they won no ribbons—not with Sal Lloyd singing off-key—but Mary Markham won a first prize for her solo recitation.

Gwladys and Zakrzewska rode into Freeland on the back of an ice wagon to buy themselves new clothes. Her old dresses were getting too shabby to mend, and he needed a suit. Unable to decide which pattern and color she preferred, Gwladys splurged and ordered three from the dressmaker—a high-waisted rose, a two-piece forest green, and a beige with blue trim—a trousseau that Mrs. Markham herself would have envied, or so Gwladys chose to believe.

"These dresses are in place of a honeymoon," she told herself. "He'll not take me anywhere, that's for sure. Not to Niagara, not to the sea-shore. Well, at least I'll look the part!" She bought a new hat, too, and a parasol to match her green ensemble.

Zakrzewska was fitted for a brown serge suit. He bought shoes, a silk bow tie, and a cotton shirt, then produced four dollars from his purse as down payment for the lot, and promised to pay the rest COD.

June brought change. Mrs. Owen Williams passed away. The funeral was large and filled the tiny church. Myfanwy didn't attend. She couldn't bring herself to face the churchwomen, whose husbands had cruelly spurned her Hugh. Later, she took wildflowers down to the cemetery and placed them on the grave.

Dick Morrissey drowned in Crystal Pond. He went diving off the rocks with Patsy and Dennis Riley, hit his head on a submerged log, and sank like a stone, never to be found. The cold water kept his body imprisoned at the bottom of the pond. The day after Dick died, Patsy showed up for work as though nothing had happened.

"Hain't he sorry 'bout his brother then?" Cyril Lloyd asked.

Jenkin shrugged. "I guess not."

After that, whenever the boys saw Patsy coming down the street, they asked him if Dick had floated up yet. Hitting the wall passed out of favor. Instead, the boys hiked out to Crystal Pond every chance they got to see if their cohort had finally risen from the murky depths, although those who'd been around awhile knew it would be late August at least before Crystal Pond relinquished its deadly grip on poor Dick.

It was a time of turning beds and turning soil, of airing-out rooms, of picking wildflowers or sitting in the warm sun for no reason. Three June babies arrived on Polish Hill. Razor and his boys played at four weddings.

June brought surprise. One day Euan picked a silver pocket watch from his chute. Except for a few scratches, it had survived the trip up from the pits and had somehow slid through the grinders unscathed.

"Keep it, pawn it! It's worth plenty!" Jenkin told him.

When Euan pried the watch open, a tiny photograph fell out—a girl in white, sitting in front of a church. He wound the stem. It ticked.

"Don't let Bryfogle see it, or he'll take it for his own!"

At quitting, Euan turned the watch over to Ned the Splicer, who told him that if no one claimed it by week's end, the watch would be his to keep. The next day, the owner came forward. Euan never learned his name or got a reward or even so much as a thank you, but Ned told him the owner cried when he got his watch back, because he was so happy. "That's a kind of reward," Euan comforted himself. "At least a kind of thank you."

"You're a dumb one!" Jenkin said. "You could've had it for your own!"

"But it wasn't mine."

"Think of all you could've bought with it! Now you've got nothin'!"

Euan *had* thought about that. He could have paid off some of the debt or bought a present for his *mam* or a year's worth of sweets and coffin nails. But the watch wasn't his to pawn. The money wasn't his to spend.

Two days later, a letter arrived in the mail from Gwen and Meb containing two train tickets to Wilkesbarre and an invitation to their *mam* and *dada* to come visit for a day.

As much as he wanted to see his daughters again, Hugh didn't relish a trip to the city. "I don't feel up to it yet," he told Myfanwy, knowing how disappointed she would be. "There's no stopping you, though. You take the train down with the boys. It'll do all of you good to get away."

"And who'll watch after you?"

"I can take care of myself for a day."

"No, no," she demurred. No matter how hard Hugh tried to convince her, she would not hear of going off and leaving her husband alone at home.

"Then let the boys go!" Hugh said finally, exasperated.

And that is how Rhys and Euan found themselves on a crowded platform at Jeddoh Station early one morning, waiting impatiently for the train that would take them to Wilkesbarre for a visit with their sisters.

❖

THE train roared in with its steamcocks open wide, spewing cinders and clouds of white smoke high into the air. Picnickers lined the platform, and couples holding hands. Little children waved American flags bigger than they were.

Hugh and Myfanwy were there to see the boys off. Myfanwy gave Rhys a quarter for each of them to spend. Behind her back, Hugh gave each a dime—money he'd saved from payday last. The boys looked handsome in their Sunday trousers and shirts.

The Markham family was there, too—the girls wearing matching cotton shifts and candy-striped ribbons in their hair, Mrs. Markham in a yellow silk dress and picture hat, trimmed with ostrich feathers and puffs of white tulle. Mr. Markham looked more dapper than usual in a beige suit and straw hat.

"All a-bo-ard!" the conductor called. "All a-bo-ard!"

"Put your return fares in your shoe then, so you won't lose them," Hugh warned Rhys as the crowd surged toward the steps between cars.

"It's not too late to come, *Mam*," Euan urged as he climbed up.

"The way I'm dressed? Go on!" she scoffed, wanting nothing more than to board the train with her family and never come back to this place.

Rhys and Mary boarded at opposite ends of the same car. Rhys couldn't help but notice and caught a trace of a smile as she looked his way.

"You got your money tucked safe then?" Hugh asked again when the boys appeared a moment later at the open window.

"Yes, *N'had*," Rhys assured him, patting his pants pocket. "Shall I say hello to Gwen and Meb for you then, *Mam*?"

Myfanwy nodded. She looked unhappy but smiled to hide it. "Tell them I said . . . tell them we miss them."

And then the whistle blew, and the train lurched forward.

"You be careful! Watch after him, Rhys!" Myfanwy called.

Euan waved both arms as the train pulled from the station. "Goodbye!" he shouted even though the belching steam and rumbling wheels drowned him out. "Good-bye! Good-bye!"

It was 9:06 in the morning. There wasn't a cloud in the sky. Already the temperature had soared to 86 degrees. This was Independence Day, 1900.

Wilkesbarre, Pennsylvania, was a bustling river city, full of railroad energy and coal-rich prosperity. Early settlers along the Susquehanna spotted outcrops of the shiny black mineral as far back as the early 1700s, but coal was worthless then, except to blacksmiths, who stoked it in their forced-draft forges. It took until 1808, when Judge Jesse Fell demonstrated how to kindle stone coal in a house grate, for the potential of coal to be realized. A new industry burgeoned overnight. Wilkesbarre's isolation, however, made shipment to markets in New York and Philadelphia impractical. The mountain roads were impassable just when the coal was needed most. Attempts to float it down the Susquehanna on flat-bottom boats to Columbia and Baltimore for off-loading to other destinations were subject to the whims of nature. The river was low in summer, ice-bound in winter. By 1828, the North Branch Canal, which ran along the river, enabled coal to be shipped year-round, but the rise of railroading made river traffic obsolete. A fast and direct route to tidewater was carved across the mountains on gleaming iron rails. New markets for coal flourished and thrived. Wilkesbarre became the capital of an empire.

Gwen and Meb were waiting at the red brick station when the train from Jeddoh pulled in. Euan spied them first and waved his cap.

"Look, he's grown so!" Meb said as Euan jumped down onto the platform. "Hasn't he, sis? Pretty soon he'll be as big as Rhys."

"Did you have a good trip then?" Meb asked, hugging him.

"Yes," Euan said and squirmed away before she could give him a kiss.

"How's *N'had* then?" Gwen asked.

"He's good. He's back at work now. *Mam* sent these," Euan said handing over a basket full of biscuits and bread. "They're tasty. I had some."

"And how is *Mam*?" Gwen asked, trying to hide her ambivalence.

"She's good, I guess. She says to give . . . no, to say hello and to tell you she misses you."

"We miss her, too," Meb said.

"Rhys? Come on, let's see you!" Gwen said to her brother, who was busy watching Mary and her family climb into an ornate carriage and drive off.

"The Markhams," Rhys said sullenly, nodding in their direction. He resisted the urge to wave as Mary passed.

"I thought so," Gwen answered, eyeing Mrs. Markham's fine dress.

"Where's our carriage then?" Rhys said, brightening.

"We gave the help the day off," Meb replied with mock snootiness and took his arm and led him down the street. "We'll just have to walk!" Gwen and Euan brought up the rear.

"What are we going to do today?" Euan asked.

"See the parade first," Gwen said, "hear the speeches, have a picnic, and there's fireworks tonight."

"Do we have to listen to speeches?"

"Only one," Gwen said with a laugh. "Mother Jones is speaking on the steps of the courthouse at one o'clock."

"Who's she?"

"She's staying at Mrs. Archer's," Meb said. "She's part of the union."

"She's such a sweet old lady," Gwen added.

"We didn't come all this way to hear some old fogey," Rhys moaned.

"Just for a short while," Gwen assured him. "Besides, we promised . . ."

* * *

Every Fourth of July, half the population of Wilkesbarre turned out to watch the other half march in the annual parade, a parade that was less a celebration of independence than it was a glorification of the city's prosperity. The march began at the north end of River Street, where the foundation of the new courthouse was being dug. It proceeded down River Street, past the Music Hall and the new iron bridge that crossed over the Susquehanna to the town of Kingston, past the imposing Coal Exchange Building, the elegant Wyoming Valley Hotel, past "Coal Baron's Row"—the mansions of Andrew Todd McClintock, Fred Kirby, A. A. Sterling, Stanley Woodward, Philo Packard, William L. Conyngham, and other members of the famed Cheese and Crackers Club, Wilkesbarre's leaders of business and social life.

The parade turned left at South Street and left again onto South Main for the final stretch to Public Square. Every store on South Main was decked with red, white, and blue bunting. Every window was crowded with flag-waving spectators, who cheered and tossed confetti onto the marchers below. Vendors snaked their way through the mob, selling balloons, flags, hot dogs, and ice. Children sat along the curbs. It was hot. At noon, the thermometer outside Frank Clark's Jewelry Store read ninety-five degrees.

There were twelve brass bands in the parade, dignitaries in motorcars, and men walking on stilts. The 109th Artillery was there. Fire Company No. 1 brought its new horse-drawn pump. The Knights of the Irem Temple marched, and the American Order of True Ivorites. Behind them marched the Ancient Order of Hibernians, the Ladies Club of Queen Dabrowska, and the Branch of Saint Kinga of the Polish Alma Mater. Even Sheriff Frostbutter marched.

Winnie Davis, another boarder at Mrs. Archer's, had saved the Morgans a spot along the curb on the shady side of South Main, across from the Boston Store. Gwen bought chunks of ice for each of them from a vendor. Rhys held his above his head and let it drip down his forehead.

The girls rubbed their cold fingers across their faces. Euan was too excited to notice the heat.

Near the end of the parade, between the Society of the Virgins of the Holy Rosary and the Alexander's 9th Infantry Regiment Band, came the United Mine Workers.

"There she is! There's Mother!" Meb cried.

Euan turned, expecting to see his *mam,* come down to Wilkesbarre after all. Instead, he saw an old lady with white hair, smiling and waving to the crowd. A phalanx of men surrounded her, towered over her, almost seemed oblivious to her passing in their midst—they in their straw hats, bow ties, and rolled-up sleeves, fanning themselves with folded newspapers—she in a black dress, trimmed with white lace and buttoned to the neck, and a matronly black empire hat.

"Hello, Mother! God bless you, Mother!" voices around them shouted.

"Hot enough for you, *Maithir*?"

"*Matka! Matka!*"

"Hello, Mother! Over here!" Gwen called, and the old woman nodded in their direction. Her face was round and cheery, her smile, beatific.

"She wasn't supposed to speak at all today," Meb told the boys. "They didn't want her to rile up the people with union talk. Isn't that silly—a harmless old woman like her?"

"Are these your brothers?" a voice behind them suddenly asked. "Or are you romancin' behind my back?"

"Oh, you!" Gwen exclaimed as a straw-hat dandy knelt and put his arms around her. "Rhys, Euan, this is my . . . my *friend* Richard Goldberg."

"Your 'friend'? Did you hear her, Duckie?" Richard asked his sidekick, a beanpole, who wore suspenders to hold up his pants and elastic bands to hold up his sleeves. "Last week, she was beggin' me to marry her, now I'm just her 'friend'!"

"Stop it, Richard!" Gwen said, blushing. "They'll believe you!" Then, turning to the boys, "Don't listen to him. He's just a . . . a talker, he is!"

"A talker! You pegged him right!" Rhys said to himself, taking an immediate dislike to the dashing intruder. Everything about Richard, from his bone-white pants and shoes to his blue striped shirt and jauntily tipped hat, rubbed Rhys the wrong way.

"You're the clerk at the five-and-dime?" Rhys asked.

"I'm the assistant manager now," Richard replied, as though Rhys should have known. "Assistant to Mr. Gaylord Steere."

"And this is Duckie Walsh," Meb added, twining her arm with his. "He's a conductor on the trolley."

"Pleased to meet you," Duckie said, smiling.

"Same here," Rhys grinned back. At least Duckie's smile seemed genuine. "Can't you say hello?" Rhys said, nudging Euan.

"Hello," Euan said.

"We're off to hear Mother Jones speak," Gwen told them.

"That old windbag!" Richard jeered. "We wanted to take you rowing.

"And you shall," Gwen said. "As soon as we've heard Mother Jones."

"Mr. Steere says she's an anarchist," Richard said smugly. "He says she's trying to overthrow the government."

"How can you say that?" Meb exclaimed, shocked at Richard's accusation.

"And how does he know?" Gwen said with more than a little irritation in her voice.

"He knows. They say she started a riot down in Maryland, earlier this year, in Lonaconing. She's been chased out of every town in West Virginia . . ."

("Chased out? Chased out of every town?" Euan asked himself, trying to remember where he'd heard those words before.)

". . . and she's been in jail more times than you can shake a stick!"

("Me *da* says he heard yer folks was chased outta the last town ye lived in . . . chased out chased out . . .")

"Mr. Steere says she's nothing but a professional gadfly," the assistant manager continued. "He says somebody ought to . . ."

"I don't care!" Gwen said flatly. "I promised her we'd be there, and a promise is a promise."

"I promised, too," Meb chimed.

"The way you're going on, Dick, you've got me wanting to hear her now," Duckie confessed.

Even Euan's curiosity was piqued. He wondered if this Mother Jones was a scab, too.

The Luzerne County Courthouse sat in the middle of Public Square, like the palace of a gingerbread kingdom. Rising six stories to the full height of its ornate clock tower, it was a landmark in that part of the state, but in a city busy with the future, the old courthouse remained a vestige of the past. It simply got in everyone's way. As soon as the new courthouse was in place, the gingerbread palace would be torn down.

Today, it reflected its former glory. A huge American flag hung like a starched sail across its granite portals. Smaller flags perched on every windowsill, and a bunting-draped dais covered its front steps. Today, thousands crowded its lawn and spilled into the street. Thousands had come to hear the speeches, just as they had come in years past. Today wasn't 1900. Today was 1888. It was 1872. It was 1856, when the old courthouse was new, having just replaced the first courthouse that had stood on the west side of Public Square since anyone could remember. Today was a reprieve. Today, the old courthouse would stand forever, or seemed like it would just as everyone crowding around it would live forever. Or thought he would.

With Richard and Duckie clearing a path, the small band made its way to a spot beneath a remarkable old beech on the edge of the square. Here, Duckie lifted Euan onto a limb so he could see over the heads of the crowd, and Rhys climbed up beside him.

At the stroke of one, the Reverend Dr. Royal Joy stood and delivered an invocation. Miss Tryphena Graves sang the national anthem, followed by the introduction of the dignitaries on the dais by Dudley W. Dawes, the president of the Wilkesbarre Board of Commerce and chairman of today's event, who asked the speakers to keep their remarks as short as possible, owing to the heat.

"Amen!" cried a voice, and a wave of appreciative laughter swept across the crowd. "Amen, brother!"

"If they're so hot, why don't they go home and sit in the shade?" Euan wondered. It seemed liked the sensible thing to do, but the Independence Day speeches were special. They were important. People came to listen, to be reminded of their country's struggle for freedom. It was their duty, heat or no heat, so they stood, thousands strong, fanning their faces and shielding their eyes from the sun's furnace.

"Amen, brother!"

The principal speaker of the afternoon was to be Philo Packard, a local merchant who had gained national prominence the year before by memorizing the Declaration of Independence and reciting it on the lawn of the White House for President McKinley. In the interim, he had begun to memorize the Constitution of the United States but today he would confine his speech and recitation to the former in his remarks entitled, "Our Forefathers and the Glorious Gift of Freedom."

"I know you're all anxious to hear Mr. Packard," Dawes said "but first we shall have some brief words from Mrs. Mary Jones, who is representing the United Mine Workers during her visit to our fair city. Without further ado, it gives me great pleasure to present you a great . . . a great . . ." Dawes paused, unsure of just what it was that made Mrs. Jones great. "A great humanitarian!—Mother Jo . . . !"

"Get it right!" the tiny lady interjected. "I'm not a humanitarian! I'm a hell-raiser!"

"Mother Jones!" he announced, blushing. The crowd roared its approval as she rose from her seat and walked to the center of the dais.

"I want to thank you, Mr. Dawes," Mother continued good-naturedly, "for having the good sense to invite me here today after trying so hard to keep me away. When I announced I'd be here, he sent a note telling me this gathering was not a union rally and would I please stay away? Well, I wrote right back and asked if there'd be working men and women in the crowd today. 'Of course,' he said. 'Then I'll be there,' I said, ' 'cause I'm a working woman, and the workers of America will not be stopped by you or anyone else! The workers of America are going forward!' '' she exclaimed amid joyful laughter and applause, then raised both her arms to the sky in an expansive gesture of strength and pride. She had won over the crowd already.

"I'm going to pass this hat around for the miners in the throng who are broke and need a glass of beer, or who can't pay their way home," Mother then said. "See that you all put something in, 'cause God is watching. You, too, Mr. Dawes. He's watching you *extra* close," Mother added sternly, extended the hat to Mr. Dawes, and waited till he contributed a dollar bill, then passed it along to the dignitary next to him.

"How many out there are miners or work in the mines or have menfolk or children who do?" Mother asked next. Nearly everyone in the crowd raised his hand, including the Morgans. "And how many belong to the union?" This time, only a smattering went up. "There you have it!" she growled with disgust.

"This may be Independence Day, brothers and sisters of anthracite, but you are not free! I spent the last two weeks traveling through your towns and mine patches. Over and over, I saw miners living lives of slavery worse than many Negro slaves did before the Civil War."

Richard scoffed. "She's talking through her hat!"

"Shhh!" Gwen cautioned.

"If the slave was ill, his master cured him," Mother tore on. "If he was hungry, he was fed. When he was naked, he was clothed. Who does this for the American miner today? Certainly not the railroads which own most of the mines *and* the miners, I might add, body and soul! Not the independents, like George Glasscock, Alonzo

McCandless, and John Markham, men who go to church on Sunday and pray to Lord Jesus to give them their daily bread, then ask Him if He'll fix it so's they can get three or four other fellows' daily bread, too!''

"You tell them, Mother!" a voice called from the crowd.

"Glory be to God, Mother! Ain't it the truth?"

"My lifework has been to try to educate the worker to the series of wrongs he has had to suffer—and still does—and to stir up the oppressed to the point of getting off their knees and demanding that which is rightfully theirs. You cannot expect the goddamned railroads to give you a better life, or Alonzo McCandless, or John Markham, or George Glasscock, whom for modesty's sake we shall call 'Crystal Peter'. . . ''

The crowd hooted and howled with laughter.

"What's 'aprest?' '' Euan asked.

"Hush!" Gwen said. "I'll tell you later."

". . . you cannot expect those sons of bitches to give you a better life, for that shall mean they will have less caviar and bonbons for them and their fat wives, and their poodle dogs might have to sleep on the hard floor instead of embroidered pillows! I wish I was God Almighty! I would throw down something some night from heaven and get rid of the whole bloodsucking bunch!"

The intensity of her voice became something the crowd could almost feel physically. Although she stood less than five feet tall, her voice commanded the huge throng, sometimes not seeming to rise above a resonant whisper, while at other times, booming with unexpected power.

Her gestures were just as bold, just as impassioned. Her hands sliced the air like swords or waved like cudgels. Just as quickly, they could twirl and mince with savage mockery.

To Euan, she looked and sounded like Pastor Wheat on a Sunday tirade.

"I see your Sheriff Frostbutter over there, lurking behind that tree," she continued, changing her tone from her previous harangue. "Hello, Sheriff! Working hard? I first met your fine sheriff a week ago. I was up on Rolling Mill

Hill talking union to a bunch of miners—wonderful boys! —and along came Sheriff Frostbutter, asking me if I had a permit for street-speaking. I told him, 'Of course I do!' He said, 'Oh? And who gave it to you?' I said, 'Patrick Henry, Thomas Jefferson, and John Adams!' '' She paused, hands on hips, for the people to laugh. ''He didn't know what the hell to say after that.

''But the story of coal is always the same, and it is a dark story. For the privilege of seeing their children's eyes by the light of the sun, fathers must fight like beasts in the jungle. That life may have something of decency—a tinted picture; a new dress; a bit of cheap lace, fluttering in the front window. For this, men who work in the mines must struggle and lose, struggle and lose, struggle and win. . . .''

''I've had enough of this gabble! Are we going rowing or not?'' Richard asked but Gwen demurred. ''Well, if you don't want to go, Duckie and me'll go ourselves. Right, Duck? We'll meet you later at Finch's boathouse.''

''All right,'' Gwen conceded. ''Come on, everybody.''

''Do they have to?'' Richard said as the boys leaped down from the tree. His expression gave her no choice.

''Rhys . . . ?'' Gwen asked hesitantly. ''I know you came down special to see us, but I bet there's lot's you'd like to do on your own that we'd only put a damper on. And, well, we only get to see our fellas on Sundays and days like this. I mean, could we . . . ? You know what I mean.''

''I guess so,'' he said, disappointed at being left behind.

''At four o'clock then! We'll meet right here! Under this same tree,'' she said and whisked off with Meb to catch up to Richard and Duckie.

''What are we going to do now?'' Euan asked.

''I don't know,'' Rhys answered sourly. ''Dickie and Duckie!''

''Do we have to stay and listen to her?'' But Rhys didn't answer. When Euan looked up, Rhys was staring off and smiling at someone in the crowd.

It was Mary Markham.

''What a surprise!'' she said, her face aglow after Rhys

had elbowed his way across thirty feet of spectators to reach her side.

"What are you doing here?" he asked.

"We've come to hear the notorious Mother Jones."

"Us, too."

"We just got here," Mary explained.

"Rhys! Come on! Let's go!" Euan moaned as he caught up.

"You're not leaving so soon?" Mary asked.

"No, no!" Rhys lied.

"Father would die if he knew we were here," Mary added mischievously. "We sneaked away from our picnic. It was terribly dull."

Mary's companion cleared her throat. Rhys remembered seeing her in the carriage earlier with Mary.

"Oh, excuse me," Mary said. "This is my cousin Blodwen Shovlin. Her father's a banker in Wilkesbarre." Slightly older than Mary, Blodwen wore a frown as her permanent expression.

"How do you do? I'm Rhys."

Blodwen smiled cursorily or, rather, her frown became less pronounced.

"Rhys!" Euan moaned again and got an elbow in the ribs as a warning to keep still.

"I missed you last Saturday in front of the church," Rhys said matter-of-factly, trying to conceal the disappointment that had haunted him since.

"I, too," Mary replied, carefully choosing her words. "I wanted so to join you, but my mother . . . my mother had other plans for me."

"I see," he said, grateful that she hadn't simply forgotten, delighted that she seemed to share his regret. "It was a beautiful day, too."

"I remember."

"Maybe we could . . . maybe next Saturday?"

"I'm afraid not. You see, mother . . ."

"Then why not now? Today? Right now?"

"Now?" she asked, amazed at the audacity of his solution, and its simplicity.

Rhys nodded.

"Why not then?" she said. "Yes, why not? We could walk to the River Commons. The gardens are so pretty there. Yes! Why not!"

Euan wondered what was going on. He had noticed Rhys's glances toward Mary Markham in church, but he didn't think they spoke or met behind his back or held hands, as they were doing now on Market Street for all the world to see, all the world except Mary's cousin, who scowled anyway. Each time she craned her neck to confirm her worst suspicions, their hands parted, only to couple again as soon as her snooty gaze had turned away. Euan would have found it amusing if he weren't so chagrined himself.

They walked toward the river, Rhys, then Mary in between, then Blodwen. Euan tagged behind, sulking, feeling ignored, betrayed even. "Why would Rhys want to spend his time with her?" he wondered. "She's just a silly girl, and a Markham girl to boot." He was beginning to wish he'd stayed in Jeddoh.

On the Wilkesbarre side of the river, a wide, grassy lawn sloped gently from the street to the water's edge. Here, they wandered on tree-shaded paths that crisscrossed among beds of geraniums and elephant ears, rhododendron and silverlace, among urns filled with pansies, through a sea of roses to the Palm Conservatory, where tropical plants sunned themselves beneath a veil of glass.

"So many flowers!" Rhys gasped in astonishment. "I've never seen the likes of it! Look, Euan, aren't they grand?" Euan couldn't have cared less.

Suddenly Mary looked faint and faltered against a bough.

"What is it?" Rhys asked.

"Are you all right, cousin?" Blodwen chirped excitedly.

"Yes, I'm . . . I'm . . . it's this infernal heat!"

"Let me loosen your buttons," Blodwen offered and undid several at the top of Mary's blouse. "Is that better?"

"Not really," she said with a sigh, then fell back into Rhys's arms.

"Perhaps I should run and fetch the carriage?" Blodwen suggested.

"I could run faster," Rhys offered. "Or Euan!"

"But you . . . you don't know the way to Aunt Jane's," Mary replied weakly. "Blodwen you go."

"But . . . but who . . . who'll stay with you?" Blodwen stammered.

"I'll be happy to," Rhys volunteered.

"Yes, Blod! Go on!" Mary urged. "And take your time! I wouldn't want you to be overcome in this heat, too."

Blodwen's mouth tightened with anger. She started to protest, thought better of it, then turned to leave. "I shall be back sooner than you think," she said sternly and padded off, still scowling, leaving Rhys and Mary in a fit of laughter.

Euan wondered what was going on. One minute this Markham girl, this hand-holder, was dizzy with the heat, the next she and Rhys were giggling like two silly sisters. Then their eyes, imploring, fell on him, and finally even he understood. He was next to go. "Four o'clock?" he asked.

"Four o'clock," Rhys answered, smiling. "Here's a dime for you then. Just think, you'll be on your own in the big city."

Euan roamed back through the streets of town, looking in store windows at mannequins in straw hats and thought that one day he'd like to have a straw hat. He passed the Poli Theater where Modjeska, the Polish actress, was playing in *The Peasant Aristocrats of Anzyc,* alternating one night as Kogycina and the next as Queen Jadwiga. Except for the Christmas pageant in church, he had never seen a drama before, and thought that one day he probably would but that it would have to have knights in it, or soldiers. There was vaudeville, whatever that was, at the Music Hall and boxing at the Savoy. He was awed by the automobiles, the noise, the people, running here, crossing there—"Watch out for that trolley, boy!"—"Give! Give to the Salvation Army!''—''Would you like to buy a rubber monkey on a stick?''

He ended up back on Public Square, where Mother Jones, in defiance of the heat and Dudley Dawes's icy stares, still held the crowd under her spell.

He lay on the grass beneath a secluded bower, tapping a pencil against his brow, staring off through motionless leaves at motionless sky. Mary lay next to him on the shirt he had gallantly removed and spread across the grass in order to keep her dress from getting soiled.

''It's odd,'' she said, brushing his chest with a sprig of juniper. ''We had to come all this way just to be together.''

''Quiet! I'm thinking!'' he said with great seriousness. ''I'm trying to remember.'' He thought for a moment before the words re-formed in his head, then scrawled them quickly in her memory book, which she had carried to Wilkesbarre for Blodwen to sign. ''There!'' he said proudly, admiring his verse.

''Let me see!''

''No, it's not done yet. There's more.''

''Well, hurry! I want to read it!''

''Oh, no! You've got to promise you won't. Not till...till later!''

''But why?''

''You can't, that's all,'' he said firmly. ''It's bad luck.''

''It is not!''

''It is, too! And if you keep hounding me, I'll never remember what I wanted to write.''

''I'll be quiet then.''

''Good.''

She lay back and listened to the buzzing of the heat bug. The heat bug only sounded on the hottest days, she wanted to tell him. Today was the first she'd heard it all summer, she wanted to tell him. She wanted him to know her heart was fluttering, that she was bursting to read what his bashfulness would not let her see, that she had never been happier than she was right now. This day was now perfect, she wanted to tell him.

"You can kiss me if you like," she said.

"Isn't it supposed to be the fella who asks the girl?" he wondered. He pretended he didn't hear her.

"I thought about you all week," she said. "I felt terrible, not seeing you on Saturday. After I promised. I thought you'd hate me. I thought you'd never speak to me again. And then I saw you at the train station . . ."

"I couldn't hate you."

"I thought about you all the way to Wilkesbarre," she said. "I wanted to sit beside you on the train and hold your hand. I wanted you to kiss me."

"I thought about you the whole way, too."

"Go ahead. You can kiss me now. I want you to," she insisted.

He wanted to kiss her, too, but he didn't know how. "Kissing's silly if you really think about it," he announced instead. "What's so special about two people rubbing their lips together?"

"Have you ever kissed a girl?"

"No. Have you? Ever kissed a boy, I mean."

She smiled. "Only my father."

"I've only kissed my mother. And my sisters."

"This will be different," she said. "Go ahead, I'm waiting," she said and closed her eyes.

Rhys lifted himself to his elbow, looked down at her perfect face, and leaned in to rub his lips against hers but stopped and fell back laughing on the grass. "I can't!" he said giddily.

"Why?" she asked, perplexed.

"I don't think I could ever kiss somebody who kissed John Markham," he said and laughed his throaty laugh.

"That's not nice at all!"

"I'm . . . sorry!" he gasped, unable to stop laughing. "I'm sorry!"

He charmed her; he crumbled her with smiles; he seduced without guile. Her resistance flown, she threw her arms across his shoulders and kissed him, and kissed him again, until he ceased his heaving laughter and surrendered to this new sensation, to this kissing, and then to tickling and the roaming of hands across bare flesh, to caressing, to the exultation of touch.

Euan bought a slice of watermelon for a penny and found a place to sit under a tree near the speaker's platform. Each time he collected a mouthful of seeds, he spit them one by one onto the grass.

". . . the parish priest told the men to go back and obey their masters," Mother Jones told the crowd, "and their reward would be in heaven. 'Boys,' I said, 'this strike is called so that you and your wives and little ones might have a bit of happiness *before* you die!'" Suddenly Mother stopped and scanned the crowd with a puzzled look on her face. "What the hell is that noise? Is somebody spitting seeds or something?"

"Here! Here!" those around Euan said, pointing to him.

"What's the matter, boy? Didn't your mother tell you it was impolite to spit out seeds? And, yes, I will have a bite, if you don't mind."

A moment passed before Euan realized that everyone was looking at him, that she was talking to him.

"Well? Are you coming up, or do I have to come down and help myself?"

Euan was nudged to his feet by people around him, and a path opened up before him in the crowd. At the dais, he raised up the half-eaten slice, and Mother broke off a generous piece.

"Mmmm, that's good," she said, savoring its cool succulence, then spit the seeds off to the side of the crowd. "Whoever said you had to be polite all the time was a damn fool!"

The crowd laughed. Even Euan laughed at her antics.

"What's your name, boy?"

"Euan Morgan."

"You work in the breaker?"

He nodded.

"Well, sit up by me, Euan Morgan, because I'm going to talk about you and all the other children out there who are living their lives as slaves to industrial profit."

"Mrs. Jones!" Dudley Dawes interrupted. "You really must conclude your talk. Mr. Packard has been waiting to give his speech for over an hour now!"

"And these people have been waiting all their lives for a simple breath of truth. Would you deny them that, Mr. Dawes?"

"Well . . . no. But Mr. Packard has been . . . ," Dawes said, quite flustered, before he was drowned out by a chorus of boos from the crowd.

"Let her speak, Dawes!"

"Speak, Mother! You're the one we came to hear!"

"Go on, Mother! Go on!"

"Sit down, Dawes! Let her speak!"

Dawes sat down, and Euan raised himself to the dais and sat at Mother's feet. Mr. Packard looked at his watch for the hundredth time. Mother looked out over the crowd. Her face grew grim, and as she spoke, her voice rose with indignation. "Forty years ago, there was a cry against slavery, and men gave up their lives to stop the selling of black children on the block. Today, the white child is sold for two dollars a week to the coal operators! Forty years ago, the black babies were sold COD. Today, the white baby is sold on the installment plan!

"And who in government cares? In Georgia, where children work day and night in the cotton mills, they have just passed a bill to protect songbirds. What about the little children from whom all song is gone? I saw the Congress of the United States—you know who I mean, the do-nothings who wear starched collars to keep their befuddled brains from oozing out of their mouths—in one hour I saw Congress pass three bills for relief of the railroads, but when labor cries for aid for children, Congress turns its back. I asked a man in prison once how he happened to be there. He said he'd stolen a pair of shoes. 'If you'd stolen a railroad,' I told him, 'you could have been a United States Senator!'

"Has anyone ever told you, my children, about the lives you are living here so that you may understand how it is you pass your days on earth? Let us consider this together, for I am one of you, and I know what it is to suffer. They take your young bodies, these men who own the mines, they take your strong backs and arms and legs—they wear you down so you're old before your time. They steal your youth, your strength—they steal your body—and use it to make their fortunes, and when they give it back, it ain't fit to live in! You should be in schools, my children, not breakers, learning to use the minds God gave you to raise yourselves up and give yourselves better, fuller lives. You are oppressed, my children, and you don't even know it!

"And why? Because child labor is cheap! Child labor is docile! Child labor does not strike!

"And who is responsible for this appalling slavery? *You!*" she shouted and swept her hand across the crowd. "Because *you* let it happen! Because you tell yourselves that you need the money these babies bring in! If you'd stand up for the wages that you deserve, you could all live more fruitful lives, and these children would not have their limbs and lives maimed and wasted!"

Mother wove a powerful spell that day. The crowd was stunned, shamed into silence by her words. She paused to let their full impact take effect before she resumed her diatribe. When she did, her voice crackled with anger as she recounted the horrors she had seen.

"I have gotten up at four thirty in the morning and gone with babies to the factories. They began work at five thirty and quit at seven at night. Children six years old going home to lie on a straw pallet till it was time to resume work the next morning! I have seen the hair torn out of their little heads by the machinery, their scalps torn off, yet not one single tear was shed, while the owners poodle dogs were loved and caressed and carried to the seashore. And you mothers and fathers stand idly by and endorse this thing. If it were you going to suffer, I would say, 'Let it be so,' but it is for your children and your children's children that I do this—that I fight your battles for you!"

Just then a wild-eyed man lunged forward through the crowd to the foot of the platform. "You all! You don't be tellin' me now," he said with great emotion, "this here's

Mother Jones! This is Jesus Christ come down to earth again an' playin' he's an old woman so's he can come here an' talk to us poor devils! God! God!—nobody else knows what the poor suffer that way!''

The man was quieted and led away sobbing, but his outburst had broken the mood of Mother's peroration. She suddenly looked tired, her energy spent. Overhead, thunderclouds charged across the afternoon sky. Dawes and Packard looked at each other and the other dignitaries with apprehension. The crowd started to trickle away.

"Remember, my children," she concluded perfunctorily. "I will be with you whether true or false. I will be with you at midnight or when the battle rages, when the last bullet ceases, but I will be in my joy, as the old saint said:

*Oh, God of the mighty clan!*
        *God grant that the woman who suffered for you,*
*Suffered not for a coward, but oh, for a man!*

Rain started to fall, lightly at first, then in a torrent.

"Join the union, boys!" she shouted to the scattering horde. Someone, a union man, came up behind her with an umbrella. "Hell, I was just getting started!" she groused and extended her hand to Euan. "Come on, Euan Morgan. Come help Mother get out of the rain."

The cooling rain dropped down through the leafy arbor onto his naked back. He shivered. She traced her fingers across his lips, his eyes, across his cheek, imprinting his features for the memory book of her mind. A rumble of thunder split the air.

His hand moved to her blouse. Slowly, awkwardly, he undid the column of buttons that lined her bodice—seven . . . eight . . . nine—then reached in, not knowing what to do, wanting (and fearing, too) to see the body concealed beneath her dress.

She sighed at his touch.

"Cousin! Cousin Mary, where are you?" Blodwen called through the rain.

He felt her heart begin to pound, and his own; he felt a sadness unlike any he had ever known. Their time was ending...ending...When would it ever be like this again? Suddenly, as if to hide herself or to shut out the world, she drew him closer; she embraced him; she rubbed her hands over his rain-wet back, down the seat of his pants, wanting to draw him into her.

"Hold me!" she said. "Hold me?"

He felt her body with his, his legs twining between hers, his hands now in hers, his cheeks rubbing her hair.

"Hold me, Rhys, hold me!"

"Cousin? Cousin Mary?"

He felt his lips on hers, driven by urges heretofore hidden unknown, aching in his tumescence, sighing, sighing, driving himself to the precipice of sensation...

"Hold me! Hold me!"

...sighing, sighing, and then...release, spasms of uncontrolled longing.

"Cousin Mary? Are you still here? Where are you?"

He rolled off her with a great exhalation of breath. What had he done? What had happened to him? He felt a warm wetness in his drawers. He felt suddenly naked.

The rain fell harder.

She nestled closer to him. She felt his strength. She loved him.

Mother sat under a makeshift tent that had been set up alongside the courthouse earlier to shield her from the sun. Now it sheltered her from the rain. A group of reporters huddled around her; bored photographers, grateful at least that they were dry, vied for her picture.

Euan sat, watching the rain from a stool in the corner of the tent, and wondered what Rhys was doing, where Gwen and Meb were. Suddenly two union men dashed across the square under huge black umbrellas. One carried a pitcher of beer, which he placed on a wooden carton in front of Mother.

"This'll do fine for me, Joe," Mother said, eyeing the

pitcher. "What about these vultures?" she added, nodding, to her thirsty companions.

"Frank and the boys are bringing more over now," the union man replied as he poured Mother the first glass.

"Just kidding, boys," Mother said. "Help yourselves. And, Joe, see if there are any stragglers out there in the rain. Bring 'em in, too. Never met a miner yet, or a reporter, who didn't need a glass of beer once in a while to help him forget his miseries. The way things are, it's a wonder we're not all drunk all the time."

"Mother, you've been avoiding my question," a reporter from Pittsburgh said. "Will there or won't there be a strike in anthracite this winter?"

"I heard you all right. I just needed a taste of beer to help me think clear," she said, taking a swig. "Let me say this, young man, the United Mine Workers will *not* strike this winter." There was a buzz. This is what the reporters had come to hear. "But there will be one by fall."

"Come on now, Mother!" said the reporter from New York. "You know you don't have the members."

"We don't need all of anthracite to go out. We have enough now to shut down the key operations. The others will follow once word gets around, you'll see. Like a snowball rolling down a hill!"

"You think Mitchell has the experience, the influence? He's only been president for two years," remarked the reporter from Philadelphia.

"And what is he, thirty years old, if that?" added New York.

"I can see you two know as much about Mitchell as a dog knows about his daddy," Mother observed wryly. "He's a very shrewd man, Mitchell. If anyone can bring anthracite together, it's him. Have another beer."

"When's Mitchell coming east?" asked the Hazelton reporter.

"He's here now—in Scranton—working on Bishop Hoban."

"Why Hoban?"

"These Irish priests and bishops are a stubborn lot from

what I hear," she said, shaking her head with bewilderment, "but they've got the influence in these parts. Mitchell says they're in cahoots with the operators, but if he can win over this Hoban and Father Curran and Father Phillips up there in Hazelton, chances are the Catholic miners will fall into place. Like I said, a snowball rolling down a hill. Take my word for it—Mitchell's going to have anthracite organized by Thanksgiving. Probably sooner."

"We'll believe it when we see it," Philadelphia said.

"Do you think there'll be trouble? Like down in West Virginia?" asked the reporter from Pittsburgh.

Her face turned sour with disgust. "West Virginia's ruled by illegal injunctions. You got Baldwin-Felts thugs down there, shooting miners dead in their beds while they sleep. You got slaves willing to work for twenty-five cents a day and be satisfied with that. It's bad here in hard coal, but it's worse down there. Much worse."

"We've had our own troubles, too," said the reporter from Hazelton.

"You mean Lattimer?" Mother asked.

The reporter nodded. "Nineteen dead. Hunkies, most of them, couldn't speak English. None of 'em was armed. Went out on strike because a foreman, a man name of Gomer Jones, beat up one of theirs. Went marching to drum up support at nearby collieries. Sheriff was called in. There was a stand-off just as they came into Lattimer. A gun fired, then all the deputies started shooting. When the smoke cleared, there was all those dead. More than twice that number shot. Happened just three years ago."

"And it'll happen over and over again," Mother railed, jabbing at the air with her stubby finger, "as long as all wealth is in the hands of the men who own the machinery! Think boys, did the laborers ever take nineteen capitalists and riddle their bodies with bullets?"

"What about yourself, Mother?" asked Philadelphia. "Do you ever worry for your own safety?"

"Hell, no! I've got a contract with God to stay here till the working man's chains are broken. I've lived seventy years, and I'll live seventy more if that's what it takes."

"Come on now," New York taunted. "There must be times when you'd like to give up this hell-raising, as you call it, and begin to take some comforts in your old age? You must be more than a little tired by now."

"Well, for one thing, I am not uncomfortable, nor am I weary. I'm an extraordinarily happy woman with just enough pain in my life to keep me true. If I yielded to luxury now, I might lose myself.

"You know, I lost my family, my husband—he was a union man, an iron molder—and my children to yellow fever in '67. In Memphis. All of them, gone in six weeks' time. The rich and the well-to-do fled the city. Churches and schools were shut. The dying were quarantined; the dead were everywhere. They were buried at night quickly, without ceremony. All around my house, I could hear weeping and cries of delirium. One by one, my four children sickened and died, and one by one, I washed their little bodies and got them ready for burial. Finally my husband caught the fever . . . and he died. I sat alone through nights of grief. No one came. No one could, because every house was as stricken as mine. All day long, all night long, I could hear the grating of the wheels of the death cart."

Her eyes misted over with tears as she relived her anguish. Her words sprang from some deep part of her soul.

"After that, I returned to Chicago and started a dressmaking business, but I lost it all in the Great Fire of '71. I figured God was trying to tell me something. I nearly lost Him after the Haymarket strike in '88," she said with a chuckle. "No, gentlemen, luxury makes slaves. I prefer the open road, a comrade's greeting, and the breath of freedom." Then, after a pause, "Look, it's not raining now. You can go off and write your stories."

"One more picture, Mother!" said New York.

"All right, just one!" she said. "Take me with my breaker boy here for those damn rich fools in New York. Let them see for once what an honest working man looks like. Come here, Euan Morgan. Come, stand by Mother."

Euan had never had his picture taken before. He stood next to Mother, and she put her hand on his shoulder. Suddenly there was a great flash, and smoke rose from the stick the photographer held in his hand. Euan gasped out loud, which made everyone laugh.

"Thank you, Mother. Good-bye, Mother! Good-bye!" they said and hurried off through the puddles.

"Write good!" she called after them. "And when I'm finished with the miners, I'll come organize you!"

Suddenly the boy and the old woman were alone. "You want to join the union, Euan Morgan?" she asked. "I haven't had a convert all day."

"I'll have to ask my *dada*."

"That's a new one," she said, chuckling. "You do that then."

"What does it take?"

"These days? Fifty cents and a lot of hope."

"I don't even know what a union is."

"Unions are old, my friend. The labor movement was a command from God Almighty Himself!" she said, sounding to Euan like she was giving the rest of her speech, the part drowned out by the thunderstorm. "Thousands of years ago, He commanded the prophet Moses to go down and redeem the Israelites that were in bondage, so Moses went to work and organized the men into a union, but the Israelites said, 'The masters are more cruel than they were before. What are we going to do?' And Moses said, 'A voice from heaven has come, commanding me to get you together.' So they got together, and the prophet led them out of the land of bondage and robbery and plunder into the land of freedom, and when the army of the pirates followed them, the Dead Sea opened and swallowed them up, and so for the first time, the workers were free."

Euan looked confused by this talk of Israelites and pirates, of unions and parting seas.

"A union," she said more simply, "is when people join together to give themselves the courage to say 'no.' Let me see your hands, lad. Ah, you've not been at it long, have you? 'No' is the most powerful word in the English language, my boy. Remember that.'' Then, calling over her shoulder, she rose like a whirlwind, ''Nate, Joe, if we're going to meet Mitchell in Scranton, we better shake a leg!''

Before the boy could blink, she was gone.

Would they remember? When they looked back? Would they? Or would calamity or rapture crowd out this day, erasing it forever from their minds? Would the girls ever forget the look of surprise on Euan's face when Duckie carried back the biggest watermelon he'd ever seen? Or he the look of disbelief on theirs when they asked what he'd done all afternoon, and he told them he'd had his picture taken with Mother Jones. (''You're a corker!'' Gwen said. ''God, how I miss you!'') Would Euan forget how they looked—dresses droopy, curls straight, shoes sopping wet from being caught in the rain? Or Rhys's face when he met them on Public Square half an hour late—all dreamy and glowing? How could they have known Rhys was in love? They never would. Would they remember the arm wrestling, how Rhys beat both Richard and Duckie, the trolley ride to Kingston Corners and back that Duckie got for them free, and supper at Dugan's on South Main, where Richard spilled his beer on Meb's skirt, and how she almost cried? Afterwards, the Stegmaier Band concert on River Common, then the fireworks—and weren't they grand?—the slow walk back to the station, stopping for ice cream, and just barely, barely making the train, then hurried ''good-byes'' and promises to come home soon and ''give our loves'' and ''be goods'' and waving until they couldn't see each other any more?

Would they remember? With pain. With pain.

The Markhams weren't on the train.

''Maybe they caught the earlier one,'' Rhys thought, beside himself with disappointment. ''But then they'd miss the fireworks. No, they must've stayed over at their cousin's.'' He remembered her parting words to him—

"See you in church!" Right then, he had vowed to join the choir *and* Christian Endeavor.

"Look what I bought for *Mam*," Euan said.

"Oh, cripes!" Rhys moaned. "I meant to buy something, too! What did you get her?

Euan carefully unfolded the tissue paper he had carried in his shirt pocket. Inside was a clear glass horse.

"Oh, it's pretty," Rhys said. "She'll like it."

"Hold it up to the light," Euan urged.

"Oh, yes . . . pretty. *Mam* says she always wanted to ride a horse."

"That's what I was thinking when I bought it."

"She'll put it in the parlor, I bet. On the table by the window."

Euan carefully wrapped it again. "I'll say it's from both of us."

Later, Euan stretched out across the length of the seat and fell asleep with his head on Rhys's lap. His shirt was stained with ice cream, watermelon, gravy. His hands were sticky from sweets.

Rhys stared out the open window, watching the trees and hills pass in the moonlight. He was bursting inside to talk about his afternoon with Mary, his memories of her—the smell of rosewater, the feel of her hands touching him, her sparkling eyes.

"Tomorrow will be soon enough," he thought.

He finally drifted off to sleep.

◆◆

RHYS arose before dawn, dressed, and went downstairs, where he ate the breakfast his *mam* had set out the night before—oatmeal the way he liked it, covered with maple syrup, blueberry preserves, biscuits, and tea. He stuffed handfuls of salt and brown sugar into his pockets for the mules and set off for work just as his *mam* and *dada* were stepping out of bed.

"We walked down to Crystal Pond," Hugh told Euan at breakfast. "Had ourselves a picnic. We haven't done that, have we, *Mam*, since our Rhys was little? We got caught in the rain, too, on the way back.''

''We were soaked through to the skin!'' Myfanwy called from the parlor, where she was placing the glass horse the boys had bought her on the table by the window.

''Yes, it was nice except for that,'' Hugh added.

''And you say the girls are well then?'' Myfanwy asked, returning to the kitchen. ''They're getting enough to eat, are they?''

''Yes, *Mam*,'' Euan told her. ''We ate so good our bellies nearly burst.''

''Well, they're the fine ones! And supposin' you got sick from all you ate and missed your work today? Agh! Those two are a pair—haven't got an ounce of sense between them! I take it they got you out of the rain at least so's you wouldn't catch your death of cold?''

Euan almost said no but caught himself in time. He had no wish to explain that he was alone when it rained, because the girls had left him to go boating with their beaux and Rhys was off chasing after Mary Markham.

''Yes, *Mam*,'' he said and let it go at that.

There was a breakdown at the pit head that morning before the main work force arrived. Most of the drivers, Rhys among them, had already gone down to prime their mules when it happened. A small valve froze shut, cutting off the steam that powered the lifting cables for the cage. It was a minor, even frequent occurrence. Till it was repaired, everyone up top sat and waited at the pit head, and everyone below did the same.

''Did you miss me, you old hag?'' Rhys asked Rosie, his favorite mule, as she licked salt from his hand.

''They're real frisky today,'' Gomer Davies called from across the aisle. ''Somebody must've poured whiskey in their water again.''

''Maybe we ought to take them out for a little run,'' Rhys said mischievously. ''Work off some of that piss and vinegar.''

''What if they catch us?''

"Who's to know then? Fifty cents says my Rosie here can beat the best of your lot," Rhys bragged.

"Oh, yeah?"

"Yeah!"

"No steam, no work!" Ned the Splicer told the men up top.

By half past seven, the colliery yard was overflowing with hundreds of men and boys. Their overseers stood by helplessly as the steam crew struggled to open the ancient valve.

Most of the breaker boys lazed idly on the tracks beside the loading bins, some slept. Bryfogle hovered nearby, scowling, spitting tobacco juice on the boys' boots for spite.

"And we saw fireworks!" Euan told Tadi as they pitched pebbles into a rusty bucket.

"Fire-vorks?"

"Fireworks," Euan repeated. "You know, big explosions in the sky? At night? They're pretty. All different colors. They're like shooting stars, only they explode and make the biggest racket you ever heard—hundreds, all at once. It gets so bright it's like day." The more Euan tried to explain, the more baffled Tadi looked. "And . . . and anyway, we saw fireworks."

They lined up across the gangway, three mules in all, each with a lamp affixed to its head, and three riders— Rhys, Gomer, and Wojtek Ratajczyk—all riding bareback, all wearing headlamps. With payday only a few days off, the betting was feverish. In the excitement of the moment, everyone was eager to risk money he didn't have.

The course was short but treacherous—two hundred yards down the main gangway to the muleway, a narrow cut that led to the level below, then around the "lake," the metal trough where rails were cooled after being shaped by the blacksmiths, back up through the muleway and down the gangway for the dash to the finish. The mules were held back by other drivers to keep them from bolting before Robert Rowlands called the start.

"Get ready! Get set!"

It was hard to tell which were more eager—the boys or the mules.

"You're off!"

Gomer and Wojtek's mules burst ahead, but Rhys's Rosie refused to budge.

"Come on, you lazy mule, come on!" Rhys shouted while the other drivers either laughed or cheered. He swatted the animal hard across the rump, and at last she bounded off.

Gomer and Wojtek held to the narrow paths on either side of the tracks, although this meant sitting low and leaning away from the walls to avoid sharp outcrops of rock. Rhys had two choices open to him—follow one of the other mules and hope for a chance to bolt ahead, or take the faster but more dangerous middle route, the ties between the tracks. Without hesitation, he steered Rosie straight on, with threats and slaps and promises of a pound of salt.

Halfway down the gangway, Rhys drew within a few feet of Wojtek's mule. He could see the muleway ahead, marked by a single red lantern. He knew the passage was narrow, only wide enough for one mule and rider at a time, but if he could squeeze through first, he had the best chance of leading the rest of the way.

"Come on, Rosie! You can do it, girl!"

Rhys's sweet talk worked. In no time, the surefooted Rosie had inched past Wojtek and was drawing alongside Gomer. At the last second Gomer's mule shied, and Rhys cut through the narrow passage without stopping, then down the steep path to the lake. Wojtek caught up and went through second while Gomer tried to get his mule under control.

The blacksmith's chamber was a deep cavern cut from solid rock. The floor was flat here, the ceilings high, and it was possible for the mules to gallop full out. Rhys had stretched his lead at the far end of the lake, the halfway point of the race, to several lengths, when suddenly Rosie stopped beside the long trough to take a drink of water.

"What the hell are you doing? This is a race!" he bellowed as Wojtek and his mule passed them by.

"Yahoo!" Wojtek yelled, laughing. "*Pocaluj moja dupe*, Morgan!"

Rosie suddenly seemed aware of her lapse and rejoined the race just as Gomer reached the halfway point.

"My Rosie don't like to lead," Rhys thought, "but she likes to race!" And off they went again toward the muleway.

Wojtek was first up this time, with Rhys close behind. When he reached the gangway, Wojtek guided his mule to one of the outside paths, leaving the other to Rhys, but Rhys knew he could pull ahead only if he rode the middle course, between the tracks. Gomer was too far back now to be a threat.

"Come on, Rosie! You can do it! Let's beat the son of a bitch!"

As it turned out, Rosie didn't need Rhys's urging. She knew these ties by heart, every splinter, having trod them a thousand times before, and knew her stall wasn't far beyond. In the stretch, she caught her second wind and evened up the race.

"Now you can kiss *my* ass, Wojtek!" Rhys shouted to his astonished foe.

At the finish line, the other drivers couldn't tell which lamps coming toward them were which, so they cheered for the leader and hoped it was their mule and driver. It was Rhys and Rosie who crossed first.

It didn't matter who won the race. It was danger they were after, and exhilaration. Nor was Rhys about to refuse the three dollars and eighty-five cents he won. He was about to accept a challenge when they heard the whirring of the cables and the cage start to descend.

As Rhys rode Rosie back to her stall, the other drivers crowded around him in good spirits, singing:

> *My sweetheart's the mule in the mines;*
> *I drive her without reins or lines.*
> *On the bumper I stand, my whip in my hand . . .*

\* \* \*

This last line was accompanied by a lewd gesture and loud laughter.

> *My sweetheart's the mule in the mines!*

But Rhys had written his own verse. "Listen! Here's a better one!" he said and sang it for them:

> *My sweetheart's the mule in the mines;*
> *I drive her without reins or lines.*
> *On the bumper I sit; I chew, and I spit*
> *All over my true love's behind!*

The drivers laughed and sang Rhys's verse through several times. Then, Rhys re-created the excitement of the race for them, jumping up and down one minute in the shadowy aisle between the stalls, kneeling like Rosie at the lake the next. Even the mules shared the excitement of his story, of the boys' laughter, by braying in chorus or kicking wildly in their stalls.

"And Rosie stops to drink like we're on a Sunday stroll!" Rhys shouted with disbelief. "And there goes Ratajczyk, passing me by like he's just seen a ghost, an I'm pooping in my drawers! I'm shoutin', 'Come on, Rosie! I'm countin' on you! I'm countin' on you to carry me home!' "

Just then, Helen the mule—the same recalcitrant Helen that Rhys had whipped the day the Sons of Thunder met their doom—sensed that her driver was hovering in the aisle behind her. She knew his sound, his smell. He was always making noise or bounding about, always annoying her and using his whip, and she still remembered that day, that beating.

Helen kicked out—a jolt of muscle, of sinew and hoof, driving back, blindly through the air behind her, back toward the unsuspecting boy. One hit was all she needed to pay him back. Was he in reach? Yes, yes!

Hoof to bone! Craaaack!

The tip of Helen's hoof caught Rhys along the side of his head, knocking him forward onto his hands and knees. The other drivers didn't see what happened, not really. It was dark in the stables, and he was jumping around, bouncing around, and they were laughing and just didn't see. He shook his head to clear his sight. He blinked then a sharp pain exploded in his skull, and everything went dark, darker than the deepest mine.

"I can't see! Jesus, I can't see!" he yelled, and they laughed. "Oh, my God! I think I'm hit! Oh, Jesus!" He felt a warm wetness running along his cheek—was it blood? Yes, blood! "Oh, God ! Oh, my God! I'm goin' to get hell from *Dada* now!" he cried, then toppled forward onto the straw-strewn floor, flinching and twisting like a new-caught fish. His body twitched one last time, like a dancer ending some odd jig, and then was still.

And they laughed harder.

"Morgan!" Bryfogle shouted as Euan climbed to his perch. "Yer wanted out in the yard!"

"I didn't do nothing!"

"Yer wanted!" Bryfogle said bluntly and disappeared into his office.

"Who would want me outside?" Euan wondered as he headed for the stairs.

The yard looked empty. The last of the men had pegged in. Only a few stragglers hurried up the hill to the cage. Some engineers stood with Ned the Splicer near the pit head, but no one was waiting for him. No one wanted him. He was ready to turn back inside when a fluttering kerchief caught his eye, a red kerchief like the one Rhys wore.

Then he saw a figure lying on the crushed slate beyond the men.

"Could it be Rhys playing a joke?" Euan wondered. "Or sick maybe from all he ate? If he loses time, *N'had*'ll lambaste him good."

Between the bursts of venting steam, Euan heard the men talking of test borings and strata. He circled around them for a better look, until his eyes confirmed what his heart felt. It was him. It was Rhys lying on the ground.

("He's joking! He's such a joker!")

He laughed at first, a hollow laugh...

("Rhys, why are you lying there? So still? Did you fall asleep? Get up or you'll catch hell!")

...and then, approaching, saw the mask of pain that twisted Rhys's face, the crease of blood that trickled down his cheek. His brother looked...Rhys looked de...

Euan backed away, backed into one of the engineers.

"Mister, my brother's...sick. Can you help him?"

"You're brother's not sick, boy. He's..."

Three short blasts of the colliery whistle cut him off. Euan recoiled, heard something behind him, turned, and saw Gwyndaf Pugh driving Black Maria up the hill, up toward Rhys, lying on the crushed slate so motionless, so still.

Three short blasts.

He began to tremble. He wanted to run to Rhys to wake him up, to hear him laugh again and say he was all right, but his legs wouldn't move. He was afraid to go near him, afraid to touch him, afraid, afraid...

Three short blasts.

The wagon rolled to a stop. Pugh and Ben John jumped down, opened the doors in back, and started toward Rhys.

"DON'T YOU TOUCH HIM!" a voice roared across the yard. It was his *dada* running from the cage. The drivers stopped; the engineers turned. "Leave him be! Don't...touch him!"

His *dada* looked at Rhys, lying there so still. "Oh, noooo!" he moaned and fell to his knees and cradled his beloved Rhys's head in his arms. "Oooh, noooo! Not my Rhys!"

Three short blasts.

"Come on, Morgan. Hain't got all day," Pugh said.

"Get away! You'll not get my boy!" his *dada* shouted, shooing them like vultures from the precious corpse, then regathering his son into his arms, saw the other standing in the shadow of Black Maria still trembling.

The watchers in the windows pulled back their curtains, expecting Black Maria to roll up the Hill. Instead, they saw a man most didn't know, carrying—could it be his son? It was only when they saw Euan—Little Rhysie, they called him—following behind that they realized what had happened.

Rhysie Morgan, the Welsh fiddler, the jokester, was dead.

Euan felt cut off from his *dada,* from what was happening, from himself. He knew this wasn't Rhys his *dada* was holding. It couldn't be Rhys. Rhys was somewhere down in the mine, and he would come home, and they would scrub each other's backs and box and go off and hit the wall, then sit behind the Emerald and smoke a cigarette.

Suddenly his *dada* staggered under the burden of his sorrow and fell to his knees. "Get your *mam,* lad!" he said, his voice raspy, his breathing hard.

Euan ran ahead, then hesitated, not certain he should leave his *dada.*

"Go!"

"*Mam, Mam!*" she heard, faintly at first, then unmistakably. It was her Euan. "*Mam,* come quick!" A breath escaped her, almost like a sigh of relief.

"At least it's not the little one," was her first thought. Death had been the constant in her life. She had lost her father and three brothers in the mines and countless uncles and cousins. In Swansea, in the old country. Death was a certainty in the mines. Only the when and how remained in doubt.

"*Mam!*" she heard, coming closer now. "*Mam!*"

Her legs felt weak. She wondered if she had the strength to rise from her chair, to open the door, to face what lay ahead.

"*Mam,* come quick!"

She heard his footsteps cross the porch, heard his hand fumble with the door, and then his breathless gasps. A scream died in her throat.

"*Mam!*" he said. "Come quick! It's Rhys!"

She followed Euan down the street. All she wanted was to see her son. Something inside her refused to believe it till she could see him for herself. She wouldn't believe it till then. And suddenly there he was, in his father's arms. Yes, it was true. Her boy was gone.

"I can go no farther," Hugh said.

With a calm that belied her inner agony, she lifted Rhys's legs as Hugh raised up his shoulders, and, together, with Euan at their side, they carried Rhys the rest of the way home.

They laid him on the table in the kitchen and stood, not knowing what to do next or, if knowing, not wanting to. Euan sought refuge in the corner, watched and listened to his *mam*'s quiet sobbing and wondered why he could not cry.

They took his clothes off first and found salt and brown sugar in his pockets. His body was untouched. The trickle of blood across his temple and down his cheek was the only hint of violent cause. Finally Hugh could stand it no more and reeled out the back door, sobbing, pounding the pillars of the porch with his fist. Myfanwy went to his side to comfort him, to comfort herself, leaving Euan alone with Rhys.

After a moment, he took a wet cloth from the sink, approached the table, and wiped away the blood that marred his brother's face.

They dressed him in his suit. Then Hugh walked down to the carpenter to have a casket made. At the store, he sent a telegram to Gwen and Meb. It read:

RHYS KILLT IN MINE. COME HOME.
BURIAL TOMORROW. DADA.

They laid him in the casket that afternoon and sat vigil.

The pastor called and prayed with them. No one else came. They were scabs.

❖❖

GWEN and Meb ran up to their room in Mrs. Archer's after work to change their clothes before Richard and Duckie came to call. The telegram was pinned to their door. They knew at once it was bad news. Telegrams always were.

"You do it," Meb said, handing it to Gwen.

Gwen closed her eyes. "Oh, God," she said under her breath and ripped open the envelope.

It was curious. From where he sat in their parlor, Euan could see out the front window. After work and all through the early evening, men passing on the street stopped, men he didn't know stopped, looked at their house, and stood in silence. Some held the beads he always saw them carrying to church. Some brought wives and children. They all just stood, whole families, stood and stared at the house in silence. Then they waved their hands across their faces and chests, like he always saw the Catholics do, and left. But others took their place.

Razor Kudla and his fiddlers stood out front, wiping tears from their eyes. Then Razor knelt in the street and prayed.

His *mam* and *dada* never noticed the stream of mourners. They stared at Rhys or read from the Bible or held each other's hand, and when their grief became too much to bear, they went out back or upstairs to vent their anguish or anger or guilt alone.

After supper, Myfanwy was alone in the kitchen, cleaning off their untouched plates—Hugh had taken Euan to the station to see if the girls were on the early evening train—when she heard the back gate open. "It's Rhys," she thought at first. "He's late from work, and I've not kept his meal warm!" And then she caught herself; she remembered. Her son was . . . "safe" now . . . safe in the next room. Instead, she saw two women from Polish Hill coming up the steps. She froze, her face glazed with contempt.

("What do these hunkies want of me?" she asked herself. "Don't they know? Don't they know we're . . . ?")

"*Pani* Morgan?" Mrs. Kudla called timidly, knocking at the open door.

("Money. They're begging for money.")

"No, I . . . I can't. Go away," Myfanwy managed to say, averting her eyes from them, reaching for the door, reaching out to slam the door.

"Ve . . . sorry. Sorry for Rhysie."

"Rhys? What?" Myfanwy asked, dumbfounded.

"Ve sorry," Mrs. Angieski said.

("*Sorry?* What do you . . . ? You didn't even know him!")

Mrs. Kudla stepped forward and placed a sum of money, carefully folded, into Myfanwy's hand. "*Przyjaciolmi*," she said, tears glistening in her eyes. "How you say. . . ? Frient? Ve sorry. . . for you an' *Pan* Morgan."

Then the women blessed themselves and left as quietly as they had come.

Myfanwy looked down at her hand, aghast.

("Money? For Rhys's life? How could money. . . ?")

She wanted to scatter the money to the wind or bury it. It tainted her hand. She backed toward the stove, then lifted the grate, thinking to drop it into the fire, but something stopped her. This was money she held—what her men worked for, now died for. She could refuse it or ignore it, but she could not destroy it. Still, it was hunky money. It fouled her house.

She heard Hugh and Euan returning home. Without thinking, Myfanwy concealed the bills under her bread box. There they could sit until tomorrow, or the next day or forever, for all she cared.

◆◆

MYFANWY came out of the house first, shielding her eyes from the glare of the sun, then Pastor Wheat. Euan held the door. The casket was borne by Hugh and Mr. Prodgers, the church sexton, who had dug the grave that morning and still wore his boots and work clothes. Gwen and Meb, who had arrived on the train late the night before, came last. Gwen placed the wildflowers they had picked that morning atop the casket. Then each took a handle to lighten the load. Euan walked behind in his Sunday suit, holding up the rear of the wooden box, ready to step in if the burden became too heavy for Gwen or Meb.

The procession moved slowly down Frog Street, which was deserted and quiet, even though the colliery was idle that day.

Mary Markham and her family had just returned from Wilkesbarre on the early afternoon train. Before going home, she accompanied June and Anna to the company store for some sweets.

"Isn't it sad about the Morgan boy?" she heard Mrs. Jenkins say to Mr. Beech.

"Yes, it is. He was a fine lad. Never gave me a bit of trouble."

Mary felt an ominous chill. "Excuse me," she asked. "May I inquire of whom it is you are speaking?"

Euan felt a hand on his shoulder. When he turned, he saw several men and women behind him, all dressed in their best, their Sunday clothes. Some carried flowers they had picked in their yards, or their rosaries. The hand drew him aside, and his place behind the casket was taken by a tall, bearded Polander, whose name he didn't know. Puzzled, he caught up to his *dada* and walked at his side.

A moment later, Euan saw Gwen and Meb walk by him and join their *mam*. Razor and his fiddlers had taken his sisters' places. Then, from every house they passed, more mourners poured forth to join the procession. Finally, Mr. Moczygemba and Mr. Drozda, without saying a word, came up to his *dada* and Mr. Prodgers and lifted the casket from their hands. His *dada* looked too amazed to protest. Rhys's casket was being borne by men from Polish Hill.

Euan squeezed in between his *mam* and Pastor Wheat. She looked sadder than he had ever seen anyone look. She was the last to sense the presence of others behind them, to hear their footfalls. Turning, she saw scores of unfamiliar faces following them. Up ahead, porches filled with more mourners, and they too came forward and joined the procession as it passed—a silent multitude, following the casket of one they loved.

Mary pressed her tear-streaked cheek against the window. She couldn't believe it, refused to believe it. Rhys? Rhys, whom she had kissed and held, whose laughter had tickled her so? Rhys?

("A buzzard . . . a buzzard of love with a kiss on every raindrop!")

"Could there be some . . . some mistake?" she had asked Mr. Beech. "Some other Morgan perhaps?"

"No, miss," he'd answered. He'd helped the poor boy's father carry the casket to the house himself. There was no mistake.

She felt the blood drain from her face, her neck . . .

"Can I get you something, miss?" she heard Mr. Beech say. "You don't look well. Perhaps you should . . . ?"

. . . from her breasts, the breasts he had touched, from her fingers, her hands, her arms. She felt the blood drain from her, her life drain from her. She felt hollow.

"No . . . no," she said softly and went to the window, where she watched the passing mourners and Euan, holding his grieving mother's hand.

("A buzzard of love . . . a buzzard of love!")

"It's odd," she remembered saying to him. "We had to come all this way just to be together." He was writing in her memory book then, and . . . her book! She reached into her purse, her heart pounding. Was it still there?

("Don't read it! Not till . . . till later! It's bad luck!")

Yes, yes, there it was! She flipped through its pages, looking for his writing and the silly picture he'd drawn at the bottom of the page.

"What's that supposed to be?" she had asked.

"That's me!" he had said. "Me! At the bottom of the mine! Doesn't it look like me?"

"And what's that next to you?"

"That's a mule! What do you think it is?"

"Looks more like a dog," she said, laughing.

"A dog?" he gasped. "A dog? Cripes Almighty! Maybe it's dogs I've been driving down there and didn't know it! It's so dark, I didn't know it!"

"Mary...?" June asked. "Is anything the matter?"

"No, no," Mary said, trying to read through her tears but not able not able to blink away her tears.

"What's wrong?" Anna asked when Mary's crying wouldn't stop. "Shall I run for Mama?" But Mary was huddled beneath an arbor in the rain, brushing a leaf across a boy's naked chest, hearing his words as if for the first time, words he'd written in her book, words that would be forever scarred in her memory.

> *Dear Mary,*
>
> *When twilight drops its curtain*
> *and pins it with a star,*
> *remember me and love me*
> *no matter where you are.*
>
> *Yours till the dew drops,*
> *Yours till the Dead Sea,*
> *Yours till Niagara Falls,*
> *Yours till the Statue of Liberty comes ashore.*
>
> > *Yours,*
> >
> > *Yours,*
> >
> > *Yours,*
>
> *Rhys (A buzzard of love with*
> *a kiss on every raindrop)*

◆◆

IT was a simple service, as befitted the occasion.

"Oh, Lord, we come before you with great sorrow ...,"

Pastor Wheat said in prayer. Hugh and Myfanwy stood next to him with Euan at her side, her hand resting on his shoulder, at times squeezing it to remind her that he was still there, still hers. The girls stood opposite them, dabbing their reddened eyes with handkerchiefs.

The mourners from Polish Hill lined the fence along the street. Some prayed, some wept, but most looked on in respectful silence.

"...we commend his spirit, oh Lord, to Your loving arms, in the Name of the Father, the Son, and the Holy Spirit. Amen."

Meb and Gwen sang "*Crimond*" as Hugh and Mr. Prodgers lowered the casket into the grave. Their voices blended in haunting harmony across the stillness of the yard.

> *The Lord's my Shepherd, I'll not want.*
> *He makes me down to lie*
> *In pastures green. He leadeth me*
> *The quiet waters by.*
>
> *My soul He doth restore again.*
> *And me to walk doth make*
> *Within the paths of righteousness*
> *E'en for his own name's sake.*
>
> *Yea, though I walk through death's dark vale,*
> *Yet, will I fear none ill;*
> *For thou art with me, and Thy rod*
> *And staff me comfort still.*
>
> *My table Thou hast furnished*
> *In presence of my foes;*
> *My head Thou dost with oil anoint,*
> *And my cup overflows.*
>
> *Goodness and mercy all my life*
> *Shall surely follow me,*
> *And in God's house for evermore*
> *My dwelling place shall be.*

\* \* \*

And then it was time to go. Hugh offered Myfanwy his arm for support, but she held back. "Oh, our Rhys!" she wailed. "We got to leave you here!"

"Come along," Hugh said, comforting her, fighting back his own tears.

When finally she turned and walked away from the grave, Myfanwy spied the faces that lined the fence. "Who are you?" she wanted to say. "Why are you here? Why?" Their sad, silent eyes would haunt her for nights to come.

They walked home slowly, Hugh and Gwen supporting Myfanwy between them, Meb holding Euan's hand, each nurturing unspeakable thoughts, each wiping away tears, except Euan, who did not cry. Upon their return, they found plates of food on the kitchen table—*szynke* and *chleb, pierogi* and *szparagi*—more food than they could eat in a week.

After supper, Hugh saw Gwen and Meb off at the station. Myfanwy stayed behind, unable to bear a second parting that day. She sat by the front window in the dying light, remembering.

Euan went off alone to the creek to hit the wall. At dusk, taking the long way home, he passed the churchyard where Rhys now lay at rest and climbed the fence and sat next to Rhys's grave and leaned back against the flowers that covered the grave. He looked up through the trees at the pinchfist stars that were just turning on their lights. He smoked a cigarette.

And still he did not cry.

# PART FIVE

MOTHER

WITH keen eyes, she surveyed the length of Frog Street from the top of Polish Hill. Some said she didn't need spectacles, that she only wore them to enhance the grandmotherly image she so carefully cultivated. Others said she wasn't nearly as old as she claimed to be. Still others swore she was really a man wearing a dress.

"You watch out now, Mother," warned the driver who had given her a ride from Freeland on his beer wagon. "It's payday, an' them hunkies get mean when they get to drinkin'."

"On your beer, no doubt," she said as she climbed down from the wagon. "Thank you all the same. I can take care of miners, drunk or sober."

"Then watch out for that Markham. I hear he plans to shoot the first union man sets foot on his land."

"I know!" she said with a snort. "That's why Mitchell sent me."

"Boardin'house is down past the breaker," he said and handed down her carpetbag. "Sure I can't drive you the rest of the way?"

"Thank you, but I have other plans."

"Afternoon then, Ma'am!" the driver called as he geed up his horses and entered the thirsty town.

"So, this is Jeddoh!" Mother said and spit the taste of dusty road from her mouth.

It had been nearly four months since Mitchell had summoned her north to Pennsylvania. "The time has come to turn our sight to our most pressing problem," he'd written her. "Membership in the anthracite region has fallen below 8,000. Every effort to raise this or ameliorate the conditions there has met with failure. It seems the anthracite workers have abandoned hope. Wherever our men go there, they are told that membership in the union would be followed by dismissals and blacklists, and, therefore, the anthracite men could not be organized. Thousands, however, vowed to participate in a strike if they were given assurance that such a movement would be made general. The gist of this is, Mother, that I need you in anthracite. The coal companies up there have evidently scared our boys and, of course with good reason, as they have been brutally beaten some of them. I dislike to ask you always to take the dangerous fields, but I know you are willing."

Mitchell's letter finally caught up with Mother in a jail cell in West Virginia, where she had been locked up for contempt of court. "Judge Jackson, in his infinite wisdom," she wrote in her reply, "has seen fit to jail me for being in contempt. Of what, I am not certain. It seems I called the judge a 'scab' for refusing to allow me to exercise my right of free speech, but I am not afraid of the pen, the sword, or the scaffold. I tell the truth wherever I please."

She left for Pennsylvania the next day, "medieval Pennsylvania," as she would come to call it, for if anything, Mitchell's characterization of the hard-coal region erred on the side of moderation. "Never have I seen men bow so low to their masters, or so willingly," she told Mitchell. "They haven't got enough marrow in their backbones to grease two cats' tails." Still, in the three months she spent crisscrossing the anthracite fields, she managed to form nine differ nt locals and bring over four thousand men and boys into the union. "The slaves in the caves need to be saved!" was her rallying cry. She wheedled free rides from train and trolley conductors, and when no trains or trolleys traveled to where she wanted to go, she walked. She slept in miners' homes; she ate their food. She was paid irregularly if at all.

Eventually her travels brought her to Jeddoh, "medieval Jeddoh," as she would come to call it. Mitchell had warned Mother to steer clear of Markham's domain. "Impenetrable," was how he described it. She'd heard of the evictions, of Markham's threats. She'd heard of the shooting, and still she came.

Perhaps that is why she came.

The Polish woman peered suspiciously at her unexpected visitor through a half-opened door. A squalling, naked child thrashed in her arms.

"Good day, I am Mother Jones. Could I speak with...?"

"*Nie rozumie,*" the woman said, shaking her head.

"I've been sent for to help the boys here form a union, and I...I need a place to..."

"*Nie rozumie,*" the woman repeated and shut the door in Mother's face.

Mother was confounded. She had been hounded by Baldwin-Felts guards, barred from more towns than she could remember, served with injunctions, even shot at, but never, never once, had she not been invited into a worker's home.

Across the street, women were airing out quilts on their front porch. Mother approached more cautiously.

"*Dzien dobry!*" she said, using the little Polish she knew. "I am *Matka* Jones. *Angielsku?*"

"*Nie,*" they answered with mirthless eyes.

"*Prosze,* if you might help me, I need a room—*pokoj*—in Jeddoh."

The women looked at each other nervously. "*Nie pokoj. Nie,*" they said and shook their heads.

"*Dziekuje...,*" she said, utterly bewildered by their incivility. These were not the Polish women she had come to know in Chicago, in Arnot and Spring Valley, not even those she had encountered in other towns in anthracite. "So this is Jeddoh," she muttered under her breath.

Mother knocked on the door of a third house a little farther down Frog Street. There was no answer at first. The house was quiet. She wondered if anyone was even home. Somehow this house seemed different from the others on the street. It was a single, yes, whereas the others were doubles, but there was something else that set it apart.

"*Dzien dobry*," Mother said, a bit too anxiously perhaps, when the door finally opened. Then, motioning toward herself, "*Matka* Jones. *Angielsku?*"

"I'm sorry," Myfanwy Morgan said and started to push the door closed.

"Wait!" Mother called. "I was beginning to think no one in this town spoke English."

"Oh, my heavens!" Myfanwy said, completely taken aback. "When I heard you, I thought . . ."

"No need for apology," Mother said graciously. "I'm simply looking for a room. I need a place to stay while I'm in Jeddoh. I am Mother Jones."

"I'm afraid I . . . I can't help you," Myfanwy replied.

"Then could you at least have me in for a cup of tea? I'm parched."

Mother saw Myfanwy hesitate for a moment, as though it were a burden on her time, but she saw a need in Myfanwy's eyes, too—the simple need to hear another human voice. "Of course," Myfanwy said. "Please, come in, do."

"It's the curtains," Mother thought as she waited in the parlor for her hostess to bring in the tea. It was the delicate lace curtains that set this house off from the rest. The Polish windows were gaudily curtained if at all. It was odd, too, to see a Welsh home in the midst of the Polish patch.

"How long have you been here in Jeddoh, Mrs. Morgan?" Mother asked when Myfanwy returned with the tea tray.

"Since last winter."

"And before that?"

"We lived in Sugar Notch. Do you know it?"

"Near Ashley, isn't it? And Warrior Run?" Of course, Mother knew it well. Dundee #2 colliery in Sugar Notch was the third local she'd organized since coming to these parts, and the easiest. "Is Mr. Morgan a miner?"

"Yes, he is."

"And your children?"

Myfanwy stiffened. "I have two girls. In Wilkesbarre. And one boy," she said. "Here in the breaker. He's . . . he's a good boy." Mother saw tears roll down the woman's haggard cheeks. Her voice sounded far-off, melancholy. "And my husband, of course. They . . . they keep me very . . . very busy."

"But at what cost, my dear? You don't look well."

"It's . . . what can one do? I am no stranger to work, but it *is* hard and there is . . . there is so much to do."

"What is your sorrow, madam?"

Myfanwy looked at Mother strangely.

"You hurt deeply," Mother said. "Your pain is writ all over your face. What is your sorrow?"

"We . . . we lost . . . our older boy," Myfanwy said, as though she were uttering these words, unburdening herself, for the first time. "This summer. Our Rhys. He was just sixteen."

"In the mine?"

Myfanwy nodded.

Mother looked at Myfanwy with compassion, remembering her own children taken so long ago. "Go on, Mrs. Morgan, give in to it. Let your tears flow."

And Myfanwy did. And Mother did also.

"He gave me this," Myfanwy said later, holding up the glass horse, "the day before he died."

"It's beautiful!" Mother said, peering over the rims of her glasses. "You were fortunate to have such a thoughtful son."

"Can I pour you another tea?"

"No, I must be on my way. I will not keep you any longer."

"For once, the work can wait," Myfanwy said impetuously. "What brings you to Jeddoh, Mrs. Jones?"

"You don't know?"

Myfanwy shook her head.

"I am here to organize the union."

Myfanwy was amused at first by this conceit. Then, as Mother spoke, a wall of ice formed between them.

"There is so little time left," Mother said. "A strike will be called across all of anthracite in a matter of weeks. If the strike isn't total, it could drag on for months. Therefore, I shall need the help of every woman in Jeddoh. There's to be a meeting tomorrow night. I shall needs names and . . ."

"Mr. Morgan does not approve of the union."

"And some slaves down south didn't want their freedom either," Mother said testily, "but they got it, like it or not, because the tide of history was too strong."

"Mr. Morgan says when you try to change things, you only end up making them worse."

"Then I shall have to speak to Mr. Morgan."

"And I shall have to ask you, please, to leave, Mrs. Jones."

Mother knew when to dig in and when to retreat and move on. She rose, adjusted the shawl that covered her simple black dress, and moved to the door. "Thank you for the tea. I enjoyed my visit, and I do hope you invite me back before I leave your town." Just then, Mother saw a man and boy walking along the side of the house. "Would that be Mr. Morgan then?"

"Yes," Myfanwy said and hurriedly opened the front door for her guest. "I would appreciate your leaving him be. He has suffered greatly."

"Good day to you, Mrs. Morgan. And thank you again."

As Mother stepped onto the porch, she heard Mrs. Morgan's husband enter the kitchen and the boy's voice call, *"Mam? Mam?"*

"Coming, Euan!" she heard Myfanwy say as the door closed behind her.

"Euan. Euan Morgan," Mother repeated to herself. "Now where have I heard that name before?"

◆◆

ZAKRZEWSKA emptied the contents of his pay envelope onto the kitchen table. He had a scant thirty-six cents to show for his month's labor.

"Son of a bitch Markham!" he snarled under his breath.

Markham had begrudgingly given him back his job as a miner, but with the ton at 3200 now and deductions for rent and water and powder and the rest, he was earning far less than before. What affronted him most was having to pay a share of his wages to the priest—he, who had not been in a church since the day of his marriage. His first marriage.

"And Gwladys, she eat like cow! I never see woman eat so much. Food is all she think about. And goods. Whenever she not eating, she go to pluck me to buy cloth for curtains and such. She have no time for me no more!"

Thirty-six cents. He stirred the coins, rearranged them, piled them. No matter what he did to them, they still only amounted to thirty-six cents. "All my work brings me nothing," he realized, "but Mrs. Markham will now have new trinkets to look at, new carpet to walk on, new pins for her hair."

It was not like that in Chicago in the stockyard, he remembered. Night after weary night he came home, his boots and clothes spattered with the blood of his trade—not black like now—but the money he earned was *his* to keep, *his* to spend on scarves for his Ewa, on picnics in Grant Park with little Mary and Tillie. It was his also to stuff into old stockings and shoes for a rainy day, under a rug or into an empty bottle at the back of the shelf, until all his days were rainy and filled with tears. That is why he refused to believe that Gwladys had hidden her nest egg in one glass jar. "She is more cleverer than that," he told himself, "and I am no dumb hunky neither." He was certain that she had squirreled away a greater sum. He was positive in fact. "But where?" he pondered. "Where?"

He hurried upstairs and dragged her trunk from the

closet. "It must be here, else why would she always keep hidden?" He tried to pry the lock, found it too hard to break, and went downstairs for his crowbar.

There wasn't much inside—clothes mostly, some photographs and books, papers, certificates. He scattered the contents onto the floor. There was no money. He had been wrong after all; she had hidden it elsewhere. After slitting open her crocheted pillows, emptying them of their feathers, tossing her new dresses onto the floor, and ripping out their hems and padding, he emptied her dusting powder onto the top of the bureau and pulled her photographs from their frames. And still he found nothing.

Euan walked down Frog Street with a dime in his pocket. He wished his *mam* had given him two nickels, even a nickel and five. At least with a couple of coins, he could hear them rubbing against one another. They'd fill up his pocket more. A dime was too thin, too quiet.

"Be careful with you!" his *mam* called after as he headed for the store to spend his dime. "And don't be spoiling your dinner with all them sweets!"

Euan stayed close to home these days. And nights. There were no more idle hours spent at the wall. Summer had come and gone, and he'd not hit it once. He stopped caring. There were no more nights out back of the Emerald, listening to stories, smoking cigarettes, no more dreams haunted by Hudsonryder's Ghost. His dreams were of tin chutes, thick with coal, thick with bony, endlessly flowing past. The faster he picked, the faster the coal flowed, the longer the chutes stretched.

"Where does it all come from?" he wondered in his dreams. "Won't it ever end?" He picked coal by day. He picked coal in his sleep.

After supper each night, he sat on the back porch while his *mam* rubbed liniment on his *dada*'s back. Afterwards, his *dada* prepared his blasting cartridges for the next day, and after that, he would come out and sit by Euan on the steps and listen to the crickets, to the music wafting up the

Hill from the Emerald, to hooting owls and crying babies. His *dada* never told stories.

"Little Rhysie!" Euan heard a voice call, jarring him from his thoughts of sour balls and licorice. It was Razor Kudla, grinning as he waved from his porch. "Little Rhysie, come here! I have somet'ing for you!"

"I'm on my way to the store then," Euan answered, hoping his *mam* wasn't watching him from the front window.

" 'Dis is better 'dan store! Only take minute! You vait!" Razor said, then disappeared inside his house only to reappear a moment later carrying a long, oddly shaped black case. "I look ev'ry place for you to give 'dis but never see you. Here!" he said and held it over the fence for Euan to take.

"What is it?" Euan asked.

"Is your brot'er's," Razor replied. "Go on. Open."

Euan lifted the lid. Inside was a shiny new fiddle.

"He make down payment. I finish off today," Razor said, beaming. "Go on, take. Is yours now."

"But I . . ."

"Is yours."

Euan reached out and touched a string. "I can't," he said. "You keep it then. Or sell it. Can you sell it?"

"Yeah, but . . . is goot fittle. I learn you to play, just like Rhysie."

"No," Euan said, backing away. His eyes were wide with fear. "No, I'm not like Rhys then. I'm not like him."

Razor was unable to hide his disappointment at the boy's reluctance. "You t'ink over, huh? You let me know."

Euan ran the rest of the way to the company store. "I'm not like him, I'm not!" he said over and over. "Rhys had the curse of Hudsonryder on him. He heard the story from Red Nose Mike, who told it and got killt in the mine, and Rhys told it and got killt, too. Everybody who told it got killt. I'm not like Rhys, I'm not!"

"Teofil, what happened? Who did this?" Gwladys asked when she returned from school to find her husband sitting amid a pile of debris on the bedroom floor. Her clothes lay strewn about; her papers were in shreds. The curtains were ripped, their hems torn out. His face, his fingers were white with dusting powder.

"Where is it?" he said quietly. "I know is here somewhere."

"What? What are you talking about? What have you done?"

"Your money!" he exploded. "I know you hide it here somewhere!"

"I told you, I *have no money*! Do you think I'd choose to live for one minute in this . . . this pigsty if I did?"

"Mind yourself, woman!"

"These are my things, Teofil!" she said, waving a featherless pillow. "How could you do this? Are you crazy? What kind of animal are you?"

"Shut up!" His eyes flared angrily.

"Don't you tell *me* to shut up! You hear? And don't ever touch my things again, you . . . you dumb hunky!"

"No one say that to me!"

"You are! You're just an ignorant, stupid . . . !"

He slapped her hard across the jaw, driving her back against the wall, knocking her spectacles askew. She crumpled to the floor.

"Oh, my God!" she said, dazed.

"Now go downstairs," he said brusquely, "and cook my supper."

An idea formed itself in the mist that was her awareness, words to explain why she could not rise from the floor at that precise moment to prepare this man's supper, a protest that evanesced, unspoken, as she blacked out.

Mother saw him coming up Frog Street, preoccupied as he was by a glob of molasses, which he licked from his fingers.

"Euan Morgan!" she said, stepping into his path, but the boy showed no surprise at seeing her. He looked paler since that day in July, his shoulders more drooped, his eyes less trusting. "Don't you remember me?"

The boy nodded, then hurried on, as though he didn't want to remember.

"Well, did your father say you could join the union? I haven't had a convert all day."

"No," he said almost inaudibly as he passed.

"Mother is old, Euan Morgan," she called after him. "She needs a good, strong boy to carry her bag to the boardinghouse. Without saying a word or even looking at her, Euan turned and picked up Mother's bag with his unsticky hand and began to carry it down Frog Street. "Folks in this town don't seem too friendly," she remarked, trying to keep up with his brisk pace. "I'm not used to that. Mr. Moczygemba was real nice, but he seemed scared. Seems your Mr. Markham has everybody in town scared out of his pants."

Mother followed the boy down past the breaker into Cheesetown, greeting everyone she passed with a smile and a hello. No one recognized her. For all everyone knew, she was the boy's *nain* come to visit from the old country.

By the time they reached the boardinghouse, Euan had licked his fingers clean. "Here it is then," he said and set her bag down on the front step.

"Before you go," she said, putting one hand on his shoulder and lifting his sullen chin with the other, "there's one more thing. Mother needs a place to hold a meeting tomorrow. Some place away from Markham's property. Can you help her?"

Euan thought for a moment. "A clearing. Up top of the hill beyond the breaker," he said, pointing. "They go there."

"Good. Will you take me?" Then, before he could answer, "Be here nine tomorrow morning. I'll spread the word through town tonight."

"My *dada* says he don't want no part of . . ."

"I'm counting on you, Euan Morgan," Mother said firmly, leaving the boy no choice. "You're working for the union now."

\* \* \*

Gwladys opened her eyes, saw a shadowy blur hovering over her.

"Oh, my angel! What have I done to you?" she heard him sob. "Please, don't die, please! I never hurt you no more. Never, never, never!"

"What happened?" she wondered. "Why am I lying on the bed?"

"I am sorry I hurt you, Ewa, " the voice sniveled on. "Please forgive me. I am bad sometimes. Do you forgive me? Please, Ewa!"

Her jaw began to throb. She moaned.

"I am so lucky to have you. You are such good wife. I am bastard to hurt you. I do not deserve such goodness in my life."

His tears dropped onto her cheeks.

"Please forgive me, Ewa? Please?" he begged, then, still sobbing, kissed her hands. He kissed her face and lips. "Please forgive me?"

"Yes," she said softly through her aching. "Yes, I forgive you," she said, even as she wondered who this woman was who crowded his thoughts, this Ewa. Who, she wondered, was Ewa?

Euan had eight cents left in his pocket. The molasses had tasted good. He wondered if he should buy more now or wait until tomorrow, or if he should buy some red hats, because two cents worth of red hats gave him more than two cents worth of molasses and lasted longer.

("What did she mean, 'I'm working for the union now?' I'm not part of no union. Just because I carried her bag? Or told her about the clearing on the hill? I work for Mr. Markham, not the union.")

He'd forgotten about her. He forgot her name. Mother Jenkins? Mother Jacobs? He remembered the day, how hot it was, the rain. He remembered sitting at her feet, looking out at all the faces looking back at him. He remembered having his picture taken, how she swore like a man and drank beer.

("How did she remember me then?")

He'd forgotten what she said, but it must have been very important if all those people stood in all that heat to hear it. Something about "aprest" people, whoever they were—he never did find out—and poodle dogs and a man who stole somebody's shoes and how they all better join the union.

("And why's she wanting me then? I've got chores. I can't go off just like that. She found her way here. Let her find her own way up the ridge.")

There was more. It was coming back to him. Something about saying "no." When you say no, it gives you courage. "Remember that," she said. And she talked about little ones working in the mills, and she looked at his hands and said he'd not been picking long. And then there was that man who said she was Jesus, but nobody laughed or hooted. They just looked at her as if she were, as if they'd just realized it.

("Cripes Almighty! Why'd she pick on me? I didn't say nothing. Did I ask to sit with her or carry her bag? Let her find another to do for her!")

He thought the man was being silly. How could an old lady be Jesus? How could anyone be Jesus? The man was touched with the heat, that was all. And Jesus would never say curse words or drink beer.

By the time he reached the pluck me store, he had forgotten all about molasses and red hats and spending the rest of his eight cents.

"There's to be a union meeting," he told his *dada* that night at supper. "Up on the ridge. Tomorrow morning."

"Where did you hear?" his *dada* asked.

"Outside the store," he lied.

"There was a union lady came calling here this afternoon," his *mam* said with a scowl. "A Mrs. Jones."

("Jenkins, Jacobs, *Jones!*")

"A pushy type," his *mam* added. "I wouldn't let her in."

"Don't you be going near there, you hear?" his *dada* warned. "There's nothing but trouble to be had. Nothing but trouble."

("Nothing but trouble, nothing but trouble! Suppose she comes looking for me if I'm not there at nine? She knows my name. And what if she sets off without me? She could get lost. Or hurt. But if I met her like she said and *N' had* found out, I'd be in Dutch. I'd be in Dutch for good.")

After supper, he walked down to the graveyard, where he stood, his face pressed between the posts of the wrought-iron fence. The grass was thick now over the plot where Rhys lay. He wished Rhys were here. Rhys would know what to do. Rhys would tell him what to do.

❖❖

AFTER her boardinghouse supper, Mother wrapped herself in her shawl to ward off the cool night air and set off to talk up the union. Ordinarily she would have stopped first at the town saloon, for there on a payday her likely allies would be gathered in a most receptive mood. Something about this town made her change her strategy.

The first house she stopped at looked austere. Neighboring houses had flower gardens out front or a swing on the porch or other embellishments that suggested that the inhabitants enjoyed higher status than the lowly miners up the street.

"Hell, it can't hurt!" she thought and knocked on the door.

The woman who answered looked every bit as austere as her house. Her hair was pulled back tight; her dress was dark and devoid of trim.

"Good evening," the woman said with no particular warmth. "May I help you?"

"Yes, I'm Mrs. Jones. I'm collecting for the widows and orphans."

"Isn't it late to be out collecting?" the woman asked, pinching up her mouth.

"It's never too late," Mother replied, "for the widows and orphans are always in need. May I ask what your husband does at the mine?"

"He's the paymaster."

"I see. All the better. Won't you give something then? Anything at all will be just fine."

Mother came away with an unexpected dime.

"It's only right," she told herself. "Her husband cheated men out of much more than that today. A bag full of dimes wouldn't square away the debt. It's only right."

Despite her evident satisfaction, she chose her next house more carefully. She listened for the sound of children inside before knocking. This time, a plump, red-cheeked woman came to the door. Three plump, round-faced children clung to her skirt.

"Good evening, I'm Mrs. Jones, collecting for the widows and orphans."

"I'm sorry," the woman said. "I barely got enough to keep me own, as you can see." Mother believed her. The children's clothes were barely rags. The woman's dress was patched and frayed.

"What does your husband do at the mine, ma'am?" she asked crisply.

"He's a smithy."

"Not a superintendent?"

"Heavens no!"

"Not a boss?"

"He should live so long!"

"There's to be a meeting tomorrow morning on the ridge up yonder. Tell your husband. Tell your sons, your brothers. Spread the word, ma'am. We're bringing the union to Jeddoh."

Three more houses, three steps closer to her goal—miners this time, ready to listen but scared to talk. Encouraged, she pressed on. She had to reach as many as she could before dark.

"And what does your husband do at the mine?" Mother asked at the next house she came to.

"My husband? My . . . my husband has passed away," said the widow of Ned the Splicer.

"God bless you," Mother said softly as the woman closed the door.

Past the breaker, past the saloon, up the Hill, she moved on.

"*Angielsku?*" she asked at her last stop.

"Yes."

"There's to be a union meeting. On the ridge up above town. Tomorrow morning. Can you be there?"

The man nodded. Something about his smile made her feel uneasy.

"We need all the men we can get," Mother urged. "Spread the word."

"I will," said Zakrzewska. "I will. For sure, I will."

Jeddoh was quiet that night, unusually quiet for a payday. Few houses had kegs out back. Gatherings were smaller, more subdued. Emerald House was packed to the rafters, but by ten o'clock men began drifting home in twos and threes. There were no brawls, no drunks stumbling in the street, no gunshots. Wages were down for August. That explained part of the turnabout—the men had less money to spend. Or maybe they had grown tired of drinking, fighting, and carousing. Or maybe it was the Coal and Irons that patrolled Frog Street from one end to the other. All night long.

Markham was poring over accounts in his study when he heard footsteps cross his porch. When he looked up, he saw Zakrzewska crouched outside his window, grinning.

"What do you want?" Markham asked as he raised the window.

"They have come!" Zakrzewska told him excitedly.

"Who?"

"Union."

Markham's eyes widened. He sat back in his chair as Zakrzewska climbed across the sill.

"How many?"

"One."

"One? That's all?" Markham scoffed. "Who is it?"

"Old lady."

"I was afraid of that!" Markham replied, suddenly bristling with annoyance. "Mitchell's sent Mother Jones. Has she called a meeting yet?"

"Tomorrow morning."

"You be there . . ."

"You want, I take care of her. Tonight, in her sleep," Zakrzewska said matter-of-factly. "Tomorrow she be found in creek with broken neck. They say old lady lose way in dark, fall down. Nobody know."

Markham raised his eyebrow, pondering perhaps the merits of this quick and brutal solution, or perhaps just shocked at the casualness with which it was offered. "A payment in kind?" he asked ruefully. "No, Zakrzewska, there are easier ways, believe me. Besides, she's too widely known. I'd have hell to pay. Where is she now?"

"Boardinghouse."

"In my backyard no less! You go to that meeting tomorrow. You're my only eyes and ears now. Let me ponder the fate of Mother Jones."

As Zakrzewska slipped home through the shadows, Markham's words tickled his brain. "Hell to pay! I'd have hell to pay." He liked the sound of that, liked the thought of Markham squirming in his boots. "Hell to pay!"

He decided that the old lady must die.

"I've lived here most of my life—as long as the town's been here," John Jones Owen told Mother. They sat in the parlor of the boarding-house near the hearth, watching the fire crackle and spit. She rocked peacefully in the chair Owen had moved in from his own parlor for her comfort.

"I saw the breaker go up, all the houses, helped paint some of them myself," he continued. "They were all bright red then. I was here the day the first families moved in. My *dada* was pit boss then. He was a big man.

"I was there when they brought up Old G.B.—the day he got killed. He'd gone down to inspect a new seam they'd found—a rich vein, the biggest they'd ever seen in these parts. A mule car broke loose, pinned him against a wall. Then John took over. He was just twenty-one—right out of school—but he knew more about mining than Old G.B.

"Yes, I've seen it all—up and down this street—stories that'd break your heart—some I couldn't repeat in front of a lady like yourself—but the sorriest day I ever saw in

Jeddoh was the day John brought them hunkies in. I told him not to, but he wouldn't listen. We've had nothing but trouble since. And now this.''

"Was he a good man?" Mother asked.

"Ned? Oh, yes. There were none finer than Ned the Splicer. He was liked by everyone. Markham thinks it was the union's doin', thinks they sent men in to stir up trouble, but I say it was them hunkies did it to get back at Markham for well, you see, we had a lot of trouble in town this past summer. Things were getting out of hand. Markham had to evict some families—hunky families. If you ask me, it was one of them hunkies that came back one night and shot Ned just to be mean. 'Twas two Fridays ago, late. He was on his way home from the saloon. Somebody ran up behind him in the dark and shot him in the back." Owen shook his head and stared at the dying fire. "Sad . . . sad . . ."

"Yes, this town is full of sadness . . . and fear," Mother said. "I see it everywhere. In the children, the wives, even in you, Mr. Owen."

"In me?" Owen scoffed. "Well, when the good Lord calls us yonder . . ."

"It's not fear of dying I speak of, but fear of living."

"How do you mean?"

"It appears that your John Markham has not only mined his coal but his miners as well," Mother said ruefully. "There is no hope in this town, no . . . no *life* left."

"Even so, but without John Markham, there would be no Jeddoh now, would there? John Markham *is* Jeddoh."

"I cannot deny that," Mother said with veiled sarcasm. "Nor can I deny that your John Markham is a very remarkable man. I have frequently heard his name mentioned in my travels."

"And what exactly *is* it you do, Mrs. Jones?"

"Missionary work."

"I see. Well, there are many souls hereabout need saving. You could be in these parts a very long time."

"I hope not, Mr. Owen. The Day of Reckoning is upon us!"

"It is . . . ?" Owen asked, astonished. "I mean, it is! It certainly is, Mrs. Jones! And I pray that we will all be ready when that day comes!"

"Amen, Mr. Owen. A-men to that!" the hell-raiser exclaimed heartily.

"Well, it's getting on late," Owen announced and began to tamp his pipe against a stone above the hearth. "Can I be bringing you anything else before I turn in?"

"No, thank you. I think I'll just sit here a while longer."

"As you please. The fire will burn itself out. Just close the lamps before you retire. Breakfast is at seven. Good night then."

"And good night to you, Mr. Owen."

Mother rocked gently in front of the dying fire, listening to the steps creak as Owen wheezed his way to bed. Her mission seemed clearer now and more formidable than she'd imagined.

(". . . there are many souls hereabout need saving!")

"The slaves in the caves need to be saved first," she muttered to herself, rocking, rocking.

(". . . you could be in these parts a very long time.")

"Not if I can help it . . . not if I can help it."

Rocking, rocking . . .

"Teofil?" she asked. Her mouth still hurt. Her jaw felt swollen.

He stirred beside her on the bed. The room was still in disarray—curtains in a tangle on the floor, her dresses clumped atop the trunk. The smells of powder and sweat hung thick in the air.

"Are you awake?" Gwladys asked.

He mumbled some reply.

"Teofil, who . . . who is Ewa?" she asked, as if her brain had no control over her tongue. Part of her wanted to forget she'd ever heard the name, but only a part of her.

He lay still and did not answer; her hand moved across the gulf between them and rested atop his.

"You called me Ewa," she said quietly, almost apologetically.

"I did?" he replied, managing to sound astonished.

"Who is she? What is she to you that you would call me by her name?"

Zakrzewska rolled onto his back and stared at the ceiling. "She was girl I knew... in Chicago. Long ago. We were to marry once, but my friend, Feliks, from the old country, he charmed her and took her away. Long, long ago. My Ewa."

"Like the wife in the story?"

"What story?"

"The story you told the night we met," she reminded him. "The farmer and his friend who went to America. While the farmer was away, the friend..."

"That was just story!" he interrupted, wishing to end this discussion. "It tell how I feel."

"What made you think of her then? Now? Today?"

"I was not in my right head. I was thinking crazy thoughts."

"Do you still love her?" she persisted.

"She is gone from me."

"Do you still love her?"

"No... no," he answered softly and turned back to her and took her hand and squeezed it.

She sighed, believing, because she wanted his words to be true, because believing him was easier than living with her doubt. "Teofil," she begged, tears of sadness streaming from her eyes, "let's leave this place."

"Where would we go? What would we do?"

"I don't know, I hate it here. I hate this life."

"Do not worry, my love," he said, comforting her tears. "I have plans. You will not be miner's wife for long. I have plans."

Euan lay awake that night, listening to the fence alongside the house creaking in the wind, like a rusty hinge. A sudden gust rattled the window. He tried to sleep, wanted to sleep... sleep... (But he heard his mother in the kitchen. She was singing. She sounded merry. Was it morning? Already? A golden light filled the room.

"Time to wake then," he heard the Ghost say. Euan sat up. The Ghost was sitting in the chair by the window, putting on his boots.

"I knew you'd come " Euan said. "It's been so lonely. Will you stay now?"

"For a while," the Ghost said. "I must be back."

"Please?" Euan pleaded, but the Ghost just smiled.

"I have seen wonders," the Ghost told him. "Wonders beyond belief!"

And then they were at breakfast and his *mam* was piling flapjacks onto their plates. "Just the way you like them!" she reminded the Ghost cheerily, then covered each stack with a thick stream of maple syrup.

"I'm blasting a new seam," his *dada* announced. "It must be eight feet thick in spots!"

"I know," said the Ghost. "I know."

"Is it cold there?" his *mam* then asked. "It's not like here, is it? I think about you all the time."

"You should see Jenkin's new pups," Euan said. "We can go down after work. He'll let you hold them."

"No, no . . . it's time," said the Ghost, opening the door.

"Not yet," Euan pleaded and followed him onto the porch. "Take me with you! I want to go with you!"

"You belong here," the Ghost told him. "It's up to you now. I'll show you." And they flew into the air, high over the yard, high over the trees, up into the sky. The Ghost held on to Euan tight so he would not fall.

"Be careful!" his *mam* called, waving from below. "Be careful!"

"Everything . . . it all looks so small!" Euan gasped as they flew over the town. "Look! there's the men, heading for work. They look so sad, so tired. And there's Tadi and Jenkin and Little Jake and Patsy! They look all hunched over, like old men. They're not like that! Look there's a fight! It's Tom Pryor and Mr. Moczygemba! You've got to stop them then, it's terrible! They shouldn't be fighting! Why is it like this? Can't you do something?"

"I have seen wonders," the Ghost whispered in his ear. "Wonders beyond belief!"

"I'm slipping! Hold me tight!" Euan suddenly shouted. "Don't let go! I'm . . . I'm falling! Faaaallling!")

◆◆

"The company owned both sides of the creek, you see, but not the creek itself," Mother told Euan the next morning as they climbed the rocky path to the clearing on the hill. "The company thugs said, 'Step one foot outta that water, and we'll fill you full of bullets!' So I walked up the middle of the creek all the way to Wineberg, and there the miners met me, and there we held a meeting with our feet in water up to our knees. They took the obligation to the union just like that, their shoes above their heads, their pants rolled up—it was the damnedest thing you'd ever want to see."

Mother talked endlessly as they climbed, telling of men and towns as if he'd been there himself, as if he should've remembered. Euan had never heard so many names. She talked endlessly, never out of breath, never stopping for a rest or begging him to slow down. "She's like a book," Euan thought, "she's so full of words."

He still didn't know why he'd come with her. He just knew he couldn't stay away. He'd risen early, swept the porches before his *mam* could tell him to, then sneaked off before she thought up more chores.

"I'll catch hell when I get home," he thought, "but I'd probably catch it one way or the other if I stayed."

The clearing was deserted. "We should have stood in bed, Euan Morgan!" Mother said as she sat on a large flat rock, allowing herself a few moments to rest. Then, shielding her eyes from the sun, she surveyed the surrounding terrain. "Come on, you damn yellow bellies!" she shouted. "I don't bite! This here's a union meeting, not a hanging!"

Euan looked around but saw no one.

"They're out there all right, behind trees and rocks.

They're afraid," she said quietly, with certainty. Then, bellowing again, her voice echoing in ripples off the hills, "You pity yourselves, but you don't pity your brothers! Else you'd stand together and help one another! Come on, boys! Come join the union!"

Still, no one came forward.

"I would like to get past," Myfanwy said to the ragged little girl who sat blocking the steps in front of the company store. In her arms, the child clutched a brown paper package almost as big as she was. "Can't you hear?" Myfanwy asked more insistently, but the child just stared back with piercing, stubborn eyes. She looked three, no more than four, Myfanwy thought, but her eyes evinced a wisdom beyond her years.

The child reminded Myfanwy of her Gwennie.

"*Prosze?*" the child implored. "*Czy moze mi pani pomoc?*"

It had not occurred to Myfanwy that this urchin was a hunky child, but with a torn dress and dirty hands and face, how could she be anything else? Suddenly the girl's elfin eyes looked less seductive, less like her Gwennie's. "Begone!" she commanded one last time, brushed the child aside with the back of her hand, and hurried up the steps.

No sooner was Myfanwy inside than she came face-to-face with Margaretta Jenkins. "*Bore da,*" Mrs. Jenkins said, feeling as awkward in their confrontation as Myfanwy. "We've missed you in church these past months."

Myfanwy could barely hide her fluster. She rarely went to the company store nowadays, hoping to avoid encounters just like this, preferring to send Euan when she could, but with Euan nowhere to be found this morning, she had to choose between going herself or doing without.

"My Hugh...he's not been well, you know. We've... we've been..."

"We missed you," Mrs. Jenkins repeated emphatically. "I hope we will see you tomorrow then."

Myfanwy forced herself to smile, then looked away

self-consciously, but Mrs. Jenkins pressed on. "Myfanwy, forgive me saying this, but you look so . . . unhappy. It will not do to simply shut yourself off. Take your burden to the Lord and leave it there. Come back to us Myfanwy."

For the second time in as many days, Myfanwy found herself struggling with her grief, grief that even now threatened to overwhelm her. She blamed Hugh for Rhys's death; she blamed Markham and his mine. She blamed the world for robbing her of a son, and when she ran out of others, she blamed herself.

"There is so much to say," Mrs. Jenkins continued. "We have failed to stand by you in your need, to comfort your loss. Myself, I have wanted many times to climb that hill and knock on your door. Please forgive me, Myfanwy, for I am weak."

Myfanwy's resistance crumbled. Her eyes filled with tears, tears of regret and relief, and there, beside the bolts of linen, the women embraced and made their peace. Myfanwy found some peace.

On the first Saturday of the month, Gwladys rode to Wilkesbarre on the noon train to purchase supplies for her schoolchildren. It was a journey she had not expected to be making this fall, but it was the only part of her job she looked forward to. Her classroom was more crowded than a year ago, more crowded with hunky children. Some couldn't even speak their own language. What hope had she of instilling virtue and citizenship in such a lumpish lot? With the Markham girls gone, she had no prizes left, only lumps—lumps with dirty ears and ragged clothes, who squawked like chickens in a pen, who spat at her and called her names she could not understand.

She wondered about the Markham girls as the train left Jeddoh Station. The little ones still fussed over her when they saw her, but Mary hadn't come to see her all summer, had not even stopped to say goodbye before leaving for Miss Cadwallader's School. She had seen Mary only once, riding in a carriage with her mother. The girl looked languid, as though her life were at an ebb. Her sparkle was gone. Gwladys wondered in passing what misfortune might have occasioned such a doleful demeanor—a lost locket? A strayed trinket? It didn't matter. The girls were gone from her life, gone for good. She hoped they hated their new schools as much as she hated her own.

"Ticket, please?" asked the conductor.

She handed him the scrip Markham provided for such occasions, keeping her face turned to the window to conceal her bruised and swollen face.

When Myfanwy and Mrs. Jenkins left the store, they came upon a group of children who were taunting the little girl on the steps. Their jeers were in Polish, but their intent was unmistakable. The child was in tears.

"Here now, get away! Stop that!" Mrs. Jenkins shouted as she ran into the street, waving her fist, scattering the screeching offenders like magpies in a field of wheat. They dodged and swooped until she nabbed the chief tormentor by the coattail, then slapped him hard and pulled his hair.

In her fright, the little girl ran to Myfanwy and threw her arms around her legs. "*Matka! Matka!*" she whimpered through her sobs.

"The boldies!" Mrs. Jenkins said as she returned, leading her squirming captive by the ear. "Never happy unless they're causing mischief." She gave the bully one last cuff and sent him on his way. "Oh, look! The poor child!" she said, kneeling to console the waif.

"Who is she?" Myfanwy asked.

"Do you remember the woman, the Polander, who fainted that day in the store? The husband," Mrs. Jenkins confided in whispers, as though the child might understand, "died of drunkenness not long after. She herself died some days ago . . . trying to end the life of the child in her womb with a mixture of kerosene and . . ."

"Oh, no!" Myfanwy gasped.

"No other relations hereabouts—just the six children. Families on the Hill have taken some in—the older ones, the ones who could work. This is the youngest. She's being sent to Wilkesbarre, to the Home for Friendless Children.''

"Poor child," Myfanwy said, drying the girl's eyes with a handkerchief. "Dry your tears now."

"*Matka?*" the child asked softly.

"She's asking you to be her mother," Mrs. Jenkins said.

"Me? Oh, Lord!" Myfanwy said, flinching. "That's all I need."

Moments later, the carriage from the orphanage arrived. As Myfanwy and Mrs. Jenkins said their good-byes, Mr. Beech, the store manager, came forward, lifted the little girl up, and set her in the front seat next to the attendant. Never once did the child take her eyes off Myfanwy. Nor she hers.

"I wonder what her name is?" Myfanwy thought. As she walked home, the child's face would not recede from her mind.

"The woman, a Mrs. Polk, had three children, and all of them worked alongside her at the mill," Mother told Euan as they each ate a half of the sandwich Mrs. Owen had made for her that morning.

"A cotton mill?" Euan asked.

"Yes, cotton. In fact, this was in Cottondale, Alabama," Mother said, spitting the name out with contempt. "When I get to the other side, I shall have to tell the good Lord about Cottondale, Alabama!"

Determined that her trek up the hillside would not be in vain, Mother preached to her lone companion, and Euan, captive as he was, and hungry, had no choice but to listen.

"There were children younger than you working there," she went on, her voice ripe with indignation. "Boys and girls, walking barefoot down endless rows of spindles, reaching with little hands into machinery that was built up north, built low for the hands of babies to operate, to clean and oil all day long, all night through—tiny babies six years old who looked sixty, working in twelve-hour shifts for ten cents a day. If they fell asleep, they got cold water thrown on their faces. One day, a girl of nine—little Maggie Sweeney—got her long, beautiful hair caught in the machinery. Before the men could throw the switch, her scalp was torn off.''

Euan winced. He couldn't imagine such things happening.

''Of such is the Kingdom of Heaven!'' Mother observed wryly. ''A great teacher once said that. Well, I say if heaven is crowded with undersized, round-shouldered, hollow-eyed, sleepy little angel children, then I want to go to the other place with the bad little boys and girls. Have you had enough?'' she asked without pause. ''Cheese, I mean. There's more.''

''I will, thank you,'' Euan replied, reaching as she broke off a piece.

''The father, you see, had died of tuberculosis, and Mrs. Polk and her three children had to work off the cost of his burial. They wore the amount down, penny by penny, but the end seemed nowhere in sight, so I decided to rescue those wretches from that everlasting debt, to get them out of Cottondale for good so's they could start a new . . .'' She stopped suddenly in midsentence, stood, and started to gather her things. ''I've just about given up on these coal-crackers!'' she said with irritation. ''We waited long enough, don't you think? What do you say we head back?''

Euan didn't care one way or the other. All he wanted was to hear the end of Mother's story.

''I've never seen anything like it!'' Mother tore on. ''Grown men, too cowardly to fight for their own rights! They'd rather spend a year in hell with Markham than ninety-nine in heaven! I've been in holes ten times worse than this place where the men were willing to strike until the last of them had dropped in his grave!

''Why, I remember one night in West Virginia not long ago,'' she said and sat down again, forgetting that a moment before she had wanted to leave. ''I was going up the mountainside with a comrade from Illinois. I said to him, 'John, I believe it is going to be very dark tonight,' and he agreed, for only the stars were shining to guide us. Well, when we got to the top of that mountain, besides the stars in the sky we saw other little stars—the miners' lamps—coming from all sides of the mountains." She pointed to the surrounding hills as if she could still see those lamps. "Those miners were coming to a schoolhouse where we had promised to meet them. I said to John, 'There comes the star of hope, the star of progress, the star the astronomer will tell nothing about in his great works for the ages yet to come, but that star—the star of the true miner—is going to light the way to the future. That star will shine when all the others grow dim."

When Mother's passion was spent—and her stories were never less than passionately told—she surveyed the hills one last time, then shook her head in disgust. "I don't suppose we'll be seeing any stars today. I'm beginning to wonder if the stars shine on this part of the world."

"So . . . ?" Euan asked anxiously. "Were they rescued?"

"Who? Oh, yes! The Polks! I hired a wagon from a farmer and drove them through town in the dead of night to the train station, like escaping Negro slaves. I expected any minute to hear bloodhounds on our trail. I'd asked the station agent to flag down the express train that night, and when it stopped, I put them on. By damn, I got those babies out of there into a school where they belonged! No more factories, God willing, no more!"

With that, she pulled a lace handkerchief from the tip of her sleeve and began to wave it back and forth in front of her, like a fan. Only then did Euan become aware of the glare of her probing eyes.

"Well, Euan Morgan," she added stiffly, as though she were about to collect a fee for her storytelling, "are you ready to join the union? Or did I come all this way for nothing?"

"I haven't got fifty cents," the boy said sheepishly.

"We can overlook that. We do that sometimes."

He suddenly felt trapped. "What would I have to do?"

"Just take the obligation."

Euan looked puzzled.

"It's like an oath, a pledge," she explained. "You put

your right hand up like this, and you promise before God to uphold the beliefs of the union.''

''Then do I have to go on strike?''

''Not until the others do.''

''What if I'm the only one who joins?''

''You've got more damn questions! You're just like a Welshman!'' Mother snorted. ''Think it over. When you're ready, speak up, and I'll give you the pledge.'' Just then, the sound of fiddles wafted up from Polish Hill. ''Here now! What's this?'' she asked, cupping her hand over her ear.

''There must be a wedding.''

''A wedding!'' she exclaimed, her expression brightening. ''Haven't been to a wedding in ages!''

''My brother, Rhys, plays fiddle at weddings. He plays good,'' Euan said without thinking. Almost at once, his face clouded over.

''He *did*, did he?'' Mother said matter-of-factly. ''You were very close, you two, weren't you? It's a terrible thing to lose a brother, especially in the mines, especially in the service of industrial profiteers for whom life is cheap. I tell you, men's hearts are cruel; they are indifferent. Not all the coal dug can warm the world.'' She sighed and put her hand on Euan's shoulder, as though she had momentarily run out of words. ''What do you say we go down to that wedding?'' she said finally. ''It'll cheer us both up.'' As easily as that, it was decided. In a moment, she was not only on her feet, but had started down the hill. Euan, however, lagged behind. ''Well, are you coming or not?'' she called back.

''I was thinking,'' he said, looking pensive. ''I was thinking what Rhys would do, if he would join the union.''

Mother walked back to where the boy stood. ''Your brother's not here anymore,'' she told him firmly, then wiped away a tear that had collected in the corner of his eye. ''And he's never coming back, you hear? Do you hear?''

Euan nodded.

''Pray for the dead, Euan Morgan, that's all we can do.

Pray for the dead and fight like hell for the living! Now, come on! We've got a wedding to go to," she said and trotted off down the hill.

While Myfanwy was scooping sugar for a cake—she hadn't baked a cake in months—a small amount spilled onto the oilcloth-covered shelf. As was her nature, to clean a simple spill, she cleared away every box and tin within reach. Her fear of ant armies converging on the site outweighed her distaste for whatever added work this might entail. Thus, as she lifted her bread box off the shelf, she was startled to find a wad of money underneath. It took a moment before she remembered that she had stashed it there herself.

The memory rushed back to her—women at the door, speaking in broken English, black shawls draped around their heads, a hand thrust out to hers, a handful of dollar bills.

("Money? For Rhys's life? How could money...?")

She had not thought of the money once since that day, and now here it was again, come back to haunt her. She wished she had burned it—she could still—or was it too late for that?

And then it occurred to her. "The debt! We could pay off the debt to the store. Or the burial." She started to count it, then stopped. "No! It should go for something else. Let something better come from all this pain. Why, Euan could leave the breaker and go back to school!"

She ran upstairs, scribbled Euan's name on an old envelope, tucked the money inside, and placed it in her drawer beside those she kept for the girls. She resolved to tell Hugh that night of her plan.

"Well, well, Miss Protheroe! What a pleasure!" said the unctuous Mr. Huntzinger as he descended a ladder with a book he had just plucked from the top shelf. The bookseller had a gift for making even the most casual remark seem patronizing. "And what can I do for you today?"

"I have a list. Just a few things," Gwladys replied, handing it over, trying not to look at him directly. She found him ugly and horrid, the only man she had ever seen who wore rouge on his cheeks and rings on his fingers.

"Maxwell's *Picture Book of Animals?*—yes, I have that. Richardson's *Lives of the Presidents* . . . no more love poems, Miss Protheroe? No more Robert Browning?"

"They can barely read," she answered grimly.

"I thought you had several who showed a talent for literature."

"Gone.

"The students or their talent?"

"Both."

"Oh, really? What a pity," the bookseller said with no real sympathy. "Well, then, I'll have the boy get these for you. Would you care to wait in my office, Miss Protheroe?"

"No, thank you," she said curtly.

"Suit yourself." His face curled into a frozen smile.

"And I'm Mrs. Zakrzewska now."

"Oh, really? And to a Polander? Funny, I never imagined you married, Miss Protheroe."

"Mrs. Zakrzewska."

"Whatever. Hmmm, nasty bruise that," the bookseller said, touching his hand to her cheek. "One of your ruffians?"

"No," she said, turning aside.

"Not your Polander, I hope?"

"Perhaps I'll just browse in the meantime," she said, fleeing from his touch.

"By all means," he said with a knowing smirk. "By all means."

"What a nasty man," she thought as she glanced through the shelves with no particular interest. She dallied for a moment at the front window to watch the passersby, then turned with no particular purpose to gaze upon the public notice board near the entrance. In the corner was a wanted poster. A wanted-for-murder poster.

"That's odd," she thought. "Odd for a bookstore."

Out of boredom, her eyes read down the rest of the sheet . . .

## WANTED FOR MURDER

## TEOFILIA ZWIARDOWSKI

### Last Seen in Wilkesbarre
### Believed to be Dangerous

. . . stopping at the photograph of the wanted man, a man who looked not unlike her Teofil—younger and handsomer, perhaps, but with the same broad forehead the same eyes, the same brash smile. "How *very* odd! And the same first name too!" she remarked to herself. She read on.

Suspect Is Wanted by the Sheriff of Cook County, Illinois, for Murders of EWA ZWIARDOWSKI, wife . . .

"Ewa!" she moaned under her breath. "That name again!" She stepped closer with dread. There was more.

. . . for Murders of EWA ZWIARDOWSKI, wife and FELIKS ZAKRZEWSKA

A gasp escaped her lips; her head felt light. The room suddenly seemed stiffling. She braced herself against the wall. "No, such a thing is impossible," she assured herself. "It's . . . it's a simple coincidence, is all. Polish names are all alike. And there are hundreds, perhaps thousands, of Teofils in Chicago, at least a dozen of them named Zwiardowski, and another dozen named Zakrzewska, and half of them at least have . . . *had* girls they planned to marry or wives named Ewa. . . ."

Breathing hard now, she reached out and traced the face, the eyes, the lips of the wanted man, as if the tips of her fingers would know if they were touching her Teofil, as if they could tell if he were a murderer.

("Hide it! Hide it from sight!" a voice inside her cried. "Don't let anyone know! Don't let anyone see!")

"No, no! I must show it to him so I can hear him say it is not true!" she decided and tore the poster off the board, then folded it with trembling fingers and stuffed it into her purse.

("Oh, my God! My God! What has he done?")

"Is everything all right?" asked Herr Huntzinger. "I thought I heard choking sounds. I thought perhaps you weren't well."

"No . . . no," she said with a wan smile. "I'm fine."

("I think my husband's a murderer, that's all!")

"You look rather bilious to me. Perhaps you should lie on the divan in my office for a few minutes."

"No, no!" she protested. "I'm fine! It's just so . . . so stuffy in here. I need some fresh air is all."

Gwladys lugged her books across Public Square in a daze. Then she saw it — another poster on a telegraph pole — and another on a tree — the same face, the same insolent eyes — the eyes of a murderer!

She laughed. "They're all over town! How could I hope to hide it? My God! Oh, my God! What am I going to do?"

Mother tracked the music straight to Maciejewski's yard, like a hound following a scent. Euan trailed far enough behind so that no one could say for certain that he was with her. Somehow he knew what was in her mind and wasn't sure he wanted to be there when it happened.

"Are you coming or not?" she called back as she reached the gate. "I swear, you're the slowest poke I've ever met. The future of the working man cannot wait on your dilatory habits. The working man is moving on!"

"More words and more words!" Euan thought. "She tires me out with her talk." He had long since stopped wondering what they meant. By the time he asked her to explain, she was already off on something else and had forgotten what it was she'd just said.

"Now stay close to Mother," she said when he caught

up. "I've wasted half a day already. If I'd known they were all going to be here, I wouldn't have had to climb that goddamned hill. You'd think somebody would have *said* something!" With that she headed along the path between houses and into the crowded yard, smiling, greeting strangers as if they were old friends, tickling babies, taking beers from the hands of guests as if they had been meant for her all along.

"What a brazen old goat!" Euan thought, even though he couldn't take his eyes off her. In no time she had worked her way through the guests toward the platform where Razor and his fiddlers were playing, and as one song ended, before another could begin, she hoisted herself up so everyone could see her.

"*Dziekuje! Dziekuje!*" she shouted, nudging Razor aside, acknowledging the applause for his music as her own. Razor just stared at her, dumbfounded. "Thank you, my friends, for inviting me to your celebration."

"Who invite her?" Euan heard Karl Maciejewski ask the bride's father.

"Not me," answered the bewildered man.

"You all know who I am," Mother continued, undaunted. "You've made me feel like one of you since I came here, one among friends. I'm Mother Jones, here to save the slaves in the caves! Come nearer, my brothers! Fear not, I will not take up much of your time, but what I have to say is very important."

"Ve don't vant trouble here!" a voice shouted. "Better you go home!"

Mother ignored the jeer. "You men came from far away to this land . . ."

"It's just like Wilkesbarre all over," Euan thought. "She just goes on and on, 'cause if she stopped, they might not let her get started again."

"You came here because you believed in your hearts . . ."

"Ve don't vant union here, lady!" another voice interrupted.

"What's that? You say you don't care if your wife and children starve? You say you'd rather work longer hours for less pay? I think Markham would be more than happy to arrange that.''

"Ve don't vant union! Union can go to hell!''

"Down in Wilkesbarre," she yelled back angrily, "and up in Carbondale and Pottsville, good American men are working day and night to keep the union alive, and you stand there and tell the union to go to hell! Well, I wouldn't say that too loud or too long if I were you, buster, 'cause one day some of them red-blooded union men might come through this town and give you a boot in the ass and a one-way ticket back to Gdansk! Now, watch your mouth!''

There were gasps from the crowd. No one had ever heard a woman speak so boldly, so rudely, but Mother tore on, her voice bristling with sarcasm.

"You know? I pity you men, you big, strong men who have allowed a few bullies to boss you, to starve you, to abuse your women and children, to deny you learning! I've heard what's going on in this town. What the hell's the matter with you? Are you afraid of Markham? Or the Coal and Iron goons he's hired to keep you in line? I can't believe that you great, strong men are so cowardly, but I'll tell you this, if you are, you are not fit to have women live with you!

"This fight that we are in—and you are in it whether you like it or not—is the fight of working men this world over, men who have seen through the dark clouds over their heads to the star that rose in Bethlehem nineteen hundred years ago. Look to that star, my friends! It will free you and make you stronger men. I see that star breaking your chains. For the first time, there is hope among the workers of this earth. My friends, it is solidarity of labor we want. We do not want to find fault with one another but to make ourselves strong and say to each other: 'We must stand together! Our masters are joined together, and we must do the same!' ''

Mother began to have her effect. Their cries of anger ceased. Even those who could not understand her words were mesmerized by the power of her delivery. Now it was time for the heart of her message.

"Let me tell you what it is that we are fighting for. Higher pay! A twenty-percent increase for your long hours of toil. Is that so bad? You'd take it, you're not fools. Shorter hours! An eight-hour day! The railroads got it, why not you? An end to dockage! And our own weighmen— paid by the union!—to make sure every miner gets an honest weigh-in. And last for now, a lower cost for powder! Why pay three twenty-six for a keg that cost Markham seventy-five cents?"

"Vhy shoult ve vorry 'bout dockage an' veighman an' powter?" asked Karl Maciejewski. " 'Dere are no jobs for us as miner."

"How many of you are miners?"

Only two men raised their hands.

"Well, you will be, more of you, all of you! Think about tomorrow, my friends, and the next day. It'll happen, I promise you. Now, who'll be the first to join the union, boys? Make me proud of you! Who'll be first?"

Suddenly, four Coal and Iron Policemen charged into the yard with their guns raised. "Halt there! You're under arrest!" one shouted to Mother. The crowd backed away, leaving Mother and Euan, who was sitting on the edge of the platform, surrounded by empty space and her four captors.

"And what may I ask is the charge?" Mother demanded imperiously.

"Disturbing the peace!" the officer in charge replied.

"Young man, I have not yet begun to disturb the silence of this town!"

"Come quietly," the officer threatened, "or we'll take you by force."

"You touch one white hair on this head, and I'll give you a good, swift kick where you'll remember it most! Just point the way, and I'll follow."

"This way, ma'am."

"You see what I'm up against, Euan Morgan?" she said as she reached out to lean on the boy's shoulder. "There seems to be no shortage of ignorance in this town." Then, quietly, as she stepped off the platform: "Meet me later on Frog Street. After dark. There is much to be done!"

As Mother was led off to jail through the silent crowd, she thanked and said "*Dzien dobry*" to everyone she passed.

In a season of odd sights on Frog Street, the oddest was the spectacle of four armed Coal and Iron Policemen escorting a white-haired grandmother to the town jail. The curious poured onto their porches to watch the procession. For those who had been unaware of her presence in Jeddoh, this was a startling introduction.

"The union is coming to Jeddoh!" she announced over and over, till the guards hushed her. "I should've done this in the first place," she realized. "Would've saved myself a lot of time and trouble."

Mother had been arrested so many times by now, she'd lost count—in West Virginia and Illinois, in Maryland. Getting arrested, she felt, was part of her job. It brought her attention and sympathy, both of which were needed by the cause. In Jeddoh, it only brought attention.

"What's this now?" Mother asked as her guards turned into the yard in front of the boardinghouse.

"This is the jail," said one of the policemen.

"I thought it was the boardinghouse."

"It's also the jail."

John Jones Owen emerged onto the porch as Mother was led up the steps. "Well, Mrs. Jones, did you have a nice day?"

"I did until these thugs showed up."

"Mrs. Jones is under arrest," said the officer in charge.

"Arrest?" Mr. Owen gasped. "What for?"

"She's a labor agitator. She was disturbing the peace up on the Hill."

"A labor agitator? Why, you're not *Mother* Jones, are you?" Owen asked, shuddering with distaste.

"The same!" she barked. "Now I suspect I shall be chained to that tree out front so Markham and his dogs of war can riddle my old body with bullets. Well, do what you must, Mr. Owen, but I will not surrender my right of free speech to *you* or John Markham or . . . !''

"Calm down, Mrs. Jones! Nobody's going to shoot you!''

"Hah! You got a lockup here, or will I be thrown in the root cellar?''

"We have, yes, we have a lockup—a room, really—in the back. It's very comfortable.''

"Good,'' she said. "Bring my things down from upstairs. I'm not paying for a room if you're giving me one free.''

"Right this way, Mrs. Jones,'' Owen said and led Mother and her guards back through the hallway.

"Might I use the convenience before I'm jugged?'' she asked.

"I suppose so,'' Owen said. "One of the officers can go with you.''

"I think I can manage by myself,'' she huffed.

He looked at her suspiciously. "No shenanigans now?''

"In an outhouse?'' she blurted indignantly, then stalked out through the back door and up the path, turning once to see that Owen was still eyeing her carefully. "This could take some time, Mr. Owen. Don't let me keep you.''

"I assure you, Mrs. Jones. You are not keeping me at all.''

But Mother was even more obstinate. "There's room here for two if you care to join me,'' she said as she swung open the privy door.

Perturbed by her baiting, but embarrassed, too, Owen reluctantly turned away. When he looked back again, she was gone.

Mother ran the length of the boardinghouse to Frog Street as fast as her short legs would carry her. She knew she had a minute at most before her captors had the nerve to open the privy door to confirm that she indeed had fled, a minute to reach safety before they set out after her.

On a porch a few houses up, she saw some flower pots

that looked familiar from her calls the night before. She scurried onto the porch and knocked vigorously on the door. After what seemed like an interminable wait, a woman with a spot of flour on the tip of her nose and another in her hair answered.

"Hello, I'm Mrs. Jones," Mother said, breathless from running. "I was here yesterday. Last night to be exact. And you're . . . ?"

"Mrs. Pryor. "

"Right! You see? I remembered," Mother said, pushing her way inside. "It's so nice to see you again."

"What? Is there anything . . ?" asked the startled Mrs. Pryor.

"Oh, a cup of tea will do nicely," Mother replied and looked casually out the window just as the Coal and Irons ran past.

Gwladys took the late afternoon train back to Jeddoh. She watched the sun blaze bright through early golden leaves. She counted cows.

She listened to the clackata, clackata.

She listened to gabbing club women in feathered hats and smart dresses, who were returning to Hazelton after attending a musicale at the Strand. She wondered if any of their husbands were murderers.

( . . . clackata, clackata . . . clackata, clackata . . . )

"I know so little of him really. All he speaks of is his work and his mysterious plans, nothing of his life in Chicago or in the old country. He is secretive, yes—but a murderer? At times he is bad-tempered, impatient, inconsiderate. He's a spoiled child, not a murderer," she told herself.

( . . . clackata, clackata . . . )

"He's been good to me. He has. He tells me my cooking is good even when it's not. He bought me new dresses. The house is comfortable, even if it is in the worst part of the worst town in Pennsylvania. What did he say, 'You will not be miner's wife for long?' He's advanced quickly. He'll be a boss soon, then a superintendent, and we'll have a better house and I'll be able to leave that miserable school for good and wear feathered hats and see musicales at the Strand and have other women envy me," she persuaded herself.

( . . . clackata, clackata . . . )

"It couldn't be Teofil on that poster. Lots of people look like other people. Why, sometimes I can't even tell one child in my class from another, they all look so alike. And the poster clearly mentioned that *Zwiardowski* was wanted, not Zakrzewska. Besides, Teofil didn't have a wife. He said so, and he wouldn't lie about a thing like that," she convinced herself.

( . . . clackata, clackata . . . )

"He wept. He knelt before me and wept. He begged me to forgive him. Would a man who has murdered do that? If he has faults—still—it is because I have not tried hard enough to change him. I am as much at fault. He wants to do better, he does. He is merely an imperfect man in an imperfect world," she realized.

( . . . clackata, clackata . . . )

"The wanted poster is just coincidence. Or an unfortunate confusion. He is not a man who would do such a thing. To even call his attention to it would be folly. Whose interest would it serve? Not his. Not mine. It is simply . . . not . . . him!"

( . . . clackata, clackata . . . clackata, clackata . . . )

She resolved to burn the poster as soon as she got home.


"There she was, five dollars worth of paint on her cheeks, coming down the street in an automobile," Mother said to Mrs. Pryor as they stirred their tea in the parlor. "She was a mine operator's wife—a 'lady'—for sure. You know, of course, that 'ladies' were created by the parasitical class, but women were made by God Almighty himself."

Mrs. Pryor found herself giggling at Mother's gibes despite herself.

"She had a poodle dog sitting on the seat next to her," Mother went on. "Every now and again the poodle would squint his eyes at his mistress and turn his nose up at what he saw. He seemed to be saying, 'You corrupt, rotten, decayed piece of humanity! My royal dogship is degraded by sitting beside you!' These are the same women who will stand up in a crowd and say, 'Oh, that horrible old Mother Jones, that horrible old woman!' I *am* horrible, I admit, but I have never decorated my hands and neck with the blood of innocent children.''

Mother set her teacup down and laid her hand across Mrs. Pryor's. "Do you see what I'm saying, Mrs. Pryor? No nation will ever go beyond the development of its women. Lift up the women and make them intellectual, I say, and thus, will great sons be born and men find true comrades in their wives. That is why I need you to speak to your husband. This . . . *situation* in Jeddoh cannot go on much longer. Tell him I want to speak to him and some of his comrades.''

"I doubt, Mrs. Jones, that my husband would listen to anything I . . .''

"Then I'll tell him myself,'' Mother insisted. "At supper. You did invite me, didn't you?''

"Well, I . . . I . . . ,'' Mrs. Pryor stammered. "I'm sure we have enough if . . . I mean, if you . . .''

"Good!'' Mother exclaimed, cutting the woman off. Time was too precious for needless chatter. "And tomorrow morning after church, I want you to bring all the women you can here to your house. Oh, Mrs. Pryor, my old eyes can see the dawning of a greater day! I see behind the dark clouds the star that rose in Bethlehem nineteen hundred years ago, the star that will break man's chains and free mankind!''

It was late afternoon when Gwladys arrived back in Jeddoh. The town looked as grimy and dust-choked as when she left. It looked as dreary.

She was relieved to hear fiddle music and singing as she trudged up the Hill. That meant Teofil was probably across the street in Maciejewski's yard, celebrating with his friends—or was this a funeral? Either way, she was glad that the house was empty. She couldn't bear to face him now. Not yet.

Their bedroom was still torn apart. She sifted through the rubble of her life—her immigration papers, destroyed; mementos, shredded; her photographs, unrecognizable; their marriage certificate, ripped to pieces. There was little left to pick up, nothing left to save.

She swept the dusting powder and parchment, the torn photographs and feathers into the coal bucket, carried them down to the kitchen, then threw them into the stove. Almost as an afterthought, she took the wanted poster from her purse and opened it one more time before consigning it to the fire. "I want to be certain it isn't him," she told herself. "Absolutely certain." Suddenly her eye dropped to words at the bottom that had escaped her before.

REWARD $500
If Captured Alive

She reread the poster from top to bottom twice through. Each time, her eye seemed to linger over those same provocative words; each time, they seemed more enticing. She refolded the poster. Later, she hid it in a safe place in her dresser drawer. Gwladys was still, still not absolutely sure.

The shades were drawn in Tom Pryor's parlor. Seven disgruntled miners had gathered to listen to Mother speak her piece.

"We're not against what you're saying, mind you," said Tom Pryor. "The conditions here could stand improving, but we'll not be part of any union with the likes of them roundheads."

"Mr. Pryor, the coal you dig is not Welsh or Irish or Polish," Mother huffed. "It's coal! The air you breathe down there is the same. You all take the same risks. A roundhead, as you call him, might some day save your life."

"Or take our jobs for less pay," retorted Dai Edwards.

"If you were both union, that wouldn't happen."

"You don't know Markham then."

"I'm not afraid of John Markham!" Mother snorted. "Why should you be? I would fight God Almighty if He didn't play square with me. If I have never in all my life—in all the battles I have had—taken backwater, then why should you? Now I want you boys to buckle on your armor. This is the fighting age, not the age for cowards. For the first time in history, the capitalistic machine has realized that there's been an intellectual awakening of the dog below, and that he's *barking*. Have you been *barking* in Jeddoh?"

"It's easy for you to come in here and say this and that, but it's our jobs we'll lose, and the homes we spent our lives working for," Pryor argued. The others nodded in assent.

"Do you own these homes?" Mother asked, at the end of her patience.

"No," they said.

"Well, there you have it! You don't own your homes, you don't own your jobs, right? Is that what you're saying? Markham owns them both, because he owns the machines! Machines he bought with the blood of children whose lives he has wrecked! And he owns you, too, is what you're saying!" Mother looked exasperated. She drew a deep breath and began again. "I see the problem here as one of education. You men in these mining towns have only the mine owners' preachers and teachers, the mine owners' doctors and newspapers to look to for your ideas, so you don't get many. If you could only see what I'm trying to tell you! You *do* own the mine, boys!" she said and slammed her hand down hard atop the table. Then, as she looked from one man to the next, her voice rose to its most fierce and stirring pitch. "The outside belongs to Markham, but the inside, where your job is, belongs to *you*. If you say, 'We're not going to work today,' there's not a damn thing Markham can do. He can't force you to work. This is still a free country. Until you can say, 'Markham, you've lived long and well off the sweat of our brow, go dig your own goddamn coal!' you will not be fit to call yourselves the sons of Patrick Henry and Abraham Lincoln. When you do business with this fellow, Markham you've got to have ammunition, and you've got to know how to use it! You must have a system, a force behind you, and that force is the union!''

She paused to catch her breath. The room was cast in silence, but for the first time, she felt a glimmer of heat, a stirring of passion long turned cold. "Come on, boys," she cajoled. "Now who will be first to join?"

◆◆

IT was late when Zakrzewska managed to elude the Coal and Iron Police that patrolled Frog Street and slip into Markham's study to deliver his good news.

"No one?" Markham asked, sounding almost disappointed.

"No one," replied Zakrzewska. "I watch from beyond trees. Only old lady and boy show up."

"What boy?"

"Boy who help her climb hill. Morgan boy."

"Ivor Morgan?"

"No. Other Morgan. Hugh."

Markham waved his hand as though the boy were insignificant. "Now if I just keep her out of the way."

"I tell Maciejewski to call Cossacks," Zakrzewska boasted. "When she bust in on wedding."

"Good thinking."

Zakrzewska smiled broadly, waiting for Markham to say more. Instead, Markham took a sheaf of papers from his drawer and began to spread them atop his desk. "When you leave, leave quietly."

But Zakrzewska did not leave.

"Is there anything else?" Markham asked.

Zakrzewska paused. "Yes. My reward."

Markham looked up from his papers as though Zakrzewska had just slapped him across the face. "Your reward? For what?"

"For telling you about union lady!" Zakrzewska said, pacing anxiously across the room and back. "For following old lady up goddamn hill! For following orders! For being eyes and ears! Now, you give me job of Ned Splicer. That is what I want.''

Markham tried hard not to let his rising anger show. "I gave you the job you have. You were merely returning the favor."

"That is old job! I want new job."

"Ned grew up with me, man! We started together as boys in the breaker. He knew that mine as well as I did, better even! Ned was irreplaceable."

"I *deserve* his job," Zakrzewska demanded loudly. "And I will have it!"

"Keep your voice down! Remember where you are!" Markham snapped. "Do you think for one minute I would take you on as my right-hand man? You're not a skilled miner. Your knowledge of ventilation and engineering is nonexistent—you proved that by killing five good men— or have you forgotten already? What's more, I find you personally repulsive. Go back to the job you have and be grateful."

"Do not say anything you will regret," Zakrzewska warned, his eyes narrowing to slits. "I will have that job."

"Get out of here! You disgust me!"

As he left the yard, Zakrzewska pulled a gun from his coat pocket and made sure, for the third time, that it was loaded.

"The tide has turned, Euan Morgan! We've got the pirates on the run now for sure!" Mother rejoiced when Euan finally caught up with her on Frog Street. He'd been waiting for over two hours in front of the company store, wondering, worrying about her safety.

The sky was starry, the air crisp, crisp enough for him to wish he'd worn his coat. The moon shone full and bright, bright enough to cast bold shadows of trees and fences across Frog Street, shadows of the Coal and Irons, walking their beat. As the night wore on, Euan had seen less and less of the Coal and Irons. Instead, they hovered in front of Maciejewski's yard or the Emerald, cadging cups of beer. One by one, he'd watched the lights go out in

Cheesetown, in Irish Flats, and he knew that if he didn't head home soon, his *dada* would come looking for him. Suddenly he saw her, scooting from the Pryor house, like a rabbit from a warren. When he caught up, she started in without so much as a "how do you do?" as if ten minutes instead of hours had passed since she'd seen him last, as though there'd been no arrest, as if he hadn't fretted all through supper and into the night.

"Think I got six ready to come over. Miners, all of them," Mother said excitedly. "Some have worked here twelve, thirteen years. Hahoo! Once I've got them, the rest should follow easy!"

"Were you arrested?" Euan asked.

"They tried, but I got out. I've been in worse pickles."

As they neared the cemetery, an owl hooted. A distant clamor of music echoed from the Hill. Otherwise, the night was still. Deathly still.

"Tomorrow I shall rise early and have a bath!" Mother announced. "And then I shall go to church. I want to see this man, Markham. Or maybe I'll go up to mass at Holy Trinity. That might even be better."

Euan felt uneasy as they walked. He thought he heard a rustling in the leaves near the gravestones. He felt that they were being watched.

"Where would be a good place to start?" she asked. "What men are most respected on Polish Hill? Moczygemba?"

"He's good."

"What about this Zak . . . Zakshefski?"

"Stay away from him. My *dada* says he's the devil."

"Good!" Mother exclaimed. "Then it's Mr. Moczygemba! Tomorrow I shall spend my time on Polish Hill."

As Mother chattered on, Euan nervously looked over his shoulder toward the graveyard. "There's someone . . . some *thing* there, watching. I know it!" he said to himself and tried to get Mother to walk faster, to hurry home faster. Suddenly, out of the corner of his eye, he detected movement beyond the graveyard fence. A moment later a shadowy figure emerged from the trees and followed them in a parallel course not thirty feet away. "Am I seeing things?" he wondered. "Should I tell Mother? Or will she think I've got the spooks?"

All at once Euan saw the dark figure raise his arm and point something through the wrought-iron fence at Mother, at him. In the moonlight, he could hardly distinguish the object, but the way the man held it left no doubt. It was a gun.

"Look out!" Euan cried aloud and flung himself back into Mother, knocking her out of the way as the gun exploded in fury. He heard the bullet whiz over their heads as they toppled into the dust.

"What the hell . . . ?" Mother squawked.

"Stay down!" Euan whispered as the gunman leaped the fence and advanced toward them, breathing fast, breathing heavy, holding the gun with both hands to steady his uncertain aim.

"Get away from here!" Mother hollered at the gunman. "There's Coal and Irons coming now! I can hear them!"

Indeed, they could hear voices but too far off to save them. If this man meant to kill Mother or kill them both, he had his chance but his hand shook. His finger froze on the trigger.

Suddenly, in a nearby house, a bedroom window flew up.

"Hey, there!" shouted a voice. A dog began to bark.

The gunman looked up at the window. In that instant, in that light, Euan saw his sweaty face and knew who he was. The man gasped at being seen before retreating to the graveyard. The man his *dada* called the devil sought sanctuary in the shadows from which he'd come.

"He must be the devil," Euan thought. "Only the devil would want to kill Mother Jones. Only the devil sweats on a cold night."

"This lad saved my life!" Mother boasted to the Coal and Iron Policemen and men in nightshirts who gathered around her.

"Are you hurt?" they asked her.

"It'll take more than Markham's bullets to do me in.

Now you see the lengths to which power and privilege will go to keep workers in slavery!''

"Did you see who it was?" they asked the boy.

Confused, fearful of his father's wrath if he found out where he had been, what he had been up to this day, fearful of the devil himself, the boy told them no.

"Boys, where the hell were you when I needed you?" Euan heard Mother chastise the Coal and Iron Police as they led her back to the boardinghouse. Euan, too, was escorted home, because it was late, and the gunman might still be about. Even so, Euan knew he was being watched.

"If you'd have kept where you belong, Mrs. Jones, this silly business wouldn't have happened," John Jones Owen said, opening the door to the lockup.

"I don't know what you're talking about, Mr. Owen."

"The wife brought your bag down from upstairs," he said, pointing to where it lay atop the dresser. The room was spare but tidy—a narrow bed, table, and chair, even some pictures on the wall. The single window had bars across it.

"Is this really necessary?" Mother asked.

"Just a formality, ma'am. Oh, and this, too," Owen said as he nudged a porcelain chamber pot from under the bed with his foot. "The wife's own, thank you. You'll not be needing the convenience out back."

"I should like a bath. Tomorrow morning," she said, testing the bed. "Before I go to church."

"Baths are Saturday night. You'll have to wait till next week," Owen told her as he left the room. "Good night then."

"But I won't be here next week!"

He smiled a knowing smile as he closed the door. A moment later she heard the sharp crack of a heavy bolt being slid into place.

Gwladys was awakened late in the night by sounds of thrashing in her kitchen below. At first, she feared that a wild animal—a raccoon or fox—had somehow broken in and was foraging through her foodstuffs. It was a moment before she realized that the sounds were coming from her Teofil, who had not come home from his mysterious ramblings till now.

Gwladys moved to the door and opened it a crack to listen. She heard him stumble into a chair and swear under his breath. She heard him drink a glass of water and throw a dish against the wall. And then he began to weep—no, sob—like a forsaken child.

She went downstairs to comfort him.

"There now, what's this?" she asked, seeing him with his head buried in his hands.

"Goddamn boy keep gettin' in way!" he mumbled between sobs. "Goddamn him! I should kill damn boy and have it over!"

"There, there now," she said and put her arms around him and pressed his head close to her. "It's all right. I'm here. Everything will be all right now."

"I will not . . . I will not get what I want now!" he moaned.

"Yes, you will," she comforted him. "Everything is going to be fine from now on. You'll see. You'll see. Teacher is here now. Everything is going to be just fine. Everything."

◆◆

"QUIET down in there!" the guard on duty shouted, unable any longer to endure the steady racket that Mother had been creating for the better part of the morning. First, she had pounded on the door. Now it seemed as if she was dismantling the furniture piece by piece.

"I wish to speak to Mr. Owen!" Mother shouted back.

The guard opened the small viewing panel in the door that allowed him to see into the lockup. "He's not here. He's in church!"

"Where I should be!" she growled at him through the opening. "Now unlock this door!"

"It's against the rules, madam. You're a prisoner."

"I am not a madam, and I order you to open this door!"

For a moment, the young guard was silent. This Mrs.

Jones reminded him of his own white-haired and frail grandmother in Shenandoah. The very thought of someone holding his saintly kin in a damp and dusty lockup filled him with a revulsion deeper than any he had ever known.

"How do I know. . . ? If I do, ma'am, how. . . how do I know you won't run off like you did yesterday?" he asked, his voice quivering with uncertainty. "I'd lose my job if you did."

"Son," she said in her most commanding voice, "a job like yours ain't worth having."

"That may be true, lady, but it's the only one I got," he replied and slammed the panel shut in her face.

"Sit down, lad," his *dada* told him with a stern look.

"I'm in for it now," the boy thought. "The strop or worse. He found out I was with Mother Jones on the ridge or in Maciejewski's yard. Or is it about last night? Somebody came, I bet, while *Mam* and me were in church and told him." He tried to swallow, but his throat felt like leather. "Think! Think!" he berated himself. "Think of an excuse!" But he was never as good at that as Rhys was. He just knew that he was in for it now.

"You're going back to school," his *dada* told him instead. "Your *mam* and I want you to quit the breaker."

Euan wasn't sure if he'd heard him right. Or heard it all. What did going back to school have to do with going against his father's orders?

"Did you hear me?" his *dada* asked.

Euan nodded. He'd heard him right, he guessed, but he still didn't understand. He had to quit the breaker to go back to school? Was that his punishment for talking to the union lady?"

"It's all for the best," his *dada* went on. "I never wanted you there. It pained me to see it, with you so young."

Only as his *dada* digressed about his own days picking slate, only when he saw his *mam* smiling—no, grinning!—as she went about her work in the kitchen, did Euan realize that Mother Jones was not at issue here at all.

"Quit the breaker?" he asked. "Quit my job?"

"Yes," his *dada* said. "You'll not go back come Monday."

"But . . ."

"It's no place to be. You belong in school."

"But it's my job then! I can't leave it," Euan said, choking back his tears. "I want to stay where I am."

"You'll go to school like I tell you!"

"But I don't want to!"

"You want to end up like your *taid*?" his *mam* interjected. "Coughing so bad from the asthma he couldn't catch his breath? He coughed so bad at night, my *mam*'d find blood on the pillow when he woke."

Euan could see at once that his *mam* was the engineer behind this turn of events. Her eyes burned with a fierce determination. He had never seen her so possessed.

"He worked the mines all his life, same as your dada. It's the mines that's ruined your *dada*'s health. He's not the same since his accident, don't you know? With wheezing and the like. And it'll not be long till the asthma has its way with him, too. It's the mines that's took . . . that's took our Rhys. If I got to go in there and work myself, I'll not let the mines have my little one, too." She put her arms on Euan's shoulders and hugged him close to her. "You're all I've got left," she said through her tears. "They'll not get you, too."

"On what grounds am I held here, Mr. Owen?" Mother huffed indignantly through the panel in the door.

"Unlawful flight from arrest," Owen said. His voice was full of spite.

"I thought it was disturbing the peace."

"You've been cleared of that charge. Shortly after you were arrested some came forward and spoke on your behalf. If you'd not fled like the guilty culprit you are, you'd be free now."

"And how long am I to be kept here?" Mother asked with a contemptuous smile.

"Until we decide what to do with you."

"We? I see! This is Markham's doing! He owns the

town; he owns the justice! Where's a telephone? I wish to call Mitchell in Wilkesbarre!''

"The telephones don't work on Sunday."

"A telegraph then."

"The office is closed on Sunday."

"Dammit to hell!" she shouted. Her anger made Owen wince. "If the world came to an end today, you jackasses in Jeddoh wouldn't know about it till next week!"

"It will do you no good to exercise profanity, Mrs. Jones," Owen said, grateful there was a door between them. "You're in enough hot water as it is. Now then, are you comfortable? Is there anything I can bring you?"

"Yes, a hacksaw, so I can begin to work on these goddamn bars!"

He slammed the panel shut in her face.

That afternoon, on the pretense of going to tell Jenkin and Little Jake that he had quit his job, Euan ran to the boardinghouse to inform Mother of his plight.

"How can I join her union if I don't work in the breaker anymore?" he fretted. "She'll know a way. She'll tell me what to do. She'll have a few thousand words of advice."

When Euan reached his destination, he found John Jones Owen sitting on the front veranda with his wife. Mother was nowhere to be seen.

"I'm looking for . . . I mean, my *mam* sent me to find the old Jones lady," Euan lied.

"Oh? And what would your *mam* be wanting with the likes of her?" Owen asked suspiciously.

"To have her by for tea."

"How social of her! Well, I'm sorry to say that Mrs. Jones has left us already. This very morning, the union men came up from Wilkesbarre and drove her off in a carriage, they did. You can tell your *mam*, and anybody else who asks, that she said she won't be coming back to these parts again. Not for a very long while."

Euan didn't believe him for a minute. He was getting too adept at lying to be taken in. "He's saying too much," he thought. "That's the mark of a liar for sure. Why would she leave? She was just getting started. What'd she say, 'We've got the pirates on the run'?''

As he walked back up Frog Street, he began to worry that something bad had happened to her after all. She wouldn't just leave, he was sure of that. No, he was certain she was still in Jeddoh, but where? Maybe she was meeting with the miners in the clearing. And maybe she was still locked up in jail. Maybe Mother needed him right now as much as he needed her, but who could he turn to for help? Who could he tell?

With his head down, absorbed in his dilemma, Euan failed to notice that Zakrzewska was watching him from his porch. When their eyes finally met, Euan hesitated slightly, enough to signal his recognition of the man, and his fear.

"Hey, Morgan!" Zakrzewska called, descending his steps.

Euan shuddered. It was too late to turn and run. He had to pass the house and pass the man his *dada* called the devil. He quickened his pace.

"Hey, Morgan boy! I am talking to you. Come here!"

Euan kept his eyes to the street, afraid to look over, afraid one look might be too much.

("Hurry, hurry! Got to move, got to get! Don't stop, got to get!")

Euan heard the devil's breath drawing nearer, felt the devil's finger clutching at his coat. Twisting free, he ran. Crying out, he ran.

"Next time, I will get you!" he heard the devil shout. "Next time, you not be so lucky!"

◆◆

"COME here," his *mam* said. "You look like you combed your hair with the leg of a chair."

He squirmed under her scrutiny. Why he had to have his hair combed to go to school was beyond his comprehension.

"And don't be giving Miss Protheroe, or whatever she calls herself now, a bad time of it. You're not with the ruffians no more. You're to listen and obey, you hear?"

Euan nodded. He had gotten up at dawn as usual, had

gotten dressed as usual, but at breakfast he was sullen and ate with a scowl to show his great displeasure.

"Now give me a kiss," she chirped.

He did dutifully and rushed out the door with his *dada*, a move he would regret when their ways parted at the entrance to the colliery, for he was suddenly bombarded from all sides by the gibes of his former mates.

"Euan's goin' to scho-ol! Euan's goin' to scho-ol!" the boys taunted as they marched past him to the pit head.

"Give me love to Miss Protheroe!" laughed Patsy.

"And don't be feelin' her up when she bends over," Jenkin warned him. "She's married now!"

"Teacher's pet! Teacher's pet!" Little Jake crooned.

Euan ignored them, or tried to. What pained him more than their gibes was the fact that his *mam* and *dada* had brought this sorry state upon him with their good intentions. As the boys ran up the hill to the breaker, Euan felt left behind. He wasn't one of them anymore.

He lingered outside the school and listened to the breaker start up, heard the first wagon tippled into the trough, heard the rollers chewing up the coal. "The whoop is rising now, it's rising," he thought. "The coal's barreling down the chutes, and now they're yelling, they're screaming! And the coal's exploding over their heads like fireworks!" He closed his eyes and felt the sound bursting in his ears. He felt the dust pelting his face. He tasted the coal.

He watched the loki move empty cars to the loading bins, heard the sheaves singing as their cables raised the cage, felt the ground shuddering from shots set off in the deep shafts below. Every man had a job but him. Every gear, every tool, every machine had a purpose but him.

When he finally stepped inside the classroom, the palms of his hands began to ache. The room looked twice as crowded as before; every seat was doubled up.

"Well, look who it is!" his nemesis spouted when she saw him. "Were you sacked then for loafing on the job?"

Euan bristled. Her voice was like a red top.

("Piss on her then! Make her go away! Piss on her school, and make it go, too!")

"You know what they say?" she asked cuttingly. "Once a breaker boy, always a breaker boy." She made him sit on a stool in back so she wouldn't have to look at him.

They sang that morning, silly songs about robins and sparrows, but Euan didn't sing. He didn't like to sing, not these songs. They recited multiplication tables and spelled words he'd never heard of before. The girls spelled their words right and giggled when he spelled his wrong. He wondered how long they would last, hunched over a coal chute, picking slate.

They read in turn up and down the row. Each reader stood and read ten lines while Miss Protheroe prowled the aisles, dispensing praise, but mostly castigation. She no longer patted the English and Welsh girls on the head or admired their pretty bows. She had scowls enough for everyone. Everyone was a Polander to Miss Protheroe.

She slapped faces, pulled hair, dispensing in just one morning enough punishment in advance to last the whole year. But it wasn't the slapping or the hitting that Euan hated to see, and dreaded, for the pain of that punishment wore off. It was the other kind—her loathing, her name-calling, her belittling, the hurting of the mind that could last for days and maybe never go away—that made him shudder most.

"Who was *she* to be so cruel, to break their hearts and make them cry?" he asked himself.

"Next, Euan Morgan!" she bade him, calling out of turn, as though she'd read his mind. "On your feet, Morgan. Or have you lost the place?"

He rose slowly, almost painfully.

"Well? Are you going to read? Or stand there like a clod?"

" 'The . . . crops . . . were . . . ' "

"Louder!"

" 'The crops were . . . plan-ted . . . by . . . the . . . be—' "

"Sound it out!" she clucked impatiently.

"Be ... gin ... ," he read, making "g" a soft consonant, "be ... gin ..."

"BEGINNING!"

" 'Be-gin-ning of ... plan-ting ...' " The next was even more perplexing.

"Sound it out!" she called sharply.

" 'Se ... se ...' "

" 'Season,' stupid! Sit down! NEXT!"

"Don't call me stupid, you ... you ... !"

" 'SIT DOWN!' I said! And shut your stupid mouth!"

"No! No, I won't sit down, you ... you big BIG FART!" he hollered and threw his book across the room at her. She ducked in time, but his angry missile crashed through the window and landed in the yard.

"You little bugger, get out of here! NOW!" she screamed and chased him toward the door, but Euan didn't need prodding. He was halfway there already. "AND DON'T EVER COME BACK, YOU HEAR?" she hollered shrilly. "DO YOU HEAR ME?"

Euan raced across the yard, free of her. Again. For good. It didn't matter what his *mam* and *dada* said, he would never go back there, not ever. He headed straight for the colliery, the pit head where he pegged in, then to the breaker. He reentered *his* world—the only world he wanted to know. He ran up to the picking room two steps at a time, past the old men with brooms, past rows of lunch buckets and Bryfogle's sneer. He climbed up to his old perch and pressed his feet into the swift, black stream. The rumbling machines, the cascading coal, the swirling dust and pounding noise were *his* again.

The other boys looked at him, welcomed him back, and wondered what had taken him so long.

The picking room seemed changed. Or he had changed. The boys looked the same, but somehow they were different, too. Or maybe he was different. He had grown from the timid boy who had stumbled in here five months before, but he felt different even from the boy who had left this chute at quitting Thursday last. He suddenly felt detached from this place, from these boys, as if he were standing on a high building looking down at a parade. Still, he was one of them. He understood their thoughts. He shared their suffering, their joy. He was one of them and yet remained apart.

Some things in this tight little world never changed. Bryfogle never changed. He still smelled of soiled underwear. He had gone five months more without a bath. He was still a drunkard. There was a new boy on chute no. 2 that morning. No one even knew his name. Bryfogle was brutal with him. And so were the boys.

"Ye, farmer, ye!" Bryfogle shouted as he rapped the boy's head with his oak rod, a new one that replaced the old one broken the day that Digger died. "This here's coal! I don't want to be seein' it in yer box no more, an' if'n I do, ye'll eat it! Ye hear?"

The boy was terrified. He had cried himself out. He looked weak, unfit for the rigors of the picking room. His fingers were already scraped and starting to bleed, and yet he stayed on.

At lunch they called him "nancy boy" and spilled coal dust on his food and tossed tiny bits of coal at him when he wasn't looking. They trotted out the broomstick, then filled his box with coal—the usual rites of entry that even Euan had laughed at when they were inflicted on others, just as they had been inflicted on him. This time he was sickened by it all.

"They're no different with their gibes and cracks than Protheroe and her slaps and taunts. They hurt the same, and all they do is make you want to hurt back."

The new boy looked no more than eight. Bryfogle chewed him out after lunch and rubbed his flinty whiskers across the boy's tear-stained face. When he grew weary of tormenting the greenhorn, of his crying, Bryfogle turned him back to the boys. Finally Euan's tolerance was gone.

"STOP IT!" he shouted.

And they did, astounded by his wrath and indignation. Even Euan wondered from where in him the voice had come. His head felt light as he stood over the whimpering boy, swaying slightly, dizzily, but defiantly daring any of them to go on tormenting the newcomer.

"No more! Stop it! Now!" he shouted again and glowered at them till they all took their places on the chutes. Then he took his place, and the coal started to flow, and he nearly fainted when he realized what he'd done.

At the pit head after quitting, Euan ran into his *dada,* who had to look at him twice to make sure he was seeing right. His face, his hands, his shoes were black with dust.

"You know what you're doing?" his *dada* asked him quietly.

Euan nodded.

"Let's go home then and tell your *mam.*"

His *mam* already knew. Miss Protheroe had paid a visit after school.

"*Why* did you have to call her that *word*?" his *mam* shouted as he slinked up the back steps. Her eyes were red and full of hurt. "I'm ashamed of you."

"Because she is!" he shouted back. "She's a big fart! And I won't go back! You can kill me first, but I won't go back!"

His *mam* seemed as though she'd shrunk since he left the house that morning. It seemed as if a part of her didn't love him anymore. His *mam* had changed. Or he had changed. She sounded the same, but somehow she was different.

Or he was different.

❖❖

IT was called sulfur ball. Whenever Bryfogle had his back turned, the players dug into their rock boxes for hard clumps of sulfur they kept hidden under the bony and slate and tried to hit various targets in the picking room. Most sulfur balls missed, splattering instead against catwalks and walls, but enough hit their targets to cause Bryfogle no end of aggravation, for usually he was the target.

Miners were supposed to lay aside the sulfur they found and send it up when they had enough to fill a wagon. Yardmen then dumped it among the culm banks that surrounded the colliery. Sometimes the miners would dump it into abandoned workings, but more often than not they simply loaded the worthless sulfur in amongst the coal they sent up. Thus, it was weighed, tippled into the trough and pulverized by the grinders. It was up to the boys to capture and discard the remaining pieces.

It was not surprising to anyone then, as Markham kept raising the ton, that more and more sulfur began turning up in the coal. No more could a boy get away with emptying his rock box two, maybe three times a day. Now it was four, sometimes six times a day to the throwaway chute at the far corner of the picking room, carrying fifty pounds of useless bony, sulfur, and slate—enough to make even the strongest boy groan. Sulfur became the curse of their lives. Until the day Patsy Morrissey invented sulfur ball.

The rules were simple enough. One boy challenged another. He also got to choose the target, but the other boy got the first throw. If he hit it, he won. If he missed, his challenger threw his sulfur ball. The challenger won if he succeeded in hitting the target, but he didn't automatically lose if he failed. The boy who had accepted the challenge got one more chance to redeem himself. If he missed on this try, he got to pick a new target. A challenge was never dropped until one boy or the other was victorious. The loser always had to empty the winner's rock box.

Once invented, the game became the favorite in the picking room. Hardly an hour went by without at least one challenge. The only drawback was the lack of good targets. Windows were out. The cost of broken windows could be deducted from a fellow's pay. Steam pipes and ladders were favorites, as were wood beams and handrails. The door to Bryfogle's office had been hit so many times, it was encrusted with sulfur. However, it was Bryfogle who offered the most imposing target, for he was not only large and tempting, he *moved*. What's more, as he lurched drunkenly across the catwalks, he seemed oblivious to near misses that whizzed over his head or splattered sulfur down on him from above.

It wasn't that Bryfogle didn't know what was going on. There was just nothing he could do to stop it. He could see

sulfur balls streaking past out of the corner of his eye—
sometimes when none had even been thrown. He felt the
resulting rain of sulfur on his head, and he most certainly
felt the sharp sting of direct hits. He had welts up and
down his back and across his ample behind. He began to
dread leaving his den. He walked so that he always faced
the boys, but the very moment he turned away, or in the
second it took him to blink, he was bombarded with sulfur
balls. He never once caught a culprit in the act, for every
time he wheeled about after a direct or indirect hit, the
hooligans were diligently at work.

They were insidious.

The morning after Euan returned to the picking room for
keeps, Dennis Riley challenged Patsy Morrissey to a game
of sulfur ball. The target Dennis chose was Bryfogle's
derby hat. Patsy kept a special sulfur ball tucked under his
coat. It was an unusually large specimen that had somehow survived the rollers intact. He decided to use it for his
special target.

With the challenge in place, the only ingredient missing
was Bryfogle himself. As the morning wore on, he failed
to appear from behind his closed door. Finally, just as they
were about to remove the hinges and go in after him,
Bryfogle staggered forth to relieve his bladder against the
picking room wall.

It was Patsy's throw first, the only one he would get as
far as he was concerned. He braced himself, aimed, and
threw with all his might, but all his might was not enough.
Instead of rising to Bryfogle's pate, the missile followed a
lower arc and crashed like a small cannonball against his
wooden leg, which shot out from under him and threw his
already shaky balance completely awry. For a moment,
Bryfogle wavered, like a great tree about to fall, then, with
his arms swimming backwards, toppled helplessly to the
deck. The floor shook. A great cloud of dust rose up. It
was an altogether terrifying sight.

The boys thought Patsy had killed Bryfogle for sure. It
didn't matter that he'd only been hit in the leg with a sulfur
ball, and a peg leg at that. He *looked* dead. The only vital

sign was his morning stream, which continued to shoot forth, like water from a whale's spout.

Suddenly the great "corpse" sneezed and sneezed again, then sat up and glared about the room with vengeance in his eyes. "I'll kill youse now! I'll kill youse all, ye little bastards!" he huffed as he tried to raise his fleshy bulk from off the floor.

The boys laughed at his clumsy thrashing, at his tired threats. He was a pathetic bag of farts, of smells and ugly scowls. They laughed as he tucked his privates back into his breeches and spat and waved his fist. They laughed as he began to claw his way toward the chutes. They laughed until he grabbed Tadeus Harakal by the hair and yanked him up beside him on the deck.

Tadi screamed as Bryfogle shook him, then squeezed him with his brutish fists.

"Ye smart ass! Teach ye to laugh at me! T'aint so funny, is it, when it's ye? Is it?" Bryfogle snarled and hurled the fragile boy toward the wall, the pissing wall. He landed in a clump on the floor, in a puddle of warm piss, and lay sobbing and catching his breath and sobbing some more.

The rest of the boys cowered over their chutes till one by one, sobered and contrite, they thrust their feet again beneath the rushing stream, which all the while had gone unpicked.

"The next'll get worse!" Bryfogle warned them. "Worse, ye hear?" For the rest of the morning, he prowled the catwalks overhead, daring them to step out of line.

"Now you done it good! Tadi nearly got killt on 'count of you!" Jenkin accused Patsy that noon in the yard. The boys had carried their lunches outside to escape Bryfogle's dirty looks.

"He'll forgit by quittin'," Patsy shot back. "And don't be callin' me names, ye cheese-eater, or I'll teach ye manners fast! Got me 'nother sulfur ball up top, waitin' jest for yer ugly puss!"

"You just try it! It'll be the sorriest day of your life!"

"Why should I give a damn 'bout a hunky anyways?" Patsy asked cockily.

"Tadi took your cracks!" Jenkin said sharply. "It was your doin', and he took the cracks!"

"So what?"

"You should care!" Euan blurted out. "We should care what happens to our brothers!"

The boys looked at Euan in amazement, wondering what startling words would come from him next. Ever since he shouted them down, they'd regarded him with suspicion.

"Mother said if we cared about our brothers," Euan explained, "we'd help each other out and not be fighting each other."

"*Whose* mother?" Patsy asked.

"Mother Jones," Euan replied.

"She that crazy lady?"

"She's not crazy. She . . ."

"Aw shut up, scab baby! I heard 'nough of yer poop!" Patsy balked and strode back inside.

"He's as bad as fatass himself," Jenkin said with a frown.

Little Jake disagreed. "Patsy's just stupid, but Bryfogle's mean. I hate Bryfogle."

Euan looked over at Tadi, whose face was black and blue, whose lip was cut, whose hands still shook. "It's not right then," he thought. "It's not. It's not right."

After lunch, Patsy was picked by Bryfogle to break up a jam in the top house. When he staggered back down, there was a deep gash on his forehead, and he couldn't stop trembling. The boys called his name but he didn't hear them. During the next lull, Patsy told them he'd slid halfway into the hole at the bottom of the trough and that his feet had touched the rollers before Bryfogle pulled him up.

Euan knew that something had to be done.

That afternoon, the yardmen hitched a mule to a wagon loaded with half a morning's refuse from the picking room—a long ton of bony, slate, pieces of timber, and sulfur balls that had been stored at the bottoms of twenty-four rock boxes. As the yardmen, Dai Edwards and Geoffrey Hughes, led the wagon toward the back gate and the culm banks beyond, they heard loud voices coming from Markham's office. One voice was Markham's, the other unknown to them but unmistakably foreign. They knew that Markham was second to none dealing with disgruntled or insubordinate workers and almost pitied the foreigner, who was feeling the full force of Markham's wrath.

"Glad it ain't me in there," Hughes said.

"Same here," echoed Edwards.

When they led the empty wagon back over the same route a few minutes later, Markham's harangue had ended and only the hot-blooded foreigner could be heard booming above the din of the yard.

"Dammit! You owe me!" they heard the foreigner shout. "YOU OWE ME!"

The four met that night in Jenkin's cellar. It was a secret gathering, not that many cared, but to Euan, Tadi, Jenkin, and Little Jake it was a matter of life and death.

"Did anybody see you coming in then?" Jenkin asked as he lit a lantern. The boys shook their heads no. "Jakie, stand by the other stairs in case the other side comes down." The unpartitioned cellar spread the length and breadth of Jenkin's house and the Pryor's house next door. Each side had its separate set of stairs. Each had to be guarded against intruders. Creaking footsteps crossed the floors above. Muffled voices filtered down through the cracks.

"What do we do then?" Jenkin asked Euan. "This was your idea."

"We've got to tell before one of us gets killt," said Euan.

"Ever try tellin' your *dada* the likes of that?" Jenkin snorted. "Mine'd say I was bein' a sis. He'd say take your lumps. He'd say he worked breakers that was worse than this, and it didn't kill him. That's what he'd say."

"He didn't have Bryfogle for a boss," Little Jake argued.

"*Ojciec* say, 'You got job, you lucky. Shut up,'" Tadi added.

"Tadi's right," Jenkin said. "Bryfogle'd lie like a fox to save his fat carcass."

"Then we got to watch out for ourselves," Euan said. "For each other."

"How ve do 'dat?"

"We start a union," was Euan's solution. He'd been thinking about it all afternoon.

"And what does that do us?" Jenkin asked.

"Mother Jones says a union is when people . . . people get together to say 'no' to something that's bad. It makes them feel strong."

"And when Bryfogle cracks our heads with the oak rod what do we do?"

"We say 'no,'" Euan answered calmly. "When Bryfogle tries to whack us or hurt us, we say 'no.' When he orders us up to the top house, we say 'no.' When he tries to dock us unfair, we say 'no.' We all say it. Together."

"And then he hits us all and docks us all!" Jenkin said skeptically.

"Not if we stand up for each other. Not if we're a union," Euan told them. The boys were silent as they tried to comprehend this union, this new and fearsome thing.

Little Jake spoke up first. "How do we make a union?"

"We just . . . just do it!" Euan said. "We take a . . . a obalgation."

"Vhat's 'dat?"

"A oath. It's like a secret. Between you and God."

"How 'dis go?"

"We make up our own," Euan replied. "And there's dues."

"Dues?"

"A nickel to join."

"A nickel? Jesus Christ!"

"I hain't got no nickel!"

"Me neither."

"Well . . . sometimes the union can overlook them," Euan explained. "Dues, that is.

"What would we call it?" Little Jake asked. "This union?"

Euan had never thought of a name. Mother had never mentioned what they called hers. "The . . . the Brotherhood of . . . of Breaker Boys?" he suggested.

"The *Secret* Brotherhood! That's better, that sounds good!" Little Jake added excitedly, suddenly keen to its clandestine appeal. "I'm ready! I'll join! How 'bout you, Jenkin?"

Jenkin was unconvinced. "What about the rest? You gonna get 'em all? What about Patsy? What about them them Polanders? What if we all say 'no' to Bryfogle, and they just sit there with their thumbs up their ass?" In the shadowy light, he squirmed and scowled and spit on the floor. "All right," he said finally. "But I ain't payin' no nickel!"

"Tadi?" Euan asked. "Are you in with us?"

"You t'ink I like Bryfogle? I gonna be first an' say 'no, fella' to 'dat big ox!"

"Then, all of you, raise your right hand," Euan bade them. "Your *right* hand. And say after me: I promise . . ."

" 'I promise . . . ' "

" . . . to stand up for my brothers . . ."

" 'to stand up for my brothers . . . ' "

The boys fanned out that night, after each had taken the obligation, to recruit the others. They found Gwilym Davies and Cyril Lloyd sitting out back of the Emerald and gave them the pledge in the woods by the light of the moon.

" ' . . . to stand up for my brothers, in sickness and in health . . . ' "

The next morning before third whistle, the six cornered Freddie Mooney and Mickey Figmic outside the breaker and gave them the pledge.

"If me pa finds out, I'm dead," Freddie said.

On the morning break, they got the Rykliewicz brothers and Harry Pryor, but Patsy Morrissey told them, "*Da* says ye join the union, ye lose yer job!"

At lunch they pledged three more and talked it up with the rest.

" '...fight like hell for the living, to pledge allegiance...' "

Most of them had no idea what the words meant but mumbled them anyway, with their stubby hands—and their hopes—raised high.

"Ye taken the pledge yet?"

"Raise yer right hand, an' stop wipin' yer nose! Yer *right* hand!"

"And bring yer dues to the meetin' tonight!"

"How much is dues?"

"Five cents."

"Jesus Christ!"

The new boy, Angus, thought it was a trick when they came to him—one more cruel joke—especially when Euan told him to piss on his red tops. But he took the pledge. He believed, because believing was better than fearing, because being one of many was better than being alone, and they showed him how to sit so his legs wouldn't hurt and rubbed his shoulders and back.

" '...allegiance to the Brotherhood of...' "

" '...to the Secret Brotherhood of Breaker Boys...' "

They brought in Stefan Hudock and Aldo Antonucci during the afternoon break, and Ralphie Pritchard and Tomasz Gluc, but not Patsy Morrissey.

" '...one union, indivisible...' "

" '...one union, indivigible (invisible, insavidable, indiminible)...' "

That afternoon, Bryfogle dragged Patsy to the trough again, and again he came down, looking closer to dead than alive. By then, he was ready. He took the pledge after work, and he brought in Dennis Riley.

That night they met in Jenkin's cellar and brought in the rest, and all repeated the pledge that Euan recited for them. A band of rowdies, who barely had a common language between them, each lit a candle he'd brought, paid his nickel, and joined a union.

" 'I promise...to stand up for my brothers...in sickness and in health, to save the slaves in the caves...to pray for the dead and fight like hell for the living...to pledge allegiance to the Secret Brotherhood of Breaker Boys...one union indivisible (indivigible, invisible, insavdable, indiminible) with liberty and justice for all. Amen.'"

"What do we do next?" asked Patsy. The others listened intently.

"I don't know," Euan told them. "Mother never got that far."

❖❖

THE sun splayed bright beams across the picking room.

"A boy!" the voice called down from the top house. "Send up a boy!"

The flow had slowed. The flow had stopped. The boys sat hunched over their chutes and held their breath. A feeling of dread pricked their spines, like needles, like nails, like grinders. The morning had passed with hardly a scowl from the one they once had loved to hate and now just hated.

"A boy! Send up a boy!"

Bryfogle scanned the chutes with sober eyes. Not one drop had passed his lips since Patsy's toss had laid him low. Drunk, Bryfogle was a nuisance. Sober, he was an ogre.

"We're needin' a boy! Cracker boss, send us a boy!"

"Shut yer bazoo up there!" Bryfogle shouted. "I heard ye!"

The boys stiffened as his eyes prowled the chutes, squinting at this one, frowning at that. "You!" he said and pointed at Little Jake. "I want you! Up there! Now!"

Little Jake bit his lip and looked across the chute to Euan and Jenkin and then up to Tadi. "No!" he wanted to tell Bryfogle, but the word wouldn't form on his lips.

"No!" Euan spoke for him.

"What...?" Bryfogle gasped.

"He says 'no!'" Jenkin shouted at the startled man. "And he means no!"

"No!" Tadi echoed. "He not do it!"

" 'Noooo'?'' Bryfogle bellowed, unable to comprehend this turn of events.

"Noooo!'' repeated Little Jake, finding his courage and his voice.

"What do ye mean, 'noooo'? I'm boss here! Ye do what I say, ye hear?''

"I won't do it! Not now! Not ever!''

"Git up to the trough, ye pot o'sis piss, or I'll . . .''

"A boy! Send up a boy!'' the voice from the top house called again.

Bryfogle wet his quivering lip. Sweat blanketed his brow. He wanted a taste of whiskey right now. No, he wanted the whole bottle. "Git up there or I'll . . . I'll sit on ye! I'll crush the livin' farts out of ye!''

"Make me!'' Little Jake said. "Try and make me!''

"Git up to that trough, ye little bastard! NOW!''

"No!'' the boys yelled back at him. "He won't! He won't go!''

"No!''

"NO!''

Bryfogle's hands started to tremble as his eyes darted from one boy to the next. "Ye, then! No, ye! Yer goin'! NOW! Up to the trough wit' ye or by Jesus, I'll crucify ye!'' he shouted and swung his oak rod in a broad arc. The boys in its swathe ducked low. The rest, unflinching, sat and jeered.

"Go to hell, Bryfogle!''

"Hey, stick leg! Over here!''

"You couldn't hit the side of a barn, lard ass!''

"He *is* the side of a barn!''

"When I git holt of ye, ye dungballs, I'm gonna give youse all a taste of me whiskers!'' he roared and leaped from the catwalk to the chutes, jabbing the oak rod like a saber, but the boys scattered like mice and pelted him from the catwalks with chunks of coal. "I'll get youse all! Youse won't sit fer a month!''

All his flailing and screeched threats proved futile. His heaving bulk suddenly sagged, like a sail bereft of wind. He felt the nicks, the scraps of coal against his face and neck, then raised his thick arms as shields. The oak rod clattered across the chutes.

"Stop it!" he cried as he stumbled toward his den. "Stop it, damn ye!"

Jenkin jumped the rail, retrieved the oak rod, and used it to goose the retreating tyrant.

"Goose 'im! Get 'im good!" the others urged. "Give it to 'im good!"

"Yer hurtin' me!" the cracker boss yelled, his hands darting fore and aft to protect his private parts. "Stop it! Yer hurtin'!"

Suddenly Bryfogle tripped and landed on his belly with a thud. At once the boys were swarming all over him, poking and pinching him and giggling with delight. They pulled his hair; they twisted his ears and when he begged for mercy, they dragged him into his den to finish him off.

Markham had just stepped from the cage when he was told he was wanted in the breaker.

"There's been a bit of trouble with the boys," the headman told him.

A bit of trouble, indeed.

Markham found them, not on the chutes, but swarming through Bryfogle's office. The cracker boss lay spread-eagled on the bed with a boy across each limb and two atop his belly. They had pried open his metal chest, confiscated his store of whiskey, and were pouring it now, bottle by bottle, down his gullet. Bryfogle sputtered and squirmed and choked and cursed, oblivious of the ultimate indignity they'd performed on him. Each boy, in turn, had carved his initials in the man's wooden leg.

The bolt on the door slid open, then the door itself. Mother looked up from the letter she was signing, expecting to see Owen or one of the Coal and Iron Police. Instead, she saw a face unknown to her—a man wearing a fine gray suit, who hovered beyond the doorway, trying to decide if he should enter this viper's nest.

Mother spoke first. "Mr. Markham, I presume? I'm glad you're finally here. I expected you long before this."

He entered guardedly. Her quarters, by his presence, suddenly seemed cramped.

"Please, be seated," she offered with a smile, as though he were an old friend come to pay a call, but Markham stiffly remained standing. "As you can see," she went on, her hands fluttering like spring butterflies over a welter of paper that lay atop her table, "I have been writing letters all day. If nothing else, Mr. Markham, my visit to your town has allowed me to return to a stack of correspondence I have too long ignored, and Mrs. Owen was kind enough to provide me with paper and ink."

He said nothing, just stared at her intensely as though he expected her at any moment to produce a weapon and threaten his life, but Mother refused to let his silence dampen her good mood.

"I was just writing to—it's funny you should come at this moment—to the other John—Mitchell. He's been working much too hard—his health is poor, you know? He very nearly had to put off this campaign. But as I was writing, I was suddenly filled with a wonderful feeling of joy. I thoroughly believe, Mr. Markham, that in the not far future, an era of industrial peace is awaiting us. True equality, which is the ideal of this country—our country—is nearer now than ever. The deplorable conditions that exist in West Virginia and Pennsylvania are the exceptions, the sort of medievalism that is as abhorrent to an intelligent mine owner like yourself as it is to the suffering miners. I know, employers suffer from it, too. You look as miserable as your workers! It is an extraordinary spectacle!

"This is a crude, rough business, I know, but there aren't as many in it as enlightened as you. I wish there were others like you, groping around out there for a way out of this muddle, who were searching for the source of the disease. 'Search for the mosquito!' I was just writing to Mitchell. That ought to be the slogan for both sides of the labor question. Find the habitat of the insect and drain it dry, so that it won't breed future violence. The other owners aren't on the trail of the mosquito. They're trying drugs, not drainage, as their cures. That's why I'm so glad you've come. If employers and the employed would only settle down to deep, effective thought and root out the cause of this economic disease we're suffering from and *think, think, think,* we'd come out all right. And we *will* come out all right! Don't you agree?''

Markham remained as stolid as before but Mother bore on.

"You know, Mr. Markham, the human being is most wonderful. We can do anything with him. If we would only agree to try to do the right thing with every human being over whom we have influence! So then, where shall we begin? Where shall we begin to seek out the mosquito?''

"There will be a train leaving here at ten o'clock tonight," Markham said quietly, refusing to look at her directly. "You will be put on it. I cannot have you here any longer, stirring up my men."

The smile faded from Mother's face. "The working man will be stirred up, Mr. Markham, whether I am doing the stirring or not."

"Be that as it may," he said, shifting uncomfortably, like a schoolboy in the presence of a censuring teacher, "you'll have to look for your mosquitoes someplace else. The voice of the working man has been heard in Jeddoh, and he has chosen to repudiate you."

"I beg to differ, sir. Why, just last night..."

"I have not come to bargain with you, madam, and I've heard enough of your fancy rhetoric. My men know to whom they owe their allegiance."

"Of course, because you've *hoodwinked* them and *exploited* them and taken away their manhood!" she charged, her temper suddenly inflamed. "If it was up to you, they'd work without even the paltry wages you pay them now!"

Markham refused to be provoked. "The rights and interests of the working man," he replied calmly, "will not be protected by the likes of you, Mrs. Jones, but by good Christian men like myself to whom God, in his infinite wisdom, has given control of the property interests of this country.''

"That's a lot of horseshit, Markham, and you know it! And you *know* you know it, so let's stop bandying about.'' She stood abruptly and advanced on him, but Markham tactfully backed away. "I've been shot at, arrested twice now, locked up in your bastille without recourse and without access to telephone or wire! And why? Because I dared challenge your authority in this town. You must be very afraid of me, are you? Well, I'm not scared of you. I've seen your type again and again, in Pullman, in Homestead, at Haymarket, and your kind *always* loses. Even when you beat men down and grind them into the dust, you lose! You lose your soul, and all your money can't buy it back once it's gone. You can't be a law unto yourself in this world Markham. If you had any decency left, you'd let me walk out of here right now.''

"If I did,'' he scoffed, "you'd start agitating my men to strike against me as soon as you stepped out that door.''

"You betcha!''

"Then you won't mind if I keep you here a while longer,'' Markham said with a faint smile on his face. "When the train I'm putting you on stops tomorrow, or the next day, you will be somewhere in Kansas. There, you will be free to agitate anyone you please. Have you ever been 'somewhere in Kansas,' Mrs. Jones?''

"Frequently,'' she replied, miffed at his arrogance.

"I hear it's very nice this time of year.''

"It is. I have many friends in Kansas.''

"Good. You will be well taken care of then. Farewell,'' he said and turned to go. "I cannot say that it has been a pleasure.''

"Mr. Markham?'' she called, stopping him. She had no intention of letting him leave without having the last word.

"Yes?''

"I'll be back, you know? I'm needed here!'' she said defiantly. "I've never walked away from a fight. Never, in all my life!''

"If my men wished to embrace you, they would have done so by now."

"You've seen to that by locking me up, haven't you?" Mother said her eyes flaring angrily. "So much for freedom of choice! Tell me, how can you sleep at night? How can your wife sleep, knowing the jewels she wears around her neck were paid for with the blood of innocent children who work for you?"

Markham looked stunned. Never before had anyone dared to impugn his wife. "Now see here!" he fumed. "I will not have . . ."

"Ah, you're not worth a lick of their spit anyway!" she grumbled, refusing to be intimidated by his threatening tone. "Besides, your days as a mine owner are numbered. Your friend Pierpoint Morgan is lurking over the next hill. He's going to chomp down on your neck so fast! The jackals shall devour the wolves! You'll be lucky if you don't find yourself somewhere in Kansas one of these days!"

"The train leaves at ten," he seethed, unable for the moment to match her lacerating wit. "Mr. Owen will see that you are on it." Once more, he turned to leave.

"Why exactly did you come here, Markham?" Now it was Mother's turn to wield her arrogance. "I should think you'd have more important things to do than go around announcing train schedules. Don't you have hacks to run your errands for you? Maybe Pierpoint Morgan can lend you some of his!"

Markham glared back with an expression as cold as steel. "I came to see the mighty Mother Jones," he said sardonically. "The most 'dangerous woman in America!' So far, all I've seen is a woman in her dotage, a sham, a pathetic old gadabout. If you ask me, you're the mosquito. You're the source of the disease. You raise my men's hopes for a future they will never have, and one they don't deserve. Go on, take your disease somewhere else! Go contaminate some other place!"

Mother was taken aback by Markham's vehemence. "When . . . when I get to the other . . . to the other side," she stammered, "I'm going to have to tell the good Lord about you."

"That will be soon, I hope," Markham said and left, carrying Mother's pen and ink.

After nightfall, Gwyndaf Pugh drove Black Maria around to the back of the boardinghouse. Under Owen's watchful eye, Coal and Irons escorted Mother out and lifted her into the back compartment, where an upholstered chair from Owen's parlor awaited her.

At the station, she sat on the same upholstered chair, surrounded by her cordon of guards. Owen hovered near-by, smoking his pipe and checking his watch every thirty seconds. At the other end of the platform, Bryfogle, also under guard, sat blubbering into his sleeve.

"He going to Kansas, too?" Mother asked.

"He *was* the cracker boss," Owen told her. "The boys gave him a time of it today, said they wouldn't go back to work till he got the boot."

"Well, I'll be damned!" Mother thought to herself. "That's why Markham decided to ship me out in the dead of night—he *is* afraid! The voice of the people, indeed! Atta boy, Euan Morgan!"

The late train was headed for Wilkesbarre not Kansas. The lone passengers on board were a repair crew, returning from a long day's work replacing a section of track torn up by a derailment. In preparation for the long descent down the western slope of the Nescopeck Mountain, the engineer released excess pressure from his boiler just as the train entered Jeddoh Station. Thus, on a clear but windless night, the train to nowhere pulled in with its steamcocks open wide. In a matter of seconds, the platform was shrouded in steam.

When it dispersed, Mother, too, was gone.

Jozef Moczygemba was awakened by a knocking on his door. He lit a lamp and went downstairs in his nightshirt, cursing the intruder, or intruders, who dared disturb him so late in the night.

"Who is 'dere?" he called grumpily.

"Please, open the door," the voice of the intruder said softly.

"Is 'dis joke?" he wondered, then flung open the door to deal with the jokester face-to-face. Instead, he confronted the white-haired union lady.

"I'm sorry," she said at once. "I am homeless for the night and need a place to stay. Can you help me?"

He hesitated, knowing the trouble she could bring him, but there was a chill in the night air, and the woman looked old and suddenly frail. He took her in then looked up and down the street to be sure no one had seen her enter. Frog Street was deserted. Relieved, he closed the door, but across the way, Zakrzewska was peering from his window and had spied it all.

Mrs. Kudla was certain her baby would be born before dawn. She had a sense of these things—this was her ninth child—and sent Razor to summon Dr. Koons. It was just past midnight.

"Is time!" Razor told the doctor.

"Is the water aboil?"

"Yes.

"They never come when I'm awake," the doctor grumbled, then disappeared inside to get his bag, leaving Razor to wait on the front steps.

Razor wished he'd worn his jacket as he rubbed his arms to keep himself warm. Suddenly he heard a scraping sound and looked across to Markham's house in time to see a dark figure emerging from a window onto Markham's porch. At first, he thought it was a burglar. That was before he saw Markham himself, standing in the window.

"Strange," Razor thought. "Leave by window, not by door?"

A moment later, the dark figure passed Dr. Koons's house half running, half walking. He wore a hat to hide his face but Razor knew at once who it was.

"Teofil!" he called but the man ignored him and ran on.

◆◆

It had been a delirious night for the Secret Brotherhood of Breaker Boys. They had met in force behind Emerald House, where they grubbed pints of ale from their older brothers, then passed them around, swigging and swearing, just like the men inside. Euan disliked the taste of ale but drank it anyway to show that he was regular. After that, they wrestled some, then went to hit the wall by moonlight. They unleashed a barrage of cracks and pings so loud it sounded like artillery fire, and while Euan couldn't prove it, he was sure one of those cracks or maybe a ping, was his. They threw until their arms were sore, until there wasn't a stone to be found within fifty yards of the creek. And then they went home content.

"I can't figure why Markham waited as long as he did to get rid of a man like Bryfogle," his *dada* said to Euan the next morning at breakfast. "He was nothing but a drunkard from what I heard. Who'll be the new cracker boss then, Dai Edwards?"

"I don't know," Euan answered. "Maybe Mr. Powell."

"Looks like rain," his *dada* told him before they left the house. "Best to wear your heavy coat then." Just as he predicted, the sky opened up as soon as they set out for the colliery. Thus, with hats pulled low and eyes affixed to the street, they failed to see at first what was happening farther down the Hill.

An empty lumber wagon had stopped in the middle of Frog Street. Men on horseback surrounded it, shouting orders to others carrying furniture from one of the houses and passing it to men on the wagon. It was an all too familiar sight—another eviction on Frog Street—this time in broad daylight, this time in the rain.

Euan shuddered when he saw what was happening. "Who is it this time? And how many?" he wondered. The rain pelted his face.

"All right, keep movin'!" the Coal and Irons shouted as the men headed for the colliery slowed to watch. "There's nothing to see! Keep movin'!"

It was the Moczygemba house.

"Leave it be," his *dada* said and hurried on without looking, but Euan lingered. Something kept him behind. Something made him disobey.

He saw Sheriff Frostbutter, looking more annoyed than usual, dismount to stand under an umbrella that one of his men had belatedly produced. His wide-brimmed hat had failed to keep the rain off his face. The hat, as well as his longcoat and trousers, were soaked through. His elaborate mustachios were drooping.

"Euan!" his *dada* beckoned from down the road. "Come along!"

"Yes, *Dada*!" he called and reluctantly trod off, till suddenly a voice he heard stopped him in his tracks.

"Take your hands off me, you hellcat!"

Euan turned and saw Mother being escorted brusquely from the Moczygemba house by two Coal and Iron Policemen. A third brought up the rear, holding an umbrella over her head. As usual, she was squawking and complaining.

"This is the last straw!" she yelled when she saw Frostbutter. "Never before have I seen such a town as this!"

"I hereby arrest you, Mary Harris Jones, in the name of the law," the sheriff intoned dramatically.

"On what charge this time?" she demanded.

"Trespassing private property.

"Markham owns the town *and* the magistrate, why not the sheriff, too? Well, I'd like to press charges against John Markham for kidnapping me and holding me for four days in his capitalist bastille without a writ of habeas corpus! These are not medieval times, Sheriff, and you are less than civilized! You are not two degrees from the savages!"

"Take her away!" Frostbutter said, dismissing her, then turned to the outraged crowd that was gathering, even in the rain. "And clear these people out of here!" Immediately, the deputies rode their horses into the throng to move them back, to move them on.

"You cannot treat law-abiding citizens this way!" she protested loudly.

"And shut her up!"

"The mules in the mines are treated with more respect!"

"Madam, be still!" the sheriff warned, "or I shall be forced to silence you myself!"

"I am not afraid of the pen, the sword, or the scaffold!" Mother ranted as the Coal and Iron Policemen lifted her bodily into a waiting carriage. At the same time, the Moczygembas were dragged from their house. "Leave those people be!" she shouted. "They have done nothing!"

"Mother!" Euan called, dodging the horses to run to her side. "I knew you were here! I knew it!"

"Euan Morgan!" she cried, leaning from the carriage. "As you can see, I am once more indisposed, but I heard about your cracker boss! Good for you! It's a start! I'll be back to mop up this town! We're going to box Markham's ears! The tide has turned, Euan Morgan! We've got the pirates on the run!"

Suddenly the carriage lurched forward.

"You've got to stay, Mother!" Euan cried. "We need you here!"

"I'll be back, Euan Morgan!" Mother shouted as it sped off. "I'll be back! Just remember all I've said! The slaves in the caves need to be saved! Say it! The slaves in the caves . . . !"

Euan ran alongside as long as he could, his tears mingling with the morning rain. Somehow he didn't believe the pirates were on the run or that the tide had turned. Somehow he knew he'd never see her again.

The boys sat on the chutes, waiting for the coal to flow, for their new cracker boss to appear. Bryfogle's things had been removed from his den. His pictures had been scraped off the walls.

Half an hour passed. An hour. All was quiet.

Suddenly they heard a clomping on the stairs leading from the top house—the unmistakable sound of the oak rod being dropped, then dropped again on each successive step as its bearer descended. It sounded like the rattling of bones in hell. The new cracker boss appeared gradually, legs first—"Least he's got two feet," Patsy whispered to Euan—then the dark figure, then the cruel, demonic grin.

"Who's that then?" Jenkin asked, uneasy.

Euan shuddered. "Zakrzewska," he whispered. "It's Zakrzewska!"

# PART SIX

EUAN

PART SIX

FLAN

ZAKRZEWSKA awoke Sunday morning, rolled over in bed, and looked out the window. The sky had finally cleared after two days of chilling rains. Birds were singing. He stretched and turned back to his wife. Zakrzewska was in a lovemaking mood.

"Not now," Gwladys said, resisting.

"Yes, now," he said, mauling her with his large hands.

"It's Sunday!"

"Is best time."

"No, please."

"You are my wife. Love me," he insisted, then muffled his grunting in the cleft between her breasts.

"After . . . ," she soughed. "After we come from church. After . . ."

"Now is best," he said and rolled on top of her and groped beneath her nightshirt with his large hands. "Is time to make more babies," he whispered, forgetting himself in his passion. He felt her body stiffen under his.

"Teofil," she said quietly. "We don't . . . we don't have . . ."

"We *afford* babies now," he said quickly, trying to correct the damage.

"You said 'more babies,'" she pointed out to him. "You said 'more.'"

"Did I?" he asked with a nervous laugh.

"Teofil? Did you and your Ewa have children?" she questioned. "Did you?"

"We were not married."

"That's not what I asked!" she snapped.

"My Ewa was taken from me," he replied softly, hoping that his sad tale would once more win her over. "Before we marry, my angel was taken from me."

"By your best friend, Feliks? Feliks *Zakrzewska*?" she asked snidely, wanting to hurt him, wanting to end their foolish dance of lies, but as soon as she'd blurted them, she wanted her words back. She knew at once from the slight tilt of his head toward her that he'd heard her and understood. What she had tried to deny was true. Her husband was a murderer.

"What are you saying?" he asked coldly, trying to mask the alarm that suddenly gripped him.

"I *know* you were married in Chicago!" she said, letting her frustration explode. "I *know* about Ewa! What you did to her. And about Feliks! Did you take his name? That was clever of you. You see? I know you too well."

"You talk crazy talk!"

"My God!" she gasped. "You did it, and I'm still lying here with you! I'm just as bad as you! I should be running down the street yelling, 'Help! Murder! Police!' I'm no better than you!"

"Are you crazy, woman?"

"Me, crazy? I think you mean to drive me so!" Gwladys snorted, then bolted from the bed, quickly put on her glasses, and began to rummage through her dresser.

"What are you doing?" he asked, fearful of her odd behavior.

"There, look!" she said and produced the wanted poster, then waved it in his face. "Look! Now you tell me who's crazy!"

His eyes grew large at the sight of his photograph and name.

"Read to me," he bade her.

"It says that you—whoever you are, Zakrzewska or Zwiardowski—are wanted for murdering your wife Ewa, also a man named Feliks, as well as some railroad employee in Denver! And there's a reward of five hundred dollars to anyone who assists the authorities in your capture."

"You are lying! It does not!"

"Then take it down to Markham and let him read it to you!" she shouted at the end of her patience. "I've had all I can take of your secrets, of your lying! All you've ever done is lie to me. From the first moment we met, you lied! You even lied about your name! I don't even know what my own name is—Zwiardowski? Zakrzewska? Who are you, Teofil? What kind of man would do a thing like this?"

"Kind of man only woman like you would marry," he said sarcastically and grabbed for the poster, which she refused to hand over. "So . . . ," he asked with a disarmirig smile, "why did you not turn me in when you see poster? You now would be rich lady with five hundred dollars."

She stared across the bed, the gulf, that separated them. "I *hoped* . . . that you were innocent," she replied, meaning it, wanting him to believe her. "I wanted you to be innocent."

"Now *you* are lying."

"I am not!"

"So, now you are free to call sheriff and collect reward."

"I might. I might just do that!" she said scathingly. "I might just do that today!"

"Telephone does not work Sunday," he said with a smirk. "And tomorrow I could be hundred miles away."

"Then you admit it. You admit that you killed . . . ?"

"I say nothing like that," he answered cagily. "Did I say that? You sound anxious to run to sheriff. Are you getting greedy, Gwladys?"

"When I think what I could do with five hundred dollars I am tempted," she admitted. "I am sorely tempted."

"No," he chuckled. "You would not turn me in. I know why, too. I know you better than you know me. I am not dumb like you think, like you want me to be. I find you when you are lost on empty road, and I give you home and love and fancy dresses. Without me, you would be on Rag Row by now. You turn me in, you would lose all this," he said and waved his hand expansively across the room.

"All this?" she asked, stupified. "An outhouse in the backyard? A pump that hardly ever works? Bugs? Coal dust everywhere? Everywhere?"

"You got a good home..."

"And a husband, it seems, who has murdered two people!" she said, refusing to be cowed.

"Maybe. He has not said for sure," he corrected her, then continued with his reasoning. "You got position in town, you got respect..."

"Respect? Respect from whom?" Gwladys guffawed. "These hunky women? Every time I go to the pluck me store, I hear nothing but insults. I've been spit at more than once, and these damn Welsh women are no better, calling me names and clucking their tongues like ... like a flock of self-righteous hens!"

Zakrzewska shrugged. "If you do not like the way things are, go pack your trunk and see if some other man will take you in! See if some other man will give you so much, if he will put up with your big mouth like I do! See if..."

"You're wrong, Teofil!" she interrupted. Her mind was racing, suddenly seeing, suddenly clear. "You *are* as dumb as I think. You've not given me one thing I didn't have before I met you! I had nothing then, and I still have nothing. I lived thirty-two years without you, and I would've made it through thirty-two more at least, but I wonder ... I wonder how long you would last if I turned the cards on you."

"Talk plain. What are you getting at?"

"It works both ways, Teofil," she said, smiling. She was enjoying this now. "You say you've given me so much, but you have more to lose. *Much* more. Six months ago you were nothing but a vagrant! Now, you're the first

Polish boss. You've got a home of your own, more money and more respect than you've ever had—your cronies line up to kiss your feet! But if I turned you in, you'd lose all that wouldn't you? Wouldn't you?''

He shifted uncomfortably on the bed. "Finish your speech! What do you get at?"

"*I* have nothing to lose, Teofil, but you . . ."

"What about your life?" he corrected her again.

The smile faded from her face. "Is that a threat?" she asked humorlessly. "Or were you merely reminding me that . . . ?"

"No, that was threat."

"You'd still lose it all if you killed me," she said, undaunted. "The house, your job, everything!"

"Hah!" he scoffed. "You dream!"

"Then how would you explain my lifeless body to the authorities? Besides, you love me too much to kill me."

"You think so?"

"You told me many times. You told me just last week."

"How do you know that was not another of my lies?" he shot back. "I loved my Ewa, too."

"And still you killed her?"

"I don't remember," he sighed and burrowed beneath the sheets. "Was so far back I don't remember."

Gwladys was exasperated by his evasions. She slumped onto the foot of the bed and exhaled deeply. She was as tired as he was of their sparring, as drained.

"Just tell me. What happened? In Chicago?" she asked without emotion. "What happened with you and Ewa? And Feliks? Tell me."

"Go away!" he demanded. "Enough of your questions! All day long! I cannot take it no more!"

"*You* can't take it? What about *me*?" she harped, rising from the bed, then stared aghast at his cowering form curled beneath the sheets. "Are you fair to me? Are your lies fair to me? Don't I matter?"

"You are my wife," he mumbled from his place of hiding. "You do as I say or you get out. Is simple. You obey. You don't ask no more questions. Or you get out."

"You spineless, cowardly thing!" she wanted to say. "You are not the husband I deserve. You're weak and selfish; you don't deserve me or my love. I wish I had the courage to turn you in. It would almost be worth it to see you dragged off, to see you humiliated in front of your cronies, to laugh at your shame. It would almost be worth it, reward or no reward."

"Teofil, how much will you earn in a year as cracker boss?" she asked instead.

"I say no questions! Can you not hear?"

"A thousand?" she pressed. "Maybe more, right?"

"One more question, and I throw you out for good!" he growled angrily.

"Listen here!" Gwladys snapped, just as angry now, and began to tug at the bed linens that covered his burly frame.

"Leave me be!" he protested, gathering the covers more tightly about his head.

"Damn you, Teofil!" she shouted as she yanked the bedclothes from his grip. With one great pull, she swept them aside, exposing his cringing nakedness. "Damn you anyway! Listen to me!"

"What is this?" he gasped. "Are you gone mad?"

"Yes, yes, I'm mad now! Totally mad!" she shrieked, brushing strands of hair from her wild eyes. "You've driven me to this! This is your doing, now you must pay the price!"

"Calm yourself! Calm down!" he urged warily, edging toward the side of the bed. "I will go for doctor, and he will give you powder."

"Stay where you are, you hear? Get back on that bed!" she ordered. "I know exactly what I need to bring me peace of mind!"

"Watch yourself!" he warned. "I am not one of your schoolhouse babies!"

"Oh, yes you are! From now on, you're my only schoolhouse baby," she gloated. "I'm leaving that rotten hole for good. Those mangy pups can fend for themselves from now on. I'm going to sit at home, like every other boss's wife, and be a lady of leisure! I might even bring in a girl to clean house and do cooking!''

''And who will pay for you to be fancy lady? Not me!''

''Yes, *you,* Teofil! That's the best part!'' Gwladys burst out laughing, a cruel, irksome laugh that vexed him as much as it angered him. ''If I turned you in to the sheriff tomorrow, all I'd stand to benefit is five hundred dollars, but you're a *boss* now. You make over a thousand a year. And next year the same, maybe even more! And more the year after! That's more than enough to satisfy a lady of leisure, so I'll . . . I'll only require half of that. From now on, half of what you earn will be *mine* to spend as I please. Our food and all the rest for the house will come from your share. That will be the price of your freedom.''

Zakrzewska listened, dumbfounded, on the edge of the bed, unable to move, unable to even breathe.

''If you think those terms are too high,'' she went on, smiling brazenly at his discomfort, ''then I'll gladly call the sheriff, and he'll come and fit you with a hangman's noose. And if you don't mend your ways, I'll raise my share. Do you understand?''

''Is good game you play, good woman's game,'' he almost complimented her. ''Too bad you will not live so long to win it,'' he wanted to say. Instead, he smiled submissively. ''Have you no pity?'' he moaned to prick her sympathy.

''Beware of people who have nothing to lose, Teofil.''

''Is this how you treat your schoolhouse babies?'' he asked as he rose from the bed.

''And just where do you think you're going?'' she asked petulantly.

''To sheriff to turn myself in!''

''Hah! That'll be the day!'' she said and blocked the door with her arm.

''Must I ask permission to go to outhouse?'' he balked.

''Every good schoolboy must ask permission,'' she insisted. ''You mustn't make teacher angry. Teacher can get very, very angry.''

''And so can schoolboy,'' he said with a wry smile and

kissed the palm of her hand, then swept past her and hurried down the steps. A moment later, she heard him rummaging through a cabinet in the cellar, then his muffled cursing. She heard him return to the kitchen, where he tore through her cupboards with increasing frenzy. She heard glass shatter, pots and pans, whole shelves, go crashing to the floor. He emptied the coal bucket atop the stove.

"Let him do as he pleases. He'll be the one putting it back in order," Gwladys thought as she moved calmly to the closet and reached into her winter boot for something she had hidden there the week before.

Suddenly the noise stopped. The searching stopped, and she heard his footsteps bounding up the stairs.

"Where is it?" he seethed as he burst into the room. "Where?"

"Back so soon?" she purred coyly.

"Where is it? What have you done with it?"

"Is this what you're looking for?" she asked, brandishing his gun.

"Give it!" he demanded, reaching, just as she concealed it behind her back. He moved closer. He drew closer.

"I've hidden the bullets," she teased softly. "You'll never find them. Not now. Not ever."

"Then I will shove gun down your throat and watch you choke. I would enjoy that very much," he snarled, then raised his hands to her shoulders and ran them down her arms to her waist and up across her back.

"Is that any way to talk to teacher?" she murmured. She felt his warm breath across her neck. She sighed. "I shall have to punish you severely if you don't apologize at once."

"And I will strangle you and chop you into small parts," he whispered in her ear, nuzzling her ear, and inched her nightshirt up her thigh. "Then I will feed you to bears and wild dogs."

Gwladys abruptly broke away.

"Time to get dressed for church," she announced blithely as she moved to the dresser, where, with the gun still in her hand, she began to brush her tousled hair. "Afterwards," she bade him, "after you've straightened up the mess you made below, then . . . *then* we will make love."

Zakrzewska was caught off guard by her rebuff, by her audacity. "She think like man," he said to himself. "She know how to get her way. She is cagey. I am going to enjoy killing her when time come."

At that same moment, farther up Polish Hill, Hugh Morgan sat down to eat his breakfast. "Is my good shirt washed and ironed?" he asked.

Myfanwy looked up in astonishment. "Why, yes, *N'had*."

"Where is it then?"

"Where it always is, in your drawer. You've not worn it since . . . ," she said and caught herself. She never mentioned the funeral.

"And, Euan, are my good shoes polished?"

"Yes, *N'had*," Euan answered, as astonished as his *mam*.

"Why don't you give them another spit and shine for good measure?"

"Yes, *N'had*," the boy replied, rising from the table.

"Finish your breakfast first."

"Yes, *N'had*," he said and sat again.

They continued to eat in silence. Finally, Myfanwy could stand the wondering no more.

"And just where are you planning to go then?" she asked him.

"Why, to church. With you," he replied matter-of-factly. "Where else would I be going Sunday morning?"

Neither Myfanwy nor Euan looked as if they believed him. And with good reason. He'd not been to church with them since June, since his "accident."

"Just because the congregation is a lot of hypocrites," he went on to explain, "doesn't mean I should cut myself off from the Lord, does it?"

She remained skeptical, but who was she to question his motives as long as he was returning to God's house, a place to which she had only recently returned herself?

Still, it was a lie. He couldn't tell her the truth, nor

could he let her see the fear that had been gnawing at him since he learned that the evil he had brought into this town, the scourge that he had set loose—this man, this Zakrzewska—was now cracker boss in the breaker. A man who had sworn to ruin his life, a man worse than all the Bryfogles Markham could dredge up from the scum that populated the earth, now held his boy's life in his hands.

Already he'd seen bruises on the boy as they were scrubbing down in the backyard after work—on his backside and his arm and wrist.

"I fell on the steps," the boy told him when he inquired.

"And your arm there?"

"I was scuffling with Little Jake is all."

Hugh wanted to believe his son. He wanted to believe that the boy was safe, but he knew better. He also knew he had to get Euan out of the breaker while he still could. How to do it was his problem. The boy was as stubborn as a stable full of mules. And so, he prayed for guidance. He prayed to God to let him know what to do. He prayed for a miracle, and if praying in God's house might make God more willing to listen, he would do that, too. So, Hugh swallowed his pride, his own stubbornness, and asked Myfanwy if his good shirt was washed and ironed. He knew it was, and he knew exactly where it was. He just couldn't tell her the truth.

It was late when the Morgans finally set out for church, held up by a button that had popped off Hugh's good shirt in the haste of dressing, a button that Myfanwy insisted on sewing back before she would allow her family to leave the house.

They were not the only stragglers on Frog Street that morning.

At a quick glance, one might have mistaken the pair coming toward them for the Markhams—he in his brown serge suit and starched collar; she in her green cheviot skirt, silk blouse, and Thomas G. Plant boots. She even had her arm twined with his and held a ruffled parasol, like all fine ladies carried to church, only Gwladys's new waist was too tight, her new boots irritated her corn, and Zakrzewska's Corliss collar pinched his neck.

It was too late to avoid them. Hugh and Myfanwy walked straight past them, as though the Polander and his tawdry wife didn't exist.

"Look at her! Like a fancy woman, selling her wares on Frog Street," Myfanwy thought. She'd never seen a whore, but this woman with her painted cheeks and lips, her tight-fitting clothes and blowsy hair, looked exactly like what she imagined a whore to be. "Look at her swinging her hips! Who does she think she is anyways? And going to the Catholic church, is she? Well, they can have her! Her *and* her education which ain't worth a lump of coal. All it did was get her a hunky and a fat behind!"

Hugh fought to control himself. "He is bigger than I am," he thought. "Stronger. He could crush the life out of me with his bare hands, but if it came to it, I wouldn't hesitate to fight him. If he harmed my boy, I would fight to kill him."

Euan saw them, too. The cracker boss and his "wife" out for a stroll! He hid behind his *dada* so they wouldn't see him, so they wouldn't get him. He couldn't stand to look at them. He wished he had a rock to throw at them.

"My God, look at her!" Gwladys thought. "She looks worse every time I see her, so old and dried out, like a worn shoe. Thank God I'm not like her! Thank God I've got my wits about me! It makes all the difference. All she's got left is her daily drudgery and an early grave. I was smart. I held out, and now I've got the best of it. Look at her—dead on her feet, dried out and dead. Thank God I'm not like her."

"Look at me!" Zakrzewska wanted to shout at Hugh. "Look! See the man you call dirt, then throw into street! See the man who is not good enough to work by your side, not smart enough to be miner. Look at him now! Who is he now? *He* is cracker boss! *He* make his own place! *He* is wearing new suit, and you are still digging rock, still loading coal. Goddamn you, man, *look* at me! Look at *me*! Pay notice, or you will be sorry! I am *here*, mister! Here!"

Gwladys felt his hand tighten around hers. She smiled, not wishing to show her discomfort. Her arm began to feel numb, from that and the weight of Teofil's gun, which she'd stuffed into her purse at the last minute. And her feet hurt, and his collar pinched, and Euan hid behind his *dada*.

Thus, they passed. The only sound heard was of feet squishing through two days of mud.

"*Dzien dobry, pan* Zakrzewska?" Karl Maciejewski asked with a big smile as Zakrzewska and Gwladys approached the crowd that awaited their arrival in front of Holy Trinity. Today a special mass would be sung in honor of their brother, who, in a few short months, had risen from the ranks of the laborers to become a boss. He had brought them self-respect. He had given them hope.

"Good, good! And you?" Zakrzewska replied, tipping his hat. He spoke English now. Bosses spoke only English to the men. "Good blessing to all on this shiny occasion!"

"And how are you, *pani* Zakrzewska?" Maciejewski asked, deferring to the honored guest's wife.

"I am fine, thank you," Gwladys answered pleasantly, smiling at several women who gawked at her with a mixture of curiosity and disgust. The daughter of Stefan Drozda presented her with a bouquet of limp wildflowers.

The crowd parted in a wave as the leader of their community approached. They shook his hand, some of them, or clapped him on the back, and escorted him and his wife to the front pew—the seat of honor. The congregation rose as one and applauded.

This cordiality, however, belied the mood of despair that had darkened the front of Holy Trinity in the minutes before Zakrzewska arrived. Whenever two men gathered on Polish Hill, the topic of their discussion was certain to be the latest, the Moczygemba, eviction.

"How coult Markham know?" Maciejewski asked the others. "Only man who know 'dat Moczygemba take in olt voman vas Moczygemba, an' next mornin', 'dere is

sheriff, vaitin' at his door! I t'ink maybe Markham got ears
like bat an' eyes 'dat see trough night.''

"Maybe sheriff know 'fore Moczygemba know,'' said
Roman Wojtek. "Maybe olt voman go 'dere 'cause Markham
sent her.''

"Maybe it someone from out of Jeddoh, from Latimer
or Drifton,'' said Tomasz Hudack.

"An' coult be vun of us,'' Maciejewski said and looked
across the faces of the men gathered around him.

"An' even coult be you,'' said Stefan Drozda.

"Agh! You see 'da pain 'dis blackleg bring us?''
Maciejewski growled. "He make us doubt men ve have
trust for years an' years. Ve shoult give our hate to
Markham, not to our own brot'ers.

"You know, more and more I t'ink ve vas wrong 'bout
dis Morgan,'' said Stefan Drozda. "I t'ink he vas not
blackleg. I dunno, somet'ing tell me. I t'ink vas some
ot'er.''

"Who 'den?''

Drozda shook his head. He had no answers.

The one who did stood at the edge of the crowd,
wondering if he dared speak, wondering if they would
believe him if he did.

"They will laugh at me,'' he thought. "They will call me
silly and tell me to go play my fiddle, but if I don't speak
up, what will happen? What *more* will happen? Who will
be next? And next?''

"I t'ink . . . ,'' said Razor. "I t'ink I know who 'dis man
is.''

"Razor, 'dis is not your business. 'Dis is not for boy to
say.''

"I am no boy no more. I am man, like you. I feel same
sorrow at vhat happen, like you. An' I see man who do
it.''

"Let him say, Karl,'' said Drozda.

"Who 'den?''

Razor could barely say the name it pained him so.
"Zak . . . Zakrzewska.''

"Agh! Jesus Christ, boy, you are ask for trouble 'dere!'' Maciejewski scoffed angrily.

Others could not help but laugh, as Razor feared.

"Shut up!'' Drozda told them. '' 'Dis is not laughin' business. 'Dis is our life! Now, Razor, say vhat you know, or take back. 'Dis is no joke.''

"On night 'fore Moczygemba vas evict,'' Razor began. "*Matka*, she start her baby comin', and she sent me to get doctor. Vas late. Real late. Vhile I vait, I sit on steps, and I see man come out vintow in house of Markham, an' Markham, dere in vintow, too. I see 'dem talk, 'den man go, run cross yart to street. He run past. I call his name, but he no answer, but I know . . . I know vas Zakrzewska.''

"Zakrzewska in Markham's house?'' Hudack said, aghast.

"Vhat business Zakrzewska have 'dere?'' Drozda wondered aloud. "Razor, you have no doubt 'dat 'dis is so? Do you svear to Holy Mot'er?''

"I svear! I svear to Holy Mot'er! I svear on Bible! I svear on your life 'dat 'dis is trut'!'' Razor said with tears streaming down his face. "I vish to Got vas not trut'.''

After being relieved of his terrible burden, Razor collapsed, sobbing, onto Drozda's chest. The others were stunned into silence. This revelation shook them to their very souls.

And then they saw the traitor himself, parading up Frog Street with his gun-toting wife.

"Keep silent,'' Maciejewski told them. "Act like 'dis vas not say, an' ve vill do not'in' till ve be sure.''

And so, they shook his hand, some of them, or clapped him on the back, then escorted him and his wife to the front pew—the seat of honor.

Their sons were not as civil. As the great leader passed, they hid behind their fathers or mothers or older brothers, just as Euan Morgan had done. They were afraid to look upon him, afraid he might single them out for later punishment, for *more* punishment.

It was better to be invisible.

Their fathers, their mothers and older brothers knew nothing of this. There was no use speaking out against him. He was untouchable. And so, the older Rykliewicz boy lay in bed that morning with a broken arm and concussion from the beating Zakrzewska had given him on Saturday.

"He fall down. He go climb where he not belong," Zakrzewska told the doctor, and none of the boys said otherwise, because they knew their fathers, their mothers and older brothers would not believe them. To them, Zakrzewska was untouchable.

On his first day as cracker boss, without even knowing it existed as a sacred, secret pledge, Zakrzewska managed to break the tenuous bond that held the boys together.

The boys were relieved that morning when coal finally started to flow. It took their minds off *him*, circling endlessly overhead, never out of sight, jabbing this one, clouting that one for not moving fast enough. Then, just as suddenly, the coal from the day before gave out, and the wait for the new coal began.

"You there!"

Angus, the new boy, looked up and saw Zakrzewska pointing to him from the catwalk above.

"Yes, you! Little chipmunk. Come here! Now!"

Angus crawled, trembling, up the length of the chute.

"Be careful, Angus!" Euan whispered as he passed.

"I give order, you listen quick!" Zakrzewska shouted as Angus reached the top, then swatted him so hard the boy was knocked a good six feet across the floor, where he sat dazed for a moment before he began to cry. Zakrzewska grabbed the boy's shirt, pulled him to his feet, and shook him like a sack of potatoes. "You are lazy good-for-nothing! You are worse than little girl!"

Angus only cried harder.

"Don't do that to him!" Euan shouted up.

"Who say that?" Zakrzewska demanded, turning.

"He's just new. He doesn't know better," Euan protested.

"Ah, is you, Morgan boy! Come here! COME HERE!"

Euan looked across to Jenkin and Patsy, expecting them to speak up, to stand up for their brothers, to Little Jake and Tadi, to Dick and Ralphie, but everyone had his head in the chutes. No one spoke up, no one.

Euan climbed soberly up to the landing, where Zakrzewska stood waiting with a malicious grin.

"Now, Mr. Mouth So Big," Zakrzewska said, grabbing Euan's ear, "maybe I should give you his punishment? Yeah? You like that?"

Euan shook his head no.

"Answer when I talk!" Zakrzewska shouted.

"No, sir!"

"Is all right with you I punish him then?"

Euan squirmed.

Zakrzewska raised his hand to strike. "Answer!"

"No."

"Then I punish you. One or the other. I must punish somebody. Who is it, tell me?"

Euan looked over at Angus, sobbing helplessly on the floor. "Me then."

"Ah, such brave boy! Bend over railing, and we see how brave you are!" the new cracker boss said as he undid his thick leather belt. Once off, he folded it lengthwise and cracked the two halves together as a warning to the rest. "Don't you turn away down there, or you be next!" he told them. "Now I show what happen to troublemakers!"

Then he turned back to Euan. "Hurry, or I give you this 'cross mouth!"

When Euan leaned over the railing, he had nowhere else to look but at the upturned faces of his mates. He saw guilt and pity in their eyes but no desire to prevent his pain or share it. He hated them right then for being too scared to live up to the words of their pledge, although he was just as scared. He could've closed his eyes but didn't. He wanted his mates to see him take his licks. He wanted them to know he was a witness to their shame.

"Now, boy with big eyes and big mouth, I teach you lesson you not forget," Zakrzewska said, then raised the belt and brought it down with swift stroke. "How was that? You like that, Morgan boy?"

"No!" Euan said, gritting his teeth, gripping the railing with all his might.

Zakrzewska raised the belt and whipped it down again even harder.

"And that? Is that better? You want more? I give you!"

The strap rose and fell, rose and fell. Eight times it cracked across his backside and legs. Only his heavy trousers relieved the stinging blows. Tears blurred his eyes, ran uncontrolled down his cheeks.

"You are not crying, are you? Strong boy like you?" Zakrzewska asked, grinning, and raised the belt again.

"No more, please! Hit him, not me!" Euan heard himself say. "Hit him! Hit him, not me!" He fell to his knees, sobbing, as Angus had before him and others would after, and raised his hands to ward off further blows.

"Anyone want taste of same medicine, step up!" Zakrzewska offered, but no one did.

The flow resumed, but the boys did not lock arms and whoop as the coal tumbled toward them. There was no delirious scream as the coal exploded over their heads. They were afraid to look at each other, afraid to speak, using signs. All they wanted was to be invisible. To be spared. To be invisible.

And then, at lunch break, Zakrzewska stood up before them, holding the oak rod, his scepter, his cudgel, and demanded, "How many ever see cow?"

Immediately everyone's hand shot up.

"What's this now?" Euan wondered. His rump was still sore. He wanted no part of this man's tricks yet raised his hand with the rest.

"How does cow go?" he asked next, but no one answered. "You!" he said, pointing the oak rod at Cyril Lloyd, "Make noise like cow!"

"Mooo," Cyril said, feeling very foolish.

"Louder!"

"Moooooo!"

"Good, good! You not as dumb as rest of these little girls," he said, then bade them all to moo as Cyril had done.

"Moooo," they said.

"Louder!"

"MOOOO! MOOOOOO!"

"Is better!" Zakrzewska cried, then thumped the oak rod on the wooden deck to quiet them down. "You like we play game? I show you I am not such mean man. You all be little cows. How does cow go?"

"MOOOOOO!"

"Now walk like cow," he commanded next. "How does cow walk?"

The boys stared back at him blankly. "Does he really mean for us to to crawl?" they wondered.

"I SAID WALK LIKE COW!" he roared. The boys dropped to their hands and knees at once and began to crawl across the floor. "I cannot hear you, cows!"

"Mooooo!"

"Louder!"

"MOOOOOO!"

Several of the younger boys began to laugh and bump into one another as they crawled. Even Zakrzewska joined in their mooing and their laughter while others grew bored and sat up to watch the rest. "Game is not over!" he chastised them. "Crawl, moo cows!" So, they crawled. And mooed.

It was then that Euan saw a chilling sight. As each little cow passed in front of Zakrzewska, he raised the oak rod and brought it down slowly, ever so slowly, atop the cow's head, as though he were practicing to bash out their brains.

"If we are cows," Euan wondered to himself, "then who is he?"

"What is wrong with you, Morgan? Can you not moo like rest? I could take off my belt again, easy!"

Euan crawled and mooed with the rest.

"Mooooooo!" they said.

"Is this not fun?"

"MOOOOOOOO!"

The men were accustomed to seeing their sons come home from the breaker, from time to time, sporting cuts or bruises. There would always be fights in the breaker. Fighting was part of growing up. They knew that, for they'd had their own share in their own time. There would be accidents, too. No breaker was a safe place to work. But when the boys were seen together that Sunday, both at Holy Trinity and the Presbyterian church, and they *all* bore the badges of violence—black eyes, cut lips, bruises—it gave them pause.

"What is going on here?" they wondered, but when they asked, the boys shrugged or looked away and said nothing.

"Mr. Markham? Excuse me, sir," Tom Pryor greeted the owner nervously after the morning service had ended. Caradoc Williams and Asher Davis stood nearby to lend support. "Could . . . could we be havin' a word with you then?"

"Yes, men," Markham nodded. "What is it?"

"This new cracker boss—he seems to be coming down a bit hard on the boys," Pryor said. "Some have been hurt."

"He's making them toe the line!" Markham fumed impatiently. "And it's about time, I'd say. They've gotten out of hand. It's a wonder some of them weren't hurt worse."

"Yes, sir."

"I'll talk to him, though," Markham said a bit more temperately.

"Thank you, sir."

"I'm sure everything will be all right," Markham added.

"Yes, sir. Thank you, sir," Pryor said, and the men went away assured that Markham would keep his word.

Gwladys kept her promise. She and Zakrzewska made love late into the afternoon, stopping only when they became hungry, returning to bed afterwards to continue where they had left off. And then they slept.

Later, as the sun burnt orange in the western sky, Zakrzewska brushed Gwladys's long red hair, as he had done so many times for Ewa. In the fading light, he spoke of Ewa, of their life in Chicago.

"My Ewa, she work in house of rich lady on Prairie Avenue," he said as he stroked the brush gently through Gwladys's hair. "She make dresses for rich lady and sometimes for friends of rich lady. She was such good sewer, my Ewa. We meet one Saturday night at box supper at Saint Kazimierz. She come with her sister, tryin' to find fella for her sister to marry, but her sister look like horse. Ewa, she was pretty, small with pretty, round face and eyes that shine like stars when she laugh."

"What was she like?" Gwladys asked.

"Why you want to know?" he replied testily.

"Why do you want to tell me?" she shot back. "You're the one who began this conversation."

"I figure if I tell, then maybe you stop with your damn questions and not stick your nose in my business no more."

"All right, tell me what she was like," Gwladys said to mollify him.

"You just want to see if I love my Ewa more than you."

"For God's sake, Teofil, either tell me or don't!" Gwladys said, losing her patience with his childish baiting. "I don't care one way or the other."

"You care," he said knowingly. "You are nosy woman. You will not shut up till you know all you want to know."

"Then *don't* tell me! I couldn't care less! The poor woman's dead, let her rest in peace."

"Ah, you want to know. You want to know more than ever now," he said with a leer. "You just say that to fool me."

"You're brushing too soft," she complained, trying to change the subject. "If you don't do it harder..."

"Like this?" he asked, digging the brush into her scalp, pulling hard through her hair.

"Owww! You're hurting!" she squawked. "Either do it right or not at all!"

He returned to the gentle strokes of before. "Ewa, she

like her hair brushed slow and soft. She was small woman, small and dainty.''

"You told me that already," Gwladys said sarcastically. "How did she put up with you? She must have been a saint!''

"She was good woman," he said. "Always want to help them who don't have so much. Even when we not have so much ourselves, she give clothes and food to others. Everybody come to her when they got problems. She have big heart, my Ewa."

Something seemed wrong to Gwladys. Something in his story didn't gibe. "I thought you told me that you met Ewa in the old country?"

He shook his head no. "We meet in Chicago at Saint Kazimierz and marry one month later. Feliks, he was best man."

"Feliks—he was the friend from your story, wasn't he? The one who stayed behind while you—I mean, the farmer—went to America, didn't he?"

"You ask too many questions!"

"I'm just trying to keep things straight," she protested. "Or did you make that story up as well?"

"Story is true," he said. "Story happen long, long ago."

"And you were the farmer, right? You said in the story you came here to America to find a job so you could send money back to your wife and friend, and while you were gone, your friend, this Feliks, had his way with . . ."

"Story is true!" he repeated sharply. He threw the hairbrush down and lay across the bed.

"Well, I'm totally confused now!" she exclaimed and threw up her arms. "If you met your Ewa in Chicago, how could you have brought her over from the old country, or is half of your story true and the other half a lie?"

He stared at the ceiling for a long time before answering. "It happen like I tell it," he said without emotion, "only I was not farmer."

"What's that supposed to mean?" she asked, bewildered.

"I was not farmer," he shrugged. "I was friend."

"I don't . . . I don't understand. How could . . . ?"

"You hear story you want to hear that night, not story I tell. That is all you ever hear—only what you want to believe. Your head is full of fancy ideas."

"Then dammit, Teofil, tell me the truth! Tell me, so I'll know what it sounds like just once!" she demanded flippantly. "Give me the truth, so I'll know what to tell Sheriff Frostbutter when I turn you in!"

The room was dark now, dark and growing colder. He drew a blanket over him to hide his nakedness. "Are you sure it is truth you want?" he asked her. "Maybe I am innocent. You get no reward for catching innocent man."

"You did it, damn you," she said softly and sat beside him on the bed. "I know you did," she said and leaned over him and began to stroke his chest, "now tell me why. Tell teacher the whole story. You know you want to."

He closed his eyes and sighed. He grimaced twice, as though he were trying to squeeze tears from his eyes, trying to cry.

"Tell teacher. Tell teacher how bad you've been," she urged. "Tell teacher all about it. Then teacher can decide how to punish you," she said.

"Story was just like I tell it," he began. "It begin many years ago, so long ago . . ."

She stroked his body as he told his story, stroked him and soothed his pain, the pain of remembering. She wept as he remembered. She wept for Ewa.

"Feliks," he went on, "he go off to 'Merica and leave his wife behind. I had no wife, you see. He send money every while, then nothing. Wife begin to worry, think he change his mind. Or dead. She cry all day long. She say she lonely. Time pass. She tell me I am now her man, and . . . and I crawl into her bed.

"Then, one day out of clear sky, letter come from Feliks with money to bring me to 'Merica, and just like that, I sail to Baltimore, then take train that bring me to Chicago and my friend, Feliks, and he ask me first thing how is his wife, and I tell him what happen in Poznan, in old country, but Feliks, he just smile, then wag his finger and tell me,

'Some day... some day, you will taste this same medicine,' and we both laugh and forget, 'cause we are in new country to start over, but Feliks, he... he never forget.

"One year after, I meet Ewa, and she like me, but I cannot figure why, though I like her too and bring her flowers and write her poem. And I say to her, 'Be my wife?' and she say, 'Sure, fella.' We find rooms 'cross way from Feliks and his wife, who by now he has sent for, and we are man and wife, and we are happy. I am workin' for stockyard, killin' cattle, and soon there is baby comin' to our house. Our little Mary. She is sweet as apples and bright as the sun. My Ewa stay at home now to care for baby, and I get second job to pay our debts, but soon I am not feelin' so good. I feel tired. I get angry over nothin'. Baby cry, and I get angry. Supper late, I am angry. Always I am yellin' at Ewa, and she is cryin'. And then... and then one day I get angry in stockyard and have fight. Boss tell me I have no job there no more. Then I lose other job. My Ewa, she say she go back to work, and I say no, no, no! But then, there is other baby comin', our Tillie. My Ewa go to Relief Society and beg for money for our babies. They say, 'Why can your man not go to work? He is healthy. He is strong.' And she say, 'What is wrong with you, Teofil?' And I don't know, and I begin to cry 'cause I don't know. I am so sad 'cause I have good wife and babies, and I am... I am no good for them.''

His eyes had filled with tears. He paused to wipe them.

"Go on," she urged and kissed his hand, kissed the tears he had wiped away. "Go on."

"Then I... I get angry and hurt my Ewa, and Feliks call police, and I am sent to Bridewell for sixty days to be punished. When I get home, I am sadder than before, and I swallow car... carbolic acid after Ewa go to work, but Mary, she start to cry and Feliks come, and Feliks say he not want to see me die, so he call doctor. Time go by and Ewa tell me she have 'nother baby, and I know, I know in my heart this baby is not mine. And I get so angry, I rip down curtains and burn sheets and blankets off bed, all my woman's things I can get a hold of, and I tear up our

photographs and wedding license and insurance, and then I
go to Relief Society and say to them, 'Arrest me! I cannot
live with my woman no more! She is havin' baby, and
baby is not mine!' So . . . I am sent to Bridewell for whole
year this time. For whole year, I not see Ewa. I not see our
babies. And when I get out, my little Mary, who has
grown so, let me in door and hug me, and when my Ewa
got home, I kneel at her feet. I beg her to forgive me, and
she weaken. She say I can stay if I find job. I see new
baby—our Bruno—for first time. I get work again in
stockyard, but all is not so good.

"'Somethin' is wrong,' I say to myself. My Ewa does
not seem right to me. She is not the same in bed. She does
not want to cook. House is dirty. So I ask her, I beg her
to tell me what is wrong, and she say nothin'. I ask her
again and again. Finally she tell me that couple days after I
am sent to Bridewell first time, Feliks come to visit to see
how she was doin', and after a while he seized her and put
his hand 'cross her mouth and threw her onto the bed,
and . . . and entered her by force. From this, our Bruno
was born.

"After I was sent to Bridewell again, Feliks, he come
back and tell Ewa what happen back in Poznan after he go
to 'Merica. He tell my Ewa I make his wife unfaithful to
him and tell her he make promise to do same to me some
day, and now he was satisfied he had got back at me."

There was a long, cold silence as though his story had
ended, as though there was nothing left to tell.

"So you killed him . . . ?" she asked, wiping a tear from
her eye.

"For what he did to me, yes," he admitted. "I killed
him. With gun I stole from stockyard."

". . . and her?"

He said nothing.

". . . and Ewa?"

"My Ewa, too. I could not live with woman who was
unfaithful to me.

Gwladys was dumbstruck. "You killed the mother of

your children because . . . because she was she was raped by . . . ?"

"She was unfaithful to me!" he said again with no remorse.

"You don't kill somebody for a thing like that!"

"Why not?"

"Your children, for one thing! What of them?" she berated him. "Now they are without a mother! Oh, poor Ewa! She was the innocent."

His mood perked up. "If you like, we send for my babies. This house is too big for two."

"And who will deliver them here? The Sheriff of Cook County?" Gwladys asked snidely. "I swear, Teofil, sometimes you have no sense!"

"But *you* are their mother now."

Gwladys groaned. "I'm not ready to be a mother!"

"Then shut up," he told her.

In a bedroom farther down the Hill, the older Rykliewicz boy cried out in pain. In a house across the street, Karl Maciejewski could not sleep. In Cheesetown, Ned the Splicer's widow sat in her darkened parlor and wept. Near the top of Polish Hill, Euan Morgan lay in his bed and wondered where, where was Mother Jones. At the far end of Frog Street, John Markham paced in his study, and across the way, the door of the empty Moczygemba house flapped open and shut, open and shut, open and shut.

"Where are they anyway?" Gwladys asked her silent husband. "Mary? And Tillie? And Bruno?"

"In home for wayward children," he said, staring off sadly.

"Good," she said. "Leave them there," she said.

◆◆

SOME time in the early morning hours, before even the predawn light glowed above the mountains to the east, while miners in Jeddoh and Shamokin, in Pittston and Dickson City slept, John Mitchell and the union officers of the three anthracite districts sat around a table in the union's storefront headquarters near the train station in Wilkesbarre. The table was covered with coffee mugs and half-eaten sandwiches, with telegrams and cigar butts, with maps and stacks of correspondence, train schedules and scores of lists—lists of collieries, their operators and superintendents, of union leaders and union members as of that night, the night before, and the night before that. There were lists of lists.

The air was thick with cigar smoke and wood smoke.

"Well, that's that," Mitchell said matter-of-factly as he affixed his signature to a strike authorization. The union's president was a slight man, young, with vibrant eyes. Since Mitchell only ever dressed in black and wore a thin white collar, many mistook him for a clergyman, an impression he made little effort to dispel. His men revered him.

He held the authorization in front of him to admire it, what it stood for, then blew on it to dry the ink before passing it to the man next to him, John Waldo, to sign. "My doctor wouldn't approve," Mitchell said with a sly smile as he removed a long cigar from his inside coat pocket, "but there are times when a man has to take charge of his own life, don't you agree? I think this is one of those times."

The men smiled too and voiced their approval as he lit the cigar, then blew a puff of smoke across the table.

"Besides my doctor's in Indianapolis," he added churlishly. "What he don't know won't hurt me."

By sunup, word that the strike had been called would be spreading by trolley and train, by telephone and horseback throughout the three anthracite districts. "No guns! No violence!" the miners were warned by the union, and there was none. Over ten thousand men and boys would stay out that first day, but it would take several more before word reached the outermost towns.

By chance, Jeddoh would have its own strike that morning, unexpectedly, of course, but not without violence. And it would all begin over the cooking of an egg.

"I'm writing a letter to Mr. Markham," Gwladys told Zakrzewska at the breakfast table. "To tell him I'm resigning as of today, as of this morning, in fact. I can't wait to see the look on his face."

"Resign?" Zakrzewska asked as she poured his coffee. "What does this mean?"

"I'm resigning!" she exclaimed as she adjusted her spectacles, which had slid down her nose. "I'm leaving the school, quitting my job!"

His expression grew sour. "You decide this without me?"

Gwladys looked at Zakrzewska in disbelief, then slumped into the chair across from him. "I *decided* yesterday morning," she reminded him. "Don't you remember our conversation before church?"

"That was game we play . . ."

"The hell it was!" she screamed at him. "I meant every word of what I said! Every word! I'm resigning my post first thing today, and if you don't like it, that's too bad! And if you think I've forgotten about our money arrangement, I haven't, by God! I meant every word of what I said!"

He chewed his sausage while she ranted. He refused to look at her, refused to listen.

"I've got a memory like a book," she boasted. "And you told me everything yesterday. I know the truth now about Ewa and Feliks, so you'd better keep in line, Teofil. This is no game we're playing."

"Where is my egg?" he asked, ignoring all she had said. "Have you forgot my egg?"

"No, Teofil! I've not forgotten your infernal egg!" she said and rose from the table to fetch his egg from the water boiling on the stove. Using a wooden spoon, she deftly plucked it from the pot, wrapped it in her apron, and carried it to the table. "I've waited years for this day, years!" she gushed. "God, it feels good! I think I might even take the train to Wilkesbarre this morning and go shopping at Isaac Long's." With a flourish, she set the egg in his dish. "There, love! Your egg! The last I shall ever cook! From now on, I'll have a girl in to cook and clean!"

He stared at the egg without touching it. He was seething inside.

"You want me to crack it for you, too?" she asked with a flippant tone.

He looked at her with mirthless eyes. She shrugged and sat again while he tapped the top of the egg and peeled away the shell.

"This egg is too done," he said sullenly.

"You've not even tasted it yet!" she balked.

"Don't argue with me! I know when egg is too done!"

"It's no different from any other morning," she shot back.

"Is too!" he said and spooned the top of the egg into his mouth.

"Well, if you don't like it, go down to Markham's house! I'm sure his help will fix you a proper breakfast."

He answered by spitting a mouthful of overcooked egg in Gwladys's face.

"You're disgusting!" she cried and ran to the sink.

"You can't even cook goddamn egg! What good are you?"

"Then cook your own goddamn eggs from now on!"

"Watch your mouth! As long as you are mine, you will cook my eggs!"

"And you go to hell!" she yelled back, then grabbed a raw egg from the basket on the counter and threw it at him. "How's that, soft enough for you?"

Zakrzewska raged inside as the egg oozed down his cheek and dripped in globs onto his shirt. "I wonder many times," he said, trying to control his anger, "what is best way to kill you when deed must be done. Now I know. I do it with my bare hands so I can watch you die slow, so I can see your eyes pop out and your tongue wiggle like fish in dirt."

"Don't you try anything! You hear?" she shouted. "I meant every word I said yesterday. I'll turn you in! I will!"

"You can do nothing when you are dead," he said as he

rose slowly from his chair. Even so, the chair fell back and crashed to the floor.

"Get back! Sit down, do you hear?"

"You are teacher no more! You are dead woman!" he snarled and advanced toward her with murder in his eyes.

"Get away from me!" she shrieked and threw more eggs, which splattered across his face and chest, until he grabbed her arm and twisted it behind her back. She tried to scream, but all that came out was a limp, "Aah, aah, aah!"

"Is time for student to punish teacher!" he snarled.

"Aah, aah, aah . . . !"

"You sound like chicken," he said and took an egg from the basket and stuffed it into her gaping mouth.

Gwladys's body arched with pain as he pulled her toward the stove. She gagged on her spit.

"For once, you not got so much to say, huh, Mrs. Chicken? I should'a stuck egg in your mouth long 'go!" he laughed and inserted the coiled handle into one of the grates atop the stove and yanked it back, uncovering the red-hot coals below. "I show you new way to cook egg!" he said, then forced her face down toward the opening.

Gwladys clamped her eyes against the blast of heat. Her spit drooled onto the seething coals, shooting up again as fingers of steam. She kicked at his shins; she reached for his hair or eyes with her free hand, but the more she struggled, the closer her face inched toward the rounded opening. Suddenly her flailing fingers touched the coiled handle. She grabbed it, forgetting how hot it was, and drove it like a metal spike, up and back toward his face. At the same moment, the egg flooded her mouth with thick mush.

"Jesus God!" he yelled, backing away, his hands flying to his eye.

Gwladys staggered to the sink, spitting out egg and bits of shell and doused her seared skin in a pan of water. "This time you've done it! You've gone too far!" she screamed and grabbed a carving knife from the rack beneath the cupboard.

"It hurts!" he said, like a petulant child. A trail of blood ran down his left cheek.

"Good, I hope you go blind! I wish you'd bleed to death!"

"I did not mean to hurt you," he whimpered.

"Yes, you did! Now get out of here!" she ordered him, brandishing the knife. "And don't come back! I never want to see you here again! Get out!"

"This is *my* house!"

"Get out! Get out!" she shrieked, waving the knife ever-closer to his head. He retreated to the door.

"I will be back!" he warned. "Back to finish this and finish you!" he warned, then slammed the door behind him and ran out through the yard.

It was only then that she felt the burn on her palm, felt the stinging in her eyes, and noticed her blurred vision. Her spectacles had fallen off in the fray. Gwladys found them finally, after a frantic search, lying atop the burning bed of coals.

Zakrzewska stormed down Frog Street, his face and shirt still wet with blood and shattered eggs. The handle had caught him in the corner of the eye, gouging the skin but not entering the eye itself. His head throbbed as if hit by a sledge. "I will kill her!" he repeated over and over. "I will kill her!"

Just as Zakrzewska passed Maciejewski's, Karl stepped onto his porch. "Teofil!" he called, but Zakrzewska tore on, oblivious. "Teofil! Vait!"

"I will do it so nobody know," Zakrzewska muttered under his breath. "She will suffer for this!"

"You are in such hurry for vork!" Maciejewski said, catching up. "Ve must talk, olt frient."

"She think she is such big-shot lady," Zakrzewska ranted on, "so fancy, so smart! Hah! I will show her!"

"Teofil?"

"I will have last laugh on her!"

"Vhat is wrong vit' you?" Maciejewski asked, tugging at Zakrzewska's sleeve.

"I will be laughing and she will be dead!" Suddenly Zakrzewska became aware of the man walking beside him. "Huh? What is the matter? What do you want?" he asked Maciejewski impatiently.

"You all right, Teofil?" Maciejewski said, seeing the mess across his friend's face and shirt.

"Yes, I am all right! I am fine!" Zakrzewska said loudly, catching the stares of everyone around him. "And you, my friend! Are you all right?"

"Shhh! I must talk vit' you."

"So . . . talk!"

"Not here," Maciejewski said, looking around uncomfortably.

"What is so important it cannot wait till later?"

"Come, ve must talk," Maciejewski repeated urgently. "Is important."

They turned off Frog Street and hastened along the walkway between the company store and the stables.

"Now what is this, Karl, that you could not whisper to me on street?"

"Tell no one, Teofil," Maciejewski confided, "but ve know who it vas 'dat betray Moczygemba."

Zakrzewska's eyes grew wide. "No!" he exclaimed, not having to feign great surprise, for he was greatly surprised. "Tell me who?"

"Come, ve have traitor out back. Come!" he beckoned and led Zakrzewska behind the stables. "Come!" he beckoned and led the traitor into the waiting arms of the men of Polish Hill.

There were twelve in all, twelve huddled in a conspirator's knot, their eyes bristling with uncertainty and anger.

"What is this?" Zakrzewska asked as the men closed in around him.

"Ve have qvestions for you," Maciejewski said, closing off the circle, blocking off any hope Zakrzewska might have had for retreat.

"Is time for work," the renegade protested.

"Is time you tell us trut', or you will never see breaker again," said Stefan Drozda.

"Vhy vas you in Markham's house night 'fore Moczygemba vas t'rown out?" Maciejewski demanded to know.

"Me?" Zakrzewska asked, astonished. "What are you talking? What business I got there?"

"You vas *seen* comin' out. Late. You vas *seen*!"

"But I...I was not...you don't understand...," Zakrzewska stumbled on. "You see, Markham, he ask me...he say..."

"Vas *you* 'dat tolt Markham 'dat Moczygemba took in union lady," Drozda accused. "*You* are blackleg!"

"No, no!" Zakrzewska protested loudly. "Moczygemba was blackleg! Was him all the time! *He* tell Markham that Gieryk and Zdepko and Gaca was all up on hill!"

The men looked at each other in amazement.

"An' Morgan?" asked Drozda. "He vas not blackleg?"

"No, only Moczygemba. He tell me Morgan was blackleg, and I believe him. That Moczygemba was no good! He lie all the time, that one!"

"Vhy voult Markham t'row out his own blackleg?"

"To save his goddamn neck!" Zakrzewska explained. "Markham, he know we find out soon, so he fix whole damn thing so real blackleg get away!"

"How you know all 'dis?" Antoni Wysocki asked.

"Markham tell me!"

"Vhy would Markham say such t'ings to you?"

"Why don't you ask *him*?" Zakrzewska snapped.

"You vere on hill 'dat night!" Drozda said. "You coult be blackleg!"

"So were you, Drozda! You could be blackleg, too!" Zakrzewska retorted. "And so could you, Maciejewski! And you, Zielka! And you, Gluc!" He pointed to and named each of his accusers in turn, stopping only when his hand pointed directly at the face of Jozef Moczygemba.

"*Dzien dobry,* Teofil?" Moczygemba greeted him.

"What are you doin' here?" Zakrzewska asked, shaken.

"I come to see if what 'dey say is true," Moczygemba said sorrowfully. "I cannot believe vhat my frients tell me, so I come back to hear for myself, to have peace in my heart, an' now...now you call me blackleg? How can I...?"

"I say what I say," Zakrzewska answered coldly, defiantly. "You are blackleg, Moczygemba! You betray us. You bring shame to all of us—your brothers! I alone know, and when I could not stand the stink no more, I go to Markham. Yes, I tell Markham 'bout old lady! To get rid of *you*! Now I am blamed for your evil deeds! You stink, man! I am sick to look at you!"

"Vhat...vhat do ve do to you?" Moczygemba asked, his voice trembling with emotion. "Vhy us? Vhy you bring all...all 'dis misery to us?"

The silence that followed was broken suddenly when Gwyndaf Pugh slid open the door at the back of the stable. All eyes turned.

"I thought I heard voices," Pugh said. "What do you be doin' here?"

"Nothin'," Zakrzewska said, pushing past his accusers. "We see rabbit, try to hit with stones, but no good, huh, fellas? No good?"

"This ain't no place for gatherin'. You'll scare the mules!" Pugh said and turned back inside.

"Ho, Pugh! I could use a cup of water!" Zakrzewska called, then clamped his arm on the smithy's shoulder and boldly followed him in before Pugh could shut the door.

The men hurried to the front of the stables, where Zakrzewska emerged a moment later, his arm still affixed to Pugh, and stood and watched powerlessly as the traitor crossed Frog Street in the thick of men and boys converging on the colliery, amid children scurrying past to the schoolhouse.

"You, Harakal!" Zakrzewska called to Tadi. "Don't be late or you will have hell to pay! And you, little angel," he said, caressing Tadi's sister, "be good in school today. You learn good!"

At the same time, Zakrzewska was the object of peculiar looks himself for the dried slop on his face and clothes, for his overzealous greetings. Thus, Zakrzewska went up the hill to the pit head, and, thus, did he thwart the men's every attempt to get near him, to hustle him out of there, to deal out their measure of justice swiftly and cleanly.

"Ho, boys! Why so glum? Life is beautiful!" he called to the men who surrounded him at the peg board, then strode brazenly away from their circle of hate and headed across the yard to the breaker, certain that they could not touch him, not in the open. Two or three followed at a distance, but the rest remained at the pit head in frustration.

"*Dzien dobry?*" he called to them from across the yard and shut the door of the breaker behind him. At once, two men, Zielka and Wysocki, who had concealed themselves inside, fell upon him. Wysocki seized the blackleg from behind while Zielka pounded him in the face and gut, but Zakrzewska leaned back as far as he could, then kicked forward, hurtling Zielka into the wall behind, at the same time, breaking Wysocki's grip. He then turned and clubbed Wysocki hard across the neck. Wysocki crumbled to his knees, clutching his windpipe, spitting up blood. Zielka ran forward and leaped onto Zakrzewska's back, but Zakrzewska shook his attacker off and threw him to the floor, where he kicked him repeatedly in the head and chest, rendering him senseless.

"You cannot stop Zakrzewska so easy!" he snarled at Wysocki and booted him toward the open door. "I am not little baby, tell them! Tell them, show respect for one who is smarter than them, or I will make them dress in fancy aprons and dance in the street, like women! Tell them!" he said, kicking the gasping man. "They know nothing! Nothing!"

"Stop! No more, please!" Wysocki begged.

"Tell them! Tell them to dance in the street like maidens, and I will forgive them!" Zakrzewska shouted as he shoved Wysocki out into the yard, then slammed the door and dropped the bar across it. "Now no more trouble come in, and no little cows . . ."

Suddenly the breaker shook as the grinders started up, and the first of the morning coal fell into the trough.

". . . and no little cows get out."

There was one more thing to be done before he fled this place, now that his leaving seemed certain. One more thing. He shook the blood from his eyes and began his last climb up the stairs to the picking room.

Gwladys was able to snatch her spectacles from the coal stove before they melted into a worthless lump, but in cooling them too quickly in water, a lens cracked.

"No matter," she shrugged. "When I collect my reward, I'll have money enough for a proper pair." She wasted no time getting to the company store.

"Good morning, Miss Pro . . . I mean, Mrs. Zakrzewska!" Mr. Beech said as she hurried through the door and charged to the telephone, which hung next to the dry goods counter. "Looks like you've been in the sun too long."

"Mr. Beech, I must use the telephone," she said, ignoring his remark, unaware that her nearly roasted face had turned a startling shade of pink.

"Is it a company call? I shall have to charge you otherwise."

"Most assuredly a company call. And most urgent," she said, lifting the earpiece from its hook.

"Just listen," the store manager told her. "The operator will come on before long. Tell her who it is you're calling and where."

"Thank you," she said, tapping her foot nervously on the floor. Only then did she become aware of the stares she was getting from the other women in the store. Only then did she realize she had no idea what she would tell the sheriff.

Suddenly a small voice from far away tickled her ear.

"Hello?" she responded. "Hello? Can you hear me? I wish to speak to Sheriff Frostbutter in Wilkesbarre. Yes, the sheriff please. And hurry!"

A few more seconds passed, interminable seconds.

"Hello, is this the sheriff?" she asked anxiously when a

voice finally interrupted the irritating clicks and hums that populated the line. "I see. Will he be in directly? It's very urgent. No, there is no message. I must speak to the sheriff himself. I shall call later, thank you." She hung the earpiece up, suddenly aware that the store had fallen silent, that every ear had been straining to hear her conversation. "The sheriff won't be in before nine o'clock!" she announced to the curious throng and hurried out the door.

In the picking room, all the boys were hard at work. Fingers darting, shoulders hunched, faces buried in the smooth-flowing black stream they sat in dread of their boss, who had not yet appeared that morning. This one still had slivers in his hand and the memory of a bloody nose; that one, jammed fingers and aching ribs. They all bore marks and sores as witness to his wrath. And so, they sat and shuddered every time a shadow passed across the window or they missed a piece of slate. They imagined his feet, pounding across the catwalks, his snarled threats, and they waited, cringing, for the oak rod to swing scythelike over their heads. Even when he wasn't there, he was there.

That morning, Euan had to be coaxed out of bed to dress for work. He moped through breakfast. He dallied before leaving the safety of his house. His pace quickened only as he passed Zakrzewska's.

("Get to work then. Get it done. It's what you wanted, what you asked for—picking slate.")

A cloud of gloom hung over the picking room by the time Euan arrived. There was no chatter, no jokes. The boys sat, yearning for the explosion of coal that would end the silent waiting. They prayed for work. Each yard of coal picked, each box of bony and slate filled brought them that much closer to quitting. Each minute that passed was one minute less of worry, one minute less of dread.

Finally the morning's coal began to flow, began to crowd the picking room with thick dust, but still the cracker boss did not appear.

"Maybe he's not coming then," Euan thought. "Maybe Markham gave him the heave. Maybe he quit or left town. Maybe he fell sick. Maybe he died."

"Don't ever wish a body dead," his *mam* had told him once. "Don't wish it, or it might come true."

He wished him dead. He closed his eyes and wished Zakrzewska dead, but when he opened them, Zakrzewska was standing on the catwalk, oak rod in hand, surveying his domain, his empire of frightened boys. In that same moment, the coal slowed, the coal stopped, as if willed by Zakrzewska himself, and a voice called down from above— "A boy! Send up a boy!"

"Mooooo, MOOOOOO!" Zakrzewska bellowed and pointed the oak rod at Euan. "I want yoooou, moo cow! YOOOOOU! MOOORGAN!"

"No . . . !" Euan said and began to climb down off his board. "No! No, I won't!" But before he could gain his footing, Zakrzewska had stepped over the railing and was straddling the chute in pursuit of him. The other boys dived out of reach, but they were not what Zakrzewska wanted. He wanted Euan. Euan alone. "No!" the boy screamed. "NOOOO!"

"What is this you say? Moo? Mooooo? Then come, I show you what I do to stubborn little moo cows," Zakrzewska said, then reached down, jerked Euan up bodily, and held him, high in the air as he carried him back up the chute, up the narrow stairs, past the hungry grinders, up to the pitiless trough.

"Moooo!" he bellowed. "MOOOOOO!"

"I have a boy for you," Zakrzewska said to Powell and McGuinness, the two weighmen, as he reached the top of the steps.

"Put him down then," Powell said impatiently, "let's be done with it!" It was only then that he saw the crazed look in Zakrzewska's eye, saw the boy trembling with fear as Zakrzewska lowered him over the edge. "Hold a minute!" he started to protest. "That boy's not properly tied!" But it was too late. Euan was already sliding down the side of the trough onto the bed of coal.

"We not use rope today," Zakrzewska said curtly.

"But how is he going to . . . ?"

"Is not your worry!"

"See here!" Powell objected. "Markham said we were to tie a rope on all the boys be . . . before . . ." His voice trailed off, silenced by Zakrzewska's withering stare. Instead, Powell threw an end of the rope down to Euan. "Tie this on!" he called. Euan quickly grabbed it and knotted it around his waist.

"And I tell you we not use rope today!" Zakrzewska repeated, yanked the loose end from Powell's grip, and tossed it down onto the coal next to Euan.

"Now, wait one minute, mister!" Powell said.

"You wait!" Zakrzewska sneered, then rammed the oak into the man's gut. Powell fell to his knees, gasping for breath.

"Are you crazy?" McGuinness asked, backing away warily. "Put that down, do you hear?" It was the last thing he said before Zakrzewska whacked it hard across the man's skull, knocking him backward over the railing onto the narrow steps below, where he landed with a sickening thud and did not get up.

As Powell staggered to his feet, Zakrzewska clouted him across the back of his head, knocking him forward onto a pile of canvas and old rope.

That done, Zakrzewska returned his gaze to the trough. "And so, Morgan boy, you are next! Time to dig! DIG!"

Down at the pit head, six loaded wagons sat waiting to be hoisted up to the top house. A like number were backed up outside the cage at the bottom of the shaft. It would not take long for the effect of this bottleneck to spread throughout the mine itself.

"What's going on up there?" asked the headman.

"Jam-up," answered Roy Hoskins, whose job it was to hook the cars onto the cable that carried them up to the top house.

"It's taking long enough," the headman groused, then waved his crew to take a rest.

"You want me to send a man up?" Hoskins asked. He was a former miner who had escaped the pits for a safer job up top. He was used to aggravating waits while jam-ups were cleared, and he knew that sending a man up would be a waste of time.

"Not yet," the headman told him. "Give them a few minutes more."

"I kill many cows in Chicago, in stockyards," Zakrzewska said as he sat with his legs dangling down the side of the trough, the oak rod resting across his lap. "All day long, I kill cattle. Four, five hundred maybe, every day. Some days a thousand. And I never get tired."

"Go on, talk! It gives me more time," Euan thought as he struggled to pile the largest chunks on one side of the trough. The smaller ones he cast to the other side, hoping that Zakrzewska would not notice he was building a means of escape. The pile was his only hope to climb out of the hopper alive, for he knew that this man meant for him to die. Slowly he dug deeper; slowly his escape pile grew.

"Hurry up, boy! You move like . . . like old cow," Zakrzewska taunted.

As he worked, Euan wrapped the rope around his waist to keep it from getting in his way, from tripping him. A trip could start a slide. A trip could mean his doom.

"Cow is such dumb animal. He not even know when I raise my hammer that he is dead. He look at me, think I give him oats. 'Moooo,' he say, 'feed me. I am hungry.' 'You have eaten all you need, all you will ever get,' I say and lift my hammer. 'I am killin' you, cow,' I say and look for fear in his eyes, but I see nothin'. Cow is so dumb, he just offer his head and say, 'Moooooo.' After while, I no more enjoy killin' cows. Killin' is no good unless . . . unless cow put up fight, unless cow show fear. Killin' is no good unless cow know he gonna die."

"You won't kill me. You won't get me!" Euan said over and over to himself. His pile had grown high now, but the more it grew, the harder it got to add chunks to the top. The higher it grew, the closer he came to the grinders below.

("Come closer, poor cow. We want you, to grind you! We're hungry, so hungry!")

"You won't get me! You won't grind me!"

"What's that you say, boy? What's that?" Zakrzewska asked, jumping up, moving around to another side of the trough. "You say your prayers, boy?"

Suddenly, just as Euan lifted a heavy piece, the jam shifted. The bed of coal settled a few inches, then stopped.

("Come, poor cow . . . we want you! We will grind you!")

Euan clung to the chunk with both arms, afraid to move, afraid to run. Zakrzewska had moved to a spot on the walkway directly above his escape.

"Time to put little cow in grinder!" Zakrzewska said and whooped with joy. "Grind him up small so even his mother not know him!"

The jam held for a moment longer before it broke. Euan heard the first chunks fall through the grinders. He felt his feet sinking deeper into the sinking bed of coal, but he couldn't run, not while Zakrzewska lingered above his path of flight.

"More time!" Euan thought. "I need more time!"

"Good-bye, little cow! *Do widzenia!*"

He had one chance to live now, just one. He had chosen the wrong side of the trough to build his escape. His only hope rested in luring Zakrzewska away from where he stood to the opposite side. Without losing another moment, he threw down the coal and scrambled up the short pile across from Zakrzewska.

"Hey, there! What you doin'?" Euan heard Zakrzewska yell as he leaped and clawed vainly for the rim of the walkway. Instead of getting closer, his hands fell farther, then farther from their mark. "Hey, you cannot climb out, boy!" he heard Zakrzewska shout and saw the man running toward him out of the corner of his eye. He waited till

Zakrzewska was almost on top of him before he darted down the sloped wall, across the sinking bed, and up the other side, the escape side. When he reached the top, he crouched, then leaped with all his might for the elusive rim. His hand touched wood but fell away.

"Little cow cannot get away from me!" Zakrzewska shouted as he doubled back. "I'm coming, little cow! I'm coming to get you!"

The boy crouched one last time and leaped one last time. His heart was pounding; his mouth was full of prayers. "Please! Please!" he cried as first one hand, then the other touched the wood, grabbed the wood. He dug in; he held on but was too weak to pull himself the rest of the way. 'Please!" he sobbed. "Please, God, help me!"

It was then he heard Zakrzewska's footsteps, heard the oak rod thumping on the wooden walkway. He looked up and saw Zakrzewska's boot extending over the edge, saw the tip of the oak rod, dancing above his fingers.

"You are clever, little cow, but I am more cleverer," Zakrzewska leered and knelt before the boy and looked into his desperate eyes. "Are you 'fraid little cow? 'Fraid you're gonna die? Yes, yes, I see it in your eyes. I see fear. I see it! Now is time to kill little cow," he said and raised the oak rod high over Euan's head. "Good-bye... little cow!"

"What's going on here?" a voice called. It was Hoskins, who had walked the length of the track to the top house. "What're you doin' here?" he asked, seeing Zakrzewska poised over the boy. "Where's Powell? And McGuinness?"

"Ah, boy here break jam! I help him up," Zakrzewska said, lowering the rod for Euan to take hold. "Here, boy! Grab hold."

Euan refused, calling instead to Hoskins, "Please, mister, help! Help me, mister!"

"Help that boy!" Hoskins called. "What the hell's the matter with you, man?"

"Come on, boy," Zakrzewska repeated. "Grab hold."

Euan hesitantly did so, and Zakrzewska began to pull

him up. Suddenly, from the pile of canvas and rope behind them, Powell cried out in pain.

"What's that now?" Hoskins asked, looking in Powell's direction.

"Is nothing!" Zakrzewska warned, then, dispensing with all pretense, tried to shake Euan loose, but the boy held on. Finally Zakrzewska let go of the rod altogether; Euan tumbled backwards into the hopper and landed atop the last few feet of coal.

"Good God!" cried Hoskins, seeing Euan fall. "Help him!"

"Is too late! Get out! Get out of here!" Zakrzewska warned, advancing on the man. "Why you come here? Get out!"

"Quick!" Hoskins said to Zakrzewska. "The cutoff switch! It's on the level below. It's not too late to shut down the rollers!"

"You move one step, you end up down there with boy!" Zakrzewska warned.

The bed of coal surrounding Euan grew smaller as it spilled through the hole more quickly now, like a bottle upended. One thing did not grow smaller, however—the oak rod. Euan realized that, lying flat, it could not possibly fit through the hole in the bottom of the trough. He quickly laid it between opposite corners and waited for the coal to settle beneath it. As the remaining chunks fell away, the rod remained firmly in place, with Euan precariously straddling it, several feet above the opening. The oak rod, which Euan had so often wanted to smash to pieces, had just saved his life.

"This boy, he is not so easy," Zakrzewska muttered to himself. Ignoring Hoskins as a nuisance he could deal with later, he ran to the tipple and began to clear away the last wagon that Powell and McGuinness had emptied in order to move the next loaded wagon into place.

In the meantime, Hoskins noticed the rope that Euan had knotted then wrapped around his waist. "The rope!" he shouted to the boy. "Throw me the rope!"

Euan unwound it quickly, taking care not to lose his balance or let the slack fall into the hole.

"Hurry! Throw it here!" Hoskins hollered as Euan unwrapped the last of it, then tossed the coil with all his might.

The rope fell short.

"Again! Try again!" Hoskins cried, leaning farther over the rim of the trough. "Again, lad! Try again!"

The boy recoiled the length of rope as fast as he could, but his second toss fell within inches of the Samaritan's outstretched hands, landing instead on the smooth, slanted wall of the trough. It was the last toss he would get, for Zakrzewska had moved the loaded wagon into the tipple and was beginning to tilt it over into the trough.

"What are you doing?" Hoskins hollered. "Stop! Stop!"

The first few chunks fell from the wagon into the trough, knocking Euan backwards off his perch as they caromed past. Somehow he held on, dangling by his knees and hands, upside down, like a monkey on a bar.

Hoskins intercepted Zakrzewska and prevented him from tipping the wagon all the way. Still, chunks dropped off as they struggled, but Euan only half heard them hit the metal, half felt them brush past him through the hole. All he saw was the coil of rope that had fallen short of Hoskins's reach, the coil of rope that was now slowly sliding down the slanted trough toward the abyss. Euan saw it fall, watched it drop over the edge and land on the rollers below.

He was more afraid of the falling rope than of any coal that might come crashing down, so afraid that he failed to hear the footsteps rushing up the stairs from below, the mayhem as twenty-two boys swarmed over Zakrzewska and drove him to the floor. The coal never did fall from the wagon, but Euan was certain the free end of the rope still tied to his waist was becoming tangled around the massive teeth below.

"Euan!" he half heard their voices call. "Euan, where are you!"

"He's down there!"

"Jesus Christ! Stop the rollers!"

"Stop them! Hurry!"

Then he felt the tug. Yes, he was right. The rope had wrapped itself around the rollers, had twined around the rollers. He was right; the rollers were drawing him down . . . down.

("We have you now, poor cow. Come, we will grind you.")

He held on. He held on, but the pull was stronger, getting stronger. He heard footsteps clattering on the stairs. He heard footsteps.

("Soon it will be over, all over! Come . . . come, poor cow!")

"I'm . . . I'm slipping!" he cried. "Hold me tight, Rhys! Rhys, don't let me go! I'm falling! Faaaaalling!"

Was this his dream?

No. He fell.

Markham was in his office, listening to the phonograph, when he heard the rollers shut down. Their vibrations were omnipresent, almost reassuring. Their absence was disconcerting. Their absence meant trouble.

"What the hell is it this time?" he wondered.

Gwladys noticed the silence as well, as did Myfanwy and all the women of Frog Street. They knew the machinery in the breaker, once started for the day, was never turned off till quitting. It was too rickety, too temperamental to withstand frequent start-ups. That it worked at all was a wonder.

"Is it an early quittin'?" the women asked themselves, even though they knew the breaker worked full time with winter coming. They dared not think that the rollers had shut down for some other reason, some unspeakable reason. Nevertheless, they stopped their work, sat quietly and prayed. They prayed they would not soon be hearing three short blasts from the colliery whistle.

"Are you all right in there?"

(Was it a falling, or a memory of falling?) He opened his eyes.

"Are you all right then?" Jenkin shouted again.

"I think so," Euan said, dazed. He lay between the motionless rollers, like a baby in a cradle. The boys clambered over the huge drums, looking down at him in disbelief. "Would you get me out of here then? I . . . I can't move," he pleaded. Indeed, he could not. The rope was wound tight around the drums. A few more inches, and he would have been torn in half.

The boys cut the rope and freed him again, then gave a cheer. And then they ran back up to the top house, where the rest kept watch over Zakrzewska.

"What happened? What'd he do to ye?" Patsy asked Euan as they climbed the stairs.

"Damn! What took you so long?" Euan snapped back. "What took you?"

There was blood on the steps where McGuinness had fallen. The boys had carried him, with Hoskins's aid, to an empty wagon. Others helped Powell, who could walk at least, into the wagon with him. Some formed a human chain down into the trough to fetch the oak rod. The rest sat atop Zakrzewska and wound ropes around him in every conceivable manner.

Zakrzewska saw Euan approaching and grunted to have the rag, which Tadi had stuffed into his mouth, removed. Tadi looked first to Euan for approval.

"Thank God you are 'live! I pray so hard for you!" Zakrzewska gushed. "And God, he answer my prayers!"

The boys hooted with derision.

"Tell them, untie me! I have done nothing. Tell them!" Zakrzewska begged.

Euan motioned for the rag to be replaced. His hand was still shaking from his brush with death.

"You're a very brave boy," Hoskins said to Euan. "When we get him back down, I'm going to tell Markham everything that happened here. This . . . *mad*man will not get away with what he's done."

"No, he stays here then," Euan said, the rumble of the grinders still echoing in his head. "He's ours to do with."

"What?" Hoskins asked, incredulous.

"We caught him!" Euan said with a ferocity none had seen in him before. "We caught him! He's ours!

Hoskins gave the signal—two short bells—that let the crew at the pit head know wagons were about to descend the track. To the men below, this meant the jam in the trough had been cleared. They were not prepared then to see Hoskins and the two weighmen ride the first wagon down. They gasped when they saw their bloodied heads and the unconscious form of McGuinness. Markham was summoned at once.

"Who did this?" he asked gruffly.

"It happened before I got there!" Hoskins answered excitedly. "It was terrible! I . . . I tried to stop it! The boy was already in the trough. . . ."

"What? What happened?"

"He . . . he tried to kill the weighmen, I guess, then . . . and then the boy," Hoskins babbled on. "Then the other boys came and . . ."

"Talk sense, man!"

"The boys have taken charge of the trough room!" Hoskins blurted.

It took Markham a moment to recover his voice. "What are you saying?"

"They won't let anything move in or out unless they say so. They told me to tell you . . . ." Hoskins paused, unable to finish.

"What, man?"

"They told me to tell you . . . to tell you they're on strike."

Markham's face froze over. He looked up at the top house, then back to Hoskins. "I'll see you in my office!" he seethed, then ordered the Coal and Irons to climb the track and secure the top house. "Get those boys down here at once!" he charged them. "Whatever it takes I want them out of there and down in the yard in five minutes!"

As he turned to leave Markham confronted the worried faces of the pit head crew—some who were fathers and older brothers of the rebellious boys. "Is the doctor called yet?" he asked them.

"Not yet, sir," Tom Pryor replied.

"Well, call him, dammit!" he snapped and stalked off to his office.

The fathers and older brothers looked at the Coal and Iron Police with disdain. "Let us go up there," Peter John Lloyd said. "We'll straighten this out."

"Markham gave orders," one of the Coal and Irons replied as the three checked their rifles to make sure they were loaded.

"You won't need those, lads," Caradoc Williams said.

"Markham gave us orders."

And so, the three set out to climb the track leading to the top house, not without trepidation, for they were young themselves and uncertain of what to expect, but they had their orders. They had not proceeded far before they were spotted by a lookout. The boys would be ready for them when they came.

❖❖

"WHEN I got there, he was trying to kill the boy, trying to throw him into the rollers," Hoskins told Markham in his office.

"Kill him?" Markham asked, dismayed.

Hoskins shrugged. "He'd already battered McGuinness and Powell."

"Did you see him do that?" Markham asked.

"Why, no. Not really."

"And the other boys?"

"They ran up in the nick of time," Hoskins explained. "The lad was nearly crushed. Then they tied up this . . . whatever his name is. They said they wanted to talk to you, and if you didn't, they'd throw this . . . *what* is his name?"

"Zakrzewska," Markham said with disdain.

"They said they'd throw him into the 'meat grinder.' That's what they called it."

"If only they would!" Markham thought. Suddenly he was sorry he'd sent up the three Coal and Iron Policemen.

"Hoskins, you're not to tell a soul what you just told me. No one. Do you understand?"

Hoskins nodded.

"I'll take care of this my way."

Suddenly there was a sharp knock at the door, and the headman rushed in without waiting to be asked. "There's a ruckus, sir! Up in the breaker!"

By the time Markham arrived back at the pit head, it was all over. Two bells sounded up top, and another wagon began the descent. The wagon appeared to be empty at first, but when it reached bottom, Markham found the three Coal and Irons cowering inside. They had been stripped not only of their firearms, but of their clothes as well. Markham was not amused.

"What's going on up there, John?" Dr. Koons, who had arrived moments earlier, asked.

"The boys have gone on a rampage in the top house," Markham answered, barely able to conceal his anger. "They've already tied up the cracker boss, now they've got guns, thanks to these horses' asses!" he added, gesturing to the naked Coal and Irons. "You boys are finished here!" he told them. "And if I see you in these parts again, you'll lose more than your clothes!"

"But, sir!" protested one. "We have nothing to wear!"

"Take them down to the stable! Give them horse blankets to cover their horses' asses! Now get out of here!" Markham ordered, then sulked across the yard toward the breaker.

Dr. Koons tagged behind. "What are you going to do, John?" he asked.

Markham waved him back, then shouted up to the top house through cupped hands. "Boys? Can you hear me?"

The door to the outer stairs halfway up the side of the breaker opened slightly.

"I want you to come down from there at once!" Markham demanded. "Throw down those guns, do you hear? If you don't, I will take stern measures, and you will be in bigger trouble than you already are! You are breaking the law, do you hear?''

The door opened a bit wider. A hand reached out and tossed a chunk of coal, wrapped in paper and tied with cord, onto the crushed slate a few yards from Markham's feet. He stepped closer to retrieve it. The message scrawled on the paper read:

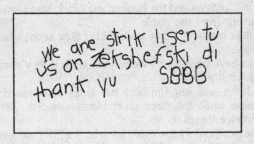

we are strik lisen tu
us on Zetshefski di
thank yu      SBBB

"The S.B.B.B.?'' Markham asked himself as he crumpled the paper. Then, shouting up, "I will not negotiate with hooligans! When I get you down out of there, and I will, I am personally going to take a cane to each of your backsides and ship you off to jail, do you hear? And you will rot there till I decide to have you set free!''

The door opened wider still.

"Do not doubt, lads, that I mean business!''

Suddenly the contents of a bucket were heaved out the open door. The clear liquid arched through the sky and plunged to earth directly on the spot where Markham stood, dousing him completely before he could take flight. He sputtered for a moment before he realized that he had been drenched with piss—a bucketful of breaker boy piss.

"I want the colliery shut down!'' Markham ordered back at the pit head. "Bring every man up! There's no more work, tell them, not until I get those boys out of there! I'll burn down the goddamn breaker if I have to!

Goddamn them!'' And he stormed back to his office to call for more Coal and Iron reinforcements.

The whistle blew one long blast. For the first time that anyone could remember, the colliery was shutting down before noon. By the time the men began to reach top, rumors were flying like sparks from a fire—talk of a riot in the picking room.

"A riot!" they laughed, and then they saw the cordon of Coal and Irons around the breaker and Black Maria wheeling up the hill from the stable.

"Move it along!" they were told if they asked what had happened.

"Our boys are in there! We want to know if they're safe!"

"Move it along!"

Gwladys was just finishing her letter of resignation to Markham when the three short blasts sounded. Her pen froze above the paper.

"Please, God! Please don't let it be Teofil!" she groaned in dread. "Not now! Not when I'm so close!" The last thing she wanted to hear right then was news of the untimely death of her husband, but somehow she knew in her heart that the whistle was sounding for him.

She crumpled the letter in her hand.

John Markham returned to his office, removed his soiled coat, and looked for something with which to dry his head and shirt. He settled finally on the curtains Mrs. Bemis had made for the office, which he'd found ugly and stuffed in an old cabinet. Twice he tried to telephone Sheriff Frostbutter in Wilkesbarre, but the lines were cluttered. On the third try, he was told that Frostbutter was out of the office, but that an assistant would call him in due time. He sat in his chair and waited.

"So, this is how it starts?" he reflected. He had taken pains to protect himself on all sides from the union's encroachment, or so he thought. The last place he expected trouble to begin was in the breaker. He wondered if the boys had been put up to this fuss by the union. He had learned that Mitchell would call a strike in the three anthracite regions before the end of the week. "Could the Glen Ellen be a testing ground?" he wondered before rejecting the thesis out of hand. "Mitchell must have better things to do," he concluded. "Still, there's got to be someone behind this farce. These boys are too simple-minded to do it on their own."

At that moment, the telephone rang.

"Markham here," he answered brusquely.

It was Frostbutter's office. The sheriff was unable to come to Jeddoh, he was told, but a deputy might be available late in the afternoon.

"I must talk to the sheriff myself, young man," Markham insisted, only to be told that the sheriff was in McAdoo on important business. "Well, what the hell is he doing in McAdoo? I've got an uprising on my hands, dammit, and I need him here!" he fumed into the tiny mouthpiece. "Now listen, young man, you'd better find your boss quick and have him telephone me or, better still, get to Jeddoh at once, or I'll have your hide stretched and hung on my office wall. Do you hear? Stretched and dried!"

A moment passed before Markham realized he was barking into a dead line.

A wind gathered in McAdoo. A whirlwind. What was it she said? "If you men are too cowardly to fight for your rights, there are enough women in this country to come in and beat hell out of you!"

Well, they marched that morning a thousand strong. A thousand women came to McAdoo and marched through the streets to the breaker, Spring Valley #2, jeering the men for not joining the union, for not joining the strike. They clanged on pot lids with broom handles, on tin pans with wooden spoons. The pandemonium reached every corner of the town.

"For shame, for shame!" a thousand voices chorused as the men arrived at the colliery. Sheriff Frostbutter had all he could do to keep the confrontation from turning into a riot. The din so frightened the mules, which were stabled in McAdoo above ground, that they refused to leave their stalls.

"Those mules won't scab today," she told the operators. "Those mules are good union mules."

It would last all day—this whirlwind—and when the men pegged out at quitting, the marchers would still be there, still berating them, abusing them. The miners feared the fury of these women more than the vindictiveness of the operators, so they would join the union. They would join the strike. Before nightfall, there would be a great celebration in McAdoo.

And so, the whirlwind gathered strength and looked for new territory to upheave. At its center stood a woman with white hair and gentle hands—the "Chicago virago" they called her—but she was known to most as Mother Jones.

❖❖

THE men of Polish Hill prowled like cats in front of the company store, waiting for the blackleg to come down from the breaker, unaware that he had already been snared in his own deadly trap.

Instead of Zakrzewska, they got his wife.

Gwladys had had enough of waiting and hurried down Frog Street for the second time that morning. As she passed the stables, she saw the black mules being unhitched from Black Maria and sighed with relief. The death wagon had completed its journey without stopping at her door. Somewhere her Teofil was alive. With renewed hope, she hastened to telephone Sheriff Frostbutter, but suddenly her path was blocked by men who only yesterday had smiled at her in front of Holy Trinity.

"Have you seen my husband?" she asked one, sounding concerned but not yet desperate. "He's not come home."

"Is this not blackleg's wife?" the man asked his cohorts, then spit in the dust at her feet.

"Soon she be blackleg's vitow," said another, laughing.

"Blackleg? Soon to be his widow? What does this mean?" she wondered. "Has anything happened to him?" she asked. "You must tell me."

"Not half of vhat gonna happen, lady," said a third.

"You come to buy casket, huh? You got black dress at home? Soon you be needin'. Soon."

Their words sent a chill down her back.

"He's still mine," she thought as she rushed up the steps to the store. "While he's still alive, he's mine!"

The store was empty, or nearly so. The only souls in sight were two of Gwladys's schoolchildren, taking advantage of their teacher's absence by buying sweets, and the dry goods clerk.

"Good morning, Miss Protheroe," the two children said with a mixture of surprise and regret.

"Is school starting then, ma'am?" asked one.

"No, children, go home! You've learned all you'll ever know," Gwladys blurted and charged toward the telephone. There she lifted the earpiece from its cradle hook with one hand and turned the crank vigorously with the other. "Hello . . . hello?" she said when the operator came on the line. "Connect me to Sheriff Frostbutter in Wilkesbarre at once, do you hear? Thank you."

"Have you heard of the accident, ma'am?" the clerk asked Gwladys timidly as the children scooted out the front door. " 'Twas terrible they say."

"Where was it?" Gwladys asked anxiously.

"In the breaker. In the top house."

"That's where he is then," Gwladys thought. "Hurry, dammit! Hurry!"

A voice came over the line.

"Hello? Hello?" she said, the tension showing in her voice. "I must speak to Sheriff Frostbutter! You said he'd be in an hour ago! Where might I reach him then? I must speak to him. This is very . . . ." Her voice halted when she caught the clerk staring at her. Gwladys turned her back on the girl and lowered her voice. "It's urgent! Desperate, in fact! Well, I would prefer to speak to the sheriff myself. I see. I wish to report the whereabouts of a man whom you are seeking to arrest. Yes, his name is . . ."

Gwladys hesitated while the clerk walked to the front of the store to watch the activity on Frog Street.

"Yes, yes. I'm still here," Gwladys said on the telephone. Then, when she was sure the girl wasn't listening, "His name is Teofil Zwiardowski, Z . . . W . . . I . . . A . . . R . . . D . . . yes, D . . . O . . . no, 'W' not 'V' . . . S . . . K . . . I. In Chicago! A reward, yes, that's the man!" Gwladys's eyes beamed with satisfaction. Just as suddenly, her face turned sour. "You what? Last week? But that cannot be! Sir, I should know! There has to be some mistake, do you hear? Sir, I am *married* to Mr. Zakrzewska . . . I mean, Mr. Zwiardowski, and I am telling you that you have arrested the wrong man!"

Euan looked out one of the windows in the top house at the fathers and older brothers near the pit head who were looking back at him. They stared at great length, shading their eyes against the sun, as if catching a glimpse of one of their boys through a grimy window might somehow make what was happening seem real. They stared and waited for something to happen, while Euan stared and tried to think of what to do next.

"Please, can we eat?" Euan heard Angus whine. "I'm hungry!"

"Stop bawlin', ye big baby!" Patsy told him. "Ye'll eat when ye eat!"

"If you two don't shut your traps, I'll throw you both in the grinder!" Jenkin shouted.

"I'm sick of his whinin'!"

"And I'm sick of you tellin' everybody what to do!"

"Stop it! All of you!" Euan said as he returned from the window. "It looks quiet out there. I guess it's all right then. Jenkin, bring over four. Tadi, did you fill up the water?"

Jenkin collected four lunch pails from the pile he had brought up from the picking room and began to divide up their contents.

"Freddie, when you've eaten," Euan said, "take Little Jake's place."

"I done me watch already!"

"I don't want that! I want my own!" Angus griped

when he saw the hunk of *kielbasa* Jenkin rationed out. "I don't like this! I don't even know what it is!"

"Angus, be quiet and eat what you got, 'cause that's all you're going to get!" Euan said, boiling over. "You hear? And Freddie, Little Jake's got to eat, too, so take it up to him or take his place till he comes down! We're a strike here, don't you know? Not a picnic to Crystal Pond! Cyril and Mickey, you watch for the other lookouts."

"I'm still hungry," Leo Drozda said after quickly gobbling his share.

"You've got to make do, Leo," Euan told him. "We don't know how long we'll be here. Could be days."

There was a general groan.

"And save some for the lookouts," he said, walking back to the window, suddenly self-conscious in his new-found role as leader.

"I don't like being on strike," Angus muttered under his breath.

"Would ye rather have that one over there beatin' on yer head?" Patsy asked him, pointing to Zakrzewska.

"What's the difference?" Cyril said. "One way or the other, we're in for it now. You heard Markham."

"Here's yours," Jenkin said, bringing Euan a quarter of a sandwich and some cheese.

"Give mine to the little ones," Euan told him.

"Can't somebody sneak out for grub? Tonight?"

"You want to go? With all them Coal and Irons they got outside?" Euan asked. Jenkin shook his head no. "We stay together. We split up, and we're done."

"You really think it'll last for days?"

Euan shrugged. The way their strike was going, they were lucky if it lasted another hour, but he couldn't say that. Leaders were supposed to have courage, and he was their leader. Mother Jones had courage, and Rhys, but he didn't, and he was afraid they'd find that out.

Just then, there was a commotion from the corner where Zakrzewska lay.

"See what he wants," Euan called to the boys who guarded the prisoner.

"What about me? I'm hungry," Zakrzewska whimpered when Leo removed the rag from his mouth. "Please? And water! My mouth is like sand."

The boys looked at each other warily.

"Let 'im starve!" said Patsy.

"Please?" the man whined. "I'm hungry."

"I'll not give him any of mine," said Cyril.

"Water!"

Euan walked back to the lunch pails, took the last piece of cheese from one and a crust of bread from another.

"What's he gonna do?" Freddie asked under his breath.

Euan knelt beside Zakrzewska and stuffed the cheese and crust into his mouth. "He's not the devil, he's a man," Euan thought as he watched him chew it hungrily. "If he was the devil, he'd be gone from here by now. He's just a man. A bad man, not fit to scrape the mud from off N'had's shoes."

"Could I have . . . water?" the man asked plaintively.

"Bring a cup of water!" Euan said to Tadi. Instead, Tadi brought over the whole bucket and dropped it roughly at Euan's feet so that water splashed across the floor.

"Get for yourself next time," he snapped at Euan.

"Thank you, you are good boy, thank you," Zakrzewska said as he gulped the water. "You saved my life. Thank you. Now maybe you loosen these ropes? They hurt so."

Euan bristled at the man's audacity. Zakrzewska had played him for a sucker, and he had fallen for it. He signaled for Leo to replace the rag and stood to confront the puzzled, disillusioned faces of his mates.

"Why you do that?" Tadi asked. "He such bad man. Why you do that?"

Euan wondered, too, but had no answer for him.

The blackleg's wife staggered up Frog Street in a daze.

("Yes, ma'am! He was caught last week and sent back to Chicago. They were mighty glad to get him, too!")

"Not half as glad as I would have been," she thought to herself. "It's not just the money I'm after but the satisfaction of knowing he's been caught, that his lies and conniving have finally done him in. I just want to see the look on his face when they throw him into chains and lead him off. I want to be sure he suffers as much as he's made me suffer, dammit!''

("Yes, ma'am! He was caught last week and sent back to . . .")

"The hell he was! He's probably on his way to Philadelphia by now, or Brooklyn. He probably sneaked home while I was calling the sheriff, took his things, and ran off. Now he can look for some other gullible woman to make his bed and cook his food, some other woman to be his drudge, then murder her when he's drained her dry! Some other dunce cap to comfort him and fornicate with him at all hours!''

As she neared the house, she half expected to see him bounding out the back gate with his satchel under his arm, but his things were still there, untouched. The house was just as she'd left it.

"Perhaps he's hiding in a closet or under the bed and means to throttle me while I'm asleep. He'd do that, too.''

She looked for him in the cellar, then went upstairs to peer under the bed and in the closet. She didn't find him, but she did find something else.

("Yes, ma'am! He was caught last week . . .")

"No, he wasn't,'' she said, suddenly soothed. "He'll come back before he leaves for good. He'll come back for this if nothing else,'' she said, loading bullets into his gun.

"And when he does, I'll be ready for him! By God, when he comes back, I'll splatter his brains across the wall,'' she vowed to herself and sat down to wait for her husband to walk in the door.

❖❖

THE fathers and older brothers were told to assemble outside Markham's office. There they waited, while Markham finished his afternoon meal, for him to come out or for them to go in, whichever he had in mind. The orders were not clear. And so, they stood or squatted by the side of the steam shanty and worried about their boys and what this furor was all about.

When Hugh arrived, he was greeted by the men of

Polish Hill, greeted in a manner befitting one held in their respect.

"*Pan* Morgan," they said simply and nodded or tipped their hats. "*Pan* Morgan." The same men who had pilloried him now passed him sheepish glances.

Finally, Markham came to the door and elected several to come inside, where they stood awkwardly, as if it were they who had done something wrong, as if they were the ones about to be punished.

"Three men were nearly killed in the breaker today," he began solemnly, "by acts of deliberate and extreme lawlessness. Another is held hostage with threats made on his life with guns taken from the Coal and Iron Police. Work is stopped. I cannot move my coal to market, and all because a gang of young devils has seen fit to break the law!"

"Are ye sayin' our boys tried to murder . . . ?" asked Joe Mooney.

"I'm saying I don't know one way or the other, and I won't until we get those boys down from there and restore this place to order."

But Mooney wasn't satisfied by this. Seeing Hoskins in the corner, he asked, "Ye were up there, man. What did ye see?"

Before Hoskins could open his mouth, Markham interrupted. "Mr. Hoskins barely escaped with his life. He's . . . confused about what happened."

"What of this hostage?" Hugh asked.

"They've taken the cracker boss, Zakrzewska, and they're threatening to throw him into the rollers." The men stared in shocked silence.

"What do they want?" Tom Pryor asked.

"I don't know, and frankly I'm not interested," Markham said and handed Pryor the boys' note to pass around. "I have summoned the sheriff. When he arrives, this whole episode will end quickly and, I fear, none too pleasantly. I've brought you here to make you aware of the gravity of the situation and to give you the opportunity to talk them down. If you wish to stay in my employ, you'll use it wisely."

"This note says they want you to . . . ," Hugh said.

"I know what it says!" Markham boomed, "and I will not be cowed by a bunch of hooligans who perpetrate a strike, be they men or boys!"

"It says they want you to *listen*! To *listen*, that's all!"

"Mr. Markham," Tom Pryor added, stepping forward. "My boy would never do a thing like this if if he wasn't pushed to it."

"By the other boys?"

"No, by this Zakrzewska. That's what this here's all about, ain't it? We told you he was hurtin' them. Did you talk to him like you said? Did you tell him to let up?"

"It's too late," Markham said and pointed toward the breaker. "They're the ones you must talk to now. I've done with it."

Euan gathered Jenkin, Tadi, Patsy, and Little Jake below in the picking room on the pretext of strengthening the barricade they had thrown up quickly across the door to the outside. "I been thinking," he said to them, "maybe . . . maybe we ought to send the little ones out."

"Let them go?" the others said as one.

Euan nodded. "They don't know any of what's going on. They're crying already. What'll it be like tonight? Or tomorrow?"

"You said we oughta stick together," Jenkin reminded him.

"I know."

"They'll think we're weakenin' and then . . ."

"I know, I know! I'm just sayin'," Euan interrupted, wishing he hadn't brought the subject up in the first place.

"We could ask them, the little ones," Little Jake suggested, in support of Euan's plan, "tell them if they want to go . . ."

"Ye know what they'd say!" Patsy balked. "None'd go anyways!"

Tadi put the final word in. He never had much to say, but he made his words count. "Ve start, ve finish. All vun or no."

"Then you've got to watch the little ones close, is what I'm sayin'," Euan urged. "Keep their mind off food, 'cause they'll be whining like cats, and they'll be wanting to go home to their own beds, and wanting to see their sisses and brothers and their...*mams* and...all the rest.'' He paused, distracted by thoughts of his own home, his own *mam*. He wondered if she'd found out yet about their strike. He was sorry she'd have more worry, more hurt on account of him. ''You hear then?'' he picked up halfheartedly where he'd left off. ''You got to watch them close is what I'm sayin'.''

Suddenly they were jarred from their quiet by the cry of danger from up top.

''Trouble in the yard!'' the lookout called. ''Trouble comin'!''

The five dashed back up the steps to the top house, where the rest of the boys were crowded at the windows, watching a line of men advance toward the cordon of Coal and Irons that ringed the breaker.

''That's me *da*,'' said Patsy.

''An' mine,'' said another.

''Mine, too.''

All their fathers and many of their older brothers came forward in a line. They came forward and stopped a few feet from the Coal and Irons and looked up at the windows of the top house.

''You think they're gonna fight the Coal and Irons for us?'' Little Jake asked, but no one replied. They were all as stymied as he was by what their fathers and older brothers had in mind.

The yard was quiet, even with all the men gathered there. A hundred men stared up at the breaker, and not a sound was made.

And then a single, haunting voice called up. ''Cyr-il! Cyr-il!''

''That's my *dada*!'' Cyril Lloyd said.

''Fred-die?'' another voice called. ''Can you hear me?''

''Leo! *To jest ojciec!*''

''Ralph? Can you hear me, lad?''

The top house was deathly still. ''What do they want?'' the boys asked themselves, and the more they heard, the more they feared the answer.

"Jenk-in! Come down, boy! Do you hear?"

"Antoni! *To jest ojciec!*"

"Ralph? Ralph, lad? They won't do anything if you come down now!"

"Eu-an? Come down, son! It's your *dada*!"

"Den-nis? Come down here now! Yer in trouble, lad! Come down now!"

"Don't listen!" Euan warned the other boys. "It's Markham makin' them call up! Don't listen!"

"Ang-us! It's poppy, lad."

"Poppy?" Angus cried softly. It was just the beginning of a flood of tears that would streak down the windows of the top house.

"Ang-us! Come down! Your mother's worried after you!"

"Come down now, boys. It'll go easier on you!"

"Stop this foolishness! You're only hurtin' the likes of others!"

"Away from the windows!" Euan shouted and began to pull the boys back one by one. "Everybody, you hear? Jenkin, help me get them away! Hurry!" Together, and with Patsy and Tadi helping, the leaders tried to clear their crew from the windows, but it was futile. As soon as one was pulled aside, another rushed back to take his place.

"Jenk-in! This is *Dada*! Come down, son!"

"Eu-an? Eu-an! Can you hear me? Answer! Can you hear me?"

The boys stood frozen, mesmerized by the sirenlike calls from below. Few, if any, had ever defied their fathers. They all knew the punishment if they dared.

"Cover your ears!" Euan told them. "Patsy, help me! We've got to get them away from the windows!"

"Little Jake? Are you up there? Can you hear me?"

"Le-o?"

"Tadeus?"

"Tadi, run down, turn the rollers back on! Hurry!" Euan ordered. When he lingered too long at the window, Euan gave him a slap across the ear. "Go, you hear? I gave an order! You hear?"

Tadi scowled at Euan. "Who are you to order me?" his

eyes said. "You, who feed the man who tried to kill you, then slug the one who saved you? Who do you think you are?" But he went. He went as Euan bade him, still scowling, still resenting.

"Pat-sy! Yer ma's waitin', boy. Come home!"

"Joz-ef!"

"Eu-an! It's no use, boy!"

"Gwilym! Listen, lad! Get down here now! This ain't no game!"

"Come home! It's no use, boy!"

"Cyr-il! Come down right now! Come home! It's no use!"

"Yer in trouble, lad! It's no use!"

The rollers kicked on with a jolt and a rumble, turning the fathers and older brothers into voiceless marionettes. Their tiny arms continued to wave, but the boys turned away from the windows, feeling betrayed. "It was no use," they'd been told. "Come down and take your licks; come down and forget; come down and submit like us."

"Our strike's for them, too!" Euan said above the rumble. "Only they don't know it."

The sudden din of the machinery came as a blessing finally. It allowed the boys to sit or slump where they were and reconsider why they had taken the top house in the first place. And when their fathers and older brothers went away, defeated, the boys were even more resolved than before.

◆◆

THE White Horse Hotel in McAdoo was the scene of the triumph. Its barroom was overrun with organizers of the new union, toasting their victory over countless rounds of beer, rubbing elbows with the very deputies who had stood opposite them all day and who now were trying to grab a meal and a beer before heading home. The women who had formed the backbone of Mother's legion of pan-beaters and broom-wavers celebrated in a side parlor with a pot of sturdy tea. Mother stood in the front hall in the midst of the reporters, who had gathered during the day as word of the siege at Spring Valley #2 had spread.

"Great masses cannot be educated in a day," she told

them. "Taking men into the union is just the kindergarten of their education, and every force is against their further education."

"How long do you think the strike will last, Mother?" asked a New York reporter.

"As long as it takes to bring Pierpont Morgan and those other pirates to their knees!"

"How long is that?"

"You fellas know him better than I do," she observed wryly.

"There's never been a strike across all of anthracite before. Do you think these coal-crackers can hold out?" a reporter from Philadelphia asked.

"Don't underestimate what you've seen here today. This strike will be a revelation to people. The working man is serving notice that he is taking his country back from the varmints who've hoodwinked him into thinking it was theirs to do with as they pleased! Now, if you excuse me, I have some other business to attend to. The strike is just beginning. There is much work to be done. Why don't you boys go have yourselves another beer?"

On the way through the hall to the parlor, Mother passed Sheriff Frostbutter, who was speaking on the public telephone. She stopped to eavesdrop.

"I can't bring my men up to Jeddoh tonight, John. I just can't. None of us have slept in three days," Frostbutter said wearily. "What do you want, another Lattimer? Look, John, we'll get there first thing in the morning. Yes, I promise, yes. Good night."

Mother couldn't help but comment. "Trouble in Jeddoh, Sheriff?"

"The union's not up there yet, is it?" the sheriff asked in reply.

"Not that I know of."

"He's got some sort of ruckus in the breaker just the same."

"Oh?" Mother asked, her voice rising with insinuation.

"Now don't be getting ideas! You stay out of there, you

hear? I had enough of you and your wild women today!"
the sheriff protested.

"Don't worry. Mitchell's called me back to headquarters."

"Good! And stay out of my hair, you hear?"

Mother smiled. "By this time tomorrow night, Sheriff, I
shall be back in Wilkesbarre, knitting mittens for the
heathens in Africa."

Mother returned to her cohorts in the side parlor and
poured herself a cup of tea, although it was something
stronger she thirsted for. The ladies' exhilaration showed
no sign of letup as they relived their long day, laughing,
applauding, shedding tears. Rarely had she seen such
enthusiasm, such determined effort behind the union's
cause. "It's a damn shame I can't take it with me," she
thought to herself, then, with a glint in her eye, turned to
the woman next to her and asked "You wouldn't happen to
know how far it is from McAdoo to Jeddoh now, would
you?"

It was after six when Hugh returned from the colliery
and told Myfanwy what he knew, what little he knew. She
was both relieved and dismayed.

"I thought when I heard the breaker start up this
afternoon," she said, "that . . . that the trouble was over."

"No," was all Hugh offered.

Myfanwy avoided setting out supper as long as she
could. She dreaded sitting at the table alone with Hugh. It
was as if she had no children left, as if they'd all been
taken from her. Before she sat, she filled Euan's plate with
food, then covered it with another dish, lest it get cold,
and set it in the oven.

Afterwards, Hugh rose from the table, put his hat on,
and made for the door. Nothing was said, but she knew
where he was going.

Other fathers and older brothers were there at the colliery, standing or sitting apart from one another on the
crushed slate or against the fences. None spoke. They
were too ashamed of what they'd done to their sons, of

what they were afraid to do themselves. They just looked up at the breaker, which was quiet again, and waited.

After the sun went down, Tom Pryor walked over to Hugh.

"Is it . . . is it all right if I sit with you?" Pryor asked awkwardly. It was the first he'd spoken to Hugh since May.

It was no time to add fuel to their grievances. "Do as you like," Hugh said, grateful to have someone to talk to. "It's been a long time."

"That it has," Pryor said. "Too long, Hugh." It took another moment before Pryor could find the courage to speak his mind. "The men I've talked to today—they're sayin' you were wronged. They're sayin' that you never named those boys up on the ridge."

"Aye," Hugh said. It was hard for him to care about all that now.

Suddenly a plaintive cry pierced the quiet of the yard. "Fred-die! I'm here, boy! Fred-die? Can you hear me?"

No answer came down from the top house. The yard grew still again as the echo died.

"This Zakrzewska lied," Pryor went on. "He bore you a grudge. He lied about it all, they say."

"Not all," Hugh admitted. "I scabbed in Sugar Notch. That part was true."

"Pat-sy! Pat-sy?" another cry went up from near the pit head. "Can ye hear me, Pats? I'm here, lad!"

"Whatever you did, Hugh, you paid a heavy price," Pryor told him.

"And here, today. I . . . I did it again," Hugh said with difficulty. "I scabbed."

Pryor thought for a moment. "We all did," he replied. "We all did."

"Aye, that we did," Hugh said and sighed deeply, painfully. He looked up toward the top house and tried to imagine what was happening up there, what they were thinking. And dreaming. "Dear God, what I'd give . . . !" he said more to himself, but to Euan, too. "What I'd give for the courage to be up there with those boys!"

"Euan? I'm here!" Hugh cried out. "I'm here, boy! I'm here!"

"Why are we here then?" Euan asked his circle of leaders.

The hour was late in the top house. The rollers had been shut down long since. Most of the boys, those not on lookout, slept under the dusty canvas.

"What do you mean, 'Why are we here?'" Jenkin asked.

"Why are we here?" Euan repeated and smoothed his hand across the head of Angus, who was sleeping on his lap. "Why are we doing this?"

"Don't you know?"

"*I* do, but suppose we have to tell Markham tomorrow or Frostbutter or the magistrate! I think we ought to write it out then, so they'll know. Do you hear what I'm saying?"

The others nodded.

"Jenkin, get the rest of them papers then," Euan said, referring to the old record sheets they'd found in scouring the top house.

Just then, another call arose from the yard. "Ang-us! Ang-us!"

Euan placed his hands over the boy's ears so he would not be awakened. The others squirmed uneasily. This caterwauling had been going on all night.

"You're the neatest writer of us," Euan said to Jenkin when he returned with the paper. "You write it down."

"What's first?" Patsy asked as Jenkin sharpened the tip of the pencil with his pocketknife. The rest looked in unison at Zakrzewska.

"A new cracker boss," Little Jake said.

"And we list what he's done to us?" Euan asked.

"Yes," they agreed.

"We got all night. We not go no place," Tadi said, having the last word as usual.

"A . . . nu . . . cra-ker . . . ," Jenkin said, reciting careful-ly as he wrote.

Suddenly another voice cried out in the yard below.

"Jenk-in! It's *N'had*! I'm here, lad!"

Jenkin froze when he heard his father's voice. The others looked at him tensely. "Why can't they leave us alone?" Jenkin said full of sadness. "It's hard enough then."

"Why are they doing that to us?" Little Jake asked, but everyone just shook his head or shrugged.

"Go on, finish it," Euan urged, trying to draw everyone's mind back to the task at hand. "Go 'head, write it!"

Jenkin took a deep breath and dropped his eyes to the sheet of paper. ". . . bos," he said as he wrote. "A nu cra-ker bos!"

Markham worked in the payroll office behind the company store late into the night. Together with Iolo Morganwyg, he withdrew the records of every boy who worked in the breaker, and of every boy's father.

Up on Polish Hill, Gwladys, still waiting in her parlor for her husband to return, drifted off to sleep. The gun slipped from her hand and thudded to the floor, discharging a shot. She awoke with a scream thinking she'd killed him, but when she looked around, she was alone and it was night.

There was no Teofil, just a gunshot echoing in her ears.

Zakrzewska lay in a corner of the top house, all but forgotten. Bound and gagged, he was no longer a menace. He had not known such impotence since his confinement in Bridewell. Tears of rage wet his cheeks.

In the far corner, in the dim lantern light, their list complete, the leaders fought sleep.

"Now's the worst time," Jenkin said. "They could try to sneak up the track. They could be on us before we know it. We gotta watch extra careful."

"He won't try nothin' tonight," Patsy argued. "Markham's a sis."

"Markham's always doin' his dirty work at night," Little Jake reminded them. "Remember the evictions?"

"He not try nothin'," Tadi said. "My *ojciec,* he holler first."

The others nodded in agreement. Their fathers and older brothers would never let the Coal and Iron Police storm the breaker. Their fathers and older brothers would warn them first, they told themselves. Still, as tired as they were, they couldn't drop their guard. Being on strike wasn't easy, they discovered. Not working was as hard as working.

"Somebody tell a story then," Little Jake suggested.

"I don't . . . know . . . none," Jenkin said with a yawn.

"Don't look at me!" Patsy balked.

"A good story'd help us keep awake," Little Jake said. "All's I know is Duncan's Goat."

"We all heard that one!" Jenkin moaned as he stretched his bony legs and yawned again.

"Tell it anyways," Patsy urged, and the others chimed in.

But Little Jake demurred. "Naw, I can't tell it good. I forget it all the time. You know it, Jenkin. You tell it."

"I ain't no storyteller. Not me!" Jenkin protested.

Euan sat against the wall, listening to their sparring, and thought how much he'd like to hear a good story, too. A ghost story. Or at least a funny one. He missed hearing stories, and he missed Rhys telling them. He wondered what Rhys would have said when he heard they'd taken over the breaker.

"Bet he would've cheered and run up the track to join us," he told himself, then realized he'd not thought once of Rhys that afternoon or night when he was busy giving orders, busy keeping his mates in line. When they drew up their list of grievances, he hadn't once stopped to think what Rhys would have written, what Rhys would have done. "There was no time for that," he tried to tell himself, but there was more to it than that. He didn't *need* to think how Rhys would've handled the strike. He had his own thoughts, his own plans.

"My brother, Rhys, told good stories," Euan spoke up. "Out back of the Emerald. Every night he had a different one."

"Tell some then."

"I only remember one."

"Tell it."

"Nobody could tell stories as good as him," Euan demurred. "Not me, not anybody."

"But he not here," Tadi said.

"No, he's not, is he?" Euan thought. " 'And he's never coming back' is what Mother said. 'Pray for the dead and fight like hell for the living!' is what Mother said."

"Does this story have shootin' and things?" Little Jake asked.

"No," Euan said, trying to remember how the story started. It had been so long since he last heard it.

"Is it scary?" Jenkin wanted to know.

"It's about a ghost."

"Tell it then! They're the best!"

"Tell it!" they echoed all around. "Tell it!"

"It happened years and years back, I think," Euan began, not knowing if he could remember it all or how well he could tell it but not caring anymore. "It happened in a town called . . . Killickinnick, and there was this big mine and a big man who owned it and a bad man who . . ."

"This true story?" Tadi asked.

"Course it's true, ain't it?" Little Jake said.

Euan shook his head. "No, it's not true. It's not real. It's just a story," he told them. "Anyway . . . there was this bad man in town, and . . . and he didn't believe in nothing. His name . . . his name was Hudsonryder. And one day . . ."

They stretched out for nearly a mile on the dusty, moonlit road. Their ranks had risen several hundred above a thousand and continued to grow as they passed through hamlets and woke the citizenry with the clamor of pots and pans and the singing of rousing anthems. In Tresckow and Junedale, in Harleigh and Drifton, scores came out and joined the march. At the head of the column, the redoubtable Mother Jones spurred the marchers on. She was bringing the union to Jeddoh, bringing the strike, unaware that the strike had beat her there by exactly one day.

❖❖

WHEN Myfanwy came down to the kitchen the next morning, she found Hugh at the table drinking a cup of tea.

"I didn't hear you come in," she said.

"Some stayed down all night," was all he said.

Her eyes begged Hugh for news of the siege, but he had nothing to tell. Nothing had changed. Even so, she only knew that the boys had gone on strike, nothing of guns or the taking of a hostage, but her imaginings had filled her with terror.

"I'm going . . . I'm going down there with you today," she announced.

"No, you're not!" Hugh said, perhaps too harshly he realized when he saw the hurt look on her face. He tried to lighten her mood, but only made matters worse. "You know it's bad luck for a wife to be seen near a mine."

Neither spoke again through breakfast. Afterwards, she packed a lunch for Euan in Hugh's pail. "He'll be hungry," she said, averting her eyes from Hugh, trying not to show the depth of her pain.

"Things'll be all right then," Hugh comforted her, although he had no reason to believe that himself. He was just as frightened as she.

He set out for the colliery just as Mother and her band of wild women were rounding the corner onto the far end of Frog Street.

At dawn, Markham climbed the hill to the pit head, where the Coal and Irons—Markham's militia, they called themselves—had set up a makeshift camp. Those who could, slept overnight in the steam shanty and were drinking coffee or washing and shaving in tin basins brought up from the company store. Markham winced when he thought how much this minor rebellion was costing him. The Coal and Irons' pay, as well as their supplies, came from his pocket. It was a question of which would drive him into bankruptcy first—the railroads or the boys and their strike.

"Well, it will end this morning one way or the other," he told himself. "With or without the sheriff. With or without violence. I'll not be made the fool by a pack of ill-bred malcontents. The breaker is mine. The colliery is mine. This town is mine. I'll turn it all into a howling wilderness before I give in to them!''

In the next moment, Markham heard a din rising from the far end of his town.

Jeddoh had never seen the likes of it. They stretched ten-wide across Frog Street, clanging their pots and pans, raising hell. Their faces wore big smiles, their eyes burned with a fervor never known in Jeddoh. In their plain gingham dresses, their shawls and dusty boots, they carried the simple message of hope to their brothers and sisters.

"Join the union! Join the union!" they chanted. "Join the union!"

Miners, bosses, yardmen, their wives and children ran from their houses and gaped open-mouthed at the prodigious sight. It was as if a fire-breathing dragon were advancing up Frog Street, raising a cloud of dust like a huge tail—unstoppable and fierce, unpredictable, yet awesome.

(Clink! Clonk! "Join the union!" Clink! Clonk! "Join the union!")

Mother waved to John Jones Owen as the dragon passed the boardinghouse. "Good day, Mr. Owen!" she called. " 'Tis a great day for a strike, is it not?"

Bewildered, the man waved back.

The dragon crawled through Cheesetown, passing the Presbyterian church, the schoolhouse, and finally the colliery, where Markham stood seething at this further incursion on his domain.

"Good day, Mr. Markham! You see, I kept my word!" Mother shouted.

(Clink! Clonk! "Join the union!" Clink! Clonk! "Join the union!")

Hugh encountered the clanging intruder as he was passing through Irish Flats. "What's this then?" he wondered. "More trouble?"

"The union needs you! Come, be a man!" a marcher taunted him. Others picked up the refrain.

("Be a man! Join the union! Be a man! Join the union!")

Gwladys was awakened by the dragon and ran to her porch.

"Get your man, missus!" a woman shouted to her. "Tell him to join the union, or we'll kick him in the pants!"

"I'll do worse than that if I ever get my hands on the son of a bitch!" Gwladys wanted to say. "He's probably a thousand miles away by now!"

Myfanwy heard the far-off roar from her kitchen and thought it was the boys come down from the top house, safe and full of spit. She hurried to the front door, expecting to see Euan racing home to hug her to lift her spirits, to calm her fears. She wasn't prepared for what she saw.

The noise was deafening.

The street was full of women, harping, screeching women, mothers chanting, wives laughing, women joining hands, women unfettered.

Who were they? What did they want, and why weren't they home doing for their men, caring for their sons, like she was? Worrying, racking their senses with grief, tormenting themselves with fear, like she was?

"Look at them!" she wanted to scream. "I am not like you! I am better than you! Better! Union wives, tossing off your cares, neglecting your duty. What'll be next then! What of your babies and your daughters! Your sons who need you? Marching off when you should be home!"

("Home, home, locked inside your home, like me!")

Dust rose from the street. Dust choked her. Her airless life choked her. She fought for breath, fought to scream.

Who were these women? What did they want?

"Come, missus! Bring your pot lids! Grab your broom!" they bade her. "Come and join the parade! Help your men! Help your sons! Help them! Help them!"

("Help *me*! Help *me*!" she wanted to scream.)

They marched in waves past her door. In waves. Young ones, like her girls, old ones. Proper Welsh women, marching beside hunky women, chanting the same words, feeling the same fervor. She wanted to scream. She covered her ears, but still she heard them, closed her eyes, but couldn't shut them out. She felt their stares reaching out, beckoning, wanting to envelop her.

"No, no!" she croaked and fled inside. "Time to scrub!" she told herself and grabbed her bucket. Her dishes rattled on the shelves. The noise followed her wherever she moved about the house.

And then it marched away. The dragon passed and flicked its tail, then lumbered back down Frog Street to the colliery. She was left more shaken then before.

She wanted to scream.

And then her body stopped. Like a watch wound too tight or an engine out of gas, it just stopped. Her hands, her heart refused to work one minute longer, to scrub or cook, to sit and fret and twist a lock of hair. Her body stopped. She lost the strength, the will, to even scream. She lost herself, that self she knew, that prison-self, that hidden, pinched-up self.

She looked around her house, her prison-house. "God, how I hate this place," she moaned. "God help me, but I do."

She felt tears on her cheeks; her body shuddered. She rushed again to the front porch to catch her breath, to keep from suffocating, to be free of this house. She sucked in the crisp air; she gulped the air, then gasped and sobbed, like a newborn child. Her body shook with sobs.

And when her eyes had cleared and her sobbing had subsided, she looked across the way and saw another who was in the same distress—a hunky woman. Myfanwy didn't know her name, but her boy was in the breaker, too. Like her, the woman had fled her prison-house to keep from being smothered by her fear. Her prison-eyes were wet from crying, her body, weak with sobs.

"I am like you," Myfanwy thought as she looked at the

woman. "I know how you feel. I know your heartache. I *know . . . I know.*"

She saw a woman across the way. She also saw herself. The woman was in pain, and so was she. The woman needed someone to comfort her and perhaps to comfort, and so did she.

A moment later, the Polish woman turned and saw Myfanwy. No words passed between them, but their eyes locked; their hearts locked, and they joined each other in the middle of Frog Street and clung to each other and wept with each other.

Markham wasted no time in forming his response. Leaving a few Coal and Irons to guard the breaker, he ordered the remainder to cordon off the foot of the hill to keep Mother and her horde from overrunning the colliery. Hugh was the last into the yard before the Coal and Irons, with rifles raised, scrambled into place.

From their vantage high over the yard, the boys could see everything—the cordon forming along Frog Street; the marchers gathering beyond, the mule drivers, bosses, and miners who dared pass through them to reach the colliery; their fathers, still waiting anxiously at the pit head; Markham striding back and forth across the crushed slate, like a medieval lord fending off a siege. Above it all rose the din of wood and metal pounding on metal, voices rising in challenge and discord—a roar unlike any they'd ever heard.

"Lookee!" Patsy shouted. "There! Past the cage!"

In unison, the boys' eyes turned to the fence behind the pit head.

"It's Mother!" Euan crowed. "Mother Jones come to help us!"

Indeed, it was! Mother had split from her column of marchers and had sneaked around to the back fence. With Markham and his forces distracted by the clamor on Frog Street, Mother's confederates were able to lift her over undetected. When her feet touched solid ground again, Mother rushed to the pit head to confer behind Markham's back with the fathers and older brothers.

"Dammit!" Jenkin said. "Wish we could hear what she's sayin'!"

"They're telling her about us," Euan said. "See? The men're pointing up to us. Maybe she'll come up then. And tell us what to do."

Suddenly Mother looked up toward the top house and grinned, then raised her arm in support. It was enough to make the boys whoop for joy, but theirs were not the only eyes attending Mother at that moment. Markham had spied the tiny woman in black just as she and a delegation of fathers and older brothers started toward the breaker.

"Look out! Look out!" the boys shouted as Markham charged up the hill, pausing only to grab a Coal and Iron Policeman's rifle before heading her off short of the breaker door.

The fathers and older brothers backed away, but Mother stood firm even with a rifle staring her in the face. The marchers stopped their chanting and pressed forward against the barricade of men and guns that separated them from Mother. Some hurled rocks. No longer were they an organized march. They had become a mob.

"Don't touch her! Leave her be!" Euan cried, wanting nothing more than to tear down the steps to defend her. She looked fragile and tiny, like that night on Frog Street when Zakrzewska aimed his gun at her. He saved her then, but he was helpless now. "I wish I was down there!" he murmured to himself. "Oh, God! I wish I was down there!"

"Go on, shoot, you big cheese!" Mother shouted indignantly at Markham and his gun. "Go on! Let these scared rabbits see you for the yellow belly you are!"

"How dare you come back here?" Markham bristled and leveled the rifle straight at her heart. "You have no right to come here and poison my . . ."

"Admit it!" she taunted, refusing to relent. "Those boys up there got the best of you! They spit in your eye and closed you down! Now the union's here to finish the job! You don't own these folks no more, Markham!"

"This ground you're trespassing on still belongs to me," Markham said, his face burning with rage. "If these men choose to work for me, they will, by God! And no union has the right to say other! How about it, men? Do you work for me? Or do you work for the union?"

The men stood staring at the ground.

"You're closed down," Mother gloated. "They've spoke!"

"The hell I am! Sound the whistle!" Markham shouted to all the men as he dropped the gun to his side. "There's work today. A full shift! Any man doesn't work today won't ever work for me again! Sound the whistle!"

Word was relayed to the pit head, where one of the bosses sounded one long blast on the whistle. Still, there was no rush to the peg board.

"You heard me, men!" Markham repeated as he strode through their ranks. "You know I am a fair man. Work for me now, and your jobs will be protected. If you don't, you're out for good!"

"How can we work when the breaker's shut down?" Tom Pryor asked.

"You take care of my coal, and I'll take care of my breaker!" Markham seethed. "So, which will it be, men? Your jobs? Or this hag's union?"

Their choice was clear. They had no choice.

"We'll work," Hugh said, "but go easy on our boys."

"Don't let him do this to you!" Mother shrieked at them.

"Are you trying to intimidate me, Mr. Morgan?" Markham demanded.

"I'm just sayin', is all," Hugh answered firmly. "They're our boys up there, and we'll not see them hurt is what I'm sayin'."

"As long as no man or boy brings harm to my property or anyone on it," Markham proclaimed for all to hear, "he need fear no retribution, and you have my word on that."

"Don't listen to him!" Mother warned. "He'll tell you anything!"

"Get her out of here!" Markham ordered, and two Coal

and Irons came up behind her and dragged her off down the hill.

"Are you men?" she shouted. "Then act like it! Don't let him do this to you! Join the union, do you hear? Join the . . . !"

Markham looked at the fathers and older brothers and defied them to go with her. One by one, they backed off toward the pit head.

"Now," he said, "I'll do what I should have done yesterday," and strode toward the breaker to reclaim his pride.

Gwladys had come to a decision.

She ran to her bedroom and emptied the contents of her dresser drawers and closet onto the bed. What clothes she couldn't pack into her valise, she put on—two petticoats, two skirts, numerous blouses, a ruff, gloves, a hat, two jackets, and a heavy coat—till she looked like a clothes stand about to topple over. Into her purse she placed her items of value that could be sold or pawned. Last of all, she dumped in the contents of her money jar, exactly forty-six cents. She left behind the corset Mr. Janeway had given her. It had never fit properly in the first place.

"The rest I shall come back for later," she said as she surveyed what remained. "Oh, the hell with it! I'm never coming back to this place again! Ever!" she exclaimed, then opened the window, and threw every dress and skirt and stocking she couldn't carry into the street. After discarding her own unwanted clothes, she tossed out Teofil's as well, including his new brown serge suit. "Let the hunkies fight over them! Let the hunkies have it all!" With that, she set off down Frog Street to catch the next train out of town.

The Coal and Irons broke through the barricade into the picking room in a matter of minutes and charged toward the steps leading up to the top house.

"Wait, I'll handle this myself!" Markham cautioned and motioned them to return to the passageway under the picking room. They looked at him, puzzled, but retreated as ordered. To the last one, Markham turned over his rifle. He would proceed not only alone, but unarmed. Such was his confidence.

Euan wiped sweat from his forehead and looked at the faces of the other boys, faces as tense as his, as scared.

"Please, God," he said silently. "Please, help us." And then he heard Markham's footsteps on the stairs.

Markham climbed to the level of the rollers, then circled around them, listening carefully to gauge whether a trap had been set for him above, but the only sound he could hear was the creaking of rope pulled taut by a heavy weight.

His hand reached for the switch that powered the rollers. Once again, the ancient gears groaned, then rumbled into motion. The breaker shook. The breaker was coming alive again.

The boys quaked, too, with fear. What was Markham doing, and why the rollers? Could he know what they'd done? Euan squeezed the shoulder of the boy next to him, and he the boy next to him, till they had reached all around.

Markham slowly climbed the stairs to the top house. His face betrayed no emotion—none, that is, until he saw the full extent of what they'd done, and then his eyes grew wide with disbelief.

They had strung Zakrzewska over a beam high above the trough. Gagged, bound, and stripped to his drawers, he swayed back and forth over the yawning hole. Upside down. The other end of the rope was gripped tightly by several of the larger boys. The rest anchored them to the floor like human ballast. They were all that kept Zakrzewska from falling into the trough below. The only boys not holding on to the rope—Cyril, Patsy, and Tomasz Gluc—aimed their captured rifles at Markham.

"I think you've made your point," Markham said drily. "Now put those guns down and heave that man to the side. He could die that way."

They made no move.

"Do it!" he demanded. "This breaker is going back to work! NOW!"

"This breaker is on strike!" Euan retorted, mustering all the courage he could find. "And we're not going back! Not till we get what we want!"

"Are ye come to listen?" Patsy asked as he moved closer with his rifle. Cyril and Tomasz quickly circled around behind Markham's back.

"I am unarmed," Markham exclaimed haughtily, extending his hands.

"Shut yer bazoo or I'll blow ye to kingdom come!" Patsy threatened defiantly. "Are ye here to listen to what we want?"

"Not until you put that rifle down!" Markham said.

Instead, Patsy raised the rifle to Markham's head.

"Yes," Markham conceded, choking on the word. "Yes, I'll listen."

"I thought ye would," Patsy said with a grin as he pulled the trigger. Markham stiffened, but the chamber was empty. There was just a loud click as the hammer struck nothing more than air. A few of the boys laughed nervously. "Don't git yer hopes too high," Patsy said flippantly. "The others are still loaded.'

"Now him," Markham said, trying to recover his dignity. "Let that man down. I'll not have his death on my hands."

The boys deferred to Euan, who looked back at Markham distrustfully but gave the signal to have Zakrzewska hauled in.

"And the guns. I won't listen unless the guns are put aside."

"No!" Jenkin exclaimed. "We're boss here! We make the rules!"

"Then there's no deal. I won't listen."

"Careful, Markham!" Patsy warned. "Ye still might find yerself hangin' over the trough in yer skivvies, jest like this one. Tell 'im, Euan."

"The guns stay," Euan said.

"Then you might as well shoot me," Markham answered

coolly. "I will not yield. I will not listen. You will not get anything you want."

The boys looked back at Euan. It was his decision, now, his burden.

"Do you want to lose it all?" Markham pressed. "I've come this far!"

"If we can't get what we want without guns, we're just as bad as him," Euan decided, and he motioned for Cyril and Tomasz to lay their weapons aside.

"No, down there!" Markham said and pointed to the trough. "I want you to throw them down there. Then I will listen to your grievances."

Once more the boys looked to Euan.

"No, Euan!" Patsy snapped angrily. "No! We're nothin' without guns!"

"If it'll end this all the sooner, let it be," Euan thought. "Do it," he told them. "Toss 'em in!"

"Euan, what the hell?" Patsy exploded.

"Do it!" Euan ordered, his eyes glaring. "Hurry up!"

Cyril and Tomasz came forward and hurled their weapons into the trough. They clattered down the side and disappeared through the cavity at the bottom. Then came the chilling sound of metal and wood being torn apart and crushed.

Markham gloated silently. The boys didn't know it yet, but the strike was over.

Mr. Beech looked up from his cash drawer to see an oddly over-dressed Gwladys Protheroe emptying the contents of her purse onto his counter.

"I haven't much time," she said, tilting her head to the side so that Mr. Beech wasn't squarely in the middle of the crack that ran across the left lens of her spectacles. "I'll take what I can get. Here's a brooch from the old country. Real tin, it is. And the hairbrush is imitation mother of pearl. From the Orient. And this gun, too."

"Well, this is highly irregular, Mrs. Zakrzewska, but . . ."

"I'm Miss Protheroe again," she said impatiently. "This time for good."

"Of course, Miss . . . er, Protheroe."

"How much can I get for the lot? I need it *now*!"

"It will take me a few minutes to figure it out," he said, scooping the items into a box.

"I'll wait."

Just as Mr. Beech started back to his office, he asked to his regret, "Did they get your husband out yet, Miss Protheroe?"

Gwladys looked at him strangely. "I beg your pardon?"

"Your husband, ma'am. Did they free him yet from the breaker?"

She felt a sudden sinking feeling. Her heart began to pound. "My . . . husband is here? In Jeddoh? Still?"

"You didn't know?" Mr. Beech replied, astonished.

"Mr. Beech!" she demanded. "*Start* at the beginning!"

Sheriff Frostbutter and six of his deputies had taken the early train up from Wilkesbarre, still weary from the ordeal of the day before, that and their night of drinking at the White Horse Saloon.

"Five bucks says we came for nothing," Frostbutter grumbled as they walked the half mile to Jeddoh. Before any of his deputies could accept the wager, the lawmen turned onto Frog Street and saw the crowd ahead and heard the chanting.

(Clink! Clonk! "Join the union!" Clink! Clonk! "Join the union!")

Their faces turned white. It was McAdoo all over.

Gwladys rushed to the porch at the front of the store, looked up at the breaker, and broke into a wide and greedy grin.

"You bastard! I've got you now!" she shouted. "I've *got* you!"

The Coal and Irons, the marchers, the roar of the dragon were a million miles away. It was just her and the breaker, and he was in there, and she had him now! Then, as if to seal her good fortune, she saw Sheriff Frostbutter up the road, proceeding with dispatch in her direction.

"Sher-iff Frost-but-ter!" she called, waving uselessly,

her voice overpowered by the chanting mob gathered at her feet. She ran from the porch to intercept him but found her progress slowed by her enormous bulk of clothing. She threw off her hat first, then shed her winter coat then one jacket, then another, and blouses and vests and skirts, all of which dropped helter-skelter to the dusty street.

"Sheriff! Sheriff!" she shouted, flailing her arms desperately. "It's mine! The money's all mine!" She ran, huffing, past the chanting women, past the noisy throng, till she was all that stood between the sheriff and the mob. "Sheriff, stop!" she begged and fell to her knees, gasping for breath. "*Stop,* I say! I've found him, Sheriff! I've found your man!"

Frostbutter took one look at the crazed woman and strode on.

"First," Euan began nervously, twisting the sheaf of grievances in his hand, "we want, I mean . . . our union wants . . ."

"Union?" Markham asked with dismay.

Euan's throat was dry; his head spun dizzily. "The S.B.B.B. That's what we call us. The Secret Brotherhood of Breaker Boys."

Markham flushed with anger. Euan's words lit a spark deep inside him.

"We want . . . the *union* wants . . . a new cracker boss."

"'Dis vun bad!" Tadi blurted out. "He bad man!"

"He's twice as bad as Bryfogle," Jenkin added. "Ten times!"

The man in question lay, still tied and gagged, on the walkway beside the trough. The rope, slackened now and tied off to a pillar, still ran from his feet up and over the crossbeam.

"We made a list—who he hurt, what he did," Euan continued, holding out the papers to Markham, who waved them away.

"He beats us even if we do our jobs right," Little Jake stood and said. The others joined the litany.

"It gets so bad we can't work! He keeps us from doin' our job!"

"Ask Mick Rykliewicz! He near had his arm tore off!"

"And yesterday, he beat the weighmen, too, real bad," Euan said. "You saw. And he tried to . . . to throw me into the grinders. He tried to kill me!"

"We save him in nick of time!"

"And we ain't goin' down into the trough no more to break up the jams," Euan said further. "Not even with ropes tied around us. Let the weighmen do it. We ain't doin' it no more!"

"Don't give me that rot," Markham interrupted when he could stand it no more. "When I was your age, younger even, I worked in the breaker. This same breaker. For longer hours and *no* pay, because my father made me. I hated it, too, but I did it, and I didn't complain."

"We had a cracker boss," he went on. "Carried a long switch, he did. If you so much as sneezed or farted when you shouldn't have, he'd whip that switch across your nose or your ass like lightning! I saw him take a boy's ear off with it once. If you ask me, Zakrzewska wasn't hard enough on you!"

"Does somebody have to get killt before you believe us?" Jenkin asked.

"We ain't dyin' fer yer coal, Markham!" Patsy shouted angrily. "We want a new cracker boss! Say it! Give us yer word!"

"I will not!"

"Say it!" Patsy repeated, his anger rising. "Give us a new boss!"

"As long as I am owner of this mine," Markham retorted, "I'll not take orders from a little snot-nosed, piss-the-pants like you! All of you! Secret Brotherhood! Who in hell do you think you are?"

The boys were startled by his sudden outburst.

"You, you little turd!" Markham said to Angus. "You speak English?"

"Yes, sir."

"What's your name, turd?"

"Angus. Angus McLaglan.

"Angus? I'm going to start counting. If you're not down those steps by the time I reach ten, your father and your brothers, and anyone else named McLaglan who works for me, will lose his job! Every McLaglan in Jeddoh will be on the road to nowhere by nightfall. Now get moving, Angus! One!"

Angus began to shake.

"Two!"

He looked to his mates all around.

"Three!"

But they were powerless to help him. Powerless, like him.

"Four!"

He looked at Euan, whose eyes were filled with terror.

"Five!"

"Do something quick then!" Euan told himself. "Quick! Before it's too late. Quick! Think quick!"

"Six! Time's wasting, Angus. Seven!"

Tears welled in the boy's eyes. He looked again at Euan . . .

"Eight!"

. . . and fled! He ran for the stairs. He was free. He was gone, but he would not be the last.

"You, roundhead! Yes, you!" Markham spat. "Your name? *Nazywa?*"

"Tadeus Harakal."

"Tadeus, you'd best leave here now. Leave! Or your *matka* will have to find a ditch to sleep in tonight! One!"

(Clink! Clonk! "Join the union!" Clink! Clonk! "Join the union!")

"Where's Markham?" the sheriff asked, pushing his way through the crowd at the pit head. Scores of men stood waiting to go down to the pits. Fathers and older brothers anxiously marked time. It was a quiet, sullen swarm at the top of the hill, unlike the mob at the bottom, but Frostbutter didn't like the looks of either. Both spelled trouble, yet neither seemed as bothersome right then as the scold who had attached herself to his sleeve and refused to let go until he accepted her demands.

"Sheriff!" Gwladys shrieked. "How dare you ignore me? I have information regarding the whereabouts of a wanted criminal, a murderer! And you will not listen!"

"Somebody tell me where the hell I can find Markham," Frostbutter said, continuing to ignore her, "or I go back to Wilkesbarre on the next train."

"He's up in the breaker with the boys," one of the bosses told him.

"Thank you!" Frostbutter said sarcastically. "And what in the name of God is he doing up there?"

"He's been some ten minutes now," Tom Pryor offered. "We've not heard a sound since he went up."

"Jesus, you couldn't hear a *cannon* go off with this racket," the sheriff muttered to his deputies.

(Clink! Clonk! "Join the union!" Clink! Clonk! "Join the union!")

"Sheriff, you are a public servant! I order you to arrest my husband!" Gwladys persisted.

"You go up 'dere!" Stefan Drozda urged Frostbutter. "'Dat man Markham. Maybe he hurt our boys."

"I'm sure Markham knows what he's doing," Frostbutter said. He no more wanted to climb those stairs than he did this hill or take the train to Jeddoh in the first place. "Besides, there's no telling what might happen if I moved in there at the wrong time."

"Sheriff! Go! Go up there before it's too late!" Gwladys pleaded.

"Madam, can you not see that I am preoccupied?" Frostbutter growled in frustration. "I have a dangerous situation here, and I cannot listen to . . ."

"Sheriff, time is running out!" she insisted. "Have you no conscience?"

"Madam, will you please shut up, or I will have you arrested!"

"The man is wanted for murder!"

Just then, a scuffle broke out between some marchers and the Coal and Irons. "We'll be lucky, madam, if there aren't more killed here today. From what I hear, your husband's not going anywhere till those boys let him free, so stop your fretting. I've got more important . . ."

"Sheriff!" she shouted imperiously. "I demand that you do your duty!"

Suddenly the breaker door flew open and a lone boy ran out, almost unnoticed in the confusion.

"Look! They're coming out!" someone shouted.

The chanting quickly died as everyone turned to see whether more would appear, but nothing happened. The boy just stood there, dazed and blinded by the sun.

"Angus!" a harried voice called to him.

"Poppy?" his plaintive voice replied.

Just then, Tadi burst through the door behind Angus, tripped over his own feet and went sprawling on his belly across the crushed slate.

It ended quietly.

Markham took the grievances from Euan's hand and pitched them into the trough. The papers fluttered prettily, like petals shaken from a tree, before they cascaded into the hungry mouth below.

"You will wait for me down in the yard," Markham said. "There I will carry out your punishment as I promised I would."

"What of him?" Patsy asked of the still-muzzled Zakrzewska.

"Don't worry, I will tend to him," Markham said. "Now, go!"

The boys hurried from his presence. Their hearts ached. None of them thought it would end this way—nothing to show for their pains. Such noble thoughts, such dreams, all for naught. Their hearts ached.

As they descended the stairs, shreds of their grievances, torn apart by the rollers and scattered by the drafts, fell around them like bits of snow.

"We had 'em," Patsy said to Euan, fighting back his sobs. "We had em, an' ye gave our guns away. Why?"

There was nothing Euan could say. His heart ached most of all.

"He's a bastard, that Markham!" Patsy said bitterly. "I wish I'da shot him when I had me the chance!"

And then Markham was alone with Zakrzewska.

"Ah! Ah! Ah!" Zakrzewska gasped as the rag was pulled from his mouth. "I thought they kill me sure! I pray to Blessed Virgin. She hear my prayer, and she bring you to me. I thought I was dead man. Please, free me? Untie my hands?"

Markham first undid the rope that had held the man aloft, then pulled at the knots that slowly loosened his binds.

"I . . . I hear such things you not believe!" Zakrzewska blurted excitedly. "Oh, jeez, I hear so much! This time you have to make me Ned Splicer. You will say, 'Zakrzewska, he is such a good man! I am lucky to have man like him at my side!' "

"What in God's name were you trying to do up here?" Markham said coldly.

"What do you mean?"

"With the boy. In the trough. With McGuinness and Powell. You nearly killed three people!"

"Achh!" he growled distastefully. "Boy—he ruin everything! He was there that night with old lady. He see it all. He see me! He think he know so much! Him and his father!"

"What old lady? What boy?"

"Union lady. Boy get in way. Bam! Boom! No good!"

"Slow down, man! I'm not following you," Markham said impatiently.

"Jones lady! I tell you I take care of her!" Zakrzewska gloated.

"Wait a minute!" Markham said, trying to make sense of Zakrzewska's babbling. "You mean, that night on Frog Street? When someone tried to shoot Mother Jones? That was . . . that was *you*?"

Zakrzewska grinned. "Bam! Boom! I do it for you."

Markham was stunned. "My God!" he managed to utter; his face grew even grimmer when he realized what this man had just confessed. "That means . . . that means it was *you* then that killed Ned the Splicer?"

"Bam! Boom!"

"It doesn't look good," Mother said. The marchers had fallen silent as one by one the boys staggered into the light.

Slowly their fathers and older brothers went to them, their estranged sons. There were awkward words, some tears, but mostly silence, painful and bitter silence.

"See what Markham does to your sons?" Mother shouted. "Don't let him get away with it! Those boys are twice the men you'll ever be! Strike back! Strike now!"

The men were only dimly aware of her cries. They had their boys back safely. They still had jobs. For that they were grateful. That was enough. What need had they of more trouble?

But Mother would not relent. "Show your sons you still got a backbone! Make 'em proud of you!" she called to the men on top of the hill. "Join the union! Do it for your sons! Who'll be first then to join the union?"

Mother's words echoed off the breaker. Mother's words echoed and died. No one on the hill was listening anymore. The dragon's breath was stilled.

"Son of a bitchin' bastards!" she hooted under her breath, then grabbed a pot lid from one of her cohorts and a wooden spoon from another. "When I get to the other side," she announced, her voice stoked with righteous anger, "I'm going to have to tell the good Lord about his goddamn coal-crackers! Trouble is, he'll never believe me!"

And she began to bang the spoon against the pot lid once again.

"You . . . despicable . . . loathsome creature!" Markham hissed at his still-entangled captive.

"These words mean what?" Zakrzewska asked as he

twisted to free himself of the clinging ropes. "I do not like their sound."

"Kill old women! Little boys! Kill men for no reason! Is there anything you would not do?"

"You are no angel, Markham."

"And you think I would have someone like you work at my side?"

"I have carried your dirty baggage this far. I will carry it the rest of the way," Zakrzewska assured him as, at last, he freed his hands. He then began to work on the ropes that bound his legs.

"No, no you won't. Not this time! You have pushed me too far this time," Markham protested, rising as if to separate himself from the man's stench, from his evil. "When you leave this place, or they drag you out of here, you are going straight to jail, and you will never go free! You will die there for your pains, and the sooner the better!"

"And what will happen to you when I tell everyone what I know? When I open up your dirty baggage? You cannot shut me up. Never!" Zakrzewska said, laughing. "I will drag you down!"

"No. No, you won't!" Markham said with calm assurance.

"Yes, yes! Wait, you see!"

"Never, Zakrzewska. Never! Not in a lifetime, not in a million years, because I am more clever and ruthless than the people I choose to deal with."

"Meaning what?"

"Meaning this!" Markham said and, with his foot, shoved the unsuspecting Zakrzewska over the edge into the trough.

The man slid down, straight down, like a stone to the bottom of a pond. To check his slide, he spread his powerful arms, but he couldn't stop his feet, which were snarled in the ropes, from sliding into the hungry maw. Straining, lifting, he braced himself against the slanted walls, then raised his legs to safety.

"You cannot kill me so easy, Markham!" the dead man

bragged. "You will suffer for this! I will make you sorry you . . . !"

His threats were cut short when he felt the first tug from below. The grinders, which had been cheated of one meal, were stubborn and refused to be robbed so easily of another. It did not take him long to realize that he was caught. The loosened ropes pulled tight and yanked him into the abyss.

He looked at Markham one last time. "This was not to happen," his eyes said, full of fear. "Not to me! This was not to happen!"

The scream was horrible when it came.

The teeth tore through his flesh, cracked his bones like twigs. They ripped that scream right out of him. The cattle killer fell silent. He was no more.

Markham ran below and watched the grinding with a gruesome fascination. Since his boyhood, his breaker boyhood, since his own days freeing jam-ups in the trough, he had wondered what this horror would be like, this falling, this grinding. Thus seen, he prayed to never see another and descended to conclude the unfinished business that awaited him below.

He got as far as the picking room before he was met by the sheriff, his deputies, and a distraught Gwladys Protheroe.

"John! What has happened? Are you safe?" Frostbutter asked.

"It's all over, Sheriff. I've cleared the trough room."

"And the cracker boss? This lady here insists that . . ."

"Mr. Markham," Gwladys interrupted. "My husband, Teofil Zakrzewska, is wanted for murder in Chicago. There is a small reward if he is captured alive—which I am claiming, of course—but I am more interested in justice being served."

"I'm sure you are, madam," Markham said, seeing through her cupidity.

"He is still up there?" Gwladys asked anxiously.

"In a manner of speaking, he is," Markham replied.

"Then, Sheriff, I beseech you to go up and arrest my husband at once!"

Frostbutter took a deep breath and motioned his deputies to proceed up the stairs. As they did, one took out a set of handcuffs from his coat.

"You won't be needing those," Markham informed the deputy. "There was a scuffle. The man was clearly deranged. He tripped on a rope and fell into the rollers. He was killed almost instantly. If you had only come a few minutes earlier . . ."

Gwladys's eyes grew round. Surely there was some mistake. Perhaps she didn't hear him correctly. Teofil dead? *Her* Teofil?

"I'm sorry, ma'am."

She staggered past them, disbelieving. "*You're* sorry?" she wanted to say. "What about my five hundred dollars? All my suffering, all my misery, to be left with no compensation? No reward? I've no one to go home to now. Who'll take care of *me* then? What about *me*? What's going to happen to *me*? To *me*!"

"I had him!" she wailed instead. "He was here all the time, and he slipped through my hands!"

And then she saw his blood streaming down the chutes, like tears, the blood of a man a part of her still loved.

She swooned.

Euan cowered beneath the stairs by the door that led out to the yard, lacking the courage to leave the breaker, to face his *dada*, to face Mother. The stairs were dark and well hidden. He wanted to stay there and never go out again. He was a scab for sure now—the worst sort. He'd gone against his own strike, the strike he'd started. He was the lowest kind of scab.

"You're our leader now," the boys had said when the strike began.

"No, not me," he'd begged. "Somebody else. Jenkin. Or Patsy."

"But you began it. You know what to do. We don't know. You're the one who knows, you. You!"

"But I'm . . . I'm afraid," he wanted to say, but he said

nothing. They would've laughed at him. And now they hated him for sure.

"We had 'em!" he sobbed in his dark corner. "We had 'em! And I gave it away! We lost it because of me! Please, God! Make me an ant, so nobody will see me, so somebody can step on me and not care."

He heard voices approaching and footsteps coming down the stairs.

"They wanted Zakrzewska replaced," he heard Markham tell the sheriff. "The man was clearly a menace, but I said 'no' just to be contrary. Most of them seemed feeble-brained to me. Can you believe they actually handed me a list of grievances? What's this world coming to?"

"You're lucky, John. It could have ended very badly."

Markham! As long as he lived, Euan would never forget his boss's face when the bucket of piss landed on his head. How they'd laughed! He'd never laughed so hard or so long.

"Throw it, Patsy! Now!"

"Not yet! Not yet! He ain't close 'nough!"

"Throw the note then!"

"There, there! He's got it! Throw it now!"

"Let 'im read it first!"

"Now! Throw it now!"

"What's he sayin'?"

"Who cares? Throw it, dammit! Throw!"

Whooooosh!

And they laughed like they never laughed before. And Patsy danced a jig. Euan's sides hurt from laughing. Tadi nearly choked.

"Well, it's over now," Euan heard Markham say as he opened the door for the sheriff. Suddenly the blinding sun poured in, and a wave of sound rolled up from the bottom of the hill.

(Clink! Clonk! "Join the union!" Clink! Clonk! "Join the union!")

"You think so?" the sheriff asked, shielding his eyes. "Then take a look out there."

("Men of Jeddoh! Join the union! Men of Jeddoh! Join the union!")

The dragon had come alive. The dragon was breathing fire again.

"Damn her!" Markham said before going out. "Damn her anyway! Come on, let's get it over with."

Euan looked toward the open door with dread, afraid to step out, afraid of what punishment lay beyond, but sooner or later he had to leave this hiding place. Sooner or later they'd come looking for him, his *mam* and *dada*. Sooner or later.

"Why? Why do these things happen? And all for naught?" he asked himself. "Why a strike? And why Rhys dead? And why Mother come and gone, then back again? And why Zakrzewska? And why me? Why not some other? Why?"

He sighed and wondered and wiped his eyes and remembered how tired he was, and hungry, then stepped out into the blinding light.

(Clink! Clonk! "Join the union!" Clink! Clonk! "Join the union!")

He half stumbled across the rough slate toward the pit head, where the men were gathered, shading his eyes as best he could.

"There he is!" he heard a voice say above the others.

"Is that him?" asked another.

"Yes, that's him!" It was Markham's voice. "I want you to arrest him and that one over there! And that one! All three!"

"No! No!" he heard the fathers and older brothers shout.

Euan saw Patsy's face as a deputy dragged him, struggling, toward the top of the hill. He'd never seen Patsy so scared before.

"Leave our boys alone! You've done enough to them!"

"For God's sake, Markham, stop it now!"

("Men of Jeddoh! Join the union! Men of Jeddoh! Join the union!")

Suddenly, rough hands grabbed Euan and started to drag him toward Markham and the sheriff.

"Euan! EU-AN!" he heard his *dada* call. He squinted and saw his *dada* rushing toward him through the crowd of men before a deputy stopped him in his tracks with a hard blow to the gut from the butt of his rifle. His *dada* fell to his knees.

"*Dada!*" he shouted and tried to break away, but the deputy caught him, lifted him, and threw him on the ground at Markham's feet.

"Yes, that's the one. The ringleader," Markham said brusquely.

Euan looked over to Patsy, who lay next to him with a bloody nose, and at Tomasz Gluc beyond, who lay squirming under a deputy's boot.

"I want these boys arrested as an example of what happens to those who break the law on my property," Markham announced so everyone could hear. Only a scattered circle of Coal and Irons separated him and the sheriff from the fathers and older brothers. "And I will personally see that they receive the harshest penalties possible!"

(Clink! Clonk! "Join the union!" Clink! Clonk! "Join the union!")

Are you sure you want to do this, John?" the sheriff asked, sensing rightly the volatility in the mood of the men atop the hill.

"These boys," Markham continued, "through their wantonness, have willfully destroyed property and . . ."

"Markham, you do 'dis, you be sorry!" Stefan Drozda shouted as the angry fathers and older brothers edged in closer.

"Enough is enough! Let them be!"

"Damn ye, Markham! We can't take much more!"

"If you don't let those boys go," Tom Pryor warned, "then, dammit, we're walking down that hill to that union!"

"Yes! Yes!" the men agreed all around.

"Oh? And who will be first?" Markham asked indignantly. "Who will be first to lose his job and lose his home!"

Euan looked up, saw his *dada* kneeling on the ground beyond the line of Coal and Irons. His *dada* looked old; his *dada* looked broken.

"And what if we all marched down that hill? Together?" Tom Pryor asked Markham.

"I would evict every man!" the owner boasted in reply.

"An' who voult you get to dig your coal?" Wladislaw Glue demanded.

Markham was unbowed by their growing unrest. "There are many out there who would gladly take your places!"

"An' vhat if dey join union also?"

"I would evict every man of them as well," he answered coldly.

"Ye can't be evictin' the whole damn world, Markham!"

(Clink! Clonk! "Join the union!" Clink! Clonk! "Join the union!")

"Then if you're so brave, go ahead!" Markham challenged. "Go on! Walk down that hill!"

But no one did.

Euan, ignored in the anger that swirled around him, helped Patsy to his feet, then wiped away the blood that smudged Patsy's face.

"I'm waiting," Markham taunted. "I guess none of you are the men you say you are! I guess no one will be walking down that hill!"

Euan looked around, saw Tadi and Little Jake and Billy and Angus, who was still crying, and Cyril and Antoni and Mickey and Ralph. They were all, all still there, and they were all looking at him, waiting for him.

"All right, Sheriff," Markham said unceremoniously. "Let's have this done with. Take these boys away!"

Euan recoiled.

"NO! NO!" the men cried.

("Men of Jeddoh! Join the union! Men of Jeddoh! Join the union!")

A pair of large, hairy hands reached out for Euan. He

backed away. He retreated in the only direction open to him—down the hill.

"Come here, boy!"

"No!" he said. He said, *"No!"* And he backed away, each step taking him farther down the hill, farther from the pit head and from Markham.

"Come here, boy!" called the deputy who had reached out.

"Where's he going? Where's the boy going?" asked another.

"Sheriff, get that boy!" Markham shouted. "He's under arrest!"

"All right, lad, come back now," the sheriff called to Euan. "Don't be making it harder on yourself."

But Euan continued his slow retreat. He wanted no more of this squabbling, this ranting. He was tired and wanted to go home. He was hungry and wanted a meal of his *mam*'s. He looked at Patsy. "Come on, Pats!" his eyes said. "Let's get out of here. Let's go home." And Patsy started down the hill after him, and Jenkin followed, too.

"There goes the other one! Shoot them both!" Markham ordered the Coal and Irons, who turned toward the defiant boys and raised their guns. "They're trying to escape!"

"Shoot them, John?" the sheriff asked incredulously.

"Yes, dammit!"

The fathers and older brothers saw what was happening. Quickly, unobtrusively, they pushed forward till they were standing between their boys and the Coal and Irons, whose guns were poised. "If you're going to shoot, shoot through us," their steely eyes dared. "Kill us first!"

Euan kept the deputies at bay as he drifted closer to Frog Street, till he lost sight of Markham through the maze of shifting men, till Markham's voice was drowned in waves of chanting. Then he saw his mates tagging after, moving as one down the hill behind him. There were too many to catch now, too many to stop.

(Clink! Clonk! "Join the union!" Clink! Clonk! "Join the union!")

So Euan turned his back on Markham, on his hatred and

his threats, and looked for the first time at the glorious pandemonium rising from the street below, and there in its midst, with her arms outstretched to him, was Mother.

"Come!" she seemed to beckon. "Come, boy! Come to me!"

And he decided there was one thing more to do before he headed home. He quickened his pace down the hill, and Patsy followed, stride for stride, and Jenkin hurried close behind with Tadi and Little Jake and Tomasz and Leo and Mickey and Freddie and Angus. They all strode down the hill together.

"Shoot them!" Markham shrieked. "Shoot them, dammit! They're getting away!"

But the sheriff did nothing. The Coal and Irons did nothing.

And Tom Pryor fell in behind the boys and followed them down the hill toward Mother, as did Stefan Drozda and his brothers and Caradoc Williams and Joe Mooney and Wladislaw Gluc and Peter John Lloyd and, finally, Hugh Morgan, who struggled to his feet and followed the rest.

("Men of Jeddoh! Join the union! Men of Jeddoh! Join the union!")

The cheering marchers broke through the confused cordon of Coal and Irons at the foot of the hill, opening up the way for Euan and his crew to enter their ranks. Tears streamed down Mother's cheeks. Her arms beckoned to embrace him, to embrace them all.

And then he was there, standing before her with Patsy and Tadi and the others crowding close behind. The men hurried to catch up, until there was a knot of men circled around.

Mother raised her hand for silence.

"I've come . . . I've come to join the union," he said to Mother, holding back his tears.

"Thank God for that, Euan Morgan!" Mother replied, her voice quivering. "I haven't had a convert all day!" And she took the boy in her arms and held him, and everyone cheered, because the union had finally come to Jeddoh.

# Acknowledgments

A writer must love his own company if he is to become a novelist, but that is not to say he alone is responsible for the work he ultimately brings forth. In the case of this book at least, there were many people as well as both private and public foundations without whose assistance this book would not have gotten beyond the dreaming stage.

I am grateful to the Writers Guild of America, East, Foundation, which provided support during the early research and writing process by means of the Paddy Chayefsky Memorial Fellowship, and particularly to Ernest Kinoy, a member of the Guild, for his encouragement and expert advice. The final stages in the completion of the book were supported by a grant from the Commonwealth of Pennsylvania Council on the Arts. In between, the following writers' colonies not only made their comfortable surroundings available to me, but also provided both moral and financial support: Cummington Community for the Arts in Cummington, Massachusetts; The Dorset Colony House in Dorset, Vermont; The Ragdale Foundation in Lake Forest, Illinois; The Ucross Foundation in Ucross, Wyoming.

Perry Blatz, director of the Oral History Program of the

New Jersey Historical Commission shared with me his extensive research into the working conditions and militant labor exploits of breaker boys. Dr. Ellis Roberts, mining historian and poet, explained the Welsh language and customs to me and provided a first-hand account of his experiences working as a breaker boy. William Woodburn, Steven Gaca, and Joseph Lopoka also regaled me with rich and touching stories of their careers in the breakers. Mrs. Lois McLean, Mother Jones's biographer, offered critical advice and historical references. Carl Oblinger and Matt Madga of the Pennsylvania Historical and Museum Commission offered enthusiastic assistance in exploring their WPA collection of oral histories of miners and their families.

The Eckley Miners' Village Museum gave me access to explore and photograph their numerous and fascinating exhibits. Anthony Zito of the Department of Archives and Manuscripts of the Catholic University of America offered his assistance in my search through the Mother Jones papers housed there.

I wish to express my gratitude to Sy Lesser and my friends at the Arts and Entertainment Network for their patience and understanding. A number of other individuals at one time or another also offered research assistance or logistical support: Joel Kubicki, Dr. Charlotte Lord, Josephine Carroll, Saul Schniderman, Thomas Graham, David Maharty, Joyce Kubicki, Gwladys Jones, Dr. John Bodnar, Maryanna Errard, Alice Jones, Leslie Pelak, Aida Cabezas Irrizarry, Joseph Nocc, Jane Tollinger, and Craig Fisher.

Finally, I extend my special thanks to Stevie Phillips; to my editor, Upton Brady, and my agents, Evarts Ziegler and Lydia Galton, for their confidence; and again to Lydia Galton and her husband, James Galton, for their generosity and friendship.